"These violent delights have violent ends. And in their triumph die, like fire and powder. Which, as they kiss, consume"

~ William Shakespeare

CHAPTER 1

NICCO

"Come on, Nicco, is that all you've got?" Dane came at me, his fists swinging and teeth snarling. He was a cocky little fucker. Reckless and impulsive with impressive strength for a seventeen-year-old.

He reminded me of myself when I was his age.

"Keep talking shit, kid, and you're going down." I jabbed my finger at him.

"Is that a threat? Because I'm shaking in my fucking boots." His friends snickered, fist bumping and high-fiving as if the result was inevitable.

A couple of the older guys caught my eye and smirked. They knew how it was. They knew Dane was one hit from getting his ass handed to him.

The truth was though, I needed this. I needed to feel his sloppy fists curled against my ribs. The flash of pain as he clipped my jaw. I needed the deep burn radiating through every one of my muscles.

I needed it all.

He came at me again, but this time I anticipated his move, ramming my fist into his stomach.

"*Oomph.*" He went down like a sack of bricks.

"Stay down, kid," I said, running a hand down my face. Sweat coated my skin and my knuckles were split open again, the new skin not hardy enough to withstand the impromptu sparring session with my cousin.

"I almost had you." He grinned up at me, blood trickling down his mouth as he did so. I held out my hand, and he grasped it so I could help pull him up. Dane staggered to his feet, shaking his head. "Next time, your ass is mine, Marchetti."

"Yeah, yeah, keep talking, kid." I ruffled his hair before shoving him toward his friends.

Grabbing a towel, I dried myself off. "Looking good out there," Benny said, approaching me. He was one of my uncle's capos. A typical southie who had worked his way up the ranks to become a made man.

"Yeah, well, I've got a ton of anger to work off."

He handed me a bottle of water and I uncapped it, chugging the thing down.

"I smell trouble with a broad." My expression fell and he cussed under his breath. "Shit, Nic, that bad?"

Inhaling a ragged breath, I rubbed my jaw. "Just how much did Uncle Al tell you?" My brow rose.

"He said you needed to come lay low until the dust settled."

Until the dust settled...

It was going to take a lot more than the dust settling to fix this.

I hesitated. The less people who knew the truth about Arianne, the better, but word would get out eventually. Besides, I really needed to talk to someone because it was killing me. Every second that I was here, and she was back in Verona County, destroyed another piece of my soul.

"Come on, I think I have some of the good stuff laying around here. You can tell me all about her over a drink." His big hand landed on my shoulder and squeezed.

I didn't get out to Boston much. Uncle Alonso and his guys handled business here, just like my father and our guys handled business in Rhode Island. But Benny was as good as family. Whatever I confided in him tonight would be between us. Capo to capo. Man to man.

I looked at him and grimaced, feeling the fight ebb away. The clench of my jaw mirroring the ache in my chest. "You'd better make mine a double."

∼

"Thanks, Lyra," Benny said to the server, letting his eyes linger on her ass as she sauntered off. She was dressed the same as every other woman in Opals, in very little.

It was one of my Uncle Al's clubs in South Boston. I would have preferred to go somewhere quieter, but Benny's gym was right around the corner and he had some business to attend to here, so I went with the flow.

Checking my cell for the hundredth time today, I tapped my foot against the stool. Despite going a few rounds with Dane at the gym, restless energy still vibrated through me. I knew the only thing that would settle me was the one the thing I couldn't have.

Not right now at least.

Arianne.

I could vividly picture her big, honey eyes. Her soft, full lips. Her irresistible smile.

My sweet, strong, compassionate Bambolina.

Fuck, I missed her.

It hadn't even been twenty-four hours since I left Verona County. Since I walked away from the only woman I would ever want.

The woman who held my heart in the palm of her hands to do with as she pleased.

I was here for her. To keep her safe until my father discovered a way to fix my mess. But nothing about it felt right.

Not a single fucking thing.

"Easy, Nicco." Benny pushed a glass of scotch toward me. I unclenched my fist, curling my fingers around the glass. "Now tell me about this girl of yours."

"I don't even know where to start," I admitted, flicking my weary gaze to his.

"Al hinted that she was forbidden fruit." He gave me a knowing look. Benny was at least twenty years my senior, as were many of the capos in Dominion. Age was but a number when you were the son of the boss though.

I ran my thumb around the rim of the glass, trying to focus on something—*anything*—except the shitstorm brewing.

"Loving her could start a war." My voice wavered.

"That bad, huh?" There was a teasing edge to his words. "She must be some broad."

"She's..." *Everything*, the word teetered on the tip of my tongue.

"It takes a strong woman to stand by a mafioso's side, Nicco. And you're so young..." I cut him with a hard gaze and he smirked, a deep rumble of laughter shaking his shoulders. "All I'm saying is, are you sure she's the one? Because from the sounds of it, ain't no coming back from this. And the family has enjoyed a certain amount of peace for the past two decades."

"That's what we're calling it?" My brow rose. "So what was that bullshit with Dane a few weeks back?"

"The kid's a hothead. Wades into a situation all guns blazing. Like we weren't all the same at his age."

I knew what he was saying, but Dane should have known better. Uncle Alonso might have been second in the chain of command, but he was still the head of the family in Boston. One day that responsibility would fall to Dane. He would be Alonso... and I would be my father.

And if Dane was going to hold the power one day, he needed to learn how to respect it.

Bringing the glass to my lips, I knocked back the scotch in one. The burn was sharp, but I didn't flinch.

I couldn't resist digging my cell phone out of my pocket again and checking for any messages.

"You could call her, you know."

"She's pissed at me."

"When ain't a broad pissed at her guy?"

"I left her." I'd just upped and left without saying goodbye. But I'd known if I woke her, if I held her and kissed her, that I would never let her go.

Arianne was having a hard time understanding that though, refusing to take any of my calls or respond to my texts.

I didn't blame her.

I couldn't.

Not when I was the one who pulled her willingly into this world, into my life.

I should have walked away. The second I found out her true identity, I should have walked away and never looked back.

But how did you walk away from something so vital as the other half of your soul?

The answer was, you didn't.

You couldn't.

Leaving Arianne, forcing myself to deny our connection, would have killed me.

Over time, it would have killed us both.

She wasn't just some girl. A fleeting crush. Arianne Capizola was my heart. The better part of me.

She was the woman I was going to spend my life with.

I let out a long breath.

If only it were that simple.

"A wise man once said," Benny said, pulling me from my thoughts, "love keeps no record of wrongs. If she is half the woman you claim her to be, she will come around."

"Niccolò, Benny, there you two are." Uncle Alonso joined us at the bar. "Where is that hothead son of mine?"

"Nicco taught him a lesson in the ring."

Alonso chuckled. "I hope you put him on his ass enough times to drill the message into his thick skull?"

"He's not a bad kid," I said. He reminded me a little of Bailey. Misguided and confused about his place in the world. But unlike Bailey, Dane didn't have any problem throwing his weight around.

"I'll talk to him again," I said. It had only been a few weeks since me, Enzo, and Matteo had driven out to keep Dane from the clutches of one of the gangs operating out of Boston. Alonso and my father felt that perhaps I could reach him, since I was only a couple of years his senior.

"That kid will be the death of me. He turns eighteen next year." Alonso shuddered. "And then what the fuck am I going to do with him? He's lucky the Diablos didn't put a bullet through his brain for that little stunt he pulled." He drained his drink, wiping his mouth with the back of his hand.

"The Diablos don't want any trouble," I said. When we'd sat down with their leader, Manny Perez, he'd been clear he didn't want war. But he did want compensation for Dane's attempt at moving in on the Diablos' territory in and around Roxbury. A compensation my uncle had reluctantly agreed to in order to save his son's life.

"Yeah, well, it's created a problem we didn't need."

"Sounds like Dane isn't the only kid causing trouble." Benny smirked at me, clapping me on the back.

"Vai a farti fottere," I growled, my blood itching for another fight. "It wasn't like I planned on any of this."

"Relax, Nicco, I'm busting your balls. What better reason to go to war than over love?"

"Benito," Alonso hissed, motioning for his capo to leave.

"I'll see you around, Nic." Benny took off.

"Excuse Benny. He is one of my most trusted men, but he is a fool."

I smirked at that. "It's okay. I know people won't understand my reasons."

"The Capizola heir." He let out a strained breath, rubbing his neatly trimmed beard. "Antonio must have blown a fuse when he found out."

"If it wasn't for the fact she was..." I swallowed the words, pain squeezing my heart like a vise. Seeing Arianne hurt like that, the blood and bruises, it made me murderous. It made me want to drive back to Verona County and make Scott Fascini pay for his sins.

"He told me she was hurt." I nodded. "We are all guilty of losing our cool now and again, but to defile a young girl so brutally..."

The words hung between us, only fueling the anger swelling inside me. It was like a fire, sweeping through me, threatening to scorch me to nothing but ash and bone.

"It is a rare thing to find what you have found, Niccolò." Alonso's hand landed on my shoulder, heavy yet reassuring. "But don't let it consume you. I have seen many a man driven to madness by love."

"You sound like my father," I said.

A smirk tugged at the corner of his mouth. "Antonio is a wise man. It would do you well to listen to him."

"I'm here, aren't I?"

His smooth chuckle washed over me, easing some of the storm raging in my chest.

"The Family must always come first, Niccolò. It is the burden we bear."

My eyes flashed to his. I'd never heard one of my uncles refer to this life as a burden before. Being mafioso was in our blood. Ingrained on our souls. You entered this life alive and you left dead. There was no other way.

I raised a brow and he chuckled again. "We all have stories, son. But some of us prefer to keep them close to our chest."

"I keep thinking it would be easier not to love her... to let her go, instead of binding her to this life." A life of secrets and heartache.

"You truly think you could do it?"

"No." My hand curled into a fist once more. "And I hate myself for it."

"Antonio has filled me in on the details and it sounds like her life was decided long before your paths crossed, the same way your life was decided. Setting her free is not the answer here."

"So I fight?"

"You fight. This thing is bigger than you and Arianne, Niccolò. It is a broken history demanding to be righted. The Capizola and Marchetti were always supposed to be united."

It wasn't the first time someone had suggested it, but I couldn't see past the war heading our way.

And to think I'd trusted him.

I'd trusted Roberto to do the right thing and be the father

Arianne deserved. But instead he'd deceived me. He'd played me like a fool, and I'd left.

I'd fucking left her there and now she was... engaged to that piece of shit Fascini.

My knuckles turned white as they clenched the glass again.

"Niccolò." Concern coated Alonso's words. "You will get through this. We are Marchetti. It is what we do."

I gave him a sharp nod. It was all I could do, while the inferno raging inside me burned hotter and hotter. It was my duty to protect her. To shield her from harm and keep the monsters at bay. Yet, here I was. Banished to some far away land unable to reach her.

My head knew it was the right call, knew it was the only option. But my heart... my foolish fickle heart was quick to forget the vows I'd taken, the responsibility that lay squarely on my shoulders.

I wasn't just a capo in the family, I was my father's son.

The Marchetti Prince.

I had an entire legacy to uphold.

A legacy that would one day see me crowned King.

But every King needed his Queen...

Didn't he?

CHAPTER 2

ARIANNE

"How are you feeling?" Nora handed me the mug of coffee and sat down beside me.

We were in our new apartment. The one I'd convinced my father to let us move into.

My gaze was fixed on the hall and beyond that my bedroom. The same bedroom Nicco had made love to me in, less than forty-eight hours ago.

He'd loved me... and then he'd left me.

And now I was bereft, lost at sea without an anchor.

Nicco was gone.

And he'd taken my heart with him.

"I still can't believe he left." I ran my thumbs around the mug.

"He had no choice, Ari. I know it hurts, but it would have hurt a damn sight worse if you'd had to watch him be dragged away in handcuffs; or worse, a body bag."

A violent shudder ripped through me as I smothered a whimper.

"Sorry, I didn't mean—"

"No, you're right. It's not so much that's he's gone, it's that he didn't tell me himself, face to face." If I'd have known it was the last night I was going to get with him, I would have savored every second. I would have begged him to make love to me over and over again.

I would have imprinted every touch, every kiss, and sigh to memory.

"You should talk to him."

My chest tightened, my hand drifting there, as if the pain were physical. It sure felt like it. My heart felt bruised and battered.

"I know, I just... what am I supposed to say to him? He's gone, Nor." And I was stuck here, living my worst nightmare.

Tristan was still in a coma. My father had betrayed me in the worst possible way. And I was promised to Scott Fascini. The guy who had drugged me and stolen the one thing that had never been his to take.

Tears pricked the corners of my eyes as I pushed down the hazy memories. Cruel touches and dirty words. He'd tainted me. Beaten and bruised me. But I hadn't let him take my heart.

He could *never* have that, for it belonged to another.

It belonged to Nicco.

He knew about the engagement. Luis, my bodyguard, had told him the second we'd left my father's estate. I had been too numb to function. Too blindsided to do anything but quietly sob the whole ride back to University Hill.

My father had promised... he'd promised to fix things.

And he'd lied.

After Nicco had beaten Scott, and accidentally hurt Tristan, I'd made a deal with my father. A deal he had broken the second my back was turned.

Anger skittered up my spine. I'd eventually confided in my father, revealed to him just exactly the type of guy Scott really was, and he'd *still* betrayed me.

Roberto Capizola had picked a side and now he might as well be dead to me.

"Ari, look at me." Nora shuffled closer, covering my hand with hers. "I know everything looks dismal now, but you'll get through this, I know you will. Antonio is working on it, and you have me, and Luis, and your mom. We'll figure it out. But I'm begging you, call Nicco. You need to talk about everything."

I gave her a slight nod. She was right. It was a conversation Nicco and I needed to have. But how did you tell the man you loved that you were promised to another? That you were expected to court him and spend time with him and—

I stopped myself.

"Now is as good a time as any." Nora handed me my cell phone. I stared at it like it was a grenade. "Take it," she urged, and I slid my trembling fingers around it.

"I'll give you some privacy."

"Thank you," I whispered, blood ringing in my ears.

Nora offered me an encouraging smile before disappearing down the hall toward our bedrooms. The apartment was only small, but it was light and airy and untainted with painful memories.

All except one.

Waking yesterday morning to find Nicco gone, reading his goodbye note, had broken something inside me. I'd thought we would face the coming storm together, but now he was there, and I was here, and like a mountain too steep to climb, Scott was wedged right in between us.

Inhaling a deep breath, I found his number and hit dial.

"Arianne?" My name was a whispered prayer that cracked my heart wide open.

"Hello, Nicco."

"Thank fuck," he breathed. "I've been so worried. Are you okay? Where are you? Is Luis there? Tell me everything."

I smiled; I couldn't help it. Nicco's protectiveness was something I would never tire of.

"I'm at the apartment with Nora. Luis is right outside. He doesn't let me out of his sight. Not that we've been far. We didn't go to classes again today. Not after..."

"Perdonami, Bambolina. I didn't want to leave like that. I didn't want to run like a coward. But I knew if I didn't... I knew if I stayed and tried to explain everything, then I wouldn't be strong enough to leave you."

"You hurt me, Nicco, you hurt me so much." Pain coiled around my heart as I swallowed the tears threatening to fall. "My father betrayed me. He said he'd fix it, he said—"

"He betrayed us both."

I gasped. "What do you mean?"

"He contacted me, before I came to the apartment. He said that there were things at play I didn't understand and that he needed some time. He asked me to let him handle it and lie low."

"He said that?" I can hardly believe what he's telling me.

"My father had already ordered me to go to Boston and lie low. So I told your father I would disappear as long as he gave me his word you would be safe."

"It doesn't make any sense. When he summoned me to the house, Mike Fascini was there with..." I can't say his name, but I know Nicco knows who I'm talking about from his sharp intake of breath.

Tears pooled in my eyes as I lost the fight to smother my heartache.

"Ssh, you don't need to say the words, Bambolina. Luis told me everything."

A garbled cry spilled from my lips. "I'm sorry. I'm so sorry."

"Don't cry." His voice wavered. "Please, don't cry. Nothing can come between us, Arianne, I need you to know that. It doesn't matter what your father says or what that piece of shit Fascini does... nothing can come between us. Not a damn thing. Il mio cuore è tuo."

I wanted to believe him. I wanted to believe him so badly. But Nicco wasn't here. He wouldn't be there tomorrow at school or tomorrow night when Scott came to pick me up for our date.

I flinched.

Just the very idea of Scott being anywhere near me made my skin crawl. But I could see no way out. Scott was out for blood—Nicco's blood. There was no telling what lengths he would go to. I couldn't risk that.

I wouldn't.

"Bambolina, say something..."

"How's Boston?"

Nicco's chuckle filled the line. It was like a balm to my broken heart, filling some of the cracks. "Boston is okay. Although my cousin Dane took an ass-beating earlier."

"You were fighting?"

"I do that sometimes..." he said warily. "It relaxes me."

"Fighting relaxes you?" I blurted out, disbelief coating my words. "What else don't I know about you, Niccolò Marchetti?"

It was a loaded question.

I'd fallen hard and fast where Nicco was concerned, which meant we were learning about each other as we went.

"Nothing important." I heard the smile in his voice. "You know my heart, Bambolina. You know my soul."

The honesty in his words twisted my insides. "I don't know if I can do this," I whispered.

There was a beat of silence, and then Nicco let out a strained breath. "You are so strong, Arianne. You can do this, I know you can."

"But what if he expects..." The unspoken words hung between us like a glacier.

My father and Mike Fascini expected me to date Scott... they expected us to behave like a couple, despite the official engagement announcement being kept under wraps for now.

My father expected me to be alone with him after he'd.... I pushed the thoughts down, swallowing the bile clawing its way up my throat. I couldn't go there. Whatever Scott had done to me in the past, I had to find a way to turn it into strength to help me survive this.

"Luis is working on it," Nicco said.

"What does that mean? What's going—"

"Bambolina, listen to me. You are not alone. I know it feels that way, but our friends, our allies, will do all they can to keep you safe. Just promise me you'll stay strong..." He hesitated, his silence deafening. "Promise me you'll fight."

"I promise." My voice trembled involuntarily. I wanted to be strong. I wanted to face the future with defiance in my heart and fury in my veins. But the truth was, I was scared.

I was scared of what would happen.

Of what I would become.

A rumble of voices filled the line, and Nicco said, "I have to go. But I'll call you soon, okay?"

"Okay." Pain was woven into every syllable.

Talking to Nicco wasn't enough. I needed to see him. To feel his arms wrapped around me, his breath fanning my face.

"I love you Bambolina. Sei tutto per me."

"I love you too," I whispered as I hung up, pain burying itself further into the cracks in my heart.

"Ari?" Nora came rushing into the room, crushing me into her slender arms as I sobbed. "Ssh, it's going to be okay. I promise."

But people kept making promises and they kept breaking them.

My father. My mother. Scott... Nicco.

People called me the Capizola heir. The kids at Montague looked at me like that meant something; something to revere and envy.

Being the Capizola heir didn't make me powerful though.

It made me a pawn.

A pawn in a game for which I didn't understand the rules.

A game I was currently losing.

The next morning didn't bring any signs of hope. Luis knocked early to inform me my father expected me to resume classes. Nora said it was a good thing—getting back to normal.

But nothing about my life felt normal anymore.

I went through the motions: showering and dressing, combing my hair and letting it hang in gentle waves around my face. I didn't bother with make-up.

Nora made coffee and heated some waffles, but I wasn't hungry. The pit in my stomach didn't want food, it wanted answers. It wanted a solution to the mess I'd found myself in.

The door opened and Luis appeared. "All set?"

I nodded, feeling the claws of uncertainty tighten around my throat.

"Nora, the car is downstairs," he said. "Could you give me and Arianne a few seconds alone?"

"Of course." She grabbed her bag and came over to me. "You've got this." Nora squeezed my hand gently before disappearing out of the apartment.

Luis closed the door and stepped further into the room. "How are you feeling?"

"Numb."

"I'll be right there," his expression softened, "every step of the way."

"And when I go tonight. Will you be there also?"

Luis' nostrils flared, but he didn't flinch. He was good at his job, able to present a calm and composed front at all times. He'd tricked my father, lied to his very face. It made me wonder if he could also lie to me.

"You can trust me," he said, as if he had heard my thoughts. "I won't let that piece of shit hurt you again. I promise."

I released a small sigh.

More promises.

Promises meant nothing when you were dealing with men like Scott Fascini and my father. Men who manipulated and lied and twisted the truth to their ends.

I'd learned that the hard way.

"Have you spoken to my father?"

Luis' expression morphed into anger. "He called me this morning."

"Did he say anything?"

"Nothing. But something doesn't add up. He's a ruthless man, Ari, but I can't believe he would hand you over to Fascini unless he thought he was doing it to protect you."

"Protect himself more like," I mumbled, indignation burning through me, betrayal and deceit lying heavy in my chest.

"Your father is many things, Ari, but he is not a monster. I have worked for him since before you were born, and everything he has ever done was to protect you."

"How can you defend him after he...?" The words got stuck over the lump in my throat. I took a deep breath, forcing myself to calm down, but my body trembled with anger. "He handed me over to Scott like I was nothing more than a possession. I told him what Scott did to me. I looked him in the eye and told him he..." I glanced away, refusing to let Luis see me break.

"I know," he exhaled a strained breath. "But there has to be more to it. There has to."

Slowly, I lifted my glassy eyes to my bodyguard. "So tell me, Luis, what am I supposed to do?"

"You are the Capizola heir, Arianne. You raise your head high and refuse to cower. Sometimes we don't realize how strong we truly are until we are faced with our greatest weakness. Try to remember that," he said around a half-smile. "Now come on, you don't want to be late for class."

I scoffed as he ushered me out of the apartment.

Being tardy was the least of my problems.

"Everyone's staring," I said to Nora as we made our way to the food court.

"They're just curious."

"Curious?" My brow rose. "*That's* what we're calling it?"

She rolled her eyes, dragging me toward the doors. I didn't want to be here. Everyone knew about Tristan. Everyone thought they knew the events that unfolded that fateful night, but they didn't know the truth.

They couldn't.

So I'd spent all morning trying to ignore the constant buzz of whispers and rumors.

"Arianne?" I stilled at the sound of Sofia's voice. Slowly, I turned to meet her tear-filled gaze. "Is there any news?"

I shook my head.

She smothered a garbled cry with her hand. "I tried to visit, but they said it's family only." Her eyes pleaded with me, as if she somehow thought I had the answer.

I didn't.

"Roberto would prefer to keep things private for now," Nora answered for me. "But I'm sure he'll let you know once Tristan is accepting visitors."

She smothered another whimper. "I know we weren't serious... but I care about him, I care about him a lot."

"I'm sorry," I said.

"Oh, Ari." Sofia threw her arms around me, hugging me tight. "If you need anything..."

"Thank you."

She stepped back, finally composing herself. "I should go. But I meant what I said... I'm always here."

As soon as she was gone, Nora let out a low whistle. "That was..."

"Don't." I made my way to the salad bar. I still couldn't bear the thought of food, but I knew I needed to eat.

"Have you seen you know who at all?"

"You can say their names, Nor."

"Can I? I don't know the rules of espionage."

My brows knitted as I met her amused gaze. "Seriously?"

"Made you smile though, didn't it?"

"Fine," I relented. "You made me smile."

Nora leaned in closer, filling her own plate. "I know things are bad right now, but we have to find flickers of light in the dark."

"We do, do we?"

"Yep. Besides, I was hoping to get another good look at Enzo's—"

I clapped a hand over her mouth. "Keep those thoughts to yourself."

"Prude."

"Hussy."

"But you love me." She grinned.

I couldn't argue with that. Nora was my best friend. My confidante.

She was the sister I'd never had.

And I was going to need her more than ever if I was going to make it through the next few months.

CHAPTER 3

NICCO

"You look like shit," Dane said as I traipsed into the kitchen.

Alonso roared with laughter. "Couldn't keep up with me and Benny."

I grumbled, rubbing the back of my neck. I didn't let myself drink a lot; I didn't like the feeling of losing control. But after speaking with Arianne yesterday, I'd been a mess. I wanted to fight, to hit and hurt. But my uncle knew I was in no state to get in the ring so instead, he'd invited Benny over, pulled out his best bottle of scotch, and the three of us had sat around the fire pit out back drinking and talking until well into the early hours.

"Niccolò," my Aunt Maria came over and kissed my cheek. "There's coffee in the pot and I'm making pancakes."

My stomach turned. "I think I'm good with coffee."

Alonso and Dane snickered. "Shouldn't you be at school?" I asked my cousin.

"Yes, he should." Maria shot her son a meaningful look.

"But, Mamma—"

"No buts, Polpetto. It's senior year, and you will graduate. Tell him, Alonso."

"Ma, don't call me that," he grumbled.

"Your mother's right. Go to school and try to learn something. And stay out of trouble."

Dane mumbled something under his breath as he tucked into a pancake drenched in syrup.

"Not sweet enough already?" I flicked my gaze to the sticky mess covering his plate.

"Fuck you," he mouthed around a smirk.

Laughter rumbled in my chest. Dane was a strange mix of Enzo and Matteo. He had Matteo's humor but Enzo's temper. It made him unpredictable and reckless and I didn't doubt he was going to cause my uncle a few more headaches before he turned eighteen.

I helped myself to coffee and moved over to the window. My uncle's house was a big corner plot overlooking South Boston's shoreline. He'd bought it a few years back for Maria who wanted to move out of the brick rows in the heart of the neighborhood. It was ostentatious and came with a hefty price tag, but Maria was his wife, his woman, and she had my uncle wrapped around her pinky finger.

My thoughts drifted to Arianne; icy fingers of regret clenching around my heart. She would be heading for class soon. I knew because Luis had already texted me to tell me of their plans. He might have been on Roberto's payroll, but I trusted him. I trusted him to do right by Arianne.

My pocket started vibrating and I pulled out my cell, surprised to see my father's name. "I'm going to take this outside," I said to my uncle and aunt before slipping out on the deck.

"Niccolò."

"Old man," I teased.

"Watch your tongue, boy."

"How's... everything?"

"Tommy is working round the clock to dig for dirt on Mike Fascini, and I have Stefan helping him."

"Did they find anything yet?"

"Aside from the fact he might be a ghost from the past coming back to haunt us, no." He let out a heavy sigh. "How's Boston?"

"It's not home."

A beat passed and then my father said, "I know, Son. I know. But you need to stay put. The last thing we need is to go to war before we've got all the facts."

My hand clenched around the rail. "He promised her to him. He fucking handed her over to that piece of shit as if she's nothing more than a—"

"Niccolò," my father's tone was sharp. "You need to keep your head. We can't have another incident."

I winced at that. "Tristan was an accident."

"I know that and you know that, but he's in a coma for fuck's sake, Son. Roberto has every right to want retribution for that."

"He was on our side," I said. "He was going to buy us some time with the Fascini."

"Was he? Or was he just trying to get you out of the picture?"

"Something doesn't add up." I released a frustrated breath. "Arianne told him about the evidence, told him she had proof that Fascini..." The words drowned in my anger, my body vibrating with unspent energy.

"You need to calm down, Son. Letting your anger get the better of you will do nobody any good."

My teeth ground together behind my lips as I pressed them into a thin line. I would never forget seeing Arianne broken and bruised in the back of Bailey's car.

"Niccolò, listen to me. You cannot lose yourself to this. Do you hear me? You're up there in Boston while your woman has to stand strong and play her part. If she can do it, then by God, you have to—"

"I know." I expelled a long breath, forcing my muscles to relax.

My father was right. I couldn't afford to drown in anger and rage. It wouldn't help me, and it certainly wouldn't help Arianne. I just felt so useless being exiled here, so powerless.

"Tell me what to do." My voice cracked, my pain filling the silence that followed.

"You stay strong and you wait. You are Marchetti, Niccolò. We don't cower to our enemies and we certainly don't run."

I scoffed at that because I had run. I was hiding out in Boston while he tried to get a handle on things.

"I know what you're thinking," he said as if he could hear my thoughts, "but we need to handle this the right way. If she's as important to you—"

"She is," I snapped.

"I know, Son." He let out a resigned sigh. "I know. That girl... she has a way of bewitching even the coldest of hearts. Arianne is as good as family now. I give you my word I'll do everything within my power to make sure she doesn't get hurt again. But you need to trust me."

"I trust you," I ground out. "That isn't the problem." I just didn't trust that piece of shit Fascini. He'd already hurt Arianne twice before. What was stopping him from doing it again?

"She has her bodyguard. And I'm putting a guy on them."

"Who?"

"Niccolò." His tone was harsher. "Trust me to do my job. We have time. You said Arianne's birthday isn't until

February. That gives us enough time to figure out how best to play this. If we go in all guns blazing it could jeopardize everything, Son. And we can't risk that, I won't. La famiglia prima di tutto." He let out a heavy sigh. "I'll call as soon as I have more."

"Okay." The word weighed heavily on me.

He was right. So long as I was in Boston and he was there, I had to trust he could handle things.

It didn't mean I had to like it though.

I spent the day with Benny and a couple of his guys, collecting pizzo. It wasn't ideal, but it was better than sitting in my uncle's house, dwelling.

"Heads up, Nic," Felix said as we approached the dingy bar. "We usually don't walk away from this place without getting our hands a little dirty."

My spine stiffened, my senses going on high alert. It looked like bad news. The flickering neon sign was busted, reading hooters instead of Shooters, and the door had seen better days. But it only seemed to amuse Benny as we ducked inside.

Some bluesy track spilled out of a jukebox in the corner of the room and a few guys sat around drinking beer and playing cards.

"Benny." One of them gave him a sharp nod.

Felix and Dimitri fanned out, one of them hovering by the door, the other moving to the door to the restrooms. One hand casually rested inside their jacket, their expressions void of emotion. The temperature in the bar cooled significantly.

The group of guys drinking seemed unaffected though, going about their game of poker as if it was just business as usual. And it probably was. People involved with the Family knew the score. They knew that at least once a month guys like me and Benny would come around to collect. Sometimes they paid for protection, sometimes they paid to do business on Marchetti territory, and sometimes they paid because they had a debt to the Family. Either way, when the date came you paid up.

And if you didn't... well, that was a whole other story.

"Yo, Gino, you back there?" Benny called out. He was standing at another doorway, this one concealed by a heavy black curtain. There was some shuffling and cussing and then a muscled guy appeared wearing a white wifebeater, tattoos snaking up his arm and around his neck.

"What the fuck, Benny? You can't cut a guy a little slack?"

I smirked. It was always the same with these coglioni. They knew the order of things, yet nine times out of ten they tried to wiggle out of paying up.

"You know, Gino, I thought you'd get a fucking clue by now."

A couple of the guys at the table glanced over, and Felix inched forward. I felt for my own piece but Benny shot me a look that said, 'we've got this'.

"Gino," a petite woman appeared, grinding to a halt when she spotted us. "Oh, hey, Benny. Gino didn't say you were coming around."

"Seems Gino has a little problem keeping a check on the date."

"Let me get you guys a drink?" She added, "Maybe something to eat?"

"For fuck's sake, Jen, they don't want a drink."

"Actually, I could take a drink." Benny glanced over at me. "What about you, Nic? You want a drink?"

I shrugged. I wasn't here to play games; I was here to distract myself.

"Sure thing, Benny, let me see to you guys." She started moving around the bar, but Gino's hand shot out grabbing her wrist. "Go out back and fucking stay there."

"Don't be that way, baby." She smiled, but it didn't reach her eyes. "We have guests. We should show them a proper Shooters welcome."

He leaned into her space, pressing his face up against hers. I lunged forward, but Benny's hand shot out. Anger simmered in my veins. She was half his size and Gino was staring at her as if she was the devil incarnate.

"I said get in the fucking back, puttana."

"Gino." She laughed, but it was strangled. "Please, we have guests." Her eyes pleaded with him, but it only made his nostrils flare.

She went to move around him, but he grabbed her wrist again, and pain etched into her expression. "Okay, I'm going... I'm going, stop making a scene."

Gino muttered to himself as she disappeared through the curtain. "Fucking broad doesn't know when to keep her mouth shut."

Benny sucked in a harsh breath. "You kiss your mother with that mouth?"

"Fuck my mother. Stupid whore didn't know her place either."

"Nice to see you keeping it classy, Gino," Felix deadpanned, his expression tight with contempt as he pulled to his full height.

"We came here to do business, not to shoot the shit, so can we move this along?" Benny raised a brow.

"More like came here to fuck me in the ass."

"I hate to break it to you, stronzo," Felix barked out a laugh. "But you're not my type."

Gino grunted, pulling out a money tin. The group of guys seated at the table paid him no attention as he pulled out a chain from around his neck and unlocked it. "It's been a slow month."

"Tell it to someone who cares." Benny smirked, advancing on the bar. "Make sure it's all there," he ordered.

"Yeah, yeah, keep your hair on."

I tsked under my breath. The guy was a real piece of work, and he was grating on my last nerve.

"Here you go." He shoved a fat envelope at Benny. "Now get the fuck out my bar."

"Tut tut, Gino. That temper of yours is going to get you into trouble one day." Benny tapped him on the cheek before heading for the door. I followed, letting my eyes run over each of the guys sitting at the table. They were obviously regulars, but I couldn't decide if they were Gino's guys or just indifferent patrons.

Felix and Dimitri exited the bar first, with me and Benny coming up behind. I'd just reached the door, when I heard Gino's raised voice. A cry pierced the air followed by a loud grunt and more muffled cries. I glanced back, but Benny's large hand landed on my shoulder.

"Leave it be, Nicco. We got what we came for."

But I saw red when I heard another faint whimper. Shrugging off Benny, I turned around and stormed through the bar. I came face to face with one of the guys as he leaped up. "I wouldn't go back there if I were you."

My hand went inside my jacket, flashing him the butt of my pistol. "You going to stop me?"

"Have at him, man." He held up his hands and stepped aside.

I ignored Benny's calls, fueled by nothing but anger and rage. She was still crying, her quiet sobs bleeding into me, turning my blood to molten lava.

"Get your fucking hands off her," I growled as I burst through the curtain. It was a small office and right there against the desk, Gino had his woman cowering, a bruise already forming around her eye.

"What the fuck?" he spat. "You don't get to come in here and tell me how to handle my shit."

"Apologize, now."

"Vaffanculo!"

I didn't give him another chance. I descended on him in a blur of fists and fury, relishing the crunch of my knuckles against his cheek, the soft tissue of his throat. He went down like a sack of bricks, blood trickling from his eye, grunts of pain spilling from his dirty fucking mouth. But I didn't stop… I couldn't.

"Don't hurt him, please…" The woman cried and I wanted to shake some goddamn sense into her. But I knew how it went. I knew how these women made excuses for their boyfriends and husbands. How they became so blinded to the cycle of abuse that they only ever had a list of excuses.

My chest heaved as I crouched down, grabbing him by his collar and yanking him forward. "Touch her again and next time it won't be my fists you have to worry about."

"Who the fuck do you think you are?" Spittle sprayed into the air as he tried to compose himself.

"Your worst fucking nightmare."

"Niccolò," Benny's voice cut through the tension. "We need to go."

"N- Niccolò?" The guy stuttered, confusion clouding his eyes. But then they grew wide as realization dawned. "Marchetti? Niccolò Marchetti?"

I didn't answer.

Shoving him hard, I stood up and smoothed down my jacket. "You should find a guy who treats you right," I said to the woman who was still sniffling.

"I- I love him."

Benny caught my eye and flicked his head to the main

bar. I ducked out of there and walked out of the place as if I hadn't just lost my cool.

"What the fuck was that?" Benny asked the second we hit the sidewalk.

"Just letting off some steam."

"Jesus, Nic, you're supposed to be laying low."

"He going to be a problem?" I flicked my head to the dingy bar.

"Nah, I'll handle it. But maybe you should stay at the house. You're a fucking liability."

He wasn't wrong. But I'd heard that woman's cries and all I heard was my mom and father arguing, his raised voice, her soft whimpers. All I'd seen was Arianne's broken and bruised body all over again. And then Alessia. My sweet, innocent sister with a faceless man, a man leveraging his power over her.

"It triggered some stuff," I confessed.

"You don't say." He clapped me on the back. "For a second there, I was worried we'd be adding clean up to our daily roster."

"It's been a long time coming if you ask me," Felix added. "Gino is a real piece of work. It isn't the first time I've seen Jenny black and blue and it probably won't be the last."

"You're right," I said around a grimace. "I probably shouldn't come around here again."

CHAPTER 4

ARIANNE

My hands shook as I finished putting the final touches to my hair. Nora had helped me style it off my face in messy bun, with stray waves framing my face. It was relaxed yet elegant.

The total opposite of how I felt.

My stomach was a tight knot and my chest felt like it was in a vise, but I had to do this.

"Ari?" Nora called, her head appearing around the door. "Are you almost… Oh my, you look beautiful." There was a tightness to her words that had me inhaling a shaky breath.

"He'll be here soon."

Emotion slammed into me like a tsunami, and I reached out for the dresser to steady myself.

"Hey," Nora rushed to my side. "Everything's going to be okay. It's just dinner. Luis said—"

"Just give me a second". Eyes screwed shut, I took three deep, cleansing breaths. I could do this.

I had to do this.

What other choice did I have?

If I didn't play my part—if I didn't paste on a smile and pretend to at least tolerate Scott—I might never get to see Nicco again.

"Okay." My eyes flickered open, my fingers curling around the edge of the dresser. "I'm ready."

It felt like preparing for battle, only my words were a weapon and my heart was the battlefield.

"Luis will be there the entire time."

"I know." I brushed a curl from my face and forced a weak smile.

Luis was to act as our chaperone. It was all part of my father's latest arrangement with Mike Fascini. Scott would court me—take me out for dinner, to business parties, family events—but our relationship would remain innocent until our wedding night.

Wedding night.

I still couldn't believe they wanted me to marry him.

My father said it was to protect me, but his words meant little considering he'd handed me over to my rapist as if I was a prized cow.

I followed Nora into the living area. Luis was waiting, his expression grim.

"Your father wishes to speak with you." He held out his cell phone and I let out a heavy sigh. Taking it, I pressed it to my ear and waited.

"Figlia mia?"

"Father."

"Mio tesoro, please... there are things you do not understand. Things I am trying to protect you from. This arrangement is the safest option for you right now."

"Very well," I clipped out. "Was there something else? Or

are you just calling to wish me a nice evening with my *fiancé?*"

He sucked in a harsh breath, cussing under his breath. "Everything I do, I do for you. One day, you will realize that."

"I will never forgive you for this," I seethed. "For handing me over to the man who…" I swallowed the words. Saying them gave them credence. It gave Scott power. And I refused to allow that. I refused to let him taint the memories I had of Nicco loving me.

He could have my company, my time, and even my hand in marriage, but he couldn't have my heart.

Never my heart.

"Arianne, please try to understand—"

"Then tell me the truth. Tell me what this is all about…"

"I can't, not yet." He let out a frustrated breath.

"Then goodbye, Father." I hung up and held out the cell to Luis. He took it, failing to hide his disapproval. But I knew it wasn't aimed at me, rather at the man I no longer called Papá.

"I'll be right there," Luis said, "every step of the way."

I gave him a sharp nod and waited for him to open the door. Scott might have held a certain amount of power over my life now, but I refused to give him my obedience. I would find pleasure in the small opportunities for dissension.

Starting with meeting him downstairs at his car.

But as Luis pulled open the door, I froze, hatred boiling my blood.

"Arianne, so early." He smirked, and I pressed my lips together, swallowing the hundred things I really wanted to say to him.

"We thought it would be less—"

"Yeah, yeah, you can save the excuses." He dismissed Luis, stepping closer. "Flowers, for the lady." Scott winked, handing me the bouquet of roses. I stared at them as if he was offering me his heart, carved from his chest, bloody and still beating in his fingers.

"Thank you," I almost choked over the words. Reluctantly taking the flowers from his hands, I doubled back only to find Nora standing there, tears and anger in her eyes.

"Burn them for all I care," I thrust them at her and she snickered.

"Ari..." Concern glittered in her eyes.

"I'll be okay. I promise."

Steeling myself, I spun around and made my way out of the apartment, not bothering to stop for Scott. He stumbled after me, his dark chuckle making my spine stiffen.

"The harder you push, the sweeter it'll be when you finally give in." He grabbed my arm, lacing it with his. I glared up at him. Anger vibrated through me, but Luis cleared his throat, moving around us to open the door.

"You'll follow in the SUV," Scott barked as if he had the power to give orders.

"Not part of the deal. I go where Arianne goes." Luis cut him with a hard look, but Scott didn't relent, the two of them locked in a silent battle of wills.

"We can always call Roberto or your father and settle this?"

"You ride in the back," Scott conceded, guiding me over to his sports car. It was so pretentious and full of bad memories. A shiver worked its way through me as he pulled open the door and pressed his hand to the small of my back. "Remember how much fun we had the last time we were in here?"

I ducked around him and slipped into the car, forcing myself to breathe. The familiar smell of the leather hit me, overwhelming me.

This was all a game to him.

A sick twisted game in which Scott wanted me afraid and

cowering. But he was forgetting one thing. When a wild animal was cornered it either surrendered or fought—and I wasn't about to cower to Scott Fascini, regardless of how much he tried to disarm me.

My fingers curled into the soft leather seat as I forced myself to slow my breathing. My senses were on high alert. For as much as I wanted to forget, I could remember every detail about the last time I was in this car. That fateful night had been the catalyst for a chain of events I couldn't have imagined even in my wildest dreams. A chain of events that had flipped my world on its head in so many ways.

The car doors slammed as Luis and Scott climbed inside.

"Well, isn't this cozy?" he sneered. "Maybe I should have made the reservation for three?"

Luis smothered a snort. "Just drive," he grumbled.

"I think you'll really like the restaurant I picked." Scott's hand landed on my knee, my body tensing. He smirked over at me. The grin of a predator tracking its prey. But I wouldn't be his victim again.

I refused.

My hand slid over his, my fingers slipping into the spaces between.

"See," he said. "That wasn't so difficult—"

I wrenched his index finger back, his pained grunt filling the car. "Fucking bitch."

Flashing him my own smirk, I said, "Who, me?"

"That's really how you want to play it?" His brows furrowed, his voice a low growl. "Because you should know, my fiancée, I never lose."

Sorrento's was a seafood lover's paradise. Nestled in one of the quaint streets of the city, it was a decadent fusion of Italy and America. I'd only been here once, when I was a child. But my parents had a monthly reservation. Anyone who was anyone in Verona County did. So I was hardly surprised that Scott had managed to get us a table.

"Mr. Fascini," the Maître D said, "we have your regular table ready and waiting."

"Thank you, Carlo." Scott urged me forward, his hand pressing the small of my back in a possessive display of ownership.

I hated it.

I hated everything about this.

Knowing Luis was close by gave me some sense of comfort, but did little to ease the tight knot in my stomach.

"Wine?"

"A bottle of champagne please, we're celebrating." Scott barely acknowledged the Maître D, keeping his eyes fixed firmly on my face.

"Of course, Mr. Fascini, I'll have someone bring it right out." He scurried away.

"Alone at last." Scott relaxed back in his chair, making no attempt to hide the way his eyes lazily appraised my body. I'd opted for black pants and a chiffon blouse. It was demure yet elegant. Date worthy but safe. If I'd have had my way, I would have worn a burlap sack, but as Nora reminded me, I needed to play my part. At least until someone figured out how to get me the hell out of this nightmare.

It would have been so easy to run; to get up and never look back. I could flee to Boston and Nicco and I could disappear across country. But he had responsibilities. He had a whole legacy weighing on his shoulders, not to mention Alessia and his cousins. I couldn't ask that of him.

Besides, Verona was my home. Nora was here. My mom... My life.

Running felt like surrender, and I refused to cower. Not

to Scott, not to my father, not to this game I didn't fully understand yet.

"Has your father talked to you about the party?"

"Party?" Dread snaked up my spine.

"The engagement party, of course. Well, at least it will be once they announce it."

Just then, the server arrived with our champagne. I wasted no time holding out my glass. "Thank you," I muttered, downing it in one. The bubbles fizzed all the way down and I covered my mouth with a hand.

Scott chuckled. "My fiancée just found out some exciting news."

"Oh, well congratulations." The server offered to refill my glass, but I declined. I needed to keep my wits about me, not succumb to the tempting distraction of alcohol.

"You should have another." Scott motioned to the bottle on ice. "Loosen up a little."

"I think I should probably stick to water."

"Spoilsport," he drawled. "I went to see Tristan today. The doctors said he could wake any day."

Pain coiled around my heart. Me and my cousin might not have always seen eye to eye, but he was still my family, my blood. I didn't want him to die.

"I hope he does."

"At least Marchetti is gone. He's lucky he isn't rotting in a cell like he deserves for what he did to Tristan." Scott said the words as if it negated his responsibility for what happened that night. If he hadn't provoked Nicco we wouldn't be sitting here right now.

Oh, who was I kidding?

I didn't know how things would have turned out because it was abundantly clear that my life was not my own. I was but a puppet and my puppet master was a man who wore many faces.

Father.
Traitor.
Sinner.
Liar.

Roberto Capizola was a man I could no longer trust. A man who spoke of protecting me and putting me first, but who locked me away in our house for five years to save me from the truth.

My father was not a good man.

My legacy was not built on the blood, sweat, and tears of an honest past. It was built on lies and secrets and a dark past he didn't think I was strong enough to know about.

I grabbed the bottle of champagne and refilled my glass.

"Are you ready to order?" The server reappeared, looking a little sheepish. Scott straightened and folded his hands on the table.

"I'd like my usual, hold the sauce with extra greens please."

"Very good, Mr. Fascini. And for the lady?"

Before I could get out the first word, Scott said, "She'll have the same, thank you."

The server gave him a tight nod and started walking away, but indignation burned through me. "Excuse me," I called after him grabbing one of the leather-bound menus. "Actually, I'd like a garden salad with a side order of the shrimp."

"Excellent choice." He gave me a small smile before hurrying away.

"I'm quite capable of ordering my own meal."

"You want to be independent," Scott relaxed in his chair again, "I can dig that. But you know, Arianne, you need to get used to being taken care of."

"I'm not looking to be somebody's arm candy, Scott." His name vibrated through me.

His lip curled with amusement. "You have so much to learn about the world, Bellissima."

"Do not call me that," I seethed, my fingers curling around the edge of my seat.

"Our union will make our families strong. It will make us a force to be reckoned with. The Capizola and the Fascini." Something flickered in his eyes. "You and me, it's happening, baby. So you can either get on board with that, or you can fight me at every turn. Either way, I'm going to enjoy the ride."

The champagne washed in my stomach, and I swallowed the acid rushing up my throat. Scott wasn't going to make this easy. He was going to push and taunt me at every turn.

He picked up his glass and inspected it, his eyes catching me through the polished crystal. "I am counting down the days until I can have you again."

I sucked in a harsh breath. I couldn't do this. I couldn't sit and listen to his sick and twisted words. "Excuse me, I need to go to the bathroom." Gingerly, I stood and grabbed my purse. Luis immediately caught my eye and moved into position to follow me. I hurried toward the back of the room and slipped into the ladies' restroom.

There was a knock and Luis' gruff voice followed. "Arianne? Are you okay?"

"Just a minute." My voice cracked, as I fought desperately to keep the tears at bay. I'd foolishly thought that if I didn't give Scott power over me, he couldn't hurt me.

I was wrong.

People like Scott—*men* like Scott—didn't wait to be given power, they took it. He wouldn't stop his tirade until he won. Until he had me broken at his feet, begging him to stop.

"Arianne, I'm coming in." Luis cracked the door open and ducked inside. "What is it, what's wrong?"

"He—" An ugly sob tore from my throat as my body trembled with frustration and pain.

"Ssh." My bodyguard wrapped me into his arms, holding me. "He's just trying to get a reaction from you."

I eased back to look at him. "Well, it's working." Luis handed me a tissue and I dabbed the corner of my eyes. "I don't think I can do this."

"You can." He gave me a sad smile. "You must."

I glanced away. In that moment, I didn't want to fight. I didn't want to stand tall and refuse to let the likes of Scott Fascini and my father walk all over me.

I wanted to run.

I wanted to beg Luis to take me far away from Verona County and never look back.

"Arianne, look at me," he let out a strained breath. Slowly, I lifted my tear-stained eyes to his. "You are one of the strongest people I know. You are kind and compassionate and you have such a big heart. Don't let him take that from you. Don't let that piece of shit win."

"O- okay. I'm okay." I slipped out of his hold and went over to the mirror, drying my eyes. "Can I have a minute?"

Luis hesitated, but after a beat, he nodded, leaving me alone.

Digging my cell phone out of my purse, I opened my messages.

Tell me something good.

It pinged straightaway, making my mouth curve into a half-smile.

. . .

I love you.

Another message came straight through.

Is everything okay?

It will be. I love you too.

Emotion clogged my throat as I awaited his reply. God, I wanted to see Nicco. To bury myself in his arms and breathe him in.

Be strong, Bambolina. Be strong for me. For us.

CHAPTER 5

NICCO

"Is that her?" Dane asked me as we sat out back with a beer. The flames from the fire pit licked high into the inky night's sky, the crackle hypnotic.

"Yeah," I said tightly, dropping my cell on the arm of the chair.

"What's she like?"

"You really want to know?"

"I can't ever imagine meeting a chick who knocks me on my ass, humor me."

"Arianne is..." I released a small breath. "She's like no one else I've ever met."

"And you had no idea that she was... you know. The enemy." He whispered the words as if they were forbidden.

"None." My chest tightened. "Do you really think I would have...?" I stopped myself. To suggest a world without Arianne seemed impossible.

I knew what Dane thought, what all of my uncles and the

guys thought. They didn't understand how I could fall so hard and fast for a girl I barely knew. Hell, even I didn't understand it. But I was done questioning it. Fate had entwined our paths that night, and I wouldn't have wanted it any other way.

Before Arianne, I had been numb; a reluctant prince wearing a crown too heavy. My only priority was the Family and fulfilling my duty. But meeting Arianne was like taking my first breath. She smiled and all the stars came out to take notice. And something inside me had come to life. I wanted to protect her. Stand by her side. I wanted to bind myself to her with permanence and loyalty and love.

I wanted things with her I had no right to want as a nineteen-year-old mafioso. A mafioso who would one day be head of the Family.

"It's rough, man," Dane let out a low whistle before taking a long pull on his beer. "The one girl you want is the only girl you can't have."

My eyes cut to his, but I found no arrogance there, just mild curiosity. Dane was still green, skirting on the fringe of the Family before he turned eighteen, graduated high school, and took his role under his father's rule.

We were the future.

Our fathers' legacies.

But it was something no one could prepare you for.

"Maybe I'll get to meet her one day. Show her I'm the better looking Marchetti." He waggled his brows and I threw my bottle cap at his head. Dane batted it away, laughter rumbling in his chest.

"Not a fucking chance."

He shrugged. "It's not like I don't already have options."

"Options?" My brow rose. Cocky fucker.

"Like you, Enzo, and Matteo didn't screw around in high

school. Enzo is one of the biggest players I've ever met. That guy is—"

"Don't ever let him hear you say that shit." The vibrations of my cell phone demanded my attention and I picked it up.

They're at some fancy place in the city. Luis is with them.

Good. Stay on them.

I hit send, unsure whether to feel relieved or more anxious. I hadn't even had to ask Bailey to keep an eye on Arianne, he'd offered. I didn't want to drag him any deeper into the shit between me, Fascini, and Roberto, but something told me he wouldn't listen anyway. And the truth was, I needed to have eyes on her, eyes I trusted with my life.

"Everything okay?" Dane asked, and I nodded. "You sure don't look like everything's okay. You can talk to me, you know. We're family. One day we're going to be running everything, together."

I didn't ever let myself look too far into the future, not when it was mapped out before me. But things were different now.

I was different.

"I'm trying to see a way through this, but I'm not going to lie, kid, it's real fucking hard."

"Hey, less of the kid. You're like two years older than me."

"Three."

"Yeah, yeah, whatever." He waved me off. "You know your old man will fix it. Uncle Toni isn't going to let some Suit piss all over him and the Family."

"You know the history between the Marchetti and the Capizola?"

He gave me a half-shrug. "I know all I need to know. They went one way, we went the other, now we're on opposite sides of the line."

I smirked. The kid sure had a way with words. "Something like that." I scrubbed my jaw. "The point is, we've got history." And history had a funny way of repeating itself.

Dane grumbled to himself. He was still young. He didn't understand the finesse required when handling certain situations. Roberto Capizola and Mike Fascini weren't just your everyday guys. They had power, money... they had connections. If we were going to finally go up against them, we needed to have an airtight plan. Because when you went to war people got hurt.

People died.

"I just hate knowing that she's there... with him. If he hurts her again..." Pure rage exploded in my veins. My body shook, my teeth grinding violently behind my lips.

I wanted to kill Scott Fascini.

I *would* kill him.

One day, when he was least expecting it, I would watch the life drain from his eyes and feel nothing but satisfaction.

"Shit, Nicco, you're a better guy than me. Some dude ever touched a girl I was seeing, I'd tear his dick off his body and feed it to him."

I smiled at that. I couldn't help it. "Trust me when I say, he'll get what's coming to him."

One way or another, Scott Fascini would pay.

Silence settled over us as we stared at the roaring fire. Boston was worlds apart from La Riva. My thoughts drifted to Enzo and Matteo and what they would be doing right now. Part of me wondered if Matt would be able to keep our hot-headed cousin out of trouble. I'd asked them both to keep an eye on Alessia. I wanted to ask them to watch over Arianne, but Enzo was still coming to terms with everything, and I knew he intimidated her. So Bailey seemed like the better option, for now. We all needed to lie low, to let the dust settle. Roberto Capizola might have double crossed me, but he'd obviously pulled some strings because I was still breathing and as far as I was aware, there had been no comeback on the Family yet.

Everything was quiet.

The calm before the unstoppable storm.

I'd beaten the crap out of Scott and put Tristan Capizola in a coma. You didn't just walk away from that.

"What's it like?" Dane finally broke the silence. "Being a capo? Being out there, working for the Family?"

Dane was a tall kid. He had broad shoulders and a trim waist, and it was obvious he worked out. But right there, with the glow of the fire dancing across his face, he looked like a little kid, scared and fascinated in equal measure.

"It is what it is." I ran my thumb around the bottle neck. "Being Marchetti means family, it means putting the Family above all else. It means being prepared to fight... to hurt... to *die* for Dominion."

"Your initiation..." His voice was quiet, a trace of uncertainty there. "What did you have to do?"

"You know what it entails." All men born into the Family did.

"Yeah but hearing about it and knowing it are different things."

I tipped my head to the sky, letting out a strained breath. I didn't think about that night often. The night me, Enzo, and Matteo were formally initiated. But I could still remember it as if it were yesterday.

They said your first kill changed you; well mine had

tattooed itself on my soul, a blood-stained shadow that would never fade.

"Come," my father beckoned us into the dimly lit room. I felt like a complete idiot in the all-black outfit. The floor was cold beneath my feet as I led my cousins—my two best friends in the whole world—to the table where my father stood.

I knew the drill; I'd heard enough stories about the making ceremony growing up around the boss.

"Niccolò, Lorenzo, Matteo, the time has come." He motioned for us to approach the table. The flames from the candelabras flickered wildly, casting shadows around the room. A half-circle of my father's most trusted men stood around him. I spotted my uncle Michele, and Enzo's father, my Uncle Vincenzo. They all looked the same in their slacks and dress shirts, their hair neat and tidy, expressions like stone. It was no surprise; they knew what was to come.

They knew what we'd have to do.

Enzo and Matteo stood quietly, flanking each of my sides. As son of the boss, they knew I would be called first.

"Niccolò Luca, how do you arrive here tonight?" My father lifted the small dagger, light bouncing off its blade. A shiver ran up my spine. This day has been inevitable for me from the moment I took my first breath. It was in my blood.

It was my legacy.

"I come ready to take the oath," I repeated the words I always knew I'd one day say.

My father motioned for me to give him my hand. I lay it palm open facing up, as he began. "Niccolò Luca, tonight you are reborn. The blood that flows through your veins is Marchetti blood," he jabbed the tip of the knife into my finger, but I did not flinch, "the blood of Dominion. It means you will put first the Family above all

47

else. You will answer the call of the Family above all else. And you will defend the Family above all else. Do you understand?"

"I do."

He pinched my finger, letting the beads of blood drip onto the card of the saint. "Swear on the saint that you will carry the secrets of the Family always."

"I swear."

My father took a lighter and ignited a corner of the card, dropping it into the palm of my hand. "As she burns so too does your soul. When the flames die, you are reborn."

The card turned to nothing but smoke and ash in my hand. I didn't know how I'd feel, finally taking my place in the Family, but as I stood there, I felt the ties snake through me, binding me to a life I'd never asked for.

A life I had to embrace anyway.

I loved my family. I loved my father, my uncles, and my elders. But to take this oath, to swear Omertà, was to sacrifice my freedom.

The flames died out as my father's large hand landed on my shoulder. He leaned in kissing my cheek. "La famiglia prima di tutto."

I stepped aside, letting Enzo take my place. He repeated the same ceremony, Matteo going last. My father's men descended on us, clapping us on the back and welcoming us to the Family. But it was all a formality. For the night was only just beginning. It wasn't enough to take the oath and swear on the saint though. You had to prove your allegiance.

"Let us eat," my father declared, moving to the long table set up behind us. "Tonight, we welcome my son and my nephews into the fold. Tonight, they become real men."

My eyes lowered to Dane. He was watching me, curiosity and fear glittering in his eyes.

You should be scared.

"Enjoy senior year," I said. "Make the most of the time you have left to be a kid. Because once you take the oath..."

I took a long pull on my beer, trying to wash down the lump in my throat.

"It's all good." Nervous laughter vibrated in Dane's chest. "I'm ready," he added.

"We're all ready," I said quietly. "Until the time comes." Until they forced a gun into your bloodied trembling fist and told you to pull the trigger.

Another vibration of my cell jolted me from the dark memory. "I need to take this," I said, standing.

"Sure thing, man. I'll catch you tomorrow."

"Is she okay?" I asked the second I was out of earshot.

"She's...." Luis let out an exasperated breath. "This shit is messed up, Marchetti. Fascini is acting like he didn't..." I heard him swallow the words.

"Did he—"

"No, no. He's said a few things and sat there with that fucking smug smirk on his face. But for the most part, he's been like a well-behaved dog."

"Where is she now?"

"He ran into some friends. They're all at the bar talking."

"You can still see them?"

"I won't let them out of my sight.... You know it would be so easy." Silence fell over the line. "So fucking easy to put a bullet between his eyes. I could do it, I could—"

"No." The words cracked my chest open. "We need to know exactly what we're dealing with first." If Scott and his father were somehow related to the Ricci, we needed to know. Ending Scott—no matter how much I wanted that—had to wait. We had to see this thing through.

"How are you holding up?"

Luis' question caught me off guard. I ran a hand down my face, feeling my days old stubble beneath my fingers.

"This isn't about me," I ground out, unable to disguise the quiver in my voice. "It's about Arianne."

So long as she was okay, I would be okay.

"That girl must have balls of steel to do what she's done tonight. But I gotta say, Marchetti, I don't trust him. Even if Roberto has managed to negotiate a celibacy agreement, he's a monster. I see it every time he looks at her. He's playing by the rules now but I'm not sure how long he'll be able to curb his hunger."

I bristled, my eyes shuttering at his words. "Just stay on her. I need you to stay on her every fucking second."

"I will. I'll check in when we're back at the apartment."

"Thank you."

Luis hung up but I was still staring at the screen long after he was gone. I couldn't see past the red mist descending in my vision. Nothing about this felt right.

Not one single fucking thing.

CHAPTER 6

ARIANNE

"I want to leave," I said through gritted teeth, forcing a smile so that Scott's friends didn't think I was rude.

I didn't care what they thought but I also didn't want to draw any attention to myself.

"Come on, baby," Scott crooned. "Just a little while—"

"You can either take me home, or I'll have Luis call for a car." He was bound to have a car nearby, just in case.

Scott laughed nervously, his gaze flicking to the couple we had spent the last hour chatting with at the bar. "Don't make a scene, Ari. Dale and Kayla are good friends. Just one more drink and then we'll go."

"You enjoy that drink." I slid off the stool, gently nudging him out of the way. "I'm leaving."

I couldn't breathe. Between the constant fake smiles and forced laughter, the rubber band around my chest had grown tighter and tighter. If I didn't get some fresh air soon, I was either going to faint, or say or do something I might live to regret.

"Is everything okay?" Dale asked.

Peering around Scott's shoulder I mustered a weak smile. "Actually, I'm not feeling so good. I think we're going to call it a night." I slipped my purse underneath my arm and tucked a stray curl behind my ear.

"Already? The night is still young. Scott was just getting to the good part."

I had to force myself not to roll my eyes. Scott hadn't stopped talking. As the evening went on, it became more and more apparent he loved the sound of his own voice. Dale had asked him about his injuries, and Scott had jumped at the chance to tell them about the night he had defended my honor against the infamous Niccolò Marchetti, who almost killed him and my cousin.

And I'd sat there silent, pretending that reliving that night wasn't like a thousand tiny blades cutting away at my skin.

"Darling, if Arianna says she needs to go, leave them be."

"It's Arianne." I almost bared my teeth at Kayla. She wasn't trying to help me out. She was trying to belittle me, the way she had the entire night. But jealousy was a powerful motivator, and I hadn't missed the way she'd made moon eyes at Scott ever since we joined them at the bar.

She obviously didn't see the monster beneath the expensive clothes and wolfish grin.

"Oh, silly me." She splayed a perfectly manicured hand on Dale's stomach, her eyes half-lidded with lust as she let them run over Scott's chest. His lip curled in a knowing smirk, causing a deep shudder to roll through me. They were being so blatant.

It was disgusting.

"Perhaps, you should stay?" I suggested. "I'm sure Layla would like that."

Dale started choking as his girlfriend narrowed her eyes at me. Scott merely chuckled, grabbing my hand in his. "Jealous, love?"

I pressed my lips into a thin line.

Breathe. Just breathe.

"It's such an unattractive quality, don't you think?" Kayla sneered.

"Now, now ladies." Dale let out a strained laugh. "Let's put the claws away. Rest assured, Ari, this one knows who she belongs to." Kayla yelped and I could only assume Dale had pinched or smacked her butt.

"Well, it was nice to meet you." I started to pull away from Scott, silently praying he wouldn't fight me on it.

"I'm sure we'll be seeing you again." Dale winked, a knowing glint in his eye.

Oh God, did he know? Had Scott already told him about the engagement?

"Enjoy the rest of your night," I said, not sticking around to hear Scott's parting words. I needed to get out of here.

Now.

Luis approached me, silently asking me if I was okay. I pursued my lips, nodding. "Come on," he said. "Let's get you home." Luis pulled open the door just as Scott caught up with us.

"Vitelli, you can drive." He thrust his keys at Luis.

"Maybe I should call for a car?"

"Worried you can't handle her?"

Luis' expression tightened. "I'll drive. But you need to figure out how you're going to get home from La Stella."

"Maybe I'll stay over?" Scott smirked in my direction.

I didn't dignify his suggestion with an answer, slipping past him and leaving the restaurant. The cool air instantly hit me, and I inhaled a deep breath in a desperate attempt to temper the storm raging inside me.

"You need to learn your place." Scott moved beside me, placing his hand on the small of my back. The intimate action was like a knife to the stomach. "Dale Manzello is a good friend and a respected businessman. It wouldn't hurt you to show a little respect."

"Like Kayla was showing you so much respect?" I all but spat the words.

"Careful, Principessa, I might mistake your venom for jealousy."

I swallowed a groan.

"This is fun." Scott dipped his head to my ear, his touch growing firmer. "It's going to be so fucking sweet watching you kneel at my feet."

My fingers curled into fists so tight my nails began to cut my skin.

"The car." Luis cleared his throat and I used the moment to my advantage, stepping away from Scott and toward my bodyguard.

"Thank you," I said as he opened the passenger side door. But Scott cut across my body, preventing my access.

"I think Ari and I will sit in the back, together." His hand brushed my waist, lingering on the curve of my butt. "After all, we have so much reacquainting to do." He leaned in, his breath hitting my face, his mouth so close I could almost taste the whisky on his tongue.

My vision began to blur, a crippling wave of nausea crashing over me.

"Arianne," someone yelled as I reached out for something —anything. But it was too late. The world began to tilt, the black abyss swallowing me whole.

∼

"Arianne?" Luis' concerned expression filled my vision. "Meno male!"

"W- what happened?"

"You fainted." He crouched down beside me. We were still on the sidewalk, a crowd of people gathered around all wearing similar expressions of concern.

"Here," someone thrust a bottle of water at me. "You should drink something until the EMTs arrive."

"EM—no." I lifted a hand, swaying slightly as everything started to spin again. "I'm fine, thank you."

"Arianne, baby, thank God." Scott burst through the crowd. "I was worried sick."

"Luis." I clutched my bodyguard's arm, confusion muddying my thoughts. "I want to go home," I whispered.

"The car should be here any second."

"Now hang on a minute." Scott began to interject, but Luis straightened to his full height and the two of them had a silent conversation while a kind-faced woman gently patted my hand.

"Is it the baby?"

"Excuse me?" I sat upright.

"Oh, I'm so sorry." Guilt flashed in her eyes. "I thought... early pregnancy knocked me off my feet more times than I can count."

"I'm not pregnant." I suppressed a shudder.

"Did you eat?"

"I'm fine. I just got a little overwhelmed."

She nodded, offering me a sympathetic smile. "Your fiancé was so concerned. It really was very sweet. And your uncle, he seemed—"

"Uncle?"

"Is he not—"

"Arianne." Luis loomed over us. "The car is here."

"What about Scott?" His name was like ash on my tongue.

"I've made arrangements for him to get home safely. Come on." Luis offered me his hand and I accepted, letting him pull me off the floor and onto my feet. "You good?"

"I think so." Embarrassment burned through me, but it was nothing compared to the memory of Scott's hand on the curve of my waist, his mouth dangerously close to mine.

I felt him watching, his stare heavy and thunderous. Glancing back, I met his eyes and held his stare. Scott was pissed, it was written all over his face. But it was more than that. There was a possessiveness in his narrowed gaze that made my body tremble. He truly believed I was his. And despite my resolve not to let him get to me, I couldn't deny I was terrified about the lengths he would go to, to make sure I remained so.

Luis led me to the sleek, black SUV and opened the door. I climbed inside, surprised when he followed me.

"Everything good?" The driver asked. I recognized him. He was the security guy who usually stayed with Nora.

"Just drive," Luis said gruffly.

"Are you okay?" I asked, peeking over at him.

"Shit, Arianne. That's supposed to be my line."

"I'm okay. I think I just..."

"It triggered you."

"What?"

"Something Scott said or did. I think it triggered you."

I curled my hands over the edge of the cool leather seat. "He wanted me to get in the car and it was like I couldn't breathe. I couldn't—" A garbled cry spilled from my lips.

"Hey, you're okay." Luis shuffled closer, pulling me into his arms. "You're okay."

Fisting his shirt, I sobbed quietly into his chest. Maybe he was right. Maybe Scott had triggered something. Despite everything being so raw, I had tried my hardest to switch off the memories. I refused to give them power over me. But the scars were real, and they did have power over me.

He had power over me.

I needed to accept that.

I needed to accept it, then find a way to wield it.

"You need me to call Nicco?" Luis whispered and I shot up.

"No, you can't tell him." If he knew what had happened... I didn't want to think about what he might do.

"Ari," Luis exhaled a strained breath. "I'm not sure we should keep this from him."

"Please, promise me. You can't tell him, Luis. Nicco needs to stay in Boston."

His expression softened. "Okay. But if it happens again... maybe you should see a doctor?"

"I don't need a doctor." I needed a miracle.

"I'm just saying, maybe talking to someone will help."

"I just got overwhelmed. It won't happen again."

"Ari—"

"I'm fine, Luis." I waved him off. "I just need to rest."

"Then rest. I won't let anything happen to you."

At his reassuring words, my eyes fluttered shut and I let myself drift, desperately wanting to believe him.

"Are you sure?" Nora asked the next morning, over coffee and pancakes.

"I need the distraction. I can't stay here all day, hiding. It'll drive me stir crazy."

"I get that but after last night..."

"Last night was... well, I don't really know what last night was. But I'm fine today. I can do this. I need to do this."

She gave me a knowing look. I'd seen it before. It was usually right before she delivered me some truth bomb.

"He raped you, Ari. Scott slipped you something and then he... *hurt* you." She took a shuddering breath. "I admire your strength. I admire the fact you want to face this head on and not let him hold the power. But I also think Luis is right, you need to give yourself space to deal with this. You need help, babe. Professional help. Maybe you should give yourself some time—"

"Time?" I shot up out of my seat, coffee spilling everywhere. "I don't need time. I need Nicco. I need for my father not to be a lying manipulative asshole. And I need to not be a pawn in some game I'm still not sure I even understand. Talking to some doctor or shrink isn't going to give me any of that. It isn't going to fix this nightmare I've found myself in.

"He gave me to Scott, Nor. My own father handed me over like a baton, and I'm terrified that if I don't comply, if I don't follow the rules, something bad will happen." Because a tiny part of me had to believe there was more to this, that my father wasn't as cruel and callous as he seemed.

Angry tears streamed down my cheeks as I inhaled a ragged breath. "So no, I don't want to talk. I don't want to try to explore my feelings about what happened. I want to carry on as normal and pretend that I still have the power to make choices about my own life. I want to pretend that I'm not just waiting for the next bomb to drop. I want—"

Nora rushed over, pulling me into her arms. "I'm sorry, I'm so fucking sorry. Whatever you need, I'm here. I just... I was so worried when Luis texted to tell me what happened."

"He did that?" I pulled back, swallowing the lump in my throat.

"He cares about you, Ari. We both do." She smiled weakly. "He also told me you made him promise not to tell Nicco."

"He can't know, Nor." Pain splintered through me. "He just can't."

"That's not... yeah, okay."

"I just need to be more aware of my emotions around Scott. He deliberately pushed my buttons most of the night. He wants to see me crack."

"Piece of shit," she sneered. "I can't wait for the day he gets what's coming to him."

"Nora." I wanted Scott to pay, I did. But I wasn't sure I wanted Nicco to spill any more blood.

Not for me.

She shrugged. "He deserves everything he has coming. I won't apologize for that."

"Who are you right now?"

"A girl who would do anything for her best friend."

"You're a little scary," I admitted around a weak smile.

"I just... God, he makes my blood boil. And don't even get me started on your dad."

"My life was never my own, I realize that now. I will always and forever be the Capizola heir."

"No. No way. I refuse to accept that." Nora shook her head. "You are so much more, Arianne. You are kind and compassionate and humble. And strong... you're so fucking strong. And what you've found with Nicco is rare. It's worth fighting for. It's worth hurting for.

"Nicco and his father will come through, babe. I don't doubt that. Because family is everything to Antonio, and you are everything to Nicco. So we'll do it. We'll keep on pretending everything is fine while we figure this out."

"Thank you," I breathed, relief spreading through me. Maybe one day, I would stop and take stock of everything that happened to me. But today was not that day.

It couldn't be.

Because if I stopped, my control on things would slip.

And if I slipped, if I lowered my guard for even a second, that's when Scott would strike.

If I'd learned anything since arriving at Montague it was that the good guys weren't always good, and the bad guys weren't always bad.

"Okay, let's go," she said, "We can stop at the coffee shop on the way."

"We already ate."

Nora shrugged. "I can always make room for a blueberry muffin. Luis," she called, and he slipped into the room. "We're going to walk to the coffee shop and then head downtown."

"It's a nice morning for it." He gave her a tight nod, his gaze flicking to mine. "How are you?"

"I'm okay, thank you."

He nodded again.

I had just grabbed my bag when my cell started ringing. "Mia cara," Mom's voice filled the line. "How are you? How was...?" She trailed off.

"It was okay." Nora caught my eye and gave me a reassuring smile. "Something happened though. I fainted."

"Oh gosh, Arianne." She smothered a cry. "I am so sorry, sweetheart. I wish things were different, I wish I could... But your father, he's withdrawn. He won't even talk to me about it. Something is happening, but I don't know how to—"

"It's okay, Mamma." It wasn't but I couldn't do this. I couldn't carry her guilt as well. "I'm just about to go out with Nora. Can we talk later?"

"Of course. Your father has asked... he wants you to come to the estate later to talk about the..." She inhaled a shaky breath. "There are arrangements to make, for the party."

The permanent knot in my stomach tightened. "Very well," I said flatly. "I will see you later."

"Wait," she rushed out. "I love you, figlia mia. I love you so much. And we'll get through this, I promise."

I mumbled goodbye and hung up.

"Everything okay?" Nora asked from the door.

"My father has summoned me. He wants to see me at the estate later."

Her expression faltered. "Did she say why?"

"The party..."

"Oh."

"Arianne?" Luis appeared over Nora's shoulder. The second his eyes landed on me he paled. "What is it?"

"Nothing."

Nothing I said right now would change anything. Not unless I asked him to take me away from here. And I couldn't do that to Nora or my mom, despite her misguided loyalty to my father.

For now, I was stuck here.

So I did the only thing within my power.

I held my head high, steeled myself, and said, "Let's go."

CHAPTER 7

NICCO

I padded into my room, shutting the door behind me. It had been a long fucking day. My aunt had tried to keep me company, but I was like a bear with a sore head. Only four days in exile and I was already starting to feel like a caged animal.

My father had no updates. Tommy, our investigator, and Stefan, the Family's consigliere, were working around the clock to dig up dirt on Mike Fascini, but there was nothing new to report. And to make matters worse, Arianne had texted earlier to say she needed to talk to me.

Dropping onto the bed, I ran a hand through my hair. It was still damp from my workout. Dane and Uncle Alonso had a fully equipped gym in the house, so I'd spent a couple of hours burning off some steam. But it wasn't enough. Restless energy coursed through my veins like lava. The whole time, I'd only been able to picture that fucker with his hands on Arianne.

My girl.

My life.

Luis had said everything had gone fine; that after dinner and drinks with Fascini's friends, he had driven Arianne home and called Scott a cab. But my mind was the enemy, working against me to concoct all kinds of nightmarish endings.

And now she wanted to talk to me about something.

I was ready to detonate.

My cell started vibrating and I scooped it up, bringing it to my ear. "Nicco?" Her voice was small, and my chest tightened.

"Bambolina."

A beat passed.

Another.

Neither of us spoke but the silence was deafening. This was our life now. Pained silence and bittersweet memories.

"How are you?" Arianne finally spoke.

"I thought it would be okay. I thought I'd come here, and knowing you were safe would be enough... but it's killing me. It's only been four days and it's killing me."

"I know," she whispered. "I looked for you today. I wandered around downtown with Nora, expecting you to appear. What are we going to do, Nicco? How are we going to survive this?"

Letting myself fall backward, I inhaled a shuddering breath. "We keep going, Bambolina. We have to keep going."

"I..." Arianne hesitated.

"What is it, amore mio?"

"My father wants to see me tonight... It's about the party."

My blood boiled. "Do you know when it is?"

"Soon, I think."

I rubbed my temples. I wanted to comfort her, to tell her

everything was going to be okay. But I couldn't find the words.

The thought of Arianne being paraded in front of everyone, introduced as Scott's fiancée, tore me up inside.

She wasn't his.

She would *never* be his.

Yet, he was there, and I was here and there wasn't a damn thing I could do about it.

"There's still time. Your birthday isn't until February. That's still five months away. My father will have a plan before then. He will—"

"Nicco, stop. Please. I don't want to keep doing this. It hurts too much."

"Bambolina," I breathed, her pain palpable even over the phone.

"Just talk to me, tell me about your day."

"There isn't much to tell," I confessed.

"Humor me."

"I had breakfast with my aunt, uncle, and Dane this morning. Then when he finally left to meet his friends, I helped my aunt around the house, then—"

"Wait, you did chores?"

I chuckled. "Surprised?"

"A little." I heard the smile in her answer. "I can't imagine big bad Niccolò Marchetti helping with the dishes."

"You think I'm big and bad?" The corner of my mouth tipped. I liked hearing Arianne like this: playful and happy.

"Well, aren't you?"

"Sometimes," I lowered my voice. "When I need to be."

There was a beat of silence, the slight ruffle of material. "What are you doing?" I asked.

"My towel slipped."

Heat flooded me, zipping straight to my dick. "Don't tell me you just got out of the shower?"

"Well, yeah..."

"Fuck, Bambolina. Do you have any idea how crazy that drives me, knowing you're there, naked—"

"I'm not naked, I have a towel wrapped around me." Arianne's soft laughter was music to my ears, but it only fueled the blood pumping through me.

"I wish I was there." It came out strained.

"Why?" Her voice was barely a whisper. "What would you do?"

"You really want to know?"

I waited with bated breath, my heart crashing against my ribcage. I hadn't planned on this, but I'd take it. I'd take anything I could get where Arianne was concerned.

"Yes, I want to imagine you're here, Nicco. I want to imagine you touching me."

"I'm right there, trailing my lips all over your damp skin. Can you feel it, can you feel my kisses?"

"Y- yes." It was a soft moan.

"Are you alone?"

"Yes, Luis is out in the hall."

Thank fuck.

"Do you trust me?"

"You know I do."

"Lie down on your bed." There was a brief pause. "Good?" I asked.

"Good." Her voice was thick with desire.

"Undo your towel, Bambolina." I heard the slight hitch in her breath. "Now trail your hand down your stomach slowly."

"It tickles."

"It's supposed to." I smiled. Jesus, I wanted to be there. I wanted to worship her. "I can picture you lying there. The swell of your breasts, the soft curve of your hips. I want to trace my tongue over every single inch of you until you beg me for more."

"God, I want that... so much." Her voice was breathy.

"See how good you feel?"

"Hmm-mm."

I was rock solid, my dick pulsing with need. Without hesitation, I worked my shorts down my hips and slid my hand around my shaft, stroking myself. I let out a long hiss.

"Nicco?"

"Touch yourself, Arianne. Imagine it's my fingers, my lips. Remember how it was when I took you to the Country Club?"

"It feels so good," she smothered a moan, inhaling a shaky breath.

"What does it feel like? Tell me..." I jacked myself harder, thrusting up into my hand, imagining it was her.

"It's soft and warm... and wet."

"Jesus, Bambolina. I wish it was me. I wish I was buried deep inside of you."

"Yes... yes." Her cries were my undoing, beads of sweat trailing down my abs as I chased my release.

"Are you close?" I groaned the words.

"It feels good... but it's not like when you touch me," she admitted.

"I'm right there, Arianne. I can hear your tiny moans, feel the way your body trembles beneath me. Come for me, Bambolina, I need you to come for me."

A tingling sensation started at the base of my spine as I let myself drown in memories of Arianne. The way it had felt when I'd made love to her. It had been the single most intense experience of my life. Two bodies fitting as one, two souls binding together.

"Nicco, oh God..." she cried. "I'm going to..."

"That's it, amore mio. Let go. Just let go.... fuck." White hot pleasure shot down my spine as I jerked into my hand. My chest heaved with exertion, my body spent and sated.

"You still there?" I asked, grabbing a tissue off the nightstand and cleaning myself up.

There was a slight pause, and then she said, "I can't believe we just did that."

"I want to do everything with you, Arianne. I want to give you everything."

"Can I ask you something?" The hesitation in her voice had my attention.

"Anything."

"Do your feelings for me ever scare you?"

"Every second of every day. I wasn't lying when I said I knew that if I stayed that morning, I wouldn't have been able to say goodbye to you. I would have betrayed everything I am... for you."

"I keep thinking about running away. Just the two of us. Going somewhere no one knows us. But then I think of Nora and my mom and Alessia and your family, and I know we can't do it."

Silence followed. Thick, ominous silence. Then Arianne let out a small sigh. "It isn't supposed to be this hard, is it?"

Fuck. Her words gutted me. Slid into me like a jagged knife and tore up my insides.

"Arianne—"

"Don't," she let out a soft sigh. "It's okay. I didn't mean to ruin the moment."

"Bambolina, never think like that. Not with me. I want all your moments. The happy ones, the sad too. Even the angry, frustrated ones. I won't lie to you and say that I know how this will all work out. But I will tell you that I will always love you, Arianne. And I will always fight for you, no matter what. I promise.

"Ti amo più oggi di ieri ma meno di domani," I whispered.

"I love you too. I should probably go and get ready. Luis wants to leave soon."

"Okay. Text me later?"

"I will. Bye, Nicco." She hung up, the sudden loss like a bucket of ice water.

I got cleaned up and found some clean sweats, before grabbing my cell phone again.

"Niccolò?" My father answered on the first ring.

"Any word from Tommy?"

"I was going to call you. He's on his way to Boston."

"He is?" Dread snaked through me.

"It was as I suspected. Mike Fascini is, in fact, son of Michael Ricci. He and his wife, Miranda Fascini, came from Vermont in the seventies. Tommy found records of a living relative in Montpelier."

"So you really think Mike and Scott are Elena Ricci's descendants?"

"It's too much of a coincidence, Son. The Ricci were going to be brought into the Family. When Elena and Emilio fled it bought great shame to her family, and they left Verona County. They never returned and it was always assumed that after Emilio's death, Elena killed herself. But what if she didn't... what if she escaped with Emilio's child?"

"Hold up, are you saying that Scott Fascini is really a Marchetti?"

"It's a possibility, Son. Tommy hit a few snags with the records, so he's going straight to the source and I want you to go with him."

"You want me to go to Vermont?"

"It'll keep you busy. Besides, Tommy could use the back up."

"Do I get any choice in the matter?" Vermont was a four-hour ride North. Another four hours away from Arianne. I didn't like it, but from my father's heavy sigh, I knew it was non-negotiable. "Fine, I'll go."

"Good, he'll be there in less than an hour."

"There's a party," I said. "An engagement party."

"I know, Son."

"You do?"

"I told you I'd keep my eye on Arianne, and I intend on keeping that promise. But we have to tread carefully if we want to avoid war."

"Then tell me how to do this? Tell me how to sit here, while her father gives her to the piece of shit who..." I couldn't say it.

"I understand your pain, Niccolò, but you have to keep your mind on the bigger picture. The Family must come first. Always. Arianne is your woman now, which means she has my protection. But we must get to the bottom of this thing with Fascini."

"I understand." I forced the words out. He kept talking about the Family and responsibility, but my head and heart were divided.

"Good. Go to Vermont and get answers and then we can figure out how to proceed." There was a pause and then he sighed. "Porca miseria. Your sister is outside hovering. Alessia, get in here," he grumbled.

I heard her voice in the background. "Sorry, Daddy. I swear I wasn't eavesdropping."

I smiled. She was too smart for her own good sometimes.

"I'll speak to you soon." There was some muffled noise and then my sister's voice filled the line.

"Nicco?"

"Hey, Sia."

"How are you? How's Boston? Tell me everything."

"Whoa, take a breath."

"Sorry." She chuckled. "I was just waiting for Dad to leave."

"Sia?" My spine went rigid.

"So… I was thinking…" I didn't like the hesitation in her voice. "What if I invited Arianne to hang out? Maybe that would help."

My heart swelled. "Shit, Sia, that's what you wanted to talk about?"

"Well, yeah. You didn't think I really give a shit ab—"

"Language!"

"Chill, big brother. I like Arianne and I keep thinking about what she's having to do… he hurt her, Nicco, he hurt and—"

"I know," I let out a pained breath, "I know."

"But maybe if I offered to hang out with her, she'd know she wasn't alone. Not that she's alone, I know she has Nora, and she seems cool and all, but I thought—"

"You're worried about her."

A beat passed and then my sister whispered, "Yeah, I am."

"Leave it with me."

I didn't want to put Alessia at risk any more than I wanted to put Arianne at risk. But maybe she was right—maybe Arianne would feel better knowing someone close to me was there for her.

"For real?"

"For real," I chuckled. "But no theatrics, Sia. I mean it. This is a delicate situation. The last thing I need is you causing more harm than good."

"I'll behave, I swear. I just want to be there for her. And it isn't like I have a ton of girlfriends to hang out with."

"You have Arabella."

"Yeah but Bella is family. It's different."

I hated that Alessia found it hard to make friends. All I ever wanted was for her to flourish. But high school hadn't been kind to my sister. Her circle was small, and she struggled to trust people.

Not Arianne though.

She'd welcomed her into the fold with open arms and a big smile. Not that I was surprised. My Bambolina had that effect on people. She'd done the impossible, and even managed to weave my father under her spell.

"I'm going to give Arianne your cell phone number, okay?"

Alessia's muted shrieks of excitement told me all I needed to know. She saw Arianne as one of us now.

And it meant everything to me.

"I need to go. But stay safe and I'll talk to you soon, okay?"

"Okay, and thank you, Nicco."

"What for?" My brow knitted.

"For trusting me with her. I know how much she means to you, so thank you."

"Shit, Sia, you're my family. My blood. Of course I trust you."

"Well, it means a lot. It's not always easy being your sister…"

"I know." I released a heavy sigh, the weight of her words like a noose around my neck. "I know. I love you."

"Love you, too. Bye, Nicco." She hung up.

Before I could talk myself out of it, I pulled up Arianne's number and started typing.

Alessia wants to know if you want to hang out. I thought it might be nice for my two favorite girls to get to know each other better. I'm going to forward you her number. I love you. Always.

. . .

I hit sent and then forwarded my sister's number. Arianne replied straightaway.

I would love that. Do you think it would be okay though? I don't want to get her into trouble.

My lip curved. They were almost as bad as each other.

Leave it with me. I'm sure Luis can think of something. I have to leave Boston for a little while. I don't want you to worry but it's important. I'll call you when I can.

This is one of those times... isn't it?

My brows furrowed as I read her text.

What times?

Your father warned me that you would have to do things, things you couldn't tell me about... even if I asked.

Are you asking?

Blood roared between my ears. Everything had happened so fast, I hadn't had time to explain things to Arianne. There was still so much she didn't know, things she didn't understand.

No. All I'm asking is that you come back to me.

I exhaled a long breath. I don't know what I'd done to deserve Arianne, but I was so fucking lucky to have her in my corner.

I will. Nothing will keep me away. Not even death.

CHAPTER 8

ARIANNE

"Oh, sweetheart." Mom gently grabbed my shoulders, letting her eyes run over my face. "You're okay?"

"I'm fine, Mamma. Is Father—"

"He's in the living room with Mike and Suzanna Fascini."

"They're here?" I blanched.

"I didn't know, I swear, baby." She gave me a sad smile. "He isn't telling me anything."

"Is Scott here?" The quiver in my voice betrayed me.

"He's not. There was a team thing he needed to attend to."

Well that was something. Perhaps I would survive a meeting with my father, and the Fascini without fainting.

"Luis, it's nice to see you again." Mom's gaze went to my bodyguard.

"Mrs. Capizola," he replied with complete indifference, giving nothing away.

"Please, call me Gabriella." She laced her arm through mine. "Last night, Scott... he didn't—"

"No, Mamma."

"Thank God," she breathed. "I was worried sick. Your father was quite clear that you are not to consummate the marriage until your wedding night, but I don't trust them, Arianne. I don't trust any of them anymore."

My brows pinched as I inhaled a deep breath.

"What is it, mia cara?"

I pulled her to one side, putting some space between us and Luis. The estate was well protected. If anything, there seemed to be extra security as we'd entered the estate. My father's team were usually like ghosts. They made their presence known but you rarely saw them. Not tonight though.

Tonight, I'd noticed the extra men posted outside the house and at the gate house.

"I need you to stop, Mamma."

"St- stop? Whatever do you mean?"

"You were happy to go along with all this until you learned the truth about Scott. You wanted me to date him."

"Arianne, that's not—"

"Don't lie to me. You were on his side." Tears pricked the corners of my eyes, but I would not cry.

"You're right." Regret glittered in her gaze, her face pale with shame. "I was blinded by my loyalty to your father, to our family's reputation. But know that it was born out of love, Arianne."

"How can you say that? I'm eighteen, Mamma. I've never dated, never experienced life outside these four walls, and you wanted to shackle me to that monster."

"Sweetheart, that's not—"

"We should join them. I wouldn't want to anger Father." I brushed past her and moved down the hall, fighting the urge to apologize to her.

Luis moved behind me, letting me have some space. It

was ironic that I felt more comforted by his presence these days than I did my own parents'.

"There you are, mio tesoro." My father stood the second I stepped foot in the room.

"Father." I didn't move toward him. "Mr. and Mrs. Fascini."

"Please, Arianne." Suzanna stepped forward. "We are going to be family soon enough." She grabbed my shoulders and planted a kiss on each cheek.

"Suzanna, let the girl breathe. Arianne," Mr. Fascini addressed me. "It's good to see you again. You too, Gabriella."

I hadn't realized my mom had entered the room, but I didn't acknowledge her. Instead, I pressed my lips together, forcing myself to nod. Mike Fascini was a real piece of work, to stand there and pretend everything was okay when he knew... he knew the kind of monster his son was. Yet he did nothing.

Not a damn thing.

"We have much to discuss; sit." He motioned to the leather couch as if it was his home, as if he was the one in control.

It occurred to me that maybe he was.

I sat down like the dutiful, docile daughter I'd once been. Defiance burned inside me like a wildfire, simmering in my blood and making my breaths come in short, shallow bursts.

Mike Fascini was like his son. Handsome. Charming. Sporting a smile that lured you in. But I wasn't fooled. Expensive suits and good looks didn't mean much in a world where money talked, and people were nothing but pawns.

"I have reserved the Michelangelo Suite at the Gold Star Hotel for next Saturday."

"That soon?" I choked out.

"We are keen to share the happy news," Mr. Fascini said. "Isn't that right, Roberto?"

Something passed between the two men, something that had a shiver rolling up my spine.

My father cleared his throat. "Indeed. Mike and Suzanna are handling the entire thing. Isn't that kind of them?"

"I think it's lovely," Mom said, patting my knee. I didn't miss the slight tremble of her hand.

"The invitations have already been sent. One-hundred and twenty of Verona County's most influential people will gather to witness the union of our two great families."

"I'm sure it will be quite the celebration." My father smiled but it didn't reach his eyes. In fact, he looked utterly defeated.

I wanted to see into his mind. To know why he was doing this.

"I have arranged extra security." Mr. Fascini's cold gaze flicked to mine. "Just in case."

"I'm sure that won't be necessary," my father added. "Arianne knows what's at stake."

"Yes, well, we can't be too careful. Nicco Marchetti is out there somewhere... I'm sure we'd all feel much safer knowing the party is well protected."

"Of course, Mike." Mom smoothed the hair from her face. "Have you decided upon a color? A theme? Is there a certain style Arianne should wear?"

"It will be a black-tie dinner," Suzanna beamed. "So break out those cocktail dresses and diamonds."

"I have just the dress." The two of them launched into a separate conversation about dresses and table centerpieces while I sat there, silent and suffocated, a storm brewing inside me.

Luis stood by the door, rigid and poised. He caught my eye, offering me a small nod of encouragement.

"Arianne?"

"Hmm, sorry?" I blinked over at my father and Mr. Fascini.

"Mike was just asking how your evening with Scott went last night?"

"It was fine, thank you." The lie wrapped around my heart, squeezing until it hurt.

"You'll have to excuse my son, Arianne. He can come on a little strong, but it's only because he likes you so much. He has been waiting a long time for this."

A violent shudder ripped through me. "He was quite the gentleman." The words almost choked me.

"I'm glad to hear it." Mr. Fascini picked up his glass and raised it slightly before knocking down the amber liquid.

I slid my gaze to my father. Guilt and pain were etched into his expression. And I was glad. I was glad he had to sit here and pretend too. Because why should I be the only one paying the price?

"We have arranged for you to arrive together," Mr. Fascini said. "We think it will really make a statement. Then we'll eat, and after the meal, I'll make a toast to Capizola Holdings and Fascini and Associates becoming partners in more ways than one." He sat back against the soft leather couch, pulling his ankle across his knee. He was the epitome of a man in control; a man holding all the chips.

"We know this has all come as quite the shock, Arianne," Suzanna said, her smile wide and honest. She was like the girls at college. Girls blinded by the Fascini name: the money, the status and power, and good genes. "But in our world, couplings like this are good business."

"Hmm." I pursed my lips, smothering a groan.

"It's just a shame Scott couldn't make it tonight," she went on. "I'm sure he would have liked to be here to reassure you that everything will be fine."

Just then Mr. Fascini's cell phone started ringing. He dug it out of his pocket and frowned. "I need to take this, excuse me." He disappeared out of the room.

"It's a lovely evening. Perhaps a nightcap on the terrace?" Mom asked Suzanna.

"That sounds like a wonderful idea." The two of them left, leaving me and my father alone.

"Figlia mia —"

"Don't," I hissed.

"Arianne, please understand..."

"I will never understand. You lied to me, Father. You *betrayed* me."

"There are things... things you don't know. Things you can't yet know. But I'm begging you, please trust me."

Staring him dead in the eye, I didn't flinch as I said, "My trust in you died the day you sold me off to the Fascini."

"Arianne, please. I only want to keep you safe."

"Safe?" I seethed through gritted teeth. "Scott raped me... he drugged me and he raped me." My body trembled with anger. "So tell me, Father, how on earth is giving me to him, keeping me safe?"

The blood drained from his face as he let out a pained sigh. "You have to trust me. I know I don't deserve it... I know I have failed you, but I need for you to—"

"Business, it never sleeps." Mr. Fascini came back into the room. He stopped, glancing between the two of us. "Is everything okay?"

"Perfectly fine." My father's lips thinned.

"Arianne?" Mr. Fascini raised a brow.

"Arianne is in agreement with all the plans, Mike."

"I'm glad we're all on the same page." His cold, hard gaze landed on my father again. Something was passing between them once more.

A silent warning.

An unspoken threat.

"Let's join the women out on the terrace," my father suggested. He stood up, smoothing a hand over his jaw. He didn't look at me.

Maybe he couldn't.

But I saw him.

I saw his mask of guilt.

And I was almost certain I saw a single tear roll down his cheek.

I was eating my lunch the next day, when my phone rang with an unknown number. "Ari?" Someone said down the line softly.

"Matteo?" My eyes widened as I recognized his voice.

"Tonight, six-thirty, be ready."

"What are you—"

"Just be ready." He ended the call. I quickly texted Alessia.

Do you know anything about tonight?

It pinged straight back.

I just got a text from Matteo. They must have figured something out. See you later?

Can't wait.

. . .

"What has you smiling?" Nora sat beside me.

"I think we're hanging with Alessia tonight."

"They managed to figure something out?"

"I guess so." I shrugged. When I'd texted Alessia to say I would love to hang out, she told me to sit tight and let the guys figure it out. It wasn't like Niccolò Marchetti's sister could just turn up at the apartment building and ask to see me. We had to be discreet. We had to make sure my father and the Fascini didn't find out about it.

"Do you think Enzo will be there?"

"Do you want Enzo to be there?" I threw back at her.

Nora chuckled, her lips curving into a smirk. "Well he hasn't been around much, and he is quite pretty to look at."

"He isn't pretty, Nor. He's terrifying."

"Oh, I don't know about that."

"Nicco said—"

"Yeah, yeah, I know what Nicco said. It's not like I want to marry the guy. I just think he'd be a good time between the sheets... or up against the wall... or over the—"

I clapped a hand over her mouth, drowning out the words. Words I did not need or want to hear. "Are you done?"

"I'm done," she murmured against my palm, and I pulled it away.

"Anyway, I thought you and Dan were a thing?"

"We're casual. I don't have time for anything serious."

"Are those your words, or his?"

"We don't all fall madly in love with the first guy we meet." She laughed but I didn't join her. "Shit, Ari, I'm joking. It's a joke. I'm just saying most of us will never have what you and Nicco share."

"Do you think I'm fooling myself?"

"What? *No!* Nicco loves you, babe. He'd go to war for you. Do you have any idea how lucky you are?"

"Sometimes I don't feel so lucky... I feel doomed."

She grabbed my hand and pulled it onto her lap. "You say you're doomed, but the way I see it, what you and Nicco could have, it gives you something to fight for. Imagine if you'd never met him, imagine if he hadn't saved you that night... you would be miserable, alone, and still engaged to Scott."

"Why is this happening to me, Nora?" I tried so hard to fight the tears building, but it was impossible to ignore the emotion rising inside me.

"I'm not a religious person, Ari, you know that. But I do believe in fate. I believe that everything we experience, everything we survive, shapes us into the person we're supposed to be.

"This is your battle to fight, babe. Own it."

"You're getting good at this." I sniffled, drying my eyes on my jacket sleeve.

"Yeah, and what's that?"

"Always knowing the right thing to say."

"Oh, I don't know," she smiled, "I still have plenty of impropriety in me. Want to hear some more?"

"I think I've heard enough for one day."

"Too bad. I had this dream the other night, about Enzo and his monster di—"

My hand shot out, smothering her words. I was always grateful for one of Nora's pep talks. But if I had to hear about Enzo's monster dick again this century, it would be too soon.

"Good job today," Brent said as we tidied up the last of the chairs. The VCTI had hosted a drop in this afternoon.

Being here, with people less fortunate than myself, put things into perspective. I'd gotten lost in their stories of hopelessness and loneliness, swept away in their candid experiences of life on the streets. The VCTI was a safe space for so many, a lifeline. And I was thankful to have a small part in that.

"What are your plans for the rest of the evening?" he asked.

"Oh, she's with me." Nora appeared from the back room. "I got your purse, all set?"

"I think so." I gave Brent a smile. "Are we okay to go?"

"Absolutely. We'll see you both again soon?"

"Definitely."

"Enjoy your evening." He called after us as we slipped out into the inky night.

"Everything good?" Luis shot to attention, and I smothered a grin. He was always so uptight. I couldn't help but wonder if he regretted taking my side in all of this.

"Yep."

"Come on then." He ushered us to the car. The driver nodded but I didn't recognize him.

"Luis?" I asked, hesitating.

"This is Jay," he replied.

"Hey, Jay." Nora slipped around me and climbed inside. "I'm Arianne's best one, Nora."

He didn't reply.

Luis leaned in. "It's okay, you can trust him. He's a friend."

My brows furrowed. Surely, he didn't mean what I thought he meant.

"You mean he's—"

Luis silenced me with a knowing look. "We need more eyes and ears. This is a good thing, I promise."

"Okay." I got inside.

"So what's the plan?" Nora asked the second Luis hopped into the passenger side.

"You'll see," he said cryptically.

Nora caught my eye and waggled her brows. Trust her to be excited by the prospect of an adventure. I couldn't find it in myself to share her enthusiasm. Because although I was excited to be seeing Alessia, I didn't want to put her at risk.

"Hey, don't do that." Nora frowned, grabbing my hand. "Don't always assume the worst. Everything's going to be fine. You'll see."

We took the road out of Romany Square toward La Riva. My heart beat wildly in my chest as I watched the landscape change, but we didn't stop. The new guy kept driving, taking the road toward Providence, until the familiar landscape of Nicco's neighborhood became nothing but trees and shadows.

After ten minutes, we turned off the main road, taking a dirt track to nowhere. The dense canopy of trees made everything eerie; their dark, twisted fingers scratching against the windows and roof of the vehicle. Eventually, the thicket started to clear, giving way to a cabin.

"What is this place?" I asked no one in particular, as my eyes strained against the darkness.

"You'll see."

The SUV rolled to a stop alongside a truck, and Luis unclipped his belt. "Wait here." He climbed out and made his way toward the cabin. After a couple of seconds, the door opened, and Matteo stepped onto the porch. My shoulders sagged with relief.

They discussed something before making their way back to us. Luis yanked open the door and Nora wasted no time getting out. I hesitated though.

Matteo stuck his head inside. "Going to sit in here all night?"

Pressing my lips together, I shook my head. Matteo chuckled, offering me his hand. "Come on, I don't bite." He helped me out.

"What is this place?" I asked.

"It's a family hideaway. We have a few places like this in and around Verona County. We should go inside. I know there's someone dying to see you."

I didn't get chance to respond. A whirlwind of blonde flew out of the cabin and down the steps. "You're here," Alessia shrieked, launching herself into my arms. I hugged her back, laughing softly.

"I've been so worried," she whispered.

"One rule, Sia," a deep voice said. My gaze lifted to find Enzo in the door, cold glare right on me. "Stay in the damn cabin."

"Lighten up, E, we're safe out here." Alessia poked her tongue out at him but Enzo was no longer looking at her. He was staring right at Nora.

"You didn't say she was bringing her."

"I have a name, douchebag." She marched right up to him, shouldered past him and slipped into the cabin.

"What?" Matteo chuckled, clearly amused. "You didn't have to come."

"Yeah," Enzo growled. "I did." He spun around and disappeared inside.

"This should be fun." Laughter rumbled in Matteo's chest. "Come on, we'll give you the tour."

Alessia pressed herself into my side. "I'm so glad you're here."

It should have felt weird or overfamiliar, but it didn't. It felt nice.

It felt right.

It felt like something was shifting, like I had finally found my place.

"We'll be right outside." Luis gave me a reassuring nod. "This place is off the grid, but we've got it covered. You're safe here."

"He's not wrong," Matteo added. "We won't let anything happen to you, Arianne, I promise."

"Yeah, you're one of us now." Alessia smiled. "And we protect our own."

CHAPTER 9

NICCO

"How do you do this day in, day out?" I asked Tommy, drumming my fingers against my thigh.

We'd been at it all day. Staking out the address he'd found. It was tedious fucking work, but Tommy seemed to like it.

"I like the solitude... and I like people-watching."

Yeah, that wasn't creepy at all.

"I don't see why we can't just go knock on the door and talk to her."

Elizabeth Monroe.

Seventy-five-year-old widow. Born and raised in Montpelier, Vermont. But she hadn't always been a Monroe. She had, in fact, been born Elizabeth Ricci, and was Mike Fascini's auntie. The only remaining Ricci in Vermont according to Tommy's findings.

"Hey, who's that?" I flicked my head to the young girl entering the house. She looked to be my age, maybe a couple years younger.

Tommy ran his hand down the notebook, flipped a page and jabbed his finger at the thing. "She has a granddaughter. Charlotte Monroe. It could be her."

"A granddaughter? You didn't say anything about family."

"It's just her and Charlotte. She's a freshman at the college in Burlington." He shrugged, lighting up a smoke.

"Do you mind?" I raised a brow. "Those things will kill ya."

"I already got a one-way ticket to hell, kid. Might as well enjoy the ride." He took a long drag, cracked the window and exhaled the smoke outside.

I cracked my own window, breathing in some fresh air. It was a little after six. Arianne would have finished her shift at the VCTI which meant Luis was driving her and Nora out to the cabin to meet Alessia.

God, I wanted to be there. I wanted to see her so fucking badly. But instead, I was stuck here with Tommy, breathing in his secondhand smoke and staking out an old woman's house.

"She hasn't left the house all day. She isn't a threat," I said, growing impatient.

"She isn't a threat, but we don't know that Fascini hasn't got eyes on her."

"You said Michael Fascini left Vermont before Mike was born."

"According to records, they arrived in Verona County in the seventies. But we still can't take any chances."

Letting out a frustrated breath, I raked a hand through my hair. "So what? We're going to just sit here all night?" It had already been hours.

"We wait for the girl to leave, then you go in."

"Me?"

"It's gotta be you, Nicco. Look at me, I'm not exactly grandma friendly."

Tommy had a point. The ugly jagged scar that ran from his left eye down to his jaw gave him a permanently angry expression. Which was ironic given that he was one of the best people I knew. But if Elizabeth Monroe saw Tommy standing on her doorstep, chances were, he wasn't going to get an invitation inside.

"Everything I dug up suggests Elizabeth and her brother were estranged. But the paper trail doesn't always paint the whole picture."

The door opened and the girl appeared. Elizabeth hovered in the door. She looked frail for seventy-five. They hugged and the girl kissed her grandma's cheeks before taking off down the sidewalk.

"Okay, you're up. You ready for this?"

"Talking to an old lady?" It was a piece of cake compared to some of the stuff we had to do.

"You packing? Just in case."

"Seriously?"

"If I've learned anything working for the Family, it's that you can never be too sure, about anyone or anything. I'll be close by." Tommy gave me a nod, and I slipped out of the car.

Cutting across the street, I jammed my hands in my pockets. The sun was just beginning to disappear on the horizon, dusk blanketing the neighborhood. I had no idea what I was going to say but the need to know the truth—to uncover the details of what led us to this point—sat heavy on my chest.

She lived in a small bungalow, a far cry from the huge place the Fascini owned in Roccaforte. Climbing the porch, I rapped my knuckles against the outer door. Nervous energy reverberated through me, which was fucking stupid. I didn't know this woman. She was no one to me.

No one.

And yet, she was.

If things had been different, she would have been family.

Maybe not by blood but her brother would have been.

It was some screwed-up shit.

A shuffle behind the door demanded my attention and then it cracked open, the fly screen separating us. "Yes?"

"Mrs. Monroe?"

"Who's asking?" she said in a soft Italian accent.

"My name is Niccolò. Niccolò Marchetti." I was already going against Tommy's advice, but something compelled me to the speak the truth.

"Marchetti, you say." She narrowed her eyes, her skin crinkled and tired. "I haven't heard that name in a very long time."

"I was hoping you can help me, Ma'am."

"Let me guess, that nephew of mine is causing all kinds of trouble?"

My spine stiffened.

She knew.

The old lady knew why I was here.

"I've been waiting for one of you to show up, you know. Didn't think it would take this long. You alone? Actually," she held up a finger. "Don't answer that. I know how you people work. Come on inside."

Elizabeth opened her door and stepped aside. I opened the screen and followed her inside. "I hope you like tea," she called. "I just made a fresh pot."

"Tea's fine."

"Well go on through there and take a seat, I'll just be a second." She motioned to the living room. It was a modest room, full of work furniture, every available surface littered with trinkets and photographs. I spotted the girl from earlier, her granddaughter, in most of them. But it was the one on the mantle above the fireplace that caught my eye. It was like staring at an older version of Scott Fascini. Same square jawline, same cocksure smirk. Except the photograph was an old faded black and white print.

"That's my brother, Michael." Elizabeth placed down a tray of tea and moved beside me, plucking the silver-framed photo off the shelf. "But you already know that, don't you?" She gave me a knowing glance. "Come, sit. I'm sure we have much to talk about.

"You keep talking like you've been waiting for this. I expected you to be more…"

"Unwilling to talk? No, I have been waiting for this moment to arrive. The past always catches up with you eventually, does it not? I am an old lady now, so I make every second count. Is he… dead?" Elizabeth deadpanned as she poured the tea.

"You didn't know?" According to Tommy, Michael Fascini had died almost twenty years ago.

"I haven't seen or heard from Michael since the day he left Vermont on his crusade."

"Crusade?"

"I'll never forget the day he found out the truth. Our mom never talked about his father growing up. We knew we had different fathers, but it didn't matter, not to me. I idolized my big brother. Even as a young boy he was strong and loyal. He doted on our mom something fierce. I think it's the reason she never found anyone else, because she feared what Michael would do.

"I was seven when she finally told him. Michael had just turned eleven. I remember because it was a bad winter and we were snowed in for days. He'd been asking more and more questions about his father and I guess she felt it was time he knew the truth."

Elizabeth gazed out at nothing, her eyes clouded with the pain of the past. "Everything was different after that. Michael became obsessed with learning all about the Marchetti and

Capizola. He became withdrawn, started fighting and getting into trouble at school. Mom was beside herself. I knew she regretted telling him the truth, but it was too late."

"She told you what had happened too?"

"Not at first, no. They both kept some things to themselves. But when she got sick, she confessed everything. How she and Emilio had sparked the chain of events that led you to be sitting here today."

"Your nephew has threatened someone I care about."

She let out a heavy sigh. "I had hoped he would break the cycle."

"You knew? You knew he would come after us?"

"You have to understand, Nicco... may I call you Nicco?" I nodded and she smiled. "Our mother fled to Vermont with nothing but the clothes on her back. When Michael discovered the truth about his father, and his murder, it left a mark on his soul. A mark that, as he grew, festered into something bigger. Something malevolent. When he met Miranda, I had hoped she would be able to bring him out of the darkness. And for a little while, she did. But when they announced their move to Verona County, I knew what he was doing.

"I begged him not to go. Miranda was pregnant and she didn't know the whole story. She thought he wanted to make a better life for them. I could have told her... I should have told, but I still hoped..."

I let out a strained breath.

It was true.

It was all true.

Mike Fascini was Elena Ricci and Emilio Marchetti's grandson. He was my grandfather's cousin.

He was my family.

"Nicco?"

"Y- yeah?" I scrubbed my jaw, trying to wrap my head around everything.

"Just tell me, has Michael Junior hurt anyone?"

"Not yet, no. But his son—"

"A son? He has a son?"

"You didn't know?"

"I did not. My granddaughter is all I have left."

"What about your husband's family?"

"Kenny, God rest his soul, was an only child. There is only me and Charlotte left. Her parents, my daughter and son-in-law, they died in a car accident a few years ago."

"She lives with you?"

"She did." The old woman smiled fondly. "She recently moved to Burlington for college. I've made my peace with the past, Niccolò, but Michael never could. I knew him moving to Verona County would mean only one thing. I'm just sorry to hear his thirst for revenge has been passed down to Mike Junior."

"So it is about revenge?" I sat forward, clasping my hands between my legs. Elizabeth had been an open book. I didn't know what I'd expected when she opened the door, but it wasn't this.

"I can't claim to know what my nephew thinks or why he does the things he does. But I knew my brother. I looked into his eyes and saw the secrets of his soul. And that man was fueled by grief and rage. The Ricci were supposed to be one of the great families of Verona County. Instead, we became nothing. What lengths would you go to for the woman who gave you life, Niccolò?"

"My mother is gone," I said flatly, feeling pain snake around my heart.

"I'm sorry to hear that. Do you have siblings?"

I nodded. "A sister."

"And what lengths would you go to in order to protect her? To right any wrong befallen on her? I don't justify my brother's actions, but I can understand them. His father was murdered because he loved the wrong woman. I understand your ways, your code... but love knows no bounds, Nicco. It doesn't adhere to codes or laws or morals... sometimes it just is."

I couldn't argue with her.

I had fallen hopelessly in love with Arianne. Even after I discovered her true identity, I couldn't stop myself. Our souls were bound. And I couldn't help but think history was reliving itself. Only this time, it wasn't a Ricci and Marchetti breaking the rules.

"What is it?" Elizabeth asked.

"Do you understand why I came here?"

"For answers... for the truth."

"And do you know what I have to do with this information? What it means?"

"I do." Her expression softened. "Like I said, Nicco, I have long made peace with things. But it was different for Michael. Our mother gave him her name to protect him. But it only fed his obsession for vengeance. My brother wanted only one thing in life, Niccolò."

"Yeah? And what's that?"

"To take everything from the people who took everything from our mother." She looked me dead in the eye, and for the first time since coming here, I felt the invisible line between us. "To make the Marchetti and Capizola pay."

"That's some heavy shit, kid," Tommy said as we sat in the bar. "So Fascini is like your distant cousin?"

"Something like that." I ran my thumb around the neck of the bottle.

Tommy wanted to break out the hard liquor, but I knew

if I let myself indulge, it would be a one-way street to doing or saying something I would regret.

He was family.

Marchetti blood flowed through Scott's veins.

It didn't change a thing.

And yet, it changed every-fucking-thing.

The sins of our forefathers had led us to this point, and now, it seemed we were the ones paying the price.

"Do you think he knows?"

"Who, Scott?" My jaw clenched, his name like acid on my tongue. "He has to, doesn't he? No one can be that twisted without some serious trauma in their lives."

Tommy shrugged, draining his beer. He slammed it down on the table and let out a heavy sigh. "Some people are just messed up. Maybe he knows, maybe he doesn't, maybe it's just in his blood... but he's the enemy, Nicco. Don't forget that."

"Forget... you think I could ever forget what he did to Arianne?" I seethed. "I will never forget." It was imprinted on my mind, engraved on every fiber of my being.

"Good." Tommy nodded. "A shitstorm is coming. I've known men like Mike Fascini in my lifetime. Men so blinded by the need for vengeance that it destroys who they are. He won't stop. There's only one way this thing ends."

He was right.

Michael Fascini had moved his family to Verona County with one sole purpose in mind: to destroy Arianne's family.

To destroy *my* family.

Even Elizabeth had resigned herself to the outcome.

The Fascini had positioned themselves as one of Verona's most powerful and influential families. The legal union of Scott and Arianne, and the business merger with Capizola Holdings would give them the resources, money, and power to destroy Roberto from the inside before going after the Marchetti.

"Why now?" I blurted out.

"Now is as good a time as any. As far as I'm aware, the Fascini aren't an organized group. It's just Mike and was just his father before that. But he's set himself up as the perfect Trojan Horse."

"Something doesn't add up. There are other ways to make the Family suffer. Other ways to make the Capizola suffer." The pieces were there but I couldn't make them fit.

"Maybe Michael tried and failed? Maybe he realized he couldn't do it alone?"

"Wait..." The pieces started moving, zipping around my head until they began to slow down, fitting together like a map.

Until everything zeroed in and became crystal clear.

"I don't like that look," Tommy said, his brows bunched together.

"I think I know," the words came out a strangled whisper. "I think I know what happened."

CHAPTER 10

ARIANNE

"This place is incredible," I said, getting comfortable on the huge soft sectional dividing the open plan living space.

There was a big real fire, the crackle of flames and smell of charred wood filling the air. It was rustic and homey and unlike anywhere I'd ever been before.

"Yeah, it's really something." Nora tracked Enzo's movements as he pulled Matteo out of earshot.

"Don't worry about them," Alessia said. "I'm so glad you're here. Both of you." She smiled at Nora. "I don't get to do this much, hang out with girlfriends."

"What about your friends at school?" Nora asked.

"School is... it's not always easy. Those three had it easy being Marchetti. But it isn't the same for us girls. Guys stay away because they're scared, and girls usually want to use us as a steppingstone to get to the guys."

"I'm sorry."

"Don't be." She shrugged. "It could be worse. If you two are sticking around," her eyes went to her cousins, "you could at least make yourselves useful."

Enzo's eyes narrowed dangerously. "Don't push your luck, Sia."

"Relax, E." Matteo slapped him on the back. "We're here now, we might as well kick back." He moved over to the kitchen and yanked open the refrigerator. "Bingo."

"This is bullshit." Enzo dropped onto one of the armchairs and pulled a blunt out of his pocket.

"Why did you come if you didn't want to be here?" I asked.

His eyes snapped to mine, hard and assessing. "You're Nicco's girl. And he's our..." Enzo pressed his lips into a thin line.

"What my cousin is trying to say is that you're important to Nicco and Nicco is important to them." Alessia flicked her gaze to Enzo. "Would it kill you be nice, E?"

He grumbled something before putting the blunt between his lips and lighting the end. The bitter scent lingered in the air, but no one seemed to mind.

"What are you hiding back there?" Nora got up and went over to Matteo. "I'll take one of those." She plucked a beer from his hands.

"You're not old enough." He teased.

"And you are?" She raised a brow.

"Touché."

"Ari, babe, there's beer or soda?"

"I'll take a soda," I replied, "please."

"I'll take a beer," Alessia said.

"No," her cousins barked in unison, and I smothered a chuckle.

"Are they always like this?"

"Worse." She rolled her eyes. "I'm surprised they haven't been trailing after you around campus."

"Actually, I haven't seen them around at all," Nora said.

Matteo glanced around Enzo who shook his head.

"What?" I asked noticing the two of them acting cagey.

"Just because you can't see us doesn't mean we're not around." Matteo uncapped his beer and took a long pull, but I didn't miss the guilt shining in his eyes.

"So you have been around?" I narrowed my eyes. "Why haven't we seen you?"

"Nicco thought it would make things easier on you if we kept a low profile."

"That makes sense, I guess." My chest tightened. The gossip mill was hot with rumors about the fight, about Tristan being in the hospital, and Nicco's sudden disappearance.

"Jeez, if I'd have known we were going to talk about this stuff all night, I wouldn't have bothered." Alessia grinned at me.

"Sorry. It's just been a lot to process."

"I know. But you're here and you're safe and I really hoped we could have some good old-fashioned girls' fun."

Enzo groaned, running a hand through his dark hair.

"You got a problem with that?" Alessia huffed.

"If it's going to be like the time you and Bella tried to braid my hair then yeah, I've got a fucking problem with it."

"Come on, E," Matteo added, "that shit was funny."

"Maybe you like getting your nails painted and hair braided but it's not exactly my kind of thing."

"You really did that to them?" Nora couldn't contain her amusement.

"We were like twelve. Nicco let me practice putting lip gloss on him."

Enzo scoffed. "We held him down and let you go at him."

Alessia rolled her eyes at him. "Your point?"

"You had him wrapped around your little finger." Matteo shifted in the chair. "And then you grew boobs."

"Gross!"

"What? It's the truth. Having a younger sister, knowing what I know about the world, it's enough to send me to an early grave."

"My older brother used to say he had two main jobs in the world," Nora said. "Making me smile and breaking the legs of any guy who ever hurt me."

Tension crackled in the air as she glanced over at Enzo who was focused solely on the wisps of smoke rising off his blunt.

"Sounds like my kind of guy," Matteo tipped the neck of his bottle at her. "What say you, Enzo?"

He grumbled again.

"Did your brother go to MU?"

"He's at UPenn, chasing dreams of pro-football, fame, and fortune."

"Enzo has a decent throwing arm."

"Fuck this, I need some air." Enzo got up and stalked to the door beyond the kitchen.

"Did you have to bring him?" Alessia grumbled. "He's so—"

"Miserable?" Nora smirked.

"That's cute." Matteo narrowed his eyes at her. "Pretending you don't care."

"I don't."

"We'll see." He got up. "Can I trust the three of you while I'm gone?"

Alessia glared at him, and his shoulders shook with quiet laughter. "I'll be back." He took off after Enzo.

"Thank God. I thought they were never going to leave."

"Leave? But Matteo said—"

"Relax. They won't go anywhere. There's a fire pit out back, some benches. It's pretty cool."

Nora looked longingly at the door.

"Down, girl," I chuckled.

"Wait a second, you and... *Enzo?*" Alessia balked. "I did not see that one coming. Have the two of you, ya know?"

"What?" Nora feigned surprise. "No. *No!*"

"But she wants to." I grinned.

"Word of warning, my cousin doesn't date. Hell, I'm not even sure he hooks up with girls in the traditional sense of the word. Enzo is... complicated."

"What's his story anyway?" Nora kicked her legs up and stretched out over the chair, making herself at home.

Alessia folded her legs up in front of her. "My Uncle Vincenzo, Enzo's dad, well he's kind of a hard ass. It was just the two of them growing up. My mom practically helped raise him. But then she..." Alessia swallowed and I reached over, grabbing her hand and squeezing gently.

"It was different for Nicco and Matteo. They had a strong female influence. They had sisters. But Enzo... he only had himself."

"That's kind of sad." Nora's eyes flicked to the door again, a look of longing there.

"Yeah. It hardened him for sure. His dad has always enjoyed bouncing from woman to woman, and I guess Enzo is the same. A lot of the men in the Family don't settle down."

"You make it sound so normal."

"It is normal, to me, at least. Our family has strong ideals when it suits them. Take me for example; you think any guy is ever going to be good enough in Nicco's eyes? Or my father's?"

"That's... rough." Nora grimaced.

"It's bullshit. They make out that their women are the most precious thing in the world but then most of them are screwing around with goomars or using them as a punching bag."

My heart sank, and I snatched my hand back, clutching the cushion in my lap.

"Shit, Ari, I didn't mean... Nicco would never do that to you. Not after what happened with our mom." Alessia gave me a weak smile. "I should probably stop talking now. Tonight was supposed to reassure you, not send you running for the hills."

"I'm not going anywhere." I smiled back. "What was she like?"

"The best. She was just a good person, you know? She was always feeding a house full of people. Loved to take care of everyone. And my brother, he doted on her."

She dropped her gaze, pretending to pick her nails. "I love my daddy, but he's a mean drunk with a short fuse. He thinks I don't know about the bruises. About all the nights Mom spent crying herself to sleep. But I see things. They think I don't, but I do. I always have."

"I'm sorry."

"Don't be." Her shoulders lifted in a half-shrug as she met my gaze again. "It could be worse. In this life, it could always be worse. But I never saw it coming. One day, Mom was there, the strong resilient woman she'd always been, and the next... she was gone."

"Do you know where she went?"

"She just vanished. Wherever she is, she doesn't want to be found." Sadness clung to Alessia's words.

I didn't know what it was like to lose a parent, but I did know what it was like to have your world ripped apart, to discover everything you thought you knew was a lie.

"I hated her for a long time, but I've made my peace with it."

Her expression said otherwise, but I didn't push. Alessia was still young. She still had to find her way in the world.

I'd felt the same when I'd arrived at MU, but everything was different now.

I was different.

The vibrations of my cell phone startled me. "It's Nicco," I said, digging it from my pocket.

"What does it say?" Alessia sat straighter, peering over to try to see. I pulled it closer to my chest.

Nora chuckled. "Trust me, you don't wanna know."

"Nor!" I shrieked, the same time Alessia grumbled, "Ew, gross. That's my brother."

Waving them both off, I read the text.

Found out some things today. We need to talk, but I want to do it in person.

You can't come back here. It isn't safe.

I know. That's why I'm going to arrange for Luis to bring you to me. But we can't tell anyone else.

"Ari, what is it?" Nora asked.

I hesitated. I knew better than most people that secrets and lies only led to heartache. Even if you thought you were protecting someone, even if they were told out of love.

I have to tell Nora. I won't lie to her.

. . .

Fine. But only Nora.

When?

Tomorrow. I'll set it up. I love you, Bambolina. Be safe and say hello to Alessia for me.

"Nicco says hey."

"Tell him he should come home soon."

"I wish he could." My heart ached.

"How is your cousin... Tristan, right?"

"There's no change. His condition is stable, and doctors say it could be any day now. It's just a waiting game."

"God, I'm so sorry." She clutched her throat. "I can't even imagine what that must be like... if it was Nicco..."

"But it wasn't." I gave her a tight smile. "And what happened was just a terrible accident."

"I really hope he gets better."

"Yeah, me too."

Tristan, despite his serious lack in judgment, was still family. I didn't want him to die. I wanted him to wake up and realize the truth about my father, about Scott.

I wanted him to do the right thing.

"Wow, we really know how to party, huh?" Nora said around a smile.

"Oh, I don't know," I glanced between her and Alessia. "This is nice."

"Yeah." Alessia beamed. "It is."

We stayed at the cabin for hours, talking and laughing. Matteo and Enzo eventually joined us, although Enzo had worn a scowl for most of the night. Luis and Jay drove us back to University Hill. Nora was half asleep by the time we made our way up to the apartment.

"I'll see you in the morning," she murmured, staggering toward her room.

"I'm making hot cocoa if you want to join me?" I said to Luis as he hovered in the doorway.

"Aren't you tired?"

"I haven't been sleeping well," I admitted.

"Nightmares?" He looked concerned.

"My demons don't haunt me in my sleep, Luis."

They were real.

Circling me like hungry piranhas waiting for their moment to strike.

"I wouldn't say no to a cocoa." He came inside and closed the door.

It was late, and I probably should have gone to bed given that I needed to return to classes tomorrow, but there was too much on my mind to switch off.

After making us each a mug of cocoa, sprinkling marshmallows on mine, I went to Luis. He'd made himself comfortable on the end of our couch. "Here you go," I said, handing him the mug.

"Thank you. Did you enjoy tonight?"

I sat at the opposite end of the couch, curling my body into the soft fabric. "Alessia is a sweetheart and Matteo seems nice. I still haven't made my mind up about Enzo."

"He's hardened. Most guys are in this life."

"You speak like you have experience?"

"Just because your family decided to walk a different path doesn't mean we don't get our hands dirty." His smile turned grim.

"What does that mean?"

I'd seen my father's true colors, but was Luis right? Was the entire Capizola empire built on lies and scandal?

"Monsters wear many faces, Arianne. Your father set out to take back La Riva and Romany Square from the Marchetti, but it was never his to take."

I stared into my cocoa, watching the marshmallows bubble and melt. "Is that why you're helping me? Because you don't agree with my father's ideals? You're his most trusted security guard."

Luis twisted his body toward me, letting out a long sigh. "I'm helping you because it's the right thing to do. Because no child should have to pay for the sins of their forefathers. This fight, the bad blood between the Marchetti and Capizola isn't yours to bear, Arianne. And what Fascini did to you... I will never forgive myself. It happened on my watch. I want to believe your father didn't know what Scott would do that night, but he knew *something* would happen." His words shook with anger.

"I never had children. My ex-wife and I, we tried. Tried for years. But it wasn't meant to be. So watching you grow, witnessing the young woman you have become, everything you have endured, I guess it spoke to me. To that part of me never fulfilled. I have served your father for the better part of twenty years, Arianne. But I serve you now. And if that means I serve the Marchetti, then so be it."

"What will happen if my father finds out?"

A dark shadow passed over his face. "Let's hope it does not come to that." He took a sip of his cocoa. "I didn't want to say anything, but I'm not sure I'll be able to get any sleep if I don't. Meeting Nicco tomorrow is a risk, Arianne. One I'm not sure you should be taking yet."

"I have to go."

"I know." He rubbed his jaw. "But if I'm going to protect

you, that means being honest with you. And I think it's a bad idea."

"You don't want to take me?"

"I didn't say that. But there's a reason Nicco left Verona County. If Mike or Scott find out…"

"They won't. We'll make sure they don't."

I was going, even if Luis didn't take me.

I needed to see Nicco, more than I needed my next breath. Every second without him here, I slipped further under the deep waters I'd found myself in.

He gave me a sharp nod. Disapproval glittered in his eyes, but Luis didn't protest any further. "I'll make the arrangements. You'll need a cover story. Something I can feed to your father, something that will keep Scott off your back."

"I won't have to worry about Scott. He'll be at practice with the team, they have a big game coming up. He'll be distracted with that."

"That makes things easier."

"Nora has invited her friend Dan over tomorrow evening, so I'll make myself scarce in my room studying." I gave him a pointed look.

"Very well. I'll get our story straight with the rest of the team."

"Thank you, for everything. I don't know what I'd do if it wasn't for you and Nora."

"Something tells me you'd survive. You have great strength, Arianne. Never forget that. I know things feel desperate now, that you can't see a way out, but you always have a choice. It's just figuring out which battles to fight."

"I won't marry him."

I'd rather die.

"I have no intention of ever letting you walk down the aisle toward that asshole. But Antonio needs time to figure out a plan. Your father has always managed to keep his hands clean, but I think we can only assume Mike Fascini will go to any lengths to get what he wants."

"Do you know what he has on my father, Luis?"

My bodyguard liked to talk in riddles, but riddles didn't help my predicament.

"I have my suspicions."

I raised a brow. "Are you going to share them with me?"

"Will it change anything?"

Silence fell over us. "No, it won't." The truth was like a knife to the heart. "He made his choice. And I made mine."

Luis placed down his mug and stood. "You should get some sleep, it's late."

"You're probably right."

"I'll handover with the night shift and get some shut eye. See you in the morning, okay?"

I nodded. "Okay. Goodnight, Luis."

He gave me a tight smile, his mask of indifference sliding back into place as he resumed bodyguard mode and headed for the door.

But he paused at the last second, glancing back. "It won't always be like this, Arianne. Sometimes the bad things that happen in our lives set us on the path to the best things that will ever happen to us. Try and hold onto that."

I wanted to believe him.

But something told me the worst was yet to come.

CHAPTER 11

NICCO

She was late.
Arianne was supposed to meet me at the motel on the edge of Blue Hills Reservation, twenty minutes ago. But there was still no sign of her.

I'd almost worn out the spongy carpet pacing back and forth, waiting for the black SUV to roll into the parking lot. I'd been tempted to ask Uncle Alonso for the keys to one of his places, but it was already risky asking Arianne here. So I'd kept it vague. The glint in his eye as I'd told him I would be gone all night was all the sign I needed that he knew exactly where I was going. He didn't try to stop me though, because he knew he couldn't.

I needed to see her.

I needed to hold Arianne as I told her everything I'd learned after talking to Elizabeth Monroe. But it was more than that. I needed to know she was okay. I needed to look her in the eye and *see* it.

I was just about to call Luis when I spotted their car. "Thank fuck," I breathed, yanking open the door.

Luis climbed out and scanned the parking lot. I'd already done a sweep of the area. Twice. Watching Arianne step out of the vehicle had the tension in my shoulders melting away. She spotted me and ran. She ran all the way until she launched herself into my awaiting arms.

"Nicco." My name was a prayer on her lips. But it was me who wanted to fall to my knees and worship her.

"You're okay." I cupped the back of her head, cradling her body against mine. "You're okay."

"I've missed you." Arianne craned her neck to look at me. "I've missed you so much."

"I know, Bambolina. I know." Dipping my head, I brushed my lips over hers. Once. Twice. Letting myself memorize their shape, reacquaint with their taste. But it was Arianne who took control, fitting her body against mine like a missing puzzle piece and deepening the kiss. Her tongue slipped between my lips, searching for my own.

Luis cleared his throat. I liked the man, I did, but right then, in that moment, I wanted him to disappear.

"We should talk," he said, when I made no effort to break the kiss.

Arianne had fisted my sweater, anchoring us together. "Bambolina," I breathed against her mouth, gently tugging her hand away. "Give me a second."

She smiled up at me, her cheeks flushed, and lips swollen.

"Go inside." I flicked my head to our room. "I'll be right there, I promise."

"Okay." Arianne hesitated, letting out a small sigh as she stole another kiss before disappearing inside.

I pulled the door shut and stepped toward Luis. "You swept the area?" he asked me.

I nodded. "It's clean. No one knows I'm out here, not even my uncle."

"Nicco," he frowned, "that's a big risk."

"She's worth it".

"You said you found something in Vermont."

"I did. But we shouldn't talk out here. You were on Roberto's security detail when someone tried to get to Arianne at the school?"

"I was."

"I need you to talk to this guy." I handed him Tommy's nondescript card. "He's expecting your call."

"We can trust him?"

"We can. I got you a room." Fishing the second card out of my pocket, I gave it to Luis. "Didn't know if you'd want it, but it's yours."

"I'm going to set up on watch, but thanks, I appreciate it. You should probably go see to her, she's getting impatient." He handed me her overnight bag.

I glanced back just in time to see the curtain twitch. "I will." My lips curved. "But first, I need to know… how is she? Really?"

"It's been less than a week. Ask me again in a month." Luis' expression hardened. He cared for Arianne, that much was obvious. But part of me sensed he disagreed with how we were handling things.

"Go, be with her. We can talk tomorrow."

"Call me if there's any problems," I said, slowly backing up toward the door.

"Same goes for you."

I watched him double back to the SUV, before entering the room. There was nothing special about it: it had four walls, a small bathroom, a queen-sized bed, and a few other pieces of furniture. But it could have been a hovel for all I cared. Because sitting there, on the edge of the bed, was the girl who held my heart in the palm of her hands.

"Bambolina." It fell from my lips on a whispered sigh, as I dropped the bag.

Arianne got up and came to me, pressing her hand against my cheek. "I can't believe you're here."

Inhaling a ragged breath, I drew her into my chest, holding her. "I had to see you."

"I know." She laid her palms on my chest, staring up at me with so much emotion, I felt winded.

I brushed a stray hair from her face, tracing the lines of her face. Arianne's breath hitched as I let my fingers glide down the slope of her neck. "Kiss me."

She complied, pushing up on her tiptoes and giving me her lips. I cupped her face with two hands, sweeping my tongue into her mouth, tangling it with her own. She tasted like love and promise.

She tasted like home.

"Nicco," she moaned softly, fitting herself closer. I kept kissing her. Peppering her face with tiny desperate kisses, licking and nibbling the skin beneath her ear. I wanted to paint every inch of her with my lips, brand her with my touch. The need to have her burned through me, a wildfire no amount of water could douse.

"God, Bambolina. I want you, I want you so fucking much."

Her hands slipped to the hem of my sweater, dipping underneath and finding my warm skin. Arianne explored my stomach, my abs and chest. Taking her time to trace every hard ridge and taut dip. "I've missed you so much," she breathed the words against the corner of my mouth. Her voice was thick with lust and want.

"I want to lie you down on the bed, strip the clothes from your body and make you mine in every way possible."

"Yes," she moaned, her hands dropping to the waistband of my jeans. "Make love to me, Nicco."

I snagged her wrist, holding it between us as I lowered my face to hers, staring into her honey-brown eyes. "We have time."

I didn't ask her here for this, no matter how badly I wanted her. We needed to talk. Arianne needed to understand the situation. But she was staring at me with such intensity, I wasn't sure I was strong enough to resist.

"Nicco, what it is?" Her eyes clouded with uncertainty.

I cupped her face, brushing my thumb over her cheek. "It shouldn't be like this. You deserve so much, Arianne, you don't deserve this." Guilt snaked through me, coiling around my heart as my eyes shuttered on a harsh breath.

"Nicco," Arianne smoothed her fingers over my jaw. "Look at me."

I opened my eyes and she smiled. God, her smile. It was enough to bring me to my knees.

"My life has never been my own, I realize that now. I have been groomed for a life I never asked for, a life I don't want. I thought going to MU was the start of my freedom, the start of me choosing my own path."

A tear slipped down her face and I swiped it away with my thumb.

"But it was all a lie. Until you. I choose you, Nicco. I choose a life... with you."

I leaned down, touching my head to hers. "There was never a choice where you were concerned."

I knew that now.

Something had changed in me that night Arianne stumbled across me and Bailey in the alley. I'd wanted to protect her, to make sure nothing ever hurt her again. And those feelings had only grown the more time I spent with her, turning into something primal, something soul-deep.

Something I couldn't fight even if I tried.

"We should talk, come on." I took Arianne's hand and led her to the bed. "I'm sorry about the room. I know it's not what you're used to."

"You think I care about that?" She sat down and kicked off her boots before crawling onto the bed and sitting against the headboard. It creaked and moaned as I joined Arianne, slipping my arm around her shoulder and pulling her into my side.

"I didn't think this through."

"Meeting me?"

"Meeting you at some dive motel." In a room that had no couch or chairs for us to sit on.

"It's not that bad." She peeked up at me. "What's really going on in that head of yours?"

"The truth?"

"Always."

"I'm having a hard time thinking about anything except getting you naked right now."

Heat flared in her eyes. "I'm right here."

A low groan bubbled in my throat. "I'm trying to do the right thing, Bambolina."

"And I love you for it." She shrugged out of my hold and moved around me.

"What are you doing, amore mio?"

"Making it easier for you." I felt her body tremble as she straddled my legs. My hands went to her waist, guiding her over me. "Is this okay?" Her voice was thick, and her pupils were blown with lust.

"More than okay." I curved a hand around the back of her neck and kissed her. Slow deep licks. "But you won't tempt me, Bambolina. We need to talk."

Disappointment etched into her expression, and I chuckled. "We have time."

"Do we though? Because it feels like the clock is already running out."

"Arianne," I breathed, pain slicing me open.

"It's okay. You said we needed to talk, so talk." My eyes narrowed, but she added, "I'm okay. You're here, that's all that matters."

"I found out some things."

"I'm listening..."

Fuck. How was I supposed to tell her this? After everything she'd already been through.

"Nicco, talk to me. Whatever it is, we'll get through it."

I guided Arianne's face to mine, inhaling a deep breath. "I think I know who ordered the hit against you."

"It really wasn't your father?"

I shook my head. "I think it was Mike Fascini."

Arianne frowned. But her confusion quickly turned to something else. Her gaze widened, fear swirling in her big brown eyes. "You think he... tried to have me killed?" She choked out the words.

"I met his aunt. That's where I went yesterday."

"What else she did say?"

"She wasn't surprised that Mike is trying start something. She knew, she fucking knew her brother moved to Verona County to come after us."

"Her brother?"

"Yeah, Mike's father. He died a long time ago. But I guess the damage was done."

"It doesn't make any sense... why would he want..." Arianne shuddered.

"Have you ever heard the name Ricci?"

"It isn't familiar, why?"

"There's a lot you don't know about our history, Bambolina."

My strong brave girl laid her palm against my cheek and gave me a sad smile. "So tell me."

∼

I told Arianne everything. She already knew about Emilio Marchetti and Elena Ricci and their betrayal. But I told her how Alfredo Capizola hunted them down and killed Emilio. I told her how the Ricci fled Verona County and became an unspoken name among our families.

"I can't believe it," she sighed, the sound making my heart ache. The last thing I ever wanted was to cause Arianne any pain. But with every revelation came a new hurt.

"Scott's your... cousin."

"*Distant* cousin." That fucker might have had Marchetti blood in his veins, but he would never be family.

"Do you think he knows?"

"Does it matter?" My brow quirked up.

"No, I guess not. Why did you tell me?"

"Because..." I pulled her closer, putting us nose to nose. "You need to understand the severity of the situation. Scott and his dad are out for blood. They want to bring down our families. I think the hit on you was a way to incite war between the Marchetti and Capizola. If it had been... successful..." I barely got the words out over the lump in my throat. "Your father would have demanded revenge."

Arianne scoffed. "You don't know that. He doesn't care about me."

"He does, Bambolina. In his own messed up way, I think he thinks he's protecting you."

"By promising me to the family who wants to see us fall?"

"But what if he doesn't know the truth? Think about it... If he suspected my father was behind the hit, maybe he turned to the Fascini to strengthen his position. Fascini and

Associates are well connected. Together, Mike and your father would be a force to be reckoned with."

"So what's his endgame? If Mike Fascini is really who you say he is, then where is all this leading?"

It was the one thing I still hadn't figured out. There were other ways to get revenge. Anyone with enough money could pay for someone to disappear or be taken out. They could make it look like an accident, a tragedy no one would question.

"Maybe he doesn't want to get his hands dirty," I said.

"Or maybe he has some bigger plan we still don't know about." Arianne let out a weary sigh.

"Hey." I kissed the corner of her mouth. "This doesn't change anything. I won't let anything happen to you."

"I'm engaged to Scott, Nicco. They want me to *marry* him."

Every muscle in my body tensed. "You will never be his," I ground out.

Arianne was mine.

"This," I pressed my hand against her breastbone, right where her heart lay. "Is mine. One day, when all this is over, I'll make you mine, Bambolina. You'll be my wife. My queen. Do you understand that?"

Her bottom lip quivered as she gazed up at me with tear-stained eyes. "Tell me you understand that," I said, desperation clinging to every word.

"I'm scared, Nicco." Silent tears streaked down her cheeks, and my heart broke for the girl who had already faced so much. "When I was at the restaurant with him... he went out of his way to make me uncomfortable, to let me know that he's the one in control."

"Did he... touch you?" My voice shook with anger. Luis had told me everything was fine, that Scott had kept his hands to himself. But I sensed it wasn't the full story.

"Not like that, no. But something happened..."

Red mist began to descend over me, my grip on Arianne's waist tightening. "I need you to move, Bambolina."

"Nicco, don't—"

"I'm okay," I said, "but I need space. Please..." My voice cracked.

Arianne crawled off my lap, pressing herself against the headboard and folding in on herself while I stood up, pacing the room like a caged animal.

"This is why I didn't want to tell you," she whispered.

"What did he do?"

"It wasn't anything really." Her eyes drifted past me as if admitting this to me was a burden too big to bear. "I wanted to leave. He wanted to stay. But I told him I was leaving. We got outside to the car and he told Luis he could drive. He got in my space and brushed my waist, that's all. But it felt so possessive, so intimate. Everything came rushing back to me. It was like this giant wave just hit me." She finally lifted her eyes to mine again. "Luis thinks I had a panic attack. I passed out."

"Fuck." My fist shot out, crashing against the solid wall. Pain ricocheted through my knuckles and down my wrist, burning like a motherfucker.

"*Nicco!*" Arianne clambered off the bed and rushed to my side.

"Wait." I held up my other hand to stop her. A dark angry storm was raging through me. I wanted to hit something, to hurt and bleed.

I needed it.

Dark rivulets of blood seeped over my hand, but I barely felt it. I was too wired. Too hungry for the kill.

"Let me take a look at it." Arianne stepped forward and I jerked back, like a caged animal being riled.

"Nicco, it's me. It's only me." She had me cornered with

no way out. My body trembled violently as I desperately tried to hold on to my frayed rope of control.

"Nicco..." Arianne brushed the hair from my face. My head hung low, my shoulders hunched and tight. I wanted to kill him. I wanted to hunt him down and kill him with my bare hands.

"Come back to me." She gently lifted my busted hand and inspected the damage. "It needs cleaning. Let me see what there is." Arianne left me and went into the bathroom. When she came back, she had a small first aid kit. "I found it in the cabinet. Sit." Her gaze went to the bed, but I remained rigid.

"I need to stand."

"Okay. Hold still." She worked in silence, cleaning me up and bandaging my hand. My pulse began to slow, the tightness in my chest easing.

It was her.

Her touch, her calmness.

"I'm sorry," I choked out.

Arianne took my face in her hands and looked right at me. God, I wanted to drown in the dark pools of honey. "Talk to me."

"I want to kill him... I should have killed him."

"So why didn't you?"

It was the last thing I expected her to say, but I knew this wasn't about her, it was about me.

"It's not that simple," I released a heavy sigh. "If I'd have killed him... it would start something we might not be able to finish. I can't do that to the Family, to you."

She nodded, dropping one of her hands to mine and lacing them together. "I hate Scott for what he did to me. I hate him so much that sometimes I wish you had done it." Arianne took a shuddering breath. "But I want a life with you. I want a future. I can't have that if you're behind bars... or worse."

"If he hurts you again, I can't promise I won't do it."

Something flashed in her eyes, but before I could decipher it, Arianne kissed me. "I don't want to talk any more, Nicco. I want you to love me. I want you to make me forget about the monsters."

"Bambolina... You deserve—"

"Don't tell me what I deserve. I can choose my own path, Nicco. And it's you. Don't you see that? It's—"

My mouth crashed down on hers, swallowing her words. She was right. I didn't want to be another man in her life taking away her right to choose. I wanted her by my side, as my equal. As the better half of me.

"I'm not sure I can be gentle," I murmured against her lips.

I was too wound up to go slow.

Arianne gripped my jaw and eased back slightly, staring at me with nothing but love and lust. "Then don't."

CHAPTER 12

ARIANNE

*N*icco looked ready to devour me.

Hunger simmered in his hooded eyes as they lingered on my lips. "Do you have any idea of how beautiful you are?" His words wrapped around me like a warm blanket.

When it was just the two of us, it was easy to forget everything else.

To get lost in him.

My hands went to the hem of his sweater, and I felt him shudder as I pulled the material up his body. Nicco took control, yanking it over his head. Reaching for him, I ghosted my fingers over the faded scars. There were so many. So many stories, so much pain. But every mark was a part of him. It made Nicco who he was. Fiercely protective and doggedly loyal. Nicco might have been mafioso but he loved with everything that he was, and I still couldn't believe I got to call him mine.

No words passed between us as he pushed the jacket from my shoulders. He worked on the buttons of my blouse next, popping each one with measured precision. His fingers traced the curve of my breasts, toying over the lace shell of my bra. "Sei bellissima."

My breath caught when his fingers found the waistband of my pants. Nicco only had eyes for me as he gently pushed the soft material off my hips, letting it pool at my feet in a silky puddle. He ran his hands down my spine, smoothing them over the swell of my hips. "I will never tire of this." It came out a rough whisper.

Without warning, Nicco picked me up, my startled shrieks filling the room. "Wrap your legs around me," he commanded, moving us in the direction of the bed.

His skin felt incredible against mine and I pressed myself closer, needing this moment with him.

Nicco stopped at the edge of the bed. I was curled around him, unwilling to ever let go. He nudged his nose against mine, inhaling a deep breath. A beat passed, delicious anticipation crackling around us. We'd only had one night together. This time felt different, like so much more. When our lips met it felt like a silent promise to everything that we were.

Everything that we wanted.

The world fell away around me as Nicco lowered me to the bed. He stood before me, strong and handsome; a dark angel put on the Earth to love me, and me alone. But there was a glint in his eye. A flash of something that had me sucking in a shaky breath.

Nicco popped the button on his jeans before dropping to his knees. His hair fell over his eyes so I couldn't see him, but I could feel him. Feel every kiss as he explored my skin, touching and tasting. He branded me with his tongue, swirling it in my navel before dragging down, down, *down*.

"Oh God," I breathed as he nibbled at the lace covering me.

"These need to go." He eased back and worked them off my hips and down my legs. Nicco gave me no warning as he dived for me, licking and sucking me into complete submission. It felt incredible, the warmth of his breath against the coolness of his tongue.

"You taste like heaven," he murmured against my damp skin. "I want to watch you fall, Bambolina. Eyes on me."

I pushed up on my elbows, gazing at him through lust-drunk eyes. "It feels so good," I breathed, my body shuddering.

Nicco watched me as he slowly worked two fingers inside me and curled them upwards.

"Oh my..." The words got stuck in my throat as he lowered his head and worked me with tongue and fingers in perfect synchrony.

"Come for me, Bambolina."

His words sent me flying off the edge. My head fell back as I screamed his name, intense waves of pleasure crashing over me. Nicco stood, pushing his jeans and boxers down his legs. I watched with rapt fascination as he stroked himself. He was long and hard and so perfect it hurt to look at him.

"See what you do to me, amore mio." His words were rough with need as he stalked toward me, kneeling on the edge of the bed. "You're mine, Arianne Carmen Lina Capizola. Nothing will ever change that." He crawled up my body until we were one.

"Yours," I whispered against his lips, hitching my legs around his waist.

Nicco thrust inside me in one smooth stroke, filling me so completely I couldn't breathe. I knew he was holding back; knew he was walking a fine line between being in control and losing it. But I didn't want him to be gentle with me. I wanted all of him. The good, the bad, and all the broken pieces. I wanted the mafia prince, the knight-in-shining-armor, the fighter, and the lover.

Simply put, I just wanted him.

Every last piece.

Tangling our hands together, Nicco pressed them at the side of my head while the other slipped to my thigh, hooking my leg higher, letting him go deeper. Harder. He kissed me like it was our first and last time together, like he wouldn't ever get enough. Our tongues danced a slow erotic dance as he rocked into me with breathtaking restraint.

"Nicco, I'm not glass. I won't break." I nipped his jaw, arching my back to meet his measured strokes.

"I don't want to hurt you."

"You won't," I breathed. "I want you. All of you." My hand slipped down his body, pressing him against me. He groaned into the crook of my neck, his pace quickening.

"You feel so good, Bambolina."

"But you need more," I said, raking my fingers over his skull.

He stilled, gazing down at me in awe. "Are you sure?"

Dragging my bottom lip between my teeth, I bit down gently, nodding.

"Hold on." Nicco moved my hands to his shoulders and rolled us without warning. My cheeks flamed at our new position. But I didn't need to worry, not with the way he was looking at me. Like I was the most precious thing on Earth.

Nicco sat up, crushing my breasts against his chest. "It'll be deep like this."

"It's okay."

His hands went to my hair as he kissed me. My body tingled with sensation, my stomach coiling tight as he moved one of my hands to his erection. I lifted myself a little, letting him guide himself beneath me and then I sank down. Slowly. Completely. Our breathy moans filled the space between us, but then he was kissing me, rocking into me. It was different. Deeper. More intense. It was like I could feel him everywhere. He curved his hand around the back of my neck and tugged gently, dropping his mouth to my collarbone, sucking the skin there.

"It feels... God..." I swallowed a moan. Everything was heightened like this, pure pleasure coursing through my veins. Nicco licked and sucked a path down to the curve of my breasts, teasing one of my nipples. I cried out, but his tongue replaced his teeth, soothing the sting.

"Perfection," he murmured against my damp skin, kissing a trail back up to my mouth.

Our bodies rocked faster... harder... *deeper*. Until our moans were a song. A rising cacophony of little sighs and breathy gasps. Nicco held me tighter, fitting our bodies so closely I didn't know where I ended, and he began. It was like he wanted to crawl inside and become a part of me.

He already was though.

His soul already entwined with mine.

"Fuck, Bambolina. Nothing," he gathered the hair off my face and pressed a kiss to the underside of my jaw, "will ever feel as good as this."

"I'm close," I panted, my body trembling.

"Together," he murmured, kissing me so intensely I felt myself begin to fall. But Nicco was there to catch me as we came together, the rise and fall of our chests quick, the beat of our hearts hard.

"I can't promise that things won't get worse before they get better..." Nicco met my heavy-lidded gaze. "But I promise I'll be waiting at the end."

I nodded, too choked up to reply. In our bubble, I felt safe.

I felt safe and loved and cherished. But out there, without him by my side, I felt lost. Adrift without an anchor.

Nicco pulled us down onto the bed and pulled the sheet over our bodies. He held me, his fingers dancing along the curve of my waist as the silence crashed down around us.

"What are you thinking?" I leaned up to look at him. He looked so good. His hair was ruffled and damp, while his eyes glowed with possessiveness and love.

"Everything... and nothing."

"Sounds complicated." I shrieked as he rolled me underneath him.

"I'm wondering how I'm supposed to leave you tomorrow. How the fuck am I supposed to let you go back there, to him? Tell me, Bambolina, tell me how?" Pain edged into his words, making my heart ache.

I lifted a hand to his cheek and gave him a sad smile. "You just do, Nicco. This is bigger than us, you said so yourself."

He grabbed my hand and kissed my palm. "I know, Bambolina. Are you tired? Hungry? I could order something..."

"Nicco, stop." My arm looped around his neck, drawing his face to mine. "I have everything I need right here." I kissed him, running my tongue along the seam of his mouth and teasing him. Nicco took control, deepening the kiss and stealing my breath. Heat pooled low in my stomach and I felt Nicco hard and ready against my thigh.

"Again?" His intense gaze pinned me to the spot.

Suppressing a coy smile, I nodded.

"Jesus, Arianne." He dropped his hand between us, finding my center. I gasped as he pushed a finger inside me. "You'll be the death of me."

I pulled him closer, until we were nose to nose. "I can think of worse ways to go." My lips curved against his.

"I love you, Arianne. With everything that I am."

"Show me," I moaned already feeling the waves of ecstasy rise inside me.

He gazed at me, his eyes looking right into my soul as he whispered, "Senza di te la mia vita non vale niente."

∽

I lifted my face into the stream of sunlight. It warmed my skin, coaxing my spent muscles from their slumber.

"Good morning." My lips curved as I reached out for Nicco, only to be met by cold empty sheets. "Nicco?" I sat up, pushing wild curls from my face.

The room was quiet. Still. I pushed back the covers and found a clean t-shirt and panties from my overnight bag. Pulling back the curtains, I scanned the parking lot, but it was as empty and still as our room. Dejection swarmed my chest. Nicco wouldn't just leave me, he wouldn't. Not again.

Not after everything.

Panic flooded me. What if something had happened...? What if—

The door handle rattled, and I froze, my heart beating wildly in my chest. I clutched my cell phone ready to call Luis.

"Morning. I have coffee."

"Nicco," I cried.

"What's wrong?" Nicco paled. "Oh, you thought I'd left, didn't you?" His head hung low, guilt swirling in his dark eyes.

"I... I didn't..."

"Hey, come here." He placed the coffee and brown paper bag down on the table and stalked toward me. "I'm sorry, I didn't think." Nicco pulled me into his arms and I went willingly, falling against his solid chest.

"I don't know what I thought." I buried my face in the crook of his neck.

"Bambolina, look at me." His fingers slid under my jaw and tilted my face up to meet his. "I won't ever do that to you again." Nicco seared me with his gaze.

"I know."

I did know.

But the deep sense of dread I'd felt when I woke up to an empty bed had been real. A natural reaction to everything I'd been through over the last few weeks.

"I was awake early, and you looked so peaceful. I didn't want to wake you." His arm looped around me, as he swayed us gently. "I have coffee and donuts."

"A man after my own heart." I smiled. "When do we have to leave?"

"We have time," he said, pulling me over to the bed. But I didn't let go and we tumbled in a tangle of limbs and laughter. Nicco gazed down at me, brushing the hair from my face. "I wish we had more time."

"Me too." The pit in my stomach was back. "Is Luis okay?"

"He's fine. Although I don't think he got much sleep."

"He stayed up all night?" My brows furrowed.

"He just wants to make sure you're safe." Nicco brushed his nose over mine, stealing a kiss.

"I need to brush my teeth." I pressed my palms into his chest, giggling when he began to pepper tiny kisses down the slope of my neck.

His soft laughter washed over me. "You think I care?"

Nudging him off me, I sat up. Nicco stood and fetched the coffee and donuts. "Breakfast, amore mio?"

"And after breakfast?" My heart sank at the thought of leaving Nicco. I was grateful for our night together, but it wasn't enough.

Not when I wanted forever.

"After breakfast, I'm going to carry you into the ridiculously small bathroom, strip the clothes from your body, and wash every inch of your skin, just so I can dirty you up again."

Oh my.

My stomach clenched. "Suddenly, I'm not feeling very hungry for coffee and donuts," I admitted.

"Eat, Bambolina. You need your strength." He gave me a pointed look, offering me the paper bag.

"Fine, but you know my mom always says a moment on the lips is a lifetime on the hips."

"Hush," Nicco said. "You're perfect just the way you are."

"Which is why eating donuts for breakfast isn't a good idea." I fought a smile. This was so nice. So normal.

"Hey," he leaned in, brushing my cheek, "don't do that." He must have noticed my expression fall. "We have time."

But it wasn't enough.

It would *never* be enough.

~

After breakfast, Nicco had made good on his promise to dirty me up. He'd loved me in the shower and again on the bed before finally succumbing to Luis' insistence that we had to leave.

Our time had run out.

"Everything good?" Nicco asked Luis as we stepped outside. He took my bag, offering us both a reassuring nod.

"We need to get back though before anyone suspects anything. I'll give the two of you a minute." Luis headed for the SUV.

"Don't cry, Bambolina." Nicco swiped the tears rolling down my cheeks.

"I'm trying to be strong," I replied. "I just hate this."

"I know." He cupped the back of my head, drawing me close. "I do too. But hopefully, it won't be for much longer. Now we know who Mike Fascini really is, we can make plans."

"What does that mean though?" My voice cracked, my heart already in tatters.

"It means we do whatever is necessary to find a way out of this."

"Okay," I conceded because what else could I do? Nicco didn't have a magic answer.

There was no answer.

"You can do this, Arianne. I know you can."

"It's easy for you to say, you're not the one—" I swallowed the words. I didn't want to argue. Not after such a perfect night. "You'll go back to Boston?"

"I will." Nicco looked gutted, guilt etched into the lines of his face. But it was more than his expression. It swirled around us, thick and heavy and suffocating.

"So I guess this is goodbye." A fresh wave of tears threatened to fall, but I swallowed them down.

"I love you, amore mio. Remember that." Nicco held me tighter. "You have to remember that."

"Arianne," Luis called from the car.

"I should go," I whispered, pain flooding my chest.

"This isn't goodbye, Bambolina."

It sure felt like it.

Nicco kissed me. Hard and bruising, not caring we had an audience of one. By the time he brushed a final kiss over my lips, I was breathless and nowhere near satisfied.

"Go," he barked roughly. "Before I ask you to come with me."

I walked away, forcing myself to put one foot in front of the other, until I reached Luis.

"Ready?" he asked.

I nodded, unable to speak. Glancing over my shoulder, I mouthed, "I love you," before climbing into the car, hoping he wouldn't hear the sound of my heart breaking or my tears falling.

CHAPTER 13

NICCO

Watching Arianne climb into the SUV was one of the hardest things I'd ever done. After their car disappeared, I didn't stick around. I grabbed my bag and hopped on my bike, the familiar rumble of the engine beneath me settling my soul.

Arianne was going back to that monster.

It wasn't right.

But it was the only choice we had right now.

Mike Fascini wasn't just some guy—he was a man out for vengeance. Arianne was right, we needed to know his endgame.

The wedding—not that I ever planned on letting her actually marry that fucker—wasn't for another four months. It would make Arianne a Fascini, and the business merger would give Mike access to Roberto's empire. But what then?

He wanted to bring down the Marchetti. To destroy the

Capizola from the inside out. But I was still missing some vital pieces of the puzzle.

One thing was for sure, if Mike was behind the failed hit on Arianne, and my money was on it being him, it meant he wasn't afraid to get his hands dirty. He wasn't afraid to murder a girl in cold blood to better his cause, which meant he was prepared to go to any lengths to get what he wanted, making him a dangerous man.

Far more dangerous than we'd first anticipated.

Blue Hills Reservation disappeared behind me as the Boston skyline came into view. I needed to speak to my father. We needed a plan. Arianne was safe for now, but what happened when Scott decided he was done playing nice?

I was biding my time. Playing by the rules and upholding the code of the Family. But if he so much as touched a hair on Arianne's head again, I wouldn't be held responsible for my actions.

Because an attack against Arianne, was an attack against me.

And an attack against me, was an attack against the Family.

I just had to make my father and his men see that.

When I arrived back at my uncle's house, I was greeted with the sight of Matteo's truck and one of my father's cars.

Nervous anticipation skated up my spine as I parked up and went inside. Haughty laughter filled the air, the familiar cadence of my father and Uncle Alonso ringing in my ears.

"Niccolò, so good of you to join us." My father cast me a knowing look. "Sit, eat. Maria was good enough to prepare a feast." He motioned to the table of food.

Just then, the back door swung open and my cousins filed in.

"Nicco." Matteo came straight over, pulling me in for a guy hug. "It's good to see you."

"You too."

"Cous." Enzo tipped his chin, his expression as cool as his greeting. He still wasn't over everything. And part of me didn't blame him. But it didn't change anything.

I was with Arianne now.

She was in my life, whether he liked it or not.

"Niccolò," Uncle Vincenzo pulled out a chair and beckoned me over. "Come, we have much to talk about."

"After we eat."

"Hell yeah," Dane piped up, dropping into a chair and loading his plate with ridiculous amounts of food.

"Where's your fucking manners, kid?"

"Can we drop the kid, already?" Dane growled at his father.

"Do you want Nicco to put you on your ass again? Because it can be arranged. In fact, now Matteo and Enzo are here, maybe I'll have the three of them teach you a thing or two."

Enzo snickered, and Dane discreetly flipped him off. He really was a cocky little fucker. I might have enjoyed sparring with him, even putting him on his ass a time or two, but given half a chance, Enzo would annihilate him.

"I'm sure we can arrange something," my cousin said, his brows drawn together.

Dane swallowed his mouthful of pancake and stuttered out, "Name the time and place."

"Oof, the kid's got balls, I'll give him that." Vincenzo roared with laughter, slamming his big hand down on the table, making the plates and dishes clink and rattle.

"He needs to learn his fucking place." Uncle Alonso glowered at his son, but Dane remained unaffected as he continued tucking into his breakfast.

"This is unexpected," I said, raising a brow toward my father. He huffed under his breath, draining his coffee.

"We'll talk after we eat."

He was pissed.

Probably because I'd gone to Arianne before calling him. But I couldn't turn back time and even if I could, I wouldn't have changed anything.

Arianne deserved to know the truth about Mike Fascini.

She deserved to know exactly what she was tangled up in.

"Well, would you look at this." Aunt Maria breezed into the room looking every bit the underboss's wife. "It's been a long time since I had this many men in my kitchen." She ran a hand over her husband's shoulder, dropping a kiss on his head.

"You're looking good, Maria."

"Thanks, Toni. Now if you all don't mind, I'm going to steal that son of mine away and make sure he actually makes it to school today. Dane." She motioned for him.

"But, Mamma..."

"You should listen to your mother, kid." Uncle Michele said.

"This is bullshit," Dane grumbled as he stood. "I can handle whatever is going down."

"That's what they all say until a pile of shit lands at their feet." Uncle Al scoffed. "Get out of here, kid. And stay the fuck out of trouble."

Maria nudged Dane out of the kitchen, and a couple of seconds later, the front door opened and then shut.

"He's going to send me to an early grave."

"He's a good kid, Al," my father offered. "Young and eager. He's hungry for it."

"Too fucking hungry if you ask me."

"He just wants to do right by you, by the Family." My father's hard gaze snapped to mine. "It's not a bad thing."

"It's good to see you, Toni. Real good. Now what's this all about?" My uncle sat back in his chair, glancing between me and my father.

"Ask Niccolò."

"You want to do this now?" I asked him.

"Now is as good a time as any, Son."

I ran a hand down my face. I hadn't expected them to come here, let alone to have to trust them all with this. But they were my family.

The Family.

I was supposed to be able to trust each and every one of them with my life. But trusting them with my life, also meant trusting them with Arianne's life.

"Niccolò..."

I stared at the men seated around the table. The men closest to me. My father, my cousins, and uncles. I couldn't carry this burden alone, and yet, to share it with them...

"Niccolò," my father rasped. "We are waiting."

"We found something out, Tommy and me," I said.

"Well, spit it out, Nic," Uncle Vincenzo scarfed down another pastry, wiping his hands on a napkin.

"Mike Fascini is Elena Ricci's grandson."

Silence enveloped us. Thick and heavy with the sins of our past.

"What the fuck did you just say?" Vincenzo sat forward, his thick fingers curved around the table edge.

"You heard him, Vin," my father said. "He speaks the truth."

"Ricci? Minchia! It is not possible."

"Elena Ricci?" Matteo balked. "As in the very reason we're all in this mess in the first place?"

"I had hoped for a different outcome," my father sighed, "but the reality is, Mike Fascini is in fact, Marchetti."

"Bull. Shit," Enzo spat, standing. No one batted an eye though, it was typical Enzo. When things went to shit, he started to pace the room like a caged tiger. "That fuck isn't one of us."

"Of course he's not one of us," Uncle Michele scoffed. "But if what Niccolò says is true, then it is far more complicated than any of us realized."

"It's true, I talked with his aunt."

"His aunt? The fuck, Nicco?"

I glanced at my father and he nodded. "Me and Tommy drove out to Vermont. It's where Elena fled to after Alfredo..." I didn't need to say the words, we all knew the story. "She had Emilio's child, a son. Michael. When he married, he took his wife's name to become Michael Fascini."

"That is some fucked up shit," Enzo let out a low whistle.

"You knew about this?" Uncle Vincenzo glanced at my father.

"I had my suspicions."

"Fuck," he breathed, running a hand over his stubbled jaw.

"There's more," I said. "I think Mike Fascini was behind the hit on Arianne five years ago. I don't have hard proof yet, but my gut tells me I'm right."

"It makes sense," my father agreed. "Take her out and pin it on us."

My stomach sank while my uncles all nodded. Talking about the failed hit on Arianne was like being gutted with a jagged blade.

"But it failed," Uncle Al said.

"It did." It came out tight. "So now he's working a different angle. Tommy thinks he's positioning himself as a Trojan Horse."

"It's smart. Move in on Capizola's empire first and then come after us."

"He's working alone?"

I gave Uncle Michele a curt nod. "We think so. There's no evidence of him having anyone outside his personal security and his team at Fascini and Associates."

Enzo loomed over us, his eyes narrowed to dangerous slits. "Let's just take him out. He's one man. End him and we end all this bullshit."

A chill rippled through the air at his words. "Lorenzo," my father let out a weary sigh. "We can't just take him out. He's one of the most influential men in the county."

"I'm with my son, Toni. Mike Fascini is a thorn in the Family's side. Taking him out makes sense."

My father clucked his tongue. "Always so quick to turn to bloodshed. We have to look at the bigger picture here. The girl is—"

"The girl is a fucking liability." Uncle Vincenzo gritted out. "I'm sorry, Nicco, I am, but she's going to be our downfall if we're not careful."

I shot up out of my chair. "She is not up for debate."

"She's a dime a dozen, kid. Of all the pussy on Earth, you had to go fall for the fucking Capizola heir."

"Don't you fucking talk about her like that," I ground out, my fists clenched at my sides.

"Niccolò, Vin means no disrespect, do you?"

"Come on, Toni. He's your capo, your son... he knew what he was doing—"

"*Basta!*" My father slammed his fist down on the table. "We did not come here to argue about Arianne. Niccolò has made his choice. She is his woman now. Which means she is as good as family. Besides, she's the only leverage we have right now."

"Fucking unbelievable," I seethed under my breath.

"Watch your mouth, Son. I might be on your side, but your uncle has a point." His brows pinched as he released a strained breath. I knew the responsibility he bore sat heavy on his shoulders. Just as I knew it would one day be mine.

"Roberto is well connected, as is Mike Fascini. We can't just take him out. Not until we know his endgame."

"I think it's pretty obvious what the endgame is, Toni." Vincenzo snorted with disapproval.

"We need more time." My lips thinned as I ran a hand through my hair.

"Time gives him the upper hand, Nicco. We need to strike now, while we have the element of surprise."

"Vincenzo," my father hissed. "This isn't helping. We can't go after Fascini until we know he doesn't have a failsafe. If we take him out, what's to say he doesn't have something set up to take us all down? When we finally cut off the head of his operation, I want to make sure another two don't grow back in its place. I will not risk everything on what ifs and maybes.

"The Marchetti have as much claim on Verona County as the Capizola. I will not bend and I will not run. But I will not rush in all guns blazing to pacify your blood lust."

My uncle's mouth twisted in disgust. I hadn't witnessed my father pull rank often, but whenever he did, it always rubbed my uncle the wrong way. Unlike Uncle Michele who sat quietly. He wasn't a soft touch like Matteo, but he was the calm to Vincenzo's storm.

"So we play their games? We might as well bend over and let them fuck us in the—"

"Vin," Uncle Michele shook his head, gently drumming his fingers on the table. "We take Toni's lead on this. He's right, it's a delicate situation and until we're sure Mike Fascini can be dealt with without kicking up a storm, we should sit tight."

"And the girl?"

"Her name is Arianne," I barked, feeling a lick of fury trickle down my spine. My uncle was pushing me. But what he probably didn't realize was, where Arianne was concerned, I would always push back.

Or maybe he did.

Maybe this was all part of his plan to demonstrate to my father that I was in over my head.

"I need some air," I said.

"Niccolò..." My father let out a resigned sigh. "Go, we'll talk later."

I didn't need telling twice.

I stormed out of there and didn't look back.

"I'd forgotten how fancy this place was." Matteo dropped down onto one of the luxurious gray rattan, egg-shaped chairs.

"It's a far cry from La Riva, that's for sure," I grumbled.

"Yeah, but La Riva is home."

"It is."

"Talk to me, Nic."

"When I saw her last night, all I could think about was taking her far away from here, from Verona County. I wanted to do it." My eyes lifted to his. "I wanted to do it and never look back. What kind of guy does that make me?"

"You love her," he said as if it was the simplest thing in the world.

"Yeah, but I also love Alessia. You and Enzo... Bailey." Running a hand down my face, I let out a frustrated breath.

"I know you do. But it's not the same. You found your person, man. The girl who makes you want more. There's nothing wrong with that."

My eyes narrowed, scrutinizing Matteo. He'd always been different to me and Enzo. Softer around the edges with a big heart. That's not to say he didn't carry out his duties, he did. He understood what it meant to be mafioso. We all did.

"What's going on with you?"

"Me?" His brows knitted.

"Yeah, something's off with you lately." Now that I thought about it, he'd been off since the semester started. But I'd been too distracted by a honey-eyed angel to give it much thought.

Until now.

"Nothing's up." He sat forward, leaning on his fists.

"You can't kid a kidder, Matt. Spill."

"I met someone."

"You met someone? What the fuck? When did you...?" I was confused. Matteo didn't date. None of us did.

At least, I hadn't, pre-Arianne.

"Remember that job we did over the summer, up in Providence?"

"Zander's club?"

He nodded. Zander DiMarco ran a chain of clubs in and around Providence, Verona County, and Pawtucket. Dominion provided him with protection in return for a good chunk of change. We'd been up there over the summer to collect pizzo and the fucker had caused a scene. So much so, my father handed future collections to Uncle Michele and his guys instead.

"I'm not sure I'm following..." I said. It had been weeks ago, and he'd not said a single word about it.

"I stayed in Providence that night. There was a storm, remember?" I nodded, it had been a big one. "Well, I ran into this girl. One thing led to another and we..."

"You hooked up with some girl in Providence and never mentioned it?"

He paled. "It sounds completely stupid, but we had this connection. It was... Nic, it was amazing. But she ghosted me."

"No shit." I rubbed my jaw. "You really liked her?"

"She was... fuck, we just clicked. And the sex, I swear I died and went to Heaven. But I got the impression she wasn't telling me the whole story and you know I wasn't entirely truthful with her."

"So why are you telling me now?"

"Because I guess I thought you'd understand. Because I look at you and Arianne and I want that. I really fucking want that."

"You should call her."

"I already told you, she blocked my number."

"Well then, you should drive up there and go see her."

"Nah, man. I can't..."

"Why the fuck not?"

"It could never work. I'm here, she's in Providence. It was just one night."

But it wasn't. I saw it in his eyes, the slight downturn of his mouth.

Matteo had it bad, and I'd been too self-absorbed to notice.

"I'm sorry."

"You don't have anything to apologize for." He raked a hand through his dirty blond hair. "I didn't tell you and you're not a mind reader. Besides, you've been a little preoccupied."

Still, it didn't ease the guilt snaking through me.

"Look at us." I sank back in the chair.

"Yeah, who'd have thought it." He chuckled but it came out strangled. "I know the Family comes first, Nic... but family is important too. I know Uncle Vin gave you a hard time in there, but it's only because he doesn't get it. He doesn't understand what it's like."

Did Matteo?

Could he?

Most of the time, I didn't even understand what Arianne and I shared.

"I'm not sure he'll ever understand," I admitted.

Matteo gave me a sympathetic nod. "Then I guess, you'll just have to make him."

CHAPTER 14

ARIANNE

"Tristan?" I rushed to the side of his bed, hardly able to fight the tears pooling in my eyes.

Tristan was awake.

"Hey, Cous," he smiled but it didn't quite reach his eyes.

"I'm so happy you're awake." Grabbing his hand, I squeezed it. "God, Tristan, I—"

"There she is."

My spine stiffened at the sound of Scott's voice. "I didn't realize you were here," I clipped out.

"Don't sweat it, baby." He roped his arm around my shoulder with complete ownership. "We can tell Tristan the good news now you're here."

My cousin frowned.

"Go on," Scott chuckled, "tell him."

I met his insistence with silence. I would never utter those words.

"We're engaged," he practically sang the words.

"Shit, Ari, for real?" Tristan grinned. "I knew he was going to pop the question, but I didn't think—"

"He didn't ask me."

"Say what?" Tristan's brows furrowed as he glanced between me and Scott. "But you just said—"

"Semantics." Scott shrugged. "After the accident things moved a little quicker than we expected. But it'll be official come next weekend."

"What's next weekend?"

"Our engagement party. Isn't that right, babe?"

I glowered at Scott, praying he'd drop the façade for just a second. I was here to see Tristan, nothing more.

"Why do I get the feeling you're not telling me everything?" Tristan's eyes bore into mine until I averted my gaze. I didn't want to do this, not here. Not with Scott right beside me.

Shrugging out of Scott's grip, I took Tristan's hand and squeezed gently. "The important thing is that you're awake."

"I still can't believe I'm out for the season. Senior fucking year." He all but growled the words.

"I'm so sorry," I choked out.

"Yeah, that makes two of us. Marchetti, is he—"

"Gone," Scott rushed out. "Won't show his face in Verona County again anytime soon if he knows what's good for him." I felt Scott drilling holes into the side of my head, but I didn't acknowledge him. I was too busy trying not to fall apart.

"What do you remember about that night?" Scott asked my cousin.

"I don't know, man. It's all a little hazy. The two of you were fighting..."

"He came at me out of nowhere. I was talking to Arianne and he just attacked me."

I smothered a whimper. That's not how it happened at all.

Nicco was defending me, he was protecting me. But I knew the truth would only fall on deaf ears so long as Scott was here. He and Tristan were best friends, and there was no love lost between my cousin and Nicco.

"First he breaks your finger and then he comes after me. The guy is a psycho—"

"What did you say?" I finally looked at Scott.

"Which bit?" He smirked.

He knew exactly which bit I was talking about, but he was going to make me repeat myself.

"He broke Tristan's finger?"

"You didn't know?" His smirk twisted into a devious grin. "At the party a few weeks back."

"He really did that?" I asked my cousin who nodded.

"He and his guys grabbed me and dragged me out to the workshop. Fucker took a hammer to my finger." My stomach washed with disbelief.

"He didn't... he wouldn't..."

"It's only what I've been trying to tell you, baby. Niccolò Marchetti is a monster."

"But why would he do that?"

I knew he and Tristan didn't see eye to eye, but breaking his finger? It made no sense.

"Why do you think?" My cousin said coolly. "Because he wanted information. He wanted to know if my cousin, the Capizola heir, was really attending MU." Tristan didn't sound mad this time... he sounded resigned.

I didn't know what to feel.

I knew Nicco wasn't inherently good; he was a mafia prince for God's sake. I'd watched as he'd beaten Scott to a bloody pulp and then lashed out at Tristan in a fit of rage. But underneath the mafioso was someone who was fiercely protective of those he loved, loyal to a fault. So not knowing what he'd previously done to my cousin felt like a betrayal somehow.

"What's wrong, baby?" Scott trailed his fingers down my shoulder. "Finally realized the kind of person Marchetti really is?"

I didn't look at him, but I felt his disapproval, heard the smirk in his words.

"Lay off her, jackass," Tristan said, throwing me a sympathetic glance.

A seed of hope took root in my chest. Maybe my cousin wasn't gone after all.

"I'm so happy you're awake," I said again, as if that erased the awkward conversation of the last few minutes. "Has the doctor said anything about when you might be able to leave the hospital?"

"They need to run a few more tests, keep an eye on my vitals for a couple of days."

"Excellent news," Scott said. "You might be able to make the engagement party."

Suppressing a shudder, my eyes fluttered closed. When I opened them again, Tristan was watching me, his lips pressed into a thin line. I gave him a weak smile, and his gaze narrowed. He sensed something was wrong, but he didn't ask.

"The team is in good hands," Scott launched into an update about the Montague Knights and I let my thoughts drift.

There had been plenty of opportunities for Nicco to tell me about him hurting Tristan.

Yet, he hadn't.

My cousin said it was when Nicco was seeking information on the Capizola heir. He didn't know it was me back then, and I couldn't help but wonder if it would have changed the outcome if he had.

Nicco lived by a code, I knew that. He was groomed for a life I would never understand. But it didn't make me love him any less. Just as him discovering I was the Capizola heir didn't make him love me any less.

Our fate was decided the second I came across him and Bailey in that dark alley.

Nicco saved me that night.

I just hadn't banked on him setting me free too.

"Okay, Tristan." A nurse breezed into the room. "You need to get some rest."

"I guess that's our cue," Scott said. "Take it easy, man, and we'll see you soon." The two of them fist bumped.

Tristan squeezed my hand. "We'll talk soon."

I gave him a small nod. "Bye."

Hurrying from the room, I didn't wait for Scott to escort me. But my attempt to escape was futile. He caught up to me and snagged my hand in his. "Anyone would think you're trying to get away from me."

"I am," I snapped.

"Tut tut, Principessa, you need to learn some respect. I am your fiancé. Your betrothed. Soon enough, I'll be the one in your bed, the one between your legs."

Bile rushed up my throat, making my eyes water. Defiance burned inside me. "I will never be yours," I spat the words at him.

It was a mistake.

Scott tightened his hold on my hand and forcefully marched me into the stairwell. It was quiet in there, even less busy than the hall we'd just left. He pushed me up against the wall, curving his hand around my throat. "Say it again."

"I'll never be yours." My eyes narrowed with hatred.

"You think you get a say in the matter?" Scott leaned in, inhaling deeply, running his nose along the slope of my neck in a way that had me swallowing a fresh wave of tears and vomit.

"I will be inside you again, and you will want it. You will fucking beg me after I'm through with you."

"Get your hands off me," my voice shook, betraying me.

"What are you going to do, baby?" He licked my skin. "Scream? Because you know it'll only get me more—"

The door on the level below opened and voices filled the stairway. I used the moment to shoulder Scott out of the way and keep walking. His dark chuckle rolled off my shoulders, sending a shiver up my spine.

"The clock's ticking, Arianne."

I marched down the stairs and into the hospital foyer. Luis shot up the second he saw me. "Arianne, what is it?"

"Nothing, can we please go?"

He'd stayed down here to give me space. Of course, I hadn't anticipated Scott being here or him being crazy enough to try something in the hospital.

I wouldn't make that mistake again.

"Vitelli, fancy seeing you here." Scott strolled up to us wearing his usual smug smirk.

Luis glared at him before glancing to me. "Are you sure everything is okay?"

"Everything's fine." The words almost choked me.

"We had some things to discuss," Scott said. "But I think she got the message."

It took everything in me not to reply. I swallowed the words. I wanted to fight him, but I had to choose my battles carefully because I would need my armor in the coming weeks.

"Come on." Luis laid a gentle hand on my shoulder. "The car is waiting."

"What, no goodbye?" Scott pouted.

I walked away from him with my head held high. Scott

could push me and taunt me, but I wouldn't let him break me.

I wouldn't.

As soon as we were clear of the hospital, Luis grabbed my hand. "What happened?"

"Just Scott being his usual creepy self."

"Did he do something?"

"It doesn't matter." I shrugged him off, fighting the tears threatening to fall.

"Arianne, it matters. If he's—"

"If he's what?" I hissed. "He holds all the cards and he knows it."

"Your father negotiated—"

"My father isn't in control here, they are. So no, I'm not okay. But I have to be. Because if I give Scott so much as an inch, he'll take everything from me, and I can't let him do that again, I won't."

"I won't leave your side again. I knew I should have—"

"Luis, this isn't your fault. We were in the hospital. You weren't to know Scott was here."

"Maybe we need to know."

"What do you mean?"

"Maybe we should start having him tailed."

I rolled my eyes. "If you think that'll help." I didn't, but I could see Luis wanted to do something, anything, to try to fix this.

"I'm going to speak to Roberto again, maybe he can—"

"No, you can't. We can't trust that he won't go to Mike with this, and if he does..." God only knew where that would land me.

My father was not an ally.

He was a pawn.

"I can handle Scott."

"You shouldn't have to deal with that piece of shit."

"You're right, I shouldn't. But what choice do I have?"

Indecision flickered in his eyes and then he leaned in and said, "I want you to carry something."

"What?" I gasped. Surely, I'd heard him wrong.

"Just a switchblade. Something discreet. You have self-defense training. I know your father made you take lessons after the attempt at the school."

"Luis, I'm not sure..."

"I know we need to bide our time, but you shouldn't be around that monster without some way of protecting yourself."

But a knife?

I didn't know what to think about that.

"It's only for self-defense and it would make me feel a damn sight better."

"Fine," I conceded.

"I'll arrange it and spend some time showing you how to—"

"I think I get it." A shudder ripped through me. "Can we go now?" Between my visit with Nicco and then Tristan, I was emotionally spent.

"As you wish." Luis guided me over to the SUV, holding the door as I climbed inside. Scott was still standing there, staring in my direction. His eyes saying a hundred things I didn't want to see.

There was no escape.

No way out.

I was his.

And he fully intended on making me realize that.

It was easy to avoid Scott at school. We shared none of the same classes, and he was a god on campus. Worshipped by the masses, it gave me a break from him while he soaked up their adoration. It should have made me feel a little better.

It didn't.

I was restless.

I missed Nicco. Despite all the questions I had about Tristan. About what happened between them. Then there was the fact I felt like I was waiting.

Waiting for Scott to make his next move.

"Ari?"

"Sorry?" I blinked over at Nora. It was Wednesday and we'd had to concede and eat lunch in the food court because of rain. But we managed to find a seating area away from everyone else. Away from the football team and their groupies.

"I said, what's up with that?" She flicked her head over to where Scott was sitting with his teammates. A girl was looming over them, her hands planted on her hips. Even from a distance, I could tell she was pissed.

"Is that Emilia?"

"Yep," I replied, watching as Emilia jabbed her finger into Scott's face.

"Man, she's really giving him what for."

Scott looked up at her, smirking. Laughter shook his shoulders as she continued her tirade. Emilia stormed off, rubbing at her eyes.

"I've got to go." I grabbed my bag and stood up.

"Go? But we only just got here." Nora stared at me like I'd lost my mind, and maybe I had.

"I'll see you later, okay? Feel free to eat mine." I nodded to my tray of untouched food.

"Should I come?"

"No, it's fine. Luis will be with me." He nodded before I took off across the food court, careful to avoid Scott and his friends.

"Emilia, wait up," I called to her retreating form.

"What?" She stopped, turning on her heel. "Oh, it's you."

"Can we talk?"

"What could we possibly have to say to one another?"

"Please?"

"Fine, five minutes. Come on." She motioned to the pergola beyond the doors. It was one of five dotted around the lawn. The rain beat down on us as we hurried to it. Luis stayed close but didn't follow us underneath the shelter.

"You have four minutes, forty seconds left," she sneered.

"Emilia, please..."

"I love him." She sighed. "I'm in love with him."

"You don't love him." She couldn't. He was a monster.

"How do you know what the hell I feel? He was mine before you came along and—" She smashed her lips together, shaking her head.

"Trust me, I wish things were different. I don't want Scott. I don't want any of this."

Emilia's brows furrowed as she studied me. "He told me you know? Taunted me about your engagement."

My heart skipped a beat. If she knew, others might. *Everyone will know soon enough.* I let out a weary sigh.

"Listen to yourself. Scott isn't a good person, he isn't..." Inhaling deeply, I chose my next words carefully. "Has Scott ever hurt you, Emilia? Made you do something you didn't want?"

"He would never... I love him. We were going to be happy together. We were going to..." Her bottom lip trembled, and I saw the realization in her eyes. Scott had hurt her; she just hadn't separated fantasy from reality yet. Maybe it was her coping mechanism, or maybe it was her way of making sense of everything, or maybe she really did love him.

But it didn't change the fact that Scott was a monster.

"You can do so much better," I said.

"Please." She rolled her eyes, indignation glittering in them. "Next to Tristan, Scott is the most eligible bachelor in MU. And he was mine." Her frown turned to a glower.

"I am not your enemy, Emilia. But I could be your ally."

"What the hell does that mean? You're engaged to him... you're going to be his wife, and you're what? Plotting some crazy revenge plan? I don't need to listen to this. Just stay away from me, okay? I don't know what you think you know, but you're wrong." Emilia started edging toward the steps.

"Just think about it, please."

If there were other girls like me and Emilia, maybe we could go to the authorities. They might be able to cover up one case, but if there were numerous someone would have to take it seriously, wouldn't they?

But my hopes were quickly dashed.

"You can't go up against a family like the Fascini," Emilia said with deep resignation. "You should remember that."

Emilia avoided me after that. The same way I continued to avoid Scott. Thursday morning rolled around, and I was almost able to trick myself into thinking I was just a normal girl living with her best friend and attending classes.

But I wasn't normal.

I was stuck in purgatory.

Living a nightmare.

I spent my time counting down the hours and minutes until my next message off Nicco. Like an addict waiting for their next high, I stalked my cell phone, desperate to hear the ping or feel the familiar vibration.

It was his words, his messages of love, that got me through the days.

It was bittersweet though. I knew I needed to ask him

about hurting Tristan, but there was never a right time. He was in Boston, and I was here, and it wasn't a conversation I wanted to have over the phone. I needed to look him in the eyes when I asked him, to see his expression.

Then there was the small matter that with every passing day, it was a step closer to the engagement party. Mom had already sent across three dresses for me to choose from. I was to coordinate with Scott which meant when I had picked a dress, I needed to inform him so he could wear the matching tie.

But informing him meant talking to him. And talking to him meant listening to him. So I'd asked Luis to pass on the message. I could have texted him myself, but it felt like a small victory to defy him.

Until I went into the living room and saw him sitting on our couch.

"If this is what you look like first thing in the morning, I'm going to be a lucky, lucky guy." He openly appraised my body, letting his hungry gaze linger on my bare legs. I was wearing an oversized MU t-shirt that finished mid-thigh.

"What are you doing here?" I wrapped an arm around my waist.

"Is that anyway to greet your fiancé? I just stopped by to bring you something for Saturday. I have extra practice today and a game tomorrow." He got up and stalked toward me. Slow, sure steps, like he owned the apartment and everything in it.

Including me.

Dipping his hand inside his jacket, he pulled out a rectangular shaped jewelry box. He flipped the lid revealing a diamond necklace. It was stunning. A delicate rope of sparkle and elegance.

I instantly hated it.

"It's too much."

"You're my fiancée, Arianne. There's plenty more where this came from." He went to take it from the box, but I laid my hand on his.

"I'll wear it Saturday." If he tried to put that thing on me now, I feared I might break.

"Very well." He snapped the lid shut and placed it on the counter beside me. "You should wear the silver dress."

"How do you—never mind."

He studied me, his sharp gaze searching my face, for what I didn't know. "I know that we didn't get off on the right foot, but it's only because you drive me fucking crazy." Scott reached out, tucking a loose strand of hair behind my ear. "We could be so good together."

My body began to tremble with indignation. Did he really think anything he could say would fix everything?

He was more deluded than I thought.

"You should go," I said, backing away ever so slightly. He was being weird, and it was unnerving.

"Yeah. But wear the diamonds and the dress. I'll see you Saturday."

Dread slithered through me, resting heavy in my stomach.

The seconds ticked by, the silence awkward and suffocating. I half-expected for Scott to make a move, to make some crude comment or try to intimidate me. But he didn't. He let out a long breath before offering me a sharp nod and leaving.

Luis rushed into the room a couple of minutes later to find me standing in the same position. "Arianne, what happened?"

"He was here."

"That sly fucker," he seethed. "I got a call there was a problem in the underground parking lot. He must have called it in to sneak up here. Did he—"

"No. He was... it was weird."

"Weird how?" Luis drew closer.

"He was almost... normal."

He smothered a grunt. "Tell me exactly what he said."

"He bought me this." I handed Luis the jewelry box. "Told me to wear it Saturday with the silver dress."

"That's all he said?"

I nodded.

"This is all a game to him." His jaw clenched. "He wanted to show us he still holds the power. I'm going to increase security here. Make sure he doesn't slip through again."

"Okay," I murmured, still rooted to the spot.

There was something about Scott's visit that bothered me, and I was beginning to think nothing would keep him away from me. He knew every trick, every blind spot.

I could handle the dirty mouthed monster who enjoyed making me cringe and cower. But cool, calm, composed Scott was a different beast entirely.

He was changing the rules. Trying to disarm me.

And I was terrified it was working.

CHAPTER 15

NICCO

"How are you?"

Silence filled the line. It was Saturday, the morning of the party. I wanted to call Arianne and reassure her that everything was going to be okay.

I'd wanted to do it all week.

But I couldn't find the words. And maybe I was growing paranoid, but she'd been off with me all week.

We still talked and texted. She told me all about her day and I told her about the monotonous routine of mine. But Arianne was distant, a lingering sadness in her voice I couldn't quite put my finger on.

It was eating me up inside.

Picking on every insecurity I had about our relationship, our future.

She hated Fascini, I didn't doubt that. My sweet Bambolina talked about him with such disdain I didn't once question her feelings toward him.

But *something* had changed.

I couldn't help wonder if it was the physical distance between us. If what we were asking her to do was too much. Luis kept an eye on her and checked in with me. But it wasn't enough. After another week apart, with no light at the end of the tunnel, I was beginning to lose faith.

Maybe Arianne was too.

"Amore mio?" I whispered. "Talk to me."

"I can't believe it's today," she finally replied, easing some of the tightness in my chest. "I lay awake all night wishing things could be different... wishing I was just a normal girl. But my life will never be normal." Her resigned sigh cut me to the bone. My girl was giving up. She was slipping through my fingers and I didn't know what the fuck to do about it.

If I went to her...

I couldn't. My father had given me strict instructions to stay in Boston. He'd given even stricter instructions to Uncle Alonso to make sure I didn't do anything reckless.

He didn't trust me where Arianne was concerned, and maybe he was right.

Because as I clutched the phone in my hand, waiting for Arianne's next words, all I could think about was driving back to Verona County.

"I only want to love you, Bambolina. With all that I am."

"I know," she took a shuddering breath. "And I want to be strong, I do. But I can't help but think tonight will change everything."

Fuck.

This was killing me.

Arianne had crawled into my soul, entwined herself with my DNA. If she hurt, I hurt. If she bled, I bled. If she cried, my soul wept with her.

"There's something else, isn't there?" I asked. "Something you're not telling me."

"How do you...?" She stopped herself.

"Whatever it is, you can tell me." My body shook violently. If Fascini had hurt... no, Luis would have told me.

"Are you having second thoughts... about us?" I barely choked out the words over the lump in my throat.

"What? *No*! It isn't like that. I love you, Nicco. There is no undoing that."

"So what is it, Bambolina? Tell me, please. You have to tell me."

Her silence was deafening.

"Arianne, please..."

"Tristan, he's awake."

"He is?" Relief flooded me. "That's good, isn't it?" I knew Arianne cared for her cousin, and I would never wish to inflict pain on her. So Tristan being awake could only be a good thing.

Yet she didn't sound pleased about it.

"I saw him at the hospital. Scott was there, he said some things... things about you."

My muscles locked up. "What things?" I tried to keep my voice even, but I couldn't disguise the trace of panic.

"I didn't want to talk about this over the phone, but I need to know... Did you hurt Tristan, Nicco? *Before* the accident?"

She knew.

That fucker had told her.

I hadn't purposefully kept it from her. Everything had just happened so fast, and now here we were.

"I should have told you," I said.

"So it's true? You broke his finger."

"It was before I knew the truth about you."

She inhaled a sharp breath. "I see."

"Bambolina, please. You know who I am. What I do."

"There's knowing it, and *knowing* it, Nicco."

"What do you want me to say?" The words came out raw.

This was who I was.

I couldn't change my legacy.

Just as Arianne couldn't change hers.

I was Marchetti. The Family came first. It would always come first unless I decided to walk away and bind us to a life in exile. It would be Emilio Marchetti and Elena Ricci all over again.

"Nothing," she breathed. "There's nothing to say. I just wish I knew. I wish Scott hadn't used the truth against me like that. I felt stupid."

"You're not stupid, Bambolina."

"No?" she seethed. "So tell me why I feel like this? I am sick and tired of having my life dictated to me by men. The only person who seems to understand that is Luis." Arianne laughed but it was bitter and strangled. Nothing like the sweet soft melody that usually spilled from her lips.

"He gave me a knife, you know. I've been practicing with him."

"He what?" My hand curled into a tight fist. Luis had never said a word during our check-ins.

"He said I should be able to protect myself."

"Bambolina, you're safe... I know it doesn't feel like it, but we're not going to let anything happen to you." Even as I said the words, I wasn't sure I believed them anymore.

This wasn't only about Arianne.

It was bigger than her, than me.

Than us.

"You're not here, Nicco." Her ragged words were like a slap to the face. "You don't get to reassure me of my safety when you're not here."

"That's not fair."

"None of this is..."

"Why do I feel like we're having our first fight?"

She let out another sigh. "I should go. I'm meeting my

mother and Suzanna Fascini for facials." The lack of emotion in her voice concerned me.

I knew it was taking its toll on Arianne, but she seemed so defeated.

"I love you, Arianne Carmen Lina Capizola. You just need to hold on for a little longer. Can you do that?" *For me?* I swallowed that thought. Arianne was already pissed at me; I didn't want to add fuel to the fire.

But I needed her to fight just a little longer.

"Bambolina, please..." I added.

"I should go. I'll talk to you soon." Arianne hung up without warning.

I let out a guttural roar, launching my phone across the room. Luckily, it missed the wall, landing with a *thud* on the spongy carpet. My cell phone was my only way of keeping in contact with Arianne. If I didn't have that, I had nothing.

Every day spent away from her was another day my soul ached. Another day the ties binding us weakened. I knew enough of this life to know that it required sacrifice. It required men to offer up a piece of their soul, to put the Family above all else.

But most men didn't find a love like ours.

It transcended familial obligation and rational thought. It lived inside me, woven into the very fiber of my being.

I feared if I didn't fight for Arianne; if I couldn't be the guy she deserved, there would be nothing of me left to serve the Family.

Because without her I was not whole.

I spent the day hanging at the house, helping my aunt. She reminded me so much of my mom, her presence brought me an unexpected comfort. Aunt Maria didn't have a housekeeper, she liked to get her hands dirty. But it was more than that, she respected my need for space, letting me help her in comfortable silence or mindless conversation.

When we were done in the kitchen, she came over to me and took my face in her small hands. "Such a good boy, Nicco. Arianne is lucky to have you."

"Is she?" My brows drew together.

"You love her, no?" I nodded. "And you would do anything make her happy? To keep her safe?"

"You know I would."

"Well, then. Stop with the pity party. You are Niccolò Marchetti." She gave me a knowing wink and tapped my cheek. "I think I heard your cell phone vibrating. You should go check it. It could be her."

I'd left it in my room to avoid checking it every five seconds.

Aunt Maria went to leave, but I called out to her at the last second. "Are you happy?"

She stopped and gave me a warm smile. "We get one life, Nicco. Love, family, and good food, what else is there?"

"The other stuff... it doesn't bother you?"

"Of course it does, but I made my choice. Just like Arianne has made hers." Her eyes twinkled with love. "Life is short. Too short to live with regrets." She disappeared into the hall, leaving me with my thoughts.

Taking her advice, I grabbed a beer from the refrigerator and went up to my room. I'd taken the smallest guest room, not wanting to be a burden. It also afforded me my own bathroom and no neighbors.

My cell was flashing, planting a seed of hope in my chest. But it was quickly dashed when I saw Enzo's name.

"Hey," he said. "I've been trying to get a hold of you."

"I was helping Aunt Maria."

"You're turning into a domesticated pussy."

"Fuck off. They were good enough to take me in, the least I could do is help out. What's up?"

"I was just calling to see how you are..." He let the words hang.

"You mean you're calling to check up on me." Irritation rippled through me.

"Uncle Toni is worried; we all are."

"I'm here, aren't I?" I gritted out.

"Yeah, and it's the right thing to do," he hesitated, "I just thought that with it being the party and all, you might..."

"You thought I'd do something stupid like get on my bike and turn up there?"

The thought had crossed my mind. In fact, I'd thought of nothing else all week.

"You need to stay away and let us handle it. Promise me, Cous."

"What would you do? Tell me what you'd do if it was the girl you loved?"

He snorted. "Un-fucking-likely."

"You'll meet her. One day you'll meet the girl who puts you on your ass and I'll be there to watch, loving every second." The words came out bitter. Enzo didn't get it. Just like his old man didn't get it. It was foolish to think otherwise.

"I didn't call to fight, Nicco." He let out a small sigh. "I called because I'm concerned. I know it's hard on you. But Uncle Toni, my dad, and Michele are trying to figure out the best course of action."

"That doesn't involve taking out Mike Fascini?" Bitterness clung to my words.

"You're still pissed over that?"

"I'm pissed that you still don't have my back." I was picking a fight, but I couldn't help myself. I needed the outlet.

I needed to get all this shit off my chest and Enzo was the unlucky bastard who was my verbal punching bag.

"That's bullshit and you know it. I have your back. I've always had your fucking back." He spat the words. "But since she came along you can't see straight. The Family comes first. Some piece of ass doesn't change that."

"I didn't ask for this, you know. I didn't go out looking for her. She barged into my life and knocked me on my ass before I even knew what was happening. You think I don't know she complicates everything? You think I don't ask myself every day if it would be easier for the both of us to just let her go?" My voice rose, my chest heaving with the weight of the words.

"Nic, that's not—"

"Loving her is killing me, E. It's fucking killing me. But not loving her, trying to walk away... there'll be nothing left of me to give." I drew in a shaky breath, feeling the weight of my words—the weight of being separated from Arianne—push down on my chest. "She's inside me, man. And I know you don't get it. I know there are so many layers of ice around your heart that you can't put yourself in my shoes and understand... but if I lose Arianne, if we can't find a way to make this work... you might as well drive out here and put a bullet between my eyes. Because she is it for me. There is no life without her. It's that simple."

Silence hung between us. "Fuck, Nicco."

"Yeah," I breathed. "One day you'll understand."

"I wouldn't bet on that. But I'm beginning to get it. I don't understand, maybe I never will. But I get it. I just don't want you to do something you can't come back from. You have to trust your father to get the job done."

"And if he doesn't?" A violent shiver ripped through me.

"He will. He knows what's at stake, maybe better than anyone."

"What's that supposed to mean?"

"He lost your mom. I know things between them weren't always easy, but he loved her. Aunt Lucia was the center of his universe. He wasn't the same after she left."

Enzo was right.

My father wasn't the same after Mom left. But he'd held it together because he had responsibilities. He had a family who needed him, and an organization that looked to him for leadership.

I let out a heavy sigh, the fight ebbing out of my system. "I know things haven't been right between us since Arianne," I said. "But you're my best friend, E. My brother in all the ways that matter."

"Don't go getting all emotional on me. You know I'll always have your back. But I'm not Matteo, Nic. I never will be. I won't always tell you what you want to hear. But I will always give it to you straight."

"And I love you for it."

"Fuck off with that shit. She's turning you into a soft touch."

"Maybe you and Nora should hook up and once this thing with Fascini is over we can all double date." A small smile tugged my lips. The chance to tease Enzo was too hard to resist.

He made some garbled choking sound, and I gave a haughty laugh. "Something tells me she could handle a guy like you."

"No one can handle a guy like me."

He had a point.

"But seriously, Cous, are you okay?"

"I'm not going to do anything stupid, if that's what you mean."

"Just sit tight. We've got tonight covered, and Vitelli will be with your girl. He won't let her out of his sight."

That wasn't the problem, not tonight.

"It should be me," I whispered.

I should have been the one at her side, the one claiming her as mine in front of all those people.

A beat passed and then Enzo let out a long sigh. "Who knows, if everything goes to plan, one day it could be."

CHAPTER 16

ARIANNE

"Ready?" Luis asked me.

Glancing at myself in the mirror on the wall, I nodded. My hair was braided in a crown atop of my head, soft tousles falling around my face. My eyes were smoky, and my lips were a deep shade of red. The diamonds Scott had given me hung like a noose around my neck. I'd almost decided against wearing them. But in the end, I'd snatched it from the box and asked Luis to fasten it for me.

Tonight, I would play my part. I would hang on his arm like the dutiful, docile fiancée I would never be, and I would do it all wearing a secretive smile.

"As I'll ever be." I grabbed my clutch purse and tucked it under my arm. We were, in fact, all staying at the Gold Star Hotel tonight, but Mike Fascini had insisted Scott and I arrive together in the limousine he had arranged for us.

"You look beautiful, Ari," he said, yanking open the door.

I felt beautiful. The dress wrapped around my body like a

silky second skin, kissing the floor as I walked. But the night was already tainted.

We made our way downstairs together, fifteen minutes earlier than planned. I refused to have Scott arrive at the door again with flowers, not when he was offering me something much more sinister.

When we reached the foyer, Luis clutched his sleeve, whispering something into the hidden mic. I was used to his discreet communications now. What had once felt like an intrusion on my life was now something I took for granted.

Luis was my shadow, my guardian angel, and I felt safer knowing he was there.

"Do you think I made a mistake?" I asked him.

He glanced down at me, his brow raised. "It is not for me to tell you how to live your life, Arianne."

"I know." I gave him a polite nod. "But I value your opinion."

"I think..." He hesitated, disapproval swirling in his eyes, but then the corner of his mouth tipped. "I don't blame you for wanting to defy him."

"But you don't think I should poke the beast?"

"You must choose your battles wisely."

A sleek, black limousine pulled up outside the building and Luis crooked his arm. "Shall we?"

I laced my arm with his, letting him lead me outside. The driver stepped from the car and came around to open the back door. Scott stepped out, his eyes instantly going to my dress. "I thought I told you wear the silver one."

"I preferred the emerald."

His eyes burned with indignation. "My parents will be disappointed you chose to disobey me."

"I'm sure they'll get over it," I said.

"I'll be up front." Luis released my arm and waited for me to climb inside. Scott followed, crowding me to the far side of the long leather seat. The car door slammed shut, reverberating through my skull.

"Is this how it's always going to be?" Scott glowered at me. "I ask you to do something and you go out of your way to defy me?"

"I wore the necklace." I flashed him a twisted smile.

"You're feisty, I'll give you that much." Scott toyed with one of the strands of my hair, twisting it around his finger. I had no choice but to lean closer unless I wanted the pinch of pain to worsen.

"I just can't decide if I like it or not." He moved away, surprising me. "Champagne? We are celebrating after all."

"You think I'd ever trust you with my drink again?"

"That was... a means to an end."

Bile clawed my throat. He spoke about it so candidly. So callously. As if that night hadn't been the single most horrific night of my life. I glanced away, giving myself a moment to catch my breath.

"Suit yourself." I heard him pop the cork and pour himself a glass. When I finally lifted my eyes to his again, Scott was watching me.

"What?" I clipped out.

"For as much as I wanted you to wear the silver dress, that looks really fucking good on you." He rubbed his jaw, letting his eyes linger on the low-cut neckline. Then a slow smirk tugged at his mouth. "Good thing I came prepared." Scott leaned over to the counter running along one side of the interior and pulled out a small drawer.

My heart sank at the emerald tie wrapped in his fingers.

"You think I don't know you, Arianne, but I do." His eyes narrowed as he undid his silver tie and replaced it with the one to match my dress.

My eyes closed as I suppressed a shudder. Something was different tonight. Maybe it was the fact I'd defied him by choosing a different dress or maybe it was the small blade strapped to my right thigh, but despite his attempt to disarm me, I no longer felt weak in his presence.

I felt strong.

Confidence coursed through me. A new sense of strength. Scott had already hurt me in the worst possible way, anything else he tried to throw at me was nothing I couldn't handle.

"I didn't wear it for you."

"No." He leaned in closer again. "But I'm going to pretend you did. I'm going to pretend you picked it out just for me." His fingers painted a trail along my arm, the emerald tie taunting me. "I have something for you. My father wanted me to wait until later, but I want to walk in there with you on my arm and my ring on your finger." His words dripped with possessiveness.

Scott pulled a small ring box out of his jacket and presented it to me. "I had it sized." He flipped the lid and removed it from its pillowed casing.

My hand trembled as he took my hand and gently slid the engagement band over my finger. It felt heavy. Unfamiliar and wrong.

It felt like he was stealing another one of my firsts.

"You're mine now, Principessa." His touch lingered, his gaze dark and hungry. My breath caught, nervous energy zipping through me. Scott was going to try to kiss me; it was there in his piercing gaze.

Thankfully, Luis chose that exact moment to lower the screen. "We're almost here. Your father has confirmed everyone is inside. You'll make your entrance and be seated for the meal."

Like I could possibly eat with the giant knot in my stomach.

"Are you ready?" Scott asked around a sly smile. He was

loving every second of this, but I refused to show any sign of fear.

Not tonight.

"I am," I said, steeling myself for the night ahead.

The door opened and Scott climbed out, offering me his hand. I took it, squeezing a little harder than was acceptable. "Nice grip," he teased.

I smoothed my dress out and glanced up at the impressive hotel. There was security posted everywhere. I'd expected it to be well-manned, but I hadn't expected such a show of force.

"Tonight, is going to be a night to remember." His breath was warm on my face. I sidestepped him, narrowing my eyes.

There was something in his inflection. A veiled threat that had alarm bells ringing in my head. But what bombshell could he possibly drop on me that was any worse than his father officially announcing our engagement?

There wasn't.

Which meant Scott was just trying to get under my skin.

I would go to the party, eat and drink, and smile in all the right places. I would stand at his side and let them believe the lie. And then I would retreat to my room where, in the cover of darkness, I would allow myself a moment to break.

This time, when he touched the small of my back and pressed his body up close behind mine, I didn't panic. I simply held my head high, rolled back my shoulders, and took a deep breath.

I could do this.

I would do this.

Because I was Arianne Capizola. I was my father's daughter.

And tonight, I would bow for no one.

The Gold Star Hotel was an opulent place decked out in rich gold and warm beige. But the Michelangelo Suite was the showstopper. A huge room with high ceilings and floor-to-ceiling sash windows, it overlooked a perfectly trimmed lawn leading to a small lake. Two identical crystal chandeliers hung over the round tables. The chairs were wrapped in beige and gold bows and each table had a candelabra centerpiece woven with fresh gold-tinted roses. It was ostentatious. A dinner fit for a king.

And exactly the kind of thing I'd expected.

"You're shaking," Scott said as we stepped into the room. No one paid us much attention at first but then the whispers started.

"There you are." Mike Fascini spotted us and made his way over.

"Son, you're looking very smart, and Arianne..." He gave me the once over before he leaned in to whisper, "My son is a very lucky man. Shall we?"

Mike motioned to the table at the front of the room. I spotted my parents and Suzanna Fascini, and Nora and her date, Dan. It felt like everyone was watching. Maybe they were. I didn't let my gaze waver to check. I kept focused on Nora who was giving me a reassuring smile, her knowing gaze silently saying, 'you've got this'.

"Mio tesoro." My father stood, coming around to greet us. He took my face in his hands, gazing at me with such reverie I felt winded. "You look..." He swallowed hard, almost choking over the words.

It gave me an odd sense of satisfaction to see him so uncomfortable.

That makes two of us, Father. I gently shrugged out of his hold and bypassed him to reach my mother.

"Arianne, mia cara. The dress is perfection on you." She

gave me a sly wink and I frowned. Did she know Scott had requested I wear the silver dress?

I got my answer when Suzanna Fascini greeted me. "Arianne, you look amazing. Did the silver dress not fit well?" She cocked a brow.

"I preferred the emerald." I shot her a saccharine smile before taking my seat. Unfortunately, we were seated male, female, male, female, so I wasn't directly next to Nora. But Dan was between us and she wasted no time sliding her hand over his lap to gently squeeze mine.

"Are you okay?" She mouthed, and I nodded.

Scott took his seat beside me just as Mike Fascini took to the stage. He unclipped the mic from its stand. "Good evening, everyone," his voice echoed through the grand room. "It's so endearing to see so many of our friends and colleagues gathered for a night of celebration. But before we get to all that, eat, drink, and enjoy good company. Cheers." He lifted his glass and the room repeated the word back at him.

An army of servers burst from a swing door carrying trays of appetizers, the rich smell of tomato and garlic filling the air.

"Wine?" Scott gently brushed my arm. The knot in my stomach twisted.

I glanced to Nora and she held up her own, reassuring me it was safe.

But I couldn't do it. I couldn't let him pour me a drink.

Laying my hand on Dan's arm, I smiled up at him. "Could you pour me a glass of the red, please?"

"Hmm, sure." His brows knitted as he glanced between me and Scott, who was still holding a bottle.

"Thank you." I lifted my glass toward Scott. "I'm good, thanks."

He snarled, his heavy hand landing on my thigh beneath

the table. I went rigid, forcing myself to breathe. "Don't play games with me, not tonight." He whispered out of the side of his mouth.

"Get your hands off me." I pushed him away, resisting the urge to break his finger.

A plate of food was placed in front of me and I thanked the server. It looked delicious. Tomato and basil bruschetta with a balsamic jus. But my appetite was back in my apartment.

"You should eat," Scott said. "We have a long night ahead."

I caught it again. The hint of warning in his voice. The slight inflection of arrogance, as if he knew something I didn't.

Refusing to play his games, I kept my gaze ahead. My mother caught my eye and smiled. She looked stunning in her Italian designer one-shoulder drape gown. It was a deep blue, a perfect match to the sapphire and diamond pendant she wore. Suzanna was in an equally beautiful gown with her hair styled in a complex updo.

At some point during the first course, Scott rested his arm along the back of my chair, his fingers dancing precariously close to my skin. If I sat straighter, putting more space between us, he shifted closer. It was a battle of the wills, neither of us prepared to lose.

"Everything okay with your food, Arianne?" Mike asked across the table. I placed down my silverware and forced a smile. I'd picked at the entrée, moving it around my plate to give the appearance of having eaten some.

"I'm saving myself for dessert."

He chuckled. "You have a sweet tooth? You'll be right at home with Scott then. He's a huge fan of dessert. Growing up he couldn't get enough of Suzanna's cannoli and tiramisu."

Pain lanced my chest. Scott and tiramisu didn't belong in

the same sentence together, not when that word reminded me so much of Nicco.

"Arianne, what is it?" My father's baritone voice reverberated through me.

"Nothing." I grabbed my wine glass and drank it down. "I'm fine."

"She's just a little nervous I suspect," Suzanna said. "It's to be expected."

"You need to relax, baby," Scott raised his voice slightly, enough that the nearby tables had to have heard him and roped his arm around my neck. "I've told you, everything is going to be fine."

Everything inside me screamed at him to get his hands off me but I swallowed it down. I couldn't cause a scene, not here. Not in the middle of this godforsaken dinner with Verona County's elite.

Grabbing his hand in mine, I removed it from my neck and placed it back in his lap. "And I've told you, I'm fine."

"You're going to have to watch that one," Mike laughed. "She's feisty."

"Don't I know it," Scott murmured under his breath.

The servers began collecting our plates, giving me a moments reprieve.

"Why don't you go see if you can get us a proper drink?" Nora suggested to Dan.

"But, babe, they have table ser—"

"There's a bar over there."

He finally took the hint and got up. Nora wasted no time sliding into her date's empty chair. "Are you okay?" she whispered.

My eyes flicked to my parents and the Fascini. They were deep in conversation and Scott was busy texting someone.

"I'm fine."

"It would be okay if you're not. It's kind of intense."

"I'll be okay. I bet Dan thinks he's entered The Twilight Zone." I let out a quiet sigh.

"After the Centenary Gala I think he knows the score where your dad is concerned."

"Abato," Scott leaned around me. "So nice of you to join us."

"I was invited, asshole," she sneered.

"Yeah, because I suggested it."

"You? Un-fucking-likely."

"Truth." His shoulders lifted in a small shrug. "I didn't want Arianne to feel out of her depth."

"How very thoughtful of you," I mocked, fighting the urge to roll my eyes.

"Fuck this, I'm going to take a piss." He got up and strolled away from the table.

"God, he's a vile asshole."

"Tell me about it. He's trying so hard to push my buttons."

Nora grabbed my hand. "And you're doing so well not rising to him. Nice little dig with the dress by the way. How'd he take it?"

"Tried to pretend he didn't mind, but it irritated him."

"Good, he deserves it, trying to tell you what to wear. Who the hell does he think he is?"

"My fiancé apparently." Bitterness clung to every syllable.

Her expression fell. "Shit, Ari, I'm sorry."

"Don't be. I'll never marry him. I'd rather—" I stopped myself.

"Don't ever say that," she gasped, concern glittering in her eyes. "It won't come to that," she whispered the next words. "Nicco would never allow it."

My breath hitched at the mention of his name and she frowned. "What is it?"

"We had an argument earlier. I said some things..."

"What things?"

"It doesn't matter." It did. But I didn't want to relive the conversation. I'd been frustrated and hurting, and I'd taken it out on him.

"Are you—"

Dan chose that moment to return, looming down over us. "I got us doubles; something tells me we're going to need it."

"My kind of guy." Nora shuffled back to her own seat and accepted the drink from him.

"I didn't get you anything, Ari, sorry, I didn't—"

"It's okay." For as much as a strong drink would no doubt settle some of my nerves, I couldn't afford to drop the ball.

Not tonight.

CHAPTER 17

NICCO

I couldn't do it.

I couldn't sit in my uncle's house knowing that she was at some flashy hotel being paraded around as his fiancée.

After our heated conversation this morning, I'd tried texting her. I'd even called again, but Arianne was freezing me out. It hurt. It hurt so fucking much that when I stormed out of the house and fired up my bike, I told myself I wouldn't go there. Told myself that I just needed to ride and clear my head. But before I knew it, the roads grew familiar... until I was in Roccaforte, the Gold Star Hotel looming in the distance like a neon fucking sign put there to taunt me.

She was in there with him.

My Arianne.

My strong, brave Arianne.

I found somewhere to park and threw my leg over the bike and just stood there. Staring at the place like it was a mirage in a scorched desert. You knew you shouldn't... but you just couldn't help yourself fall for the illusion.

It was a bad decision.

A moment of weakness that could land me in a whole heap of trouble.

But in that moment, I didn't care.

I didn't care I was defying my father's direct order, risking everything just to be near her.

Before I could stop myself, I started towards the hotel, keeping to the shadows. My hooded jacket afforded me some disguise, but I knew Roberto and Fascini's security guys would have been told to keep an eye out for any signs of me or my guys.

Part of me wondered if Fascini was banking on me showing up. That maybe this was all an intricate trap laid to ensnare me, and I was walking willingly into it.

But I had to see Arianne.

After our fight this morning, I needed to see her. I needed to look her in the eyes and know we were okay, that we could survive this.

As I drew closer to the Gold Star, I pressed closer to the rows of storefronts, careful not to draw too much attention to myself. It was heavily guarded, numerous security men posted on the entrance and beyond the glass doors. There was no way I was walking through the front door, but I knew there were multiple entrances. The hotel overlooked vast lawns that ran down to a private lake, that was my best option. It would give me a perfect vantage point of the Michelangelo Suite. I could watch, I could make sure she was okay, and then I could slip away like a ghost.

～

It shouldn't have been so easy. I'd walked right into the gardens, scaled a wall, and found the perfect place to watch from.

It all seemed very dull; dinner followed dessert. I could just make out Arianne as she sat quietly wedged between Fascini and Nora's date. There were security guys posted at every window, and the door was heavily guarded. But I wasn't going inside. Watching was enough.

At least, that's what I kept telling myself.

A crunch sounded behind me and I shot up, glancing around. My eyes strained against the darkness, my heart thudding against my ribcage. If anyone caught me out here—

"Enzo?" I frowned.

"You couldn't just do as you were fucking told, could you?"

"How did you...?"

"I know you, Nic. I knew you wouldn't be able to stay away. Just took me a while to find you."

"I had to come."

"You shouldn't have."

"I know." I looked back at the hotel. People had begun moving around while the servers worked quickly to clear away empty plates and dirty glasses. Arianne and Nora were huddled close. God, she looked fucking amazing. The emerald green dress accentuated her soft curves to perfection.

A low growl formed in my throat as I watched Scott loop his arm around her waist and guide her toward a group of people as if he owned her.

"Easy, Cous." Enzo's hand clamped down on my shoulder. "You need to relax."

"Relax?" I snapped. "She's in there with another guy. The same guy who..." The words soured on my tongue as I swallowed them down.

"I know but you need to keep your head. You shouldn't be here. If anyone were to see you that would be a shitshow of epic proportions. She's okay. You can see that. It sucks, I know it does. But she's okay."

She looked okay, smiling to the group as Scott made introductions. His hand remained possessively on her waist. I wanted to tear it from his body and beat him with it.

I wanted to watch that fucker bleed out and beg for his life. The need to hurt him never went away, it lingered under the surface. A sleeping beast waiting for its moment to strike.

"You need to go." His grip tightened, trying to guide me away from the cover of the large white oak tree. But I couldn't look away. Mike Fascini and his wife joined them, laughing and joking like they were old friends.

Like they were family.

The thought gutted me.

"Nicco, you need to—"

"I need to see her," I rushed out, slipping out of his hold, and taking a step forward. But Enzo grabbed me from behind and yanked me backward.

"What the fuck are you thinking?"

I spun around and met his thunderous expression. "I can't just stand by. It's killing me."

"Now is not the time. You're already risking everything by being here."

"I need to see her."

"Nicco, listen to me." He gave me a pointed look. "You need to get on your bike and get the fuck back to Boston before Fascini realizes you're here."

"No, I need to see her."

"Porca miseria!" he grumbled. "It's not like I can walk in there and get her out here."

"No, but Nora or Luis might be able to help." I dug out my cell and thrust it at him.

"You're serious?" His eyes bugged, glittering with disapproval.

"I just need five minutes." It would never be enough, but it would settle my soul until the next time I saw her.

"You've fucking lost your mind."

I didn't deny it.

I felt unstable.

Lost.

Like I was drowning in dark angry waters, being pulled under by the riptide.

"Wait here." Enzo glared at me. "I mean it, Nicco. You don't move a fucking muscle. If Vitelli says it's a no go, it's a no go. Do you hear me?"

All I could manage was a tight nod. I was too busy over-analyzing Arianne's every move. The way she stood close but not too close to Fascini. The smile that didn't quite reach her eyes.

Enzo gave me one last look before ducking out of the tree line. I wanted to go after him, to be the one calling Nora or Luis, and going to Arianne. But despite my evident lack of restraint, I didn't have an immediate death wish.

The minutes ticked by painfully slowly as I waited. People had begun to sit again as the servers went from table to table refilling glasses. I'd lost sight of Arianne.

Nervous energy vibrated through me as I rocked on the balls of my feet, desperate to see any sign of her.

But she didn't appear.

Enzo did.

"We need to move, now," he barked, beckoning me from the shadows.

I jogged over to him, following him around the side of the building to a small terrace area.

"Five minutes," he said. "I mean it, Nic. A second longer and I'll personally drag you from this place and kick your ass all the way back to Boston."

"You couldn't take me," I quipped back.

"Don't push me," he growled.

A door opened and Luis appeared. He shot me an irritated look. Apparently, Enzo wasn't the only one pissed at me. But none of it mattered when Arianne appeared.

"Bambolina." I rushed over to her, running my eyes over every inch of her body. "Thank fuck."

"Nicco," she sighed. "What are you doing here?"

"I had to see you. I had to know you're okay."

"You can't be here."

"Ssh." I brushed the hair from her face, moving in closer until I could smell the sweet notes of her perfume.

"Nicco." She fisted my jacket. "You shouldn't have come here."

My eyes snapped open, my brows pinched with confusion. "What do you—"

"It's not safe. If anyone were to see you..."

"They won't. After our conversation this morning... I couldn't just leave things like that." I ran my nose along Arianne's cheek, breathing her in. She shivered at my touch and the possessive part of me rejoiced at knowing I still affected her so viscerally.

I wound one hand around her neck, holding her against me. "You look so beautiful, Bambolina. I saw you... with him. Talking to his parents."

"I'm playing a part, Nicco. That's all this is." She stepped back but I snagged her hand, noticing the glint of light hit her finger.

"Is that... Fuck." I breathed through my nose, trying to rein in the tsunami of emotion crashing over me.

She was wearing a ring.

A huge diamond engagement ring.

His ring.

I was going to puke.

"Nicco, it's just for show." Arianne was the one clutching me now, her wild eyes pleading with me to calm down.

"He put his fucking ring on you?" A chill ran through me.

"Ssh," she moved closer, crowding me against the wall. "Don't do this, please. Not here, not now. It's all for show. An act. You knew what tonight was about."

"Did he get down on one knee and profess his love for you?" I sneered.

Arianne blanched, jerking back as if my words had slapped her in the face. "That isn't fair, and you know it."

"Shit, I'm sorry. I just... it blindsided me, okay. I hate knowing he's in there with his hands all over you."

"I don't exactly enjoy it." Tears pricked the corner of her eyes but my strong Bambolina forced them down.

"I know. Come here." I looped my arms around her waist and dropped my chin on her head. "You really do look beautiful, Bambolina. And I'm sorry you're having to do this. All of it."

"All I keep thinking is he's stolen another of my firsts... and I hate him so much for it."

I eased back to look at her, my spine rigid.

"You should go." She smiled weakly.

"How am I supposed to let you go back in there?"

"You just do." Arianne gave me a small shrug. She took another step back, our hands lingering between us.

"He can have your firsts," I said quietly, "but your forever... that belongs to me."

Arianne hesitated before throwing herself at me. I caught her and stumbled back with her in my arms.

"Kiss me," she breathed. "Kiss me like it's your ring I'm wearing."

Our lips met in an urgent collision of tongues and teeth. Arianne poured all her pain and frustration into every stroke and I greedily welcomed it. Her body fit against mine and our hands roamed and explored as we fell headfirst into the kiss.

I wanted forever with her.

I wanted the fairytale.

I might have been a mafia king-in-waiting, but I was nothing without my queen. And I didn't want to rule if I couldn't have her by my side.

It was that simple.

By the time I pulled away, Arianne was flushed, and her lips were swollen. Desire shone in her eyes and she looked ravished. But I couldn't find it in me to care. Because when she went back inside, when she went back to that fucker, she would be able to taste me.

And she would know exactly who she belonged to.

"Happy now?" Enzo gave me a hard shove toward my bike. "That was a close call."

"Yeah, yeah, save it for somebody who cares."

"That's just it though, Cous. You should fucking care. And I'm not talking about just the Family. What do you think that would have done to Ari tonight if Fascini's guys had found you? You're not thinking straight."

"She's wearing his ring, E." I scrubbed my jaw in frustration. "Am I supposed to just pretend this isn't happening?"

"You're supposed to trust your old man to get the job done."

My lips thinned. He had a point, and I hated it.

"Look, it's done." He let out a heavy sigh. "You saw her. Now you need to leave and stay your ass in Boston."

"Will you tell him?"

"What do you think?" He gave me a pointed look. "As long as you promise not to pull this shit again it stays between us, okay?"

"Thanks, I appreciate it."

"I know you think I don't get it, and maybe I don't, but I know you, Nicco. Nothing will ever change that."

I climbed on my bike, pulling on my helmet.

"Go straight home."

I nodded. I didn't want to lie to him, but there was somewhere else I needed to go first, and I knew he wouldn't agree.

"Did you get a glance of Nora tonight?" I asked, changing the subject. "She looked smokin' hot." I'd seen her through the window.

"Fuck you," he gritted out.

Laughter rumbled in my chest as I kicked the starter and gave him a nod before pulling into the street. The ride to County Memorial was only ten minutes. It was exactly what I needed to clear my head after seeing the ring on Arianne's finger.

I still couldn't believe it. It made perfect sense, they were engaged after all, but my mind couldn't make sense of it. Probably because my soul had already claimed her as his. So to see another guy lay claim to her went against everything I felt.

By the time I pulled into the hospital parking lot, the weight on my chest had eased a little. Arianne was mine. Something as materialistic as a ring didn't change that. But she'd looked so right standing at that fuck's side, his parents smiling at them like everything about the situation made sense.

I climbed off my bike and hung the helmet on the handlebars. This was another bad idea, but I needed to see Tristan.

Enzo was right, Arianne was changing me. Things that shouldn't have mattered before, did now. Like looking into the eyes of a guy I almost killed and asking for forgiveness.

The parking lot was empty as I crossed over to the main entrance. County Memorial was lit up against the inky backdrop, a sign that hospitals never slept. But I found the place quiet inside. Still, they probably didn't take too kindly to random people walking the halls at night.

Taking the stairwell to the second floor, I checked the hall before ducking out of the door. I knew Tristan was up there, but I didn't know where. The nurses station loomed up ahead, manned by a lone woman. I waited a few minutes, hoping she would be called away.

When she finally got up and disappeared down the hall, I took my chance, jogging up to the station and checking the huge whiteboard.

"Gotcha," I whispered, making a mental note of Tristan's room number. It was only a couple of doors behind me.

I'd half-expected there to be security, but the hall was empty. Pressing my face against the glass, I glanced inside, and sure enough, Tristan lay sleeping soundly.

Guilt flashed through me. I'd done this. I'd put him here. But he was okay.

He was going to be okay.

I grabbed the handle and gently opened the door. It barely made a sound as I slipped inside. Moonlight streamed through the blinds, casting shadows off the walls, illuminating Tristan's profile. I stuck to the corner of the room, hiding in the darkness.

I wasn't supposed to be here. But I needed to fix things.

I needed him to know I never meant to hurt him that night when I'd snapped. Now I was standing here though, I didn't know what the fuck to say.

So I started with the truth.

"I didn't mean to fall in love with her," I said to the silence. "It just happened. It wasn't some grand plan to mess with your family. She wasn't a game, never to me. I just took one look at her that night and something snapped into place."

I let my head fall back against the wall as I inhaled a ragged breath. It was late. Mike Fascini had probably made the announcement. The engagement was probably official.

Pain squeezed my heart like a vise.

"She wouldn't want me to tell you this, but you should know. As the person who is like a brother to her, you should know that he raped her. The night of the Centenary Gala, he slipped something in her drink and raped her." Tears burned the backs of my eyes. "And now she's there, at the party with him. Your uncle and his father are parading them around like a happy couple... it's messed up. This whole fucking thing is messed up.

"We weren't ever supposed to be enemies, you know." I let out a long breath. "We were supposed to be family. If history had played out the way it was supposed to, we wouldn't even be here."

Tristan shifted in his sleep, the rustle of stiff linen piercing the silence. I froze, holding my breath until he settled.

"I shouldn't be here. I don't know why I came... but everything is different now. All I want is to protect her. To put an end to all of this. But I don't know how. I don't know how to save her."

I inched closer, staring down at him. "I never meant to hurt you that night. I didn't even realize it was you until it was too late. If Arianne is going to survive this thing with Fascini she's going to need all the allies she can get. So I guess I'm not only here to apologize, I'm here to beg you to do right by her. To step up and be the cousin she needs you to be. And to promise me that if something happens to me, you'll be there to look out for her."

I was met with nothing but silence.

This was stupid.

Tristan was out cold, and I might as well have been talking to a corpse. But it wasn't like I could wake him. He'd take one look at me standing in his hospital room and call for security.

Defeated, I headed for the door. My fingers wrapped around the handle and pulled gently just as a whisper carried in the air.

"You have my word."

I glanced back, expecting to find Tristan glaring at me. But he wasn't.

And maybe I really was losing my mind.

CHAPTER 18

ARIANNE

"So... what did he say?" Nora whispered as we made our way back to our seats.

"Not here." I smiled, trying to give the illusion of everything being fine.

Everything was not fine.

Nicco was here.

Or, at least, he had been.

I hoped he was far away now, out of the reach of my father's and Mike Fascini's men.

He shouldn't have come.

Yet my heart was so relieved to see him standing there on that terrace.

"There you are." Scott rose from his chair and pulled mine back slightly. "You almost missed the most important part of the night." He smirked.

It was late and I was tired.

Tired of keeping up pretenses and putting on a smile.

All I wanted was to retire to my room, lock the door, and wash the games and fakeness off my skin. But first, Mike had to make his grand speech.

He was already on the stage, microphone in hand, a glass of champagne on the shaker table beside him. The servers were busy moving from table to table, replacing wine glasses with flutes, filling them with Dom Perignon for the toast.

Once we were all in our seats, Mike gave our table a nod and the room ushered into thick silence. "Some of you may be unaware but I have roots in Verona County. My family was here in the beginning and they will be here as we move into a new future. A prosperous future full of opportunity and growth. Together, with Capizola Holdings, Fascini and Associates will become a household name in the redevelopment of our great county. Get up here, Roberto." He beckoned for my father to join him.

He kissed my mother on the cheek, the two of them sharing a long, lingering look.

What was I missing?

The pieces of the puzzle were right there in front of me, but I still couldn't see them all.

My father climbed the steps to the stage and shook Mike's hand.

"I invited you all here tonight," he went on, "to celebrate the partnership between our two great families. But some of you may have noticed by now, that it isn't the only thing we're celebrating." His eyes found mine, dark and full of wicked intent. "My son, Scott, has asked Arianne Capizola for her hand in marriage and she said yes."

A low rumble of whispers trickled around the room. "This union will not only cement our business relationship, but it will unite our families. So I'd like you all to raise your glasses and toast the happy couple with me. To Scott and Arianne."

The words reverberated through my skull as Scott slipped his arm around me and pulled me close. "You're mine now, Principessa," he breathed, his words sending a violent shiver skittering up my spine.

"Before we continue with the celebrations, I would just like to say to you, Arianne, we look forward to officially welcoming you to our family. I don't know about Roberto, but I can't think of a better way to celebrate Thanksgiving than watching our children take their vows. Now please, the night is still young, and the drinks are still flowing. I hope to see you all up on the dance floor before we say goodnight."

Applause and cheers filled the room as the light dimmed. But I didn't move.

I couldn't.

Scott's eyes drilled into the side of my face as Nora cussed under her breath.

Thanksgiving.

He'd said Thanksgiving.

That was only weeks away.

"You knew." My gaze slid to Scott.

He wore an arrogant smirk. "I told you tonight was going to be special."

I shoved my chair back with such force, it almost toppled over.

"Arianne, sweetheart?" The color drained from Mom's face.

"I'm fine." The band around my chest tightened, stealing the air from my lungs. "I just need to freshen up."

I marched out of there with my head held high, nodding and smiling at the wave of congratulations offered from faceless guests.

I could barely breathe, let alone engage in conversation.

Thanksgiving.

"Arianne, wait up." Nora caught up with me just as I

stepped out into the hall, but I didn't stop. "Wait, just wait." She snagged my wrist and I conceded.

"Thanksgiving," I hissed.

"They really know how to ruin a girl's night, huh?"

"I need you to do me a favor."

"Anything..."

"I need you to go back in there and cover for me."

"Ari..." Her lips pursed.

"I'm only going up to my room. I need some space."

"You're sure?"

"Yeah, Luis will be with me." I glanced over at him and he nodded.

"Here," she handed me my clutch purse, "you forgot this."

"Thank you."

Nora pulled me in for a hug. "I know this is another blow, but it's just a game. They're just trying to keep the upper hand."

Nodding stiffly, I took a deep breath and met her eyes. "You should go before anyone comes looking."

"Okay, and for what it's worth, I'm so fucking sorry." She hurried back inside leaving me with Luis.

He came toward me, his brows drawn with concern. "They know," he said.

"So it would seem." We walked over to the elevator and waited.

"I'll let the Marchetti know."

I nodded. The doors pinged open and we stepped inside.

"It's a kink in the road but it doesn't change anything."

I released an exasperated breath. "I'm going to my room. I don't want you to let anyone inside, okay?"

"Arianne, maybe I—"

"Please, Luis. I need this."

"Very well," he said around a tight expression. "I'll make sure you have your space."

Good.

For the first time since all this happened, I felt out of control. Wild. I felt like a caged animal pushed to its limit.

And I was terrified that if I found myself cornered, I would do something reckless.

Something I couldn't undo.

∽

My suite in the hotel looked like a storm had blown through it.

The second the door had closed behind me, I had unleashed all my anger and frustration. Clothes lay scattered around the floor; my dress was in a crinkled heap on the bed and the pillow was stained with mascara and tears.

But I felt better.

I felt calmer somehow.

True to his word, Luis had kept any potential visitors at bay. Nora had texted me to say the party was in full swing, detracting from my absence. Everyone thought I was sick.

But Scott and my family knew the truth. And they afforded me a moment to myself. I guess I should have been grateful, but it was the least they could do given the bombshell Mike had dropped tonight.

Thanksgiving.

They wanted me to marry the man who had raped me, stolen my innocence, and hurt me in inexcusable ways, in less than two months' time.

Luis was right. The likely explanation for the sudden change in plans was that Mike Fascini knew that Nicco and his father had discovered the truth about Elena Ricci.

I grabbed the glass off the nightstand and threw it across the room, the sound of my screams piercing the silence. It hit the wall, shattering into a thousand pieces.

"Arianne?" A knock sounded on the door.

"I'm fine, Luis. I just... I broke a glass."

"Maybe I should—"

"I said I'm fine," I yelled.

He didn't reply.

Pulling a pillow into my chest, I curled into a ball and laid down. I wanted to be stronger, to be down there putting on a brave face. But I was scared that if I did, and Scott said something to me, I would snap.

In here, I was safe.

They were safe from me.

Because I felt different. Dark volatile energy coursed through me, making my skin vibrate and my body hum.

I wanted to hurt him.

I wanted to hurt his father.

I wanted to make them both pay for what they'd taken from me. What they continued to take.

The last thought I had was of Scott on his knees, begging me for forgiveness, begging me for his life, before everything went black.

I woke startled.

Fear wrapped around me as I lay frozen on the bed. "Luis?" I called out.

Where was I?

It all came rushing back like a tidal wave.

The party.

Mike's announcement.

Me fleeing to my hotel room.

I lay listening for any sound but there was nothing.

Sitting up, I pushed the wild curls from my eyes. I was a mess. Dressed only in my underwear, my hair all over the place, and no doubt with makeup streaked down my face, I was thankful I couldn't see my reflection in the darkness.

Swinging my legs over the edge of the bed, I fumbled to find my cell phone. It was almost two-thirty. The party would be over by now, guests sleeping peacefully in their expensive suites. Nora would be with Dan, curled up in his arms. Dropping my cell back on the nightstand, I reached for the lamp switch but a noise in the corner of the room caught my attention. My eyes strained, my heart beating furiously in my chest.

"What did I tell you, baby?" Scott's voice had me paralyzed. He leaned forward, appearing from the black abyss like the Devil himself. "If you push, I will always push harder."

I flicked on the light, and my eyes widened at the sight of the gun in his hand.

"What are you doing here, Scott? Where's Luis?"

"He's around."

Bile rushed up my throat as I choked out, "You shouldn't be here."

"Like Marchetti shouldn't have been here earlier? Like he shouldn't have been snooping around in Vermont?" He got up and stalked toward me, rubbing the pistol against his head like it was a comb. "I don't know how many times I have to say this but you. Are. Mine."

I pulled my legs up, shuffling back onto the bed but Scott was quicker. His hand shot out, grabbing my ankle and yanking me toward him.

"Don't, please..." I couldn't let this happen, not again. "My father will—"

"You think your old man gets a say in any of this? I am untouchable. My father has enough lawyers and cops in his pocket to protect me. I could fuck you right here and cut you up into tiny little pieces and no one would do a thing about it."

Waves of nausea rolled through me.

"You're mine, Arianne." He leaned down, running his hands up my bare thighs, the overpowering stench of liquor on his breath. "Look at you, all laid out like this. Anyone would think you were waiting for me. Waiting for your fiancé to come and dirty you up."

My hand *cracked* against his cheek, and Scott staggered back. "Fucking bitch." He grabbed me by the hair, pain shooting through my skull, and threw me down on the floor. I tried to crawl away from him, but it was futile.

Scott rounded me like a predator stalking its prey. "You look good on your knees." He waved the pistol in the air, pointing it at me. "I think we should have a little fun, don't you?"

"Fuck you," I seethed.

I wasn't going to beg for mercy.

Maybe if I made him mad enough, he would shoot me and end this sick game I wanted no part of.

"Hmm," he chuckled darkly. "Kitty grew claws." He shot forward, pressing the gun to my forehead. "Move."

My body shook, silent tears streaming down my face. I didn't want to die. But I didn't want to be his toy, not again.

He kept the gun trained on me as he sat back in the chair, fumbling with his belt. His zipper went next and then he pulled his erection free, stroking himself roughly.

I dry heaved into my hand.

"You get me so hard, Principessa. You have no idea of the things I want to do to you."

"If you touch me, Nicco will kill you."

He stopped, his eyes darkening to two obsidian slits. "Marchetti is a dead man walking. In fact, I think I might serve up his head on a silver platter for you as a wedding gift. Would you like that?"

"You're nothing but a monster."

Scott slid off the chair, dropping to his knees. His erection brushed my stomach and I retched again, But then he grabbed my throat, cutting off my airway.

He pressed the gun to my lips. "Suck it."

I smashed them together, determined not to let him break me.

But he squeezed my windpipe harder forcing me to gasp for breath. Using my desperation to his advantage, he shoved the barrel of the pistol into my mouth. He was pleasuring himself. Moving the pistol in and out as he jerked himself off. All while silent hot tears streamed down my face.

I didn't understand what had happened to make him this way.

He wasn't only a monster.

He was depraved.

Grabbing my hand, he pushed it to his hard length, making me topple slightly, forcing the pistol further between my lips until I couldn't breathe.

"Fuck yeah," he groaned, thrusting his hips wildly.

He yanked the pistol free, grabbing my hair again and forcing my head down to his crotch. I sucked in big greedy lungfuls of air.

"You're going to put those pretty lips around me and suck."

I thrashed against him but then the click of the safety pierced the air and I froze.

"Do it."

I was on all fours, his hand forcing my head in place. Frantically, I searched the floor for something, *anything*, I could use to hurt him.

Then I felt it.

The soft leather knife holster Luis had given me. It was empty, the knife must have scattered when I'd thrown it.

"I'll count to five, Arianne. Don't make me get to zero, because you won't like what happens."

Oh God.

My eyes burned as I held myself in place, desperately trying to pat the floor for the knife without giving myself away.

"Five... four... three..." I couldn't find it, my fingers meeting nothing but soft carpet. "Two..." I stretched my hand further, praying to some higher power to help me.

"On—"

My fingertips met the smooth hilt of knife.

"Time's up." He almost sounded disappointed.

"Wait," I said, lifting my head slowly. Scott narrowed his eyes. "Not like this, please..."

His brow quirked up. If he glanced down to the left, he would see my hand, see me trying to reach for the knife.

"Sit in the chair," I said trying my best to hide the quiver to my voice.

"Okay," he said, "I'll play. But you'd better fucking make it worth my while."

Scott lifted himself into the chair, keeping his legs wide, his hand wrapped proudly around his length.

Everything about him made my skin crawl.

But there was no other way.

I scooched forward on my knees, sliding one hand up his thigh letting it drift precariously close to his erection. Scott groaned, sinking back in the chair. It was enough for me to grab the blade.

His hand went to my hair, yanking me closer. "Now, Arianne. I won't ask—"

I slammed the knife into his thigh. Scott let out a grunt of pain. "You fucking bitch." He shot forward to lunge for me, but I collapsed back out of his reach, grabbing the first thing I could find and swinging it at him.

The lamp crashed against Scott's head with a sickening *thud*. Scott groaned, falling back into the chair, blood trickling from the cut above his eye.

Clambering to my feet, I grabbed my phone and a hotel robe, wrapping the soft fluffy material around my body, and I ran from the room.

"Arianne?" Luis looked gutted as he appeared around the corner of the hall, flushed and breathless.

"We need to go, now."

"What did you do?" He glanced to my room.

"I... the knife..."

"Is he dead?"

I shook my head. Luis hesitated; his eyes fixed on the door. I knew what he was thinking. It was the same thing I was thinking. It would be so easy to go back in there and finish the job.

"He has a gun," I whispered, my body racked with fear.

"Shit, okay. Come on, we should get you out of here. I'll radio for some of our guys to deal with him."

Luis wrapped his arm around me and led me down the hall. We didn't take the elevator, slipping into the stairwell instead.

"What happened?" he asked as we hurried down the stairs.

"I woke up and he was there, in my room. I asked where you were and—"

"I heard something in the stairwell, so I went to check it out." His jaw clenched. "He got the jump on me and knocked me out."

"He had a gun and tried to..." I swallowed a fresh wave of tears. "I found the knife you gave me and stabbed him. I couldn't let him do that to me again. I just couldn't."

"You did the right thing." Luis glanced down at me. "But you know what this means?"

"I can't go back." I trembled.

"No, you can't." He pulled his cell from his pocket and typed out a text. It pinged two seconds later, and he read the message. "Okay, come on. Keep your head down and don't stop for anyone, okay?"

Luis opened the door and checked the coast was clear before beckoning for me to join him. We weren't in the main foyer; it was a side entrance used for guests only. Luis fished a keycard out of his pocket and pressed it against the keypad. The door clicked open and we exited onto the street. A car pulled up alongside us and someone climbed out.

"Enzo?" I blinked sure my eyes were deceiving me.

"We need to go, now." He and Luis shared a concerned look.

"Go, Enzo will keep you safe."

"Wait." Panic rose in my voice. "You're not coming with us?"

"I need to go back and make sure he doesn't do anything stupid. Consider it damage control."

"But he has a gun..."

"Vitelli can handle himself." Enzo wrapped an arm around my shoulder and guided me toward the car. The gesture was so unlike him, I didn't resist.

"I'll see you soon, okay?" Luis offered me a warm smile, but it didn't reach his eyes.

Everything had changed tonight.

And it was all my fault.

"I'm sorry I couldn't do it," I called over my shoulder.

He frowned. "It's okay, we always knew it might come to this."

I had no idea what he meant, but Enzo didn't give me

chance to ask. He pushed me into the car and slammed the door, going around to the driver's side.

Enzo climbed in. "You okay?" he asked coolly.

"Not really." I leaned my head against the cool glass, trying to make sense of the last few hours. "But I will be."

What other choice did I have?

CHAPTER 19

NICCO

My eyes snapped open, the blare of my cell phone like a siren in the night. "What the hell?" I mumbled, trying to locate it. "Yeah?"

"Nicco?" Enzo sounded distant.

I shot upright. "What happened?"

"It's Ari, she's... fuck, man. It's messed up."

"Is she okay?" A bolt of fear shot through me, my hands trembling as I gripped the phone tighter.

"She's okay. I brought her out to the cabin."

"Okay, I'm on my way."

"Be careful." He inhaled a ragged breath. "Fascini knew you were at the hotel, so there's every chance he's watching your movements. If you're being tailed, you can't lead them here."

He was right.

The cabin was off the grid. A family hideaway few people knew about.

"I'll take precautions." My words shook. "Can I talk to her?"

"She's sleeping."

"Okay, I'll see you soon." I inhaled a ragged breath. "And E?"

"Yeah?"

"Thank you."

∽

After waking my uncle and explaining the situation to him, I packed a bag, grabbed my keys and fired up my bike. The ride to the cabin should have only been an hour, but if Enzo was right and I was being watched then I needed to take a different route.

It was the middle of the night, the roads deserted. But it worked in my favor. I'd barely made it out of Boston, when I realized I was being tailed.

The black SUV kept its distance, but when I pulled off the interstate and took the state highway, and it followed, gut instinct told me it was more than just coincidence. I didn't gun the engine. I kept a steady pace, trying to figure out how best to let things play out.

If I tried to shake them and failed, I could be leading them straight to Arianne, which wasn't an option. But if I tried to take them on, I could end up hurt … or worse. I had no fucking idea if they were here on Mike Fascini's orders or his son's. Not that it mattered. Either way, I was the enemy in their eyes. Just as they were the enemy in mine.

I pulled over at a rest stop just on the outskirts of Rhode Island. Ahead of them by a couple of minutes, I climbed off my bike and scanned the area. There was a small brick building signposted 'restroom' and a couple of vending machines, but not much else in the way of places to hide.

Slipping around the building, I pulled out my pistol and waited.

The SUV rolled to a stop. I couldn't see it, but I heard the doors open, heard heavy boots hit the gravel. There were two of them. One would have been easier, but it didn't matter.

No one was going to keep me from getting to Arianne.

Neither of them spoke, probably hoping to sneak up on me in the restroom while I went about my business. Once I heard them both enter the building, I tiptoed back around and silently slipped inside.

"He's not here," one of them said.

"He's got to be. Check—"

The shot rang out, one of the guys hitting the floor like a sack of bricks.

"Motherfucker," the other guy roared but I cocked my pistol right at him.

"Don't. Move."

He lifted up his hands, edging backward.

"Who sent you?"

His lips pressed into a thin line, but I wasn't looking to play games. Lowering my aim, I pulled the trigger and he went down on his knee, blood trickling from the hole in his leg. "Who. Sent. You?"

"Fascini."

"No shit," I grumbled. "Mike Fascini?"

"N- no. The son. Crazy sonofabitch that one."

My brow quirked up. "What were your orders?"

The blood drained from his face as he whimpered in pain. "Please man, don't kill me. I got—"

I stormed forward, pressing the barrel right against his head. "What. Were. Your. Fucking. Orders?"

"Tail you and make sure you didn't make it back to Verona."

Scott really was a crazy motherfucker.

"Look, man, I- I was just doing—"

The second shot hit him right between the eyes.

It should have bothered me, killing a man in cold blood. It wasn't something I ever relished, but this was different. This was about Arianne, about keeping her safe.

Doubling back to my bike, I didn't spare a second glance as I kicked the starter and sped off in the direction of the cabin.

In the direction of the girl I would kill for.

Thirty minutes later, I pulled up to the cabin. It was almost five thirty in the morning, the first signs of sunrise breaking on the horizon. I climbed off my bike hardly surprised when the door opened, and Enzo appeared. "You good?" he asked.

"I will be. Is she inside?" I shouldered past him.

"Hold up a minute. What happened?"

My eyes locked on his and I let out a heavy sigh. "You were right."

"About the tail?"

"Yeah."

"But you handled it?"

I knew what he was asking me. With a deep frown, I nodded.

"Hey, you did what you had to do." He squeezed my shoulder.

"Where is she?"

"In the first room. I wanted her close by."

"Thank you."

"Go see her and then we'll talk."

I took off down the hall. I hadn't been out here in a while, but everything about the place was still familiar. The door to Arianne's room was ajar and I slipped inside quietly. She looked so peaceful asleep in the middle of the queen-size bed, wrapped in a fluffy white robe. I moved closer, my mind darting in a hundred different directions. He'd hurt her again, that much was obvious. But it was hard to imagine right now while she seemed so at peace.

Leaning down, I brushed her cheek. Arianne murmured nestling further into the covers. But she didn't wake.

"I love you, Bambolina," I whispered.

Her hand was curled around the sheets, the ring on full display. Carefully, I eased her finger straight and slipped it off, placing it on the nightstand beside the bed. It didn't belong on her, but Arianne could choose what to do with it.

With one last lingering look, I left the room and went to find Enzo.

"Everything okay?" he asked as I joined him in the main room.

"She's sleeping. I didn't have the heart to wake her."

"It was a fucking shitshow by all accounts." His expression turned grim.

"What the fuck happened?" I dropped down into the chair opposite him.

"After you left, Luis called me, said he was worried about Scott's demeanor."

"Worried how?"

"Said he had a gut feeling."

"So I stuck around. Stayed in the shadows, watching. Nothing seemed out of the ordinary, but I stayed. Was half-asleep in my car when he called again." His expression morphed into one of disgust. "He said she—"

There was a knock at the door and my hand instantly went inside my jacket to my pistol.

"Relax," Enzo shot up, "it's Vitelli." He went and opened it, letting Luis inside. "I was just getting to the good part," he said to Arianne's bodyguard as if the last few hours had bonded them somehow.

"I'm sorry," Luis said, sitting on the end of the couch. "I shouldn't have let him get the drop on me like that."

"What happened?"

"Does he know?" he asked Enzo.

My best friend shook his head.

"Know what?"

"The wedding... Mike announced a new date. Thanksgiving weekend."

"That's a joke... you're joking, right?" That was less than two months away.

"I wish I were." A dark shadow passed over his face. "Fascini knows you went to Vermont."

"Fuck."

"Yeah, fuck." Enzo ran a hand down his face.

"But we have bigger problems right now." The two of them shared another look.

"Will someone just tell me what the fuck happened?" I was growing inpatient.

"Arianne left the party after he made the announcement. I think it was too much for her. She didn't want any visitors, so I posted myself outside. Everything was fine, then around two I heard something in the stairwell. I went to check it out and Scott jumped me, knocked me clean out. He managed to slip the guy we had on his room, and must have gotten an extra keycard for her room and slipped inside..." He cleared his throat clearly uncomfortable with whatever it was he needed to tell me.

"Arianne woke up and he held a gun to her head and tried to force her to..."

"He didn't just hold a gun to her head," Enzo snapped. "He made her suck the fucking thing while he got off. Your girl showed him though, drove a knife right through his thigh and knocked him out with a lamp."

"He did that?" The air was sucked clean from my lungs. It was bad enough he'd already hurt her, but to hold a gun to her head and force her to—

I swallowed the rush of bile up my throat. "Did he...?"

"No. She says he didn't touch her."

"Where is he now?"

"I stayed behind and woke up both sets of parents to let them deal with that piece of shit. Roberto was concerned and wanted to see Arianne, but I told him over my dead body."

"Nice," Enzo snorted. "You sure no one followed you out here?"

"I'm good at my job. I know how to stay off the radar." Luis almost looked offended at Enzo's words.

"I want him dead." I leaped up. "I want his head on a silver fucking platter." The red mist swallowed me whole until I could see nothing but Fascini's lifeless bloody body at my feet.

"You need to calm down." Enzo hovered on the fringe of my consciousness.

"No, what I need is to see that fucker bleed."

"Nicco?" Arianne's voice rose above the blood roaring between my ears. I turned slowly to meet her weary gaze. Her eyes were red and swollen, her face streaked with mascara. "You're here," she said shakily.

"I'm here." I went to her, falling to my knees and burying my face in her robe. I didn't care that we had an audience. In that moment, all I cared about was that she was here, and she was safe.

"Nicco." Arianne slid her hand against my cheek, coaxing my face to hers. "I'm okay."

But she wasn't.

She couldn't be.

"It's early and I'm still tired, come to bed with me." She tugged the collar of my jacket. I clambered to my feet, glancing over my shoulder.

"Go," Enzo said. "We've got your back."

I nodded, mutual understanding passing between us.

Arianne led me to our room, closing the door behind me. "I'm so fucking sorry." My voice cracked.

"Ssh," she whispered, pushing my jacket from my shoulders. Her hands went to the hem of my sweater next. I helped her work it off my body before unbuttoning my jeans and kicking them off. Arianne stood before me, drinking me in with her big, honey-brown eyes. "You're really here."

"I am." And I didn't plan on ever leaving her again.

Whatever Mike Fascini had up his sleeve we would face together.

She unbelted the fluffy robe and pushed it off her body. "Lie with me?"

I didn't need asking twice. I scooped Arianne up in my arms and laid her down on the bed. "Are you sure you're okay?"

"I am now." She leaned up, pressing a tender kiss to the corner of my mouth. "But I'm tired. I'm so tired, Nicco."

"It's okay." I climbed in beside her and rolled her onto her side away from me, tucking her into my chest. "I'm right here." My lips touched her shoulder, lingering, as a violent shudder rolled through me.

"Promise you'll be here when I wake up?"

"I promise."

Her body sagged against me as if she needed to hear the words before she could allow herself to relax. But I couldn't close my eyes, because if I did, I knew the nightmares would come. So I held her close and listened to the sound of her gentle breathing and tiny sighs.

Arianne never should have been there tonight. But she

was right, she had been forced to play a part because of the men in her life who pulled the strings.

I wouldn't let it happen again.

If Fascini wanted war, I'd meet him on the battlefield. I'd fight with all that I had, if it meant protecting her from the likes of Scott and his father.

I'd always known my life in the Family was tenuous. I respected the Omertà; respected the codes we lived by, but Arianne was my woman.

My life.

And to put the Family above her was a betrayal to my soul.

A betrayal to the future I hoped we'd one day have.

I must have dropped off, because when I woke up the bed was empty, and I had a kink in my neck. Sitting up, I stretched out my muscles before pulling on my jeans and going in search of Arianne.

The last place I expected to find her was at the cooktop making breakfast for Luis and Enzo.

"You look like shit," my cousin said around a smirk.

I flipped him off, going to Arianne. Wrapping an arm around her waist, I pulled her against my chest and tucked my chin into her shoulder. "I missed you."

"You were sleeping. I didn't want to wake you."

"You should have." She tilted her face up to mine and I stole a kiss.

"I needed to do something. Luis went out for supplies so I could make breakfast."

"What time is it?"

"A little after ten."

"Any word?" I asked Luis.

"Roberto has been blowing up my cell, but I haven't responded yet. Figured we need to get our stories straight."

"What about you?" My eyes went to Enzo.

"You think I'm going to be the one to break it to Uncle Toni that we stole the Capizola heir *again*? Yeah, not happening."

"I'll talk to him." I ran a hand down my face, reluctantly pulling myself from Arianne.

"Are you hungry?" She seemed so content standing there, as if it was just a normal Sunday morning.

It wasn't.

Luis was right.

We needed to get our stories straight and figure out what came next. There was no way Arianne was going back to that piece of shit, but if she didn't... Well, it had the potential to pull the trigger on everything, and we were still in the dark about Fascini's endgame.

Catching Luis' gaze, I beckoned for him to follow me outside. "Stay with her," I ordered Enzo and he gave me a two-fingered salute.

"Tell me everything."

Luis closed the door behind him and joined me on the porch.

"Fascini is pulling all the strings. Roberto swears he didn't know about them bringing the wedding date forward."

"What do you think Mike has on him?"

"I don't know, but whatever it is, it's big. I've known Roberto a long time, Nicco. I have only known him as scared as this one other time and that was the failed hit on Arianne."

"You think Fascini has threatened to hurt Arianne again?"

"Not Arianne. She's the key. Think about it, she's the future of Capizola Holdings. They need her to get rightful and legal access to his empire."

"So if not Arianne... her mom?"

"Aside from Tristan, she's the second most important person in his life."

"Fuck." I raked a hand down my face. The bombshells just kept coming.

If Luis was right, and Arianne didn't go back, she could potentially be sentencing her mother to death.

"It's a mess, Nicco. But you know you can't send her back there, not now. He shoved a fucking gun in her mouth and—"

"Don't, just don't," I gritted out as my fist ground against the wooden railing. I wanted to fuck something up. Preferably that psychopath's face. "He needs to be dealt with."

"She won't let you do that. She won't want his blood on your hands."

"Do you have an alternative?" Because we were running out of options.

Luis' cell started ringing and he pulled it out of his pocket.

"Roberto?" I asked.

"No." He frowned. "But I need to take this."

"I'll be inside."

He nodded, stepping off the porch and heading for the SUV.

I went back inside, smiling when I saw Enzo helping Arianne find plates. Leaning against the door jamb I watched them. Enzo still looked like a cold-hearted bastard, but the fact he was here told me all I needed to know.

He was warming to her.

"Are you going to stand there all day?" His brow rose as he glowered at me.

"Put me to work."

"Actually, we're almost done. Take a seat and breakfast will be served." Arianne flashed me a warm smile, making my insides weak.

"Where's Vitelli?"

"Taking a call."

"Problem?" Enzo mouthed.

"I don't think so." I took a seat at the breakfast counter. My stomach grumbled at the smell of freshly cooked bacon and pancakes. "This looks great, Bambolina."

Arianne smiled as she served us each a plateful of food. "This is nice," she said, taking the stool beside me.

"When are you going to call Uncle Toni?" Enzo asked.

"We have time."

I needed this.

She needed this.

We'd spent our entire relationship fighting fires, I think we'd earned one morning.

"Nora texted me." Arianne cut into a pancake, pushing it around her plate.

I held my breath, expecting her to deliver another bombshell. "And?"

"She says hi."

"You told her?" Enzo groaned.

"No, I didn't tell her, but she's not stupid. She knows there's only one place I'd be if I'm not at the hotel or the apartment."

"You can't tell her," I said thickly. "Not yet."

"I know. She knows I'm safe, that's all that matters."

"I'm proud of you." Curving my hand around the back of her neck, I drew Arianne toward me, brushing my lips over hers.

"I keep thinking I should have killed him. If I'd have done it then this would be over..." She shuddered, dropping her silverware onto the plate.

"Hey, you did the right thing." She didn't deserve to have his blood on her hands.

"But I could have..."

"Nah," Enzo said, surprising us both. "You don't want to carry that kind of burden. You did what you needed to do to protect yourself, that's what matters. You leave the rest to us."

The protective edge in his voice soothed something inside me. I needed to know Arianne had people. If things went to shit and I got caught in the crossfire, I needed to know she was protected.

We ate in comfortable silence after that. Arianne seemed lighter by the time we were done. "I'll clean up," she said, but I batted her hand away from my plate.

"Me and Enzo can handle the dishes. You go get a shower."

"You two are going to do the dishes?" She wagged a finger between us.

"Don't look at me, Princess," Enzo teased. "I'm not—"

"Grab the towel," I barked at him. "You can dry."

Arianne's laughter lingered as she left us to it.

"You are so fucking whipped, I feel like I need to check for your balls."

"You just haven't met the right girl yet."

"If it turns me into... *this*." He pointed at me. "Then count me out."

My lip curved. "Thanks for looking out for her."

"She's family."

"She is."

"Well then, it's that simple. I might not always agree with you, Cous, but we protect our own." His words hit me square in the chest.

The fact he felt that way meant everything to me.

"But do me a favor, yeah, and keep your PDA's to a minimum."

"You just had to go and ruin it, didn't you?" I chuckled as we got to the dishes.

Before long, we had the kitchen looking brand new.

"Luis has been gone a while," Enzo said. "What do you think he's doing?"

"He said he had to take care of something." I shrugged, glancing down the hall where the bathroom was.

"You really trust him, don't you?"

"Yeah." I met my cousin's hard gaze. "I do."

"I hope you're right about this."

"I am."

I had to be. Because I'd entrusted him with Arianne's life. And if he betrayed me… it would not end well for him.

CHAPTER 20

ARIANNE

"I still can't believe he did that," Nora gasped. "I mean, I can... but shit, Ari. He's a real piece of work."

"I got away, that's all that matters." I tucked my legs up beneath me. Nicco was outside on the phone to his father, and Enzo was busy off doing whatever Enzo did.

"He's sick in the head, it's the only explanation."

"He's a monster." I shuddered at the memory of Scott manhandling me in the hotel room. The way he'd shoved the gun into my mouth and—

"Babe?"

"Sorry, I just..." *Breathe. Just breathe.*

"He can't hurt you now."

"I know, but it doesn't change anything, not really."

Scott was deranged. The soulless look in his eyes as he'd attacked me would forever be imprinted to my memory. If I hadn't found the knife... I couldn't even think about it.

"They'll figure it out."

My eyes flicked to the window. I was so relieved Nicco was here. I didn't want us to be apart, not again. But I knew it wasn't as simple as him being back. Not until things were settled with Mike Fascini and my father.

"Tell me about your night with Dan," I changed the subject, "how's that going?"

"He's nice enough."

"Nor, come on. He's a sweetheart. He got dressed up in a tux and came to the party for you."

"I know, it isn't him," she let out a frustrated sigh, "it's me. There's just something missing. He doesn't set my world on fire."

"Maybe you just need to give it time?" Dan was solid. He attended classes, held open doors, and bought her coffee. "You said the sex was good."

"The sex is good, it's just not... life changing."

I chuckled. "They're some high expectations you have there."

"I know, I know. You think I'm squandering a good thing. But I don't want to settle, babe. I want epic love, like you and Nicco."

Just then, Nicco came back into the cabin. He smiled at me, his eyes so full of love and possessiveness it made my heart skip a beat.

"He's there isn't he?" I heard the amusement in Nora's words.

"Yeah, he's back."

"Well, tell him I say hey. And tell him he'd better keep you safe. You're precious goods."

"I will. I'll talk to you soon."

"Damn right you will." She hung up and I placed my cell on the coffee table.

"Nora says hi." Nicco's brows furrowed and I let out a

weary sigh. "I didn't tell her where we are. I promised you I wouldn't."

"I know, I'm sorry." He came around the sectional and sat beside me. "I just wish it wasn't like this."

"It is what it is."

"Bambolina." Nicco pressed his palm against my cheek and I leaned into his touch.

"What did your father say?"

He stiffened.

"That bad, huh?"

"He'll come around."

I sensed Nicco didn't want to talk about it, so I changed the subject. "Where is everyone?" Luis had been gone since before breakfast and Enzo was still nowhere to be seen.

"Luis had to go take care of something and Enzo has gone to pick up some supplies."

"What supplies?"

"Well, if we're going to be here awhile, we need clothes, food, toiletries."

"So that's the plan? To stay here?" I took his hand in mine and brought it to my lips, kissing his fingers.

"For now. It's safe here. You're safe."

"And we're alone?" Heat pooled low in my stomach.

"We are. But, Bambolina, I don't want to—"

"Ssh." I brushed my lips over his. "Stop talking." My arms wound around Nicco's neck as I pulled myself onto his lap, letting my legs fall to either side of his.

"Enzo could return at any second." He eased back to look at me.

"So take me to bed then."

His eyes darkened, a pained groan rumbling in his chest. "You're sure?"

I nodded.

I needed him, I needed him to erase all the memories of last night.

Nicco gripped me tightly and stood, carrying me down the hall. When we were inside our room, he kicked the door shut behind us and moved me to the bed. "I'll never let you go again," he murmured against my lips, trailing kisses along my jaw and down the slope of my neck.

"That feels so good."

But it wasn't enough.

I needed more.

I needed everything he had to give me.

Slowly, Nicco lowered me to the floor, my body sliding down his, making me whimper with need. "Tell me what you want, Bambolina?" He brushed the hair off my neck and kissed my collarbone, gently raking his teeth against the sensitive skin there. A shiver ran through me as I tilted my head to give him better access.

"You," I breathed. "I want you, Nicco."

"You have me, amore mio. Heart, body, and soul." He paused, gazing at me with complete reverie.

"Nicco?"

Snapping from his trance, he dipped his hand under my t-shirt. His warm fingers danced up my spine, higher and higher until the material was bunched around my chest. His hands kept going, and I lifted my arms letting him slide it off me.

"On the bed," he ordered, and I laid back, moving into the middle of the giant mattress. Nicco grabbed the hem of his black t-shirt, and pulled it clean off his body. My mouth watered at the sight of him, cut abs and taut, tanned muscle stretched over broad shoulders. He was a sculpted work of art.

And he was all mine.

Reaching out, Nicco brushed his hand along my ankle, his featherlight touch sending shivers skittering up my spine. He dropped to his knees, gently yanking me closer to him. Laughter spilled from my lips but quickly died as he toyed with the waistband of the boy shorts Enzo had found for me to wear. Nicco didn't break eye contact with me as he inched them over my hips and down my legs. His gaze was dark and intense.

Hungry.

He looked ready to devour me, turning my blood to molten lava.

Splaying a hand on my stomach, Nicco dipped his head and took a long, greedy swipe. I bucked against him, overwhelmed at the sensations. "Relax, Bambolina," he rasped. "I got you."

My head fell back as he began sucking and licking me. He slid two fingers inside me, curling them and rubbing until I was a quivering breathless mess beneath him.

"Nicco, it's..." My breath caught as his teeth teased the sensitive skin and his lips painted letters of love over my body.

"You taste like Heaven." His tongue circled my clit as he slowly worked me with his fingers. I shivered and moaned, arching into him, desperate for more.

"I will never let him touch you again," Nicco murmured the words against my core, making my breath catch.

"Oh my god..." I slid my fingers in his hair, gripping on tight as my body began to tremble, teetering on the edge of ecstasy. "Nicco..." His name was a prayer on my lips as I shattered around him.

He kissed my inner thigh before standing and sliding his boxers off his legs. Crawling up my body, he covered me until we were nothing but a tangle of limbs and love, skin and sweet nothings.

"I will kill him for ever looking twice at you, Bambolina."

A storm swirled in Nicco's eyes as he stared down at me. His jaw was set, his breathing shallow.

"Nicco," I gasped, "don't say such a thing."

He took my hand, pressing it against his chest. "This is who I am, Arianne. My heart beats for you, and I am done being the nice guy where you're concerned." Dipping his head, he ran his nose along my jaw, ghosting a kiss over my lips. "I will do whatever it takes to protect you. Even if it means ending him."

A shudder racked through me. I didn't like hearing Nicco talk like this, but he was right. This was who he was. How could I deny this part of him when I loved the other parts so deeply?

"I know." I wound my hands around his neck, pulling him closer. "I love you, Niccolò Marchetti, all of you."

I felt the tension leave his body. Nicco needed this. He needed my acceptance.

No words were spoken as he hitched my thigh around his hip and sank into me with one smooth glide. "Fuck, Bambolina..." His voice was thick with desire. I ran my tongue along the seam of his mouth, desperate for more. More kisses, more sensation, just *more* of him.

Nicco rocked into me in a torturous rhythm; slow measured strokes that made it difficult to breathe. He was everywhere, his lips on my neck, his tongue and teeth marking my skin, his hard body caging me to the bed, loving me. Filling me so completely I was drowning in him.

"Mine," he whispered into my ear, rocking harder. Deeper. "Sei mia."

I clung to him as he pushed me closer to the edge. Being with Nicco was like being in the eye of a storm. Wild and reckless and unpredictable but awe inspiring, nonetheless.

The way we loved, the way our bodies came together as

one, it was more than just lust. More than love. It was transcendent.

It was Fate working her will, binding two lives together until not even death could part them.

It should have terrified me.

It didn't.

With Nicco I felt whole. I felt home. I couldn't explain it, couldn't even really understand it, it just was.

"I love you," I breathed, grabbing his jaw and kissing him hungrily. Desperately. "I love you so much."

"Sei il più grande amore della mia vita."

Our skin was damp, our moans breathy. Nicco hitched my legs higher, grinding against me in the most delicious way. It created the perfect friction, making my stomach coil tight and my toes curl into the soft sheets.

"Come for me, Bambolina." He kissed me, swallowing my moans as waves of pleasure rippled through me.

My body shuddered, but he didn't stop. His pace was relentless, as if he was trying to imprint himself on my soul.

Maybe he didn't realize he was already there.

Branded on my heart.

Etched into the very fiber of my soul.

"It's okay," I dug my fingers in his hair, peppering tiny kisses over his face. "You can let go now."

A low growl built in his throat as he came inside me. His eyes were almost black, his expression lost.

"Nicco," I whispered against his mouth. "Come back to me."

He blinked, his expression softening. "You're okay." His voice cracked.

"I'm okay." I laid my palm on his cheek. "I'm right here."

Nicco's body began to tremble as he dropped his face to the crook of my shoulder. "I can't lose you," he murmured against my damp skin. "I can never lose you, Arianne."

"You won't," I whispered.

You won't.

After taking a shower together, we found Enzo in the main room.

"Don't mind me," he grunted, shoving a handful of chips into his mouth.

"We were just—"

He silenced Nicco with a knowing look. I smothered a giggle, burying myself into Nicco's side. "I'm hungry," I murmured.

"I'm not surprised." Enzo smirked.

"Watch it," Nicco jabbed a finger at his cousin.

"Where's Matteo?" I asked, slipping out of Nicco's arm and going over to the refrigerator.

"He's helping hold down the fort back home."

"What does that mean exactly?"

"Does she always ask this many questions?" Enzo raised a brow, and Nicco chuckled.

"Thanks for doing that..." the two of them fell into conversation, but I tried not to eavesdrop.

All that mattered was I was here with Nicco.

We could figure out the rest, together.

I checked the refrigerator for supplies and pulled out ingredients to make sandwiches. "You two hungry?" I called.

"Is the sky blue?" Enzo shot back and I poked my tongue out at him. He acted like the big bad wolf, but I was slowly figuring out he wasn't a bad guy. He was just guarded, layers of ice frozen around his heart.

"Are you always so smug?"

His brows drew together. "Watch it, Principessa. Just because you're Nicco's girl doesn't mean I won't—"

The box of eggs clattered to the floor, cracking in a pile of sticky yolk.

"Arianne?" Nicco rushed over to my side. "What is it?"

"Nothing." I inhaled a deep breath. "I just..."

"Something triggered you." Enzo came over, his eyes narrowed at me. "He called you that, didn't he?"

I nodded, forcing down the tears burning the backs of my eyes. "Sorry, I didn't—"

"Don't ever apologize for that fucker. I'm sorry." His expression softened. "I didn't know, or I wouldn't have..."

"It's not your fault. Sometimes I'm fine then other times, someone says something, or I remember something, and it's like I freeze."

"Come here." Nicco wrapped me in his arms.

"I'm okay, I promise." I hated that Scott still had control over me, but I knew you didn't just forget the kind of trauma he'd put me through.

"Nicco?" He was trembling again. I eased back, peeking up at him.

"Why don't you come sit down," Enzo said, gently taking my arm. "Give him a second to cool off."

He pulled me away, but my eyes remained on Nicco. His fists were clenched impossibly tight, and I could feel the anger rolling off him. It was like a storm cloud circling him. Dark and angry, and ready to unleash its destruction at any moment.

I sat down, flinching at the sound of Nicco's fist colliding with the counter.

"Should we do something?" I asked Enzo. He gave me a sympathetic look before going back to Nicco. He spoke in a low voice, making it difficult for me to hear. But I caught the odd word.

Calm down...

L'Anello's...

She needs you...

"What's L'Anello's?" I asked, trying to break the heavy silence.

Enzo glanced over at me, running a hand through his hair. "Somewhere you'll never go."

"E," Nicco sighed. "Don't."

"Fine. Have it your way." The two of them shared a look. "It's a bar. We... hang out there sometimes."

"A bar?" Suspicion clung to my words. I knew I wasn't supposed to ask questions and I knew even if I did, they weren't supposed to tell me anything. But I wanted to know as much as possible.

"Remember how I told you I fight sometimes? To burn off steam?" Nicco came over to the sectional and sat down.

"I remember."

"L'Anello's is where I fight sometimes."

"You fight in a bar?"

"The bar is a front for... other things."

"I see." My stomach twisted. "Are you good?"

"Jesus," Enzo muttered under his breath, casting Nicco a dark look. But he only had eyes for me.

"I'm pretty good, yeah."

"Okay."

Enzo snorted. "Nic just tells you he's a good fighter and all you've got to say is okay?"

I shrugged. "What else do you want me to say?"

"Nothing, I'm just surprised is all. I'm starting to wonder when any of this will freak you out."

"Oh, I'm pretty freaked out." I let out a strangled laugh. "But I also love Nicco and when you love someone you don't get to pick and choose the parts you want."

He studied me. "Yeah, I'm starting to see that." He moved over to the window, pulling back the curtains. "It looks like Luis is back. About fucking time."

I curled into Nicco's side, letting out a contented sigh.

"What the hell?" Enzo yanked open the door and Nicco moved me off him to stand.

"What is it?" Strolling over to his cousin, he peered over his shoulder.

"What did you do?" Enzo growled. I couldn't see him, but he didn't sound happy.

I got up, gingerly going to them, coming to an abrupt halt when I saw what Enzo and Nicco were looking at.

They weren't looking at Luis at all. It was the person standing beside him.

"Tristan?" I gasped, hardly able to believe my eyes.

He wasn't in the hospital anymore.

He was here.

And he looked as nauseous as I felt.

CHAPTER 21

NICCO

"Tristan?" Arianne slipped between me and Enzo and hurried down the steps to greet her cousin.

"A word?" I tipped my chin to Luis. Enzo stepped aside to let him past.

"What the fuck were you thinking?"

"Relax—"

"Relax?" Enzo seethed. "You brought the fucking enemy into our safe house. I knew we couldn't trust you, Vitelli, motherfucking—"

"E," I cut him off.

"Look," Luis said. "I knew if I gave you a heads up you would fight me on this. Tristan has intel; he might be able to help. I met him off the highway, we dumped his car, and I blindfolded him, so he doesn't know where we are. It's safe, I promise."

Enzo made a hacking sound and I jabbed him in the ribs. "You did all that?" I asked Luis.

"I covered my tracks, yeah. I'm not stupid. I know what's at stake and I don't want Arianne in harm's way anymore than you. But you're going to want to hear what he has to say."

I gave him a tight nod. He had a point. Everything he'd done up until now made him trustworthy, but bringing Tristan here still felt like a big risk.

Luis doubled back to go outside. Enzo leaned in and kept his voice low. "I don't like this, Nic."

"You don't have to like it. But maybe Luis is right, maybe he does have good intel." Lord only knew we needed it. Tommy and Stefan were still yet to dig up anything useful on Mike Fascini, and my old man wasn't exactly over the moon when I told him me and Arianne were here. But he knew I wouldn't relent again. He hadn't even bothered to try to order me back to Boston.

I wasn't going.

I'd stay in the cabin for now, but if it came to it, I would return home and face any consequences.

"We can't trust him, he's Fascini's best friend," Enzo spat the words, "or have you forgotten that?"

My mind went to two nights ago when I'd stood in the hospital room, confessing my deepest, darkest sins to Tristan. I'd assumed he was asleep... but I wasn't sure now.

"Let's just hear him out."

Enzo pursed his lips, disapproval glittering in his eyes. "You hear him out. I'm going to take a drive around the perimeter, make sure Vitelli definitely covered his tracks."

"You're sure?"

"I think it's for the best. I'm not sure I can be held responsible for my actions if I have to sit and listen to any of Capizola's bullshit."

"Okay, but don't be too long."

Enzo stalked out of the cabin just as Arianne and Tristan came inside.

"I know this is as awkward as fuck," Tristan stepped forward, raking a hand through his hair. He looked pale, his eyes sunken and ringed with dark circles.

Guilt flooded me, but it didn't override the need to protect Arianne. My hand slid inside my jacket and before giving it a second thought, I whipped out my pistol, pressing it right against his temple.

"Nicco!" Arianne shrieked and Luis moved to her side, gently holding her back.

But Tristan didn't flinch. His hands went slowly up at his sides. "I swear, Marchetti, I'm here to help that's all."

"How can I trust you?"

"You can't." He inhaled a ragged breath. "You're just going to have to take a leap of faith. She's my cousin, she's family. Surely you can appreciate that."

Family meant everything to me, but to people like Tristan, people like Roberto Capizola and Mike Fascini, even family could be pawns. They'd proved that more than once.

We were locked in an impasse. I didn't want to trust him —everything inside me screamed at me not to trust him—but we needed allies.

We needed answers.

And he was one person who could possibly give them to us.

"I'm sorry," the words were out of me before I could stop them. I pulled my pistol away and engaged the safety, shoving it back in the waistband of my jeans.

"You don't need to apologize," he said. "I think once is enough, don't you?" His expression turned smug.

So he had been awake the other night.

I didn't know whether to be relieved or embarrassed.

"Let's sit." I walked over to the sectional. Arianne sat

down beside me, sliding her hand into mine. She cast me a concerned look.

"I had to," I whispered.

"I know." She gave me a sad smile.

Tristan and Luis took the chairs opposite. Silence stretched out before us. Thick and heavy with the secrets of our past. Tense with the reality of our current predicament.

"I should probably start," Tristan said. "I got discharged from hospital yesterday."

"I didn't know." Arianne sat a little straighter.

"Mom picked me up and I crashed.

"I headed over to the estate this morning, hoping to catch Uncle Roberto. I wanted to talk to him about some things..." His eyes flicked from Arianne to mine. "I knew something was wrong the second I got there."

"You saw my father?"

He gave Arianne a sharp nod. "He was beside himself. I've never seen anything like it. Aunt Gabriella was trying to console him, but he got so angry. He trashed his office. That's when she told me everything."

Arianne stiffened. "H- how much?"

"Everything."

"Oh." She pressed closer to me.

"I want you to know I'm on your side, Ari. I didn't know..." He let out a weary sigh. "If I'd have known what he would do, I would never have pushed the relationship. I didn't—"

"Stop, just stop." She breathed. "You said I needed to grow up and live in the real world. You said it was my destiny whether I liked it or not. You said that."

"Fuck, I know, but I didn't think it meant *this*. You were supposed to date, fall in love, and get engaged." He paled. "It wasn't supposed to be like this, I swear."

"But you knew about my father's plans for me and Scott. You knew, and you never said a word."

"Shit, Ari. I know it sounds bad when you say it like that, but this is your legacy. You are the Capizola heir, one day the entire empire will be yours. Scott was my best friend. I thought you would be a great match. I thought it made good business sense. That's just how it is in this life."

"He's a monster."

Shame filled Tristan's eyes. "I realize that now. He's always been... intense. But I didn't know he would..." He swallowed hard, rubbing his jaw as if the words were just too painful to say.

"He raped me, Tristan. He slipped something into my drink at the Gala and raped me." Arianne's voice shook, but it was nothing compared to the rage boiling beneath my skin.

"You never said anything. You never—"

"Would it have mattered?" Her voice cracked. "I tried to tell my father and he acted like I was making a big deal about nothing. He downplayed my being raped because it didn't fit into his business plans." Bitterness clung to her words, but Arianne didn't cower. She didn't cry or whimper. She sat tall, her eyes locked on her cousin, on her family, as she purged her thoughts.

"He deserves your wrath," Tristan buried his face in his hands, scraping his fingers through his hair, "We both do. But the second I found out the truth, I called Luis."

"Is this true?"

Arianne's bodyguard nodded.

"You are my family, Ari, my blood. Scott hurt you which means he hurt me. I knew he could be a little forward. But I didn't know... I swear. Either way, I'm done. He's no one to me now."

"Just like that?" I scoffed. "Sounds too fucking convenient to me."

Tristan met my icy stare. He deserved some credit. Few people faced off with me like that. "We've all made mistakes, man. But Scott... he's obsessed with her. Uncle Roberto knows she isn't safe."

"So why the fuck did he promise her to that piece of shit?"

Tristan let out a heavy sigh, but it was Arianne who spoke. "I don't know that I can trust you again. You were on his side, Tristan."

"I appreciate that, and I know I don't deserve a second chance." He gave her a sad smile. "But I'd like the chance to earn it back."

She gave him a small nod,

"Okay." He sagged back into the chair. "So I always knew Uncle Roberto wanted to secure your future. After Antonio Marchetti tried to have you—"

"It wasn't Antonio," Arianne said.

"What?" Tristan's eyes almost bugged. "But it had to be. Uncle Roberto said—"

"She's telling the truth," I added. "It was Mike Fascini. We think he did it to try to set my father up and incite war between our families. When it failed, we think he decided to try another approach."

Tristan's brow drew together. "That doesn't make any sense. Why would he do that?"

"Because there's something else," I said. "Something we only recently found out."

"Go on..."

"What do you know of the name Ricci?"

"Ricci? As in Elena Ricci? The girl who betrayed our family and ran off with Emilio Marchetti?"

I nodded. "Mike is Elena's grandson."

"Cazzo!" His eyes went wide. "So this is what? Some sick attempt at righting history?"

"Michael Fascini, Mike's father, never got over what

happened. According to his aunt, he became obsessed with getting vengeance. He moved to Verona County in the seventies with the sole purpose of getting even. When he died, Mike took over the reins and here we are."

"So Mike's the puppet master? It makes sense." He scrubbed his jaw before fixing his eyes on Arianne. "I know your father doesn't seem like he has your best interests at heart, Ari, but he loves you."

"He has a funny way of showing it."

"But if Mike has been pulling the strings all along, maybe he didn't have a choice."

The thought had occurred to me, but it still didn't excuse Roberto's actions.

"Do you think Scott knows the truth?" Tristan asked.

"We don't know. If he does, he risked everything last night and his father is likely to be pissed. If he wants to keep his hands clean, he needs Capizola Holdings and Arianne was his insurance policy."

"Hold on a second." Arianne grabbed my arm. "You think I'm a bargaining chip?"

I twisted my body around to look at her. "It's possible Mike threatened to harm you again unless your father complied, yes."

"I- I don't know what to say." The blood had completely drained from Tristan's face. "I came here ready to offer to talk to Uncle Roberto, to make him see sense. I didn't realize... fuck. What are we going to do?"

"We?" I raised a brow.

"I'm here, aren't I? I want to help."

"You need to buy us some time while we figure out our next move. Arianne cannot go back now, no matter what happens."

"Agreed." Tristan gave me a sharp nod. "But what about

my uncle and aunt? If Mike wants Capizola Holdings, there are other ways to make it happen."

"I guess you need to make sure that doesn't happen. Arianne is my priority, and until we can be sure Fascini doesn't have a failsafe we can't touch him." He was one of the most prominent men in Verona County. If he turned up dead or missing, it would raise questions.

Questions that could lead back to the Family.

"What's it going to require to take him down?" For the first time since he'd arrived, I saw the fight in Tristan's eyes. He might not have been ready to bury the hatred between our families, but he was here for Arianne. And right now, that's all that mattered.

"If we want to avoid bloodshed, we need to be able to pin something on him. Something that will make sure he never sees the light of day again." He deserved to rot in Hell for what he'd done to Arianne. But a six by four cell would do all the same.

It all started with him, and it would end with him.

"And Scott?"

"He's mine," I ground out, feeling the familiar lick of fury skate up my spine.

"We have the evidence, Nicco." Arianne tugged my arm. "We can take it to the authorities."

Tristan caught my eye. He gave me an imperceptible nod, and I knew what he was telling me.

Scott was a dead man walking.

"Nicco?" Arianne spoke more forcefully this time, and I gave her my attention.

"It's okay, Bambolina. I'm okay." I pulled her into my side and kissed the top of her head.

I didn't want to lie to her.

But she didn't need to know that I wouldn't rest until I'd had my pound of Scott Fascini's flesh.

After we hatched a tentative plan, Tristan and Luis left.

Tristan would return home and try to find out everything he could about the nature of Mike Fascini's plan. He would also try and buy some time. Our enemy had become a turncoat. It was a risk, but it was better than doing nothing.

"You're quiet," I said to Arianne. She was reading a book she'd found on one of the shelves. Except, she hadn't turned a page in almost ten minutes, so she was either a really slow reader or she was using the book as a distraction.

I leaned over and snagged it from her hands.

"Hey," she protested. "I was reading that."

I gave her a pointed look and she let out a weary sigh. "Fine, you caught me."

"It's okay to need some space. If you want me to leave—"

"What? No!" She sat up. "I just... Do you think I should forgive Tristan?"

"That is not my decision to make."

"They both let me down, Nicco. When I needed them, my father and Tristan let me down."

"I know, Bambolina. Come here." I pulled her into my side. "You are so strong. It's okay to not want to forgive easily. But don't let your resentment fester. Eventually, there will come a day when you must decide to forgive or forget. But know that I'll be right here by your side and I'll support whatever decision you make, okay?"

She gave me the faintest of nods before kissing me. "Thank you," she whispered. "For everything."

"It is me who should be thanking you. You make the world a brighter place, Arianne."

Emotion swirled in her eyes as she suppressed a smile. "Tell me about L'Anello's." She cleared her throat. "About what you do there."

"You really want to know this stuff?"

"I want to know everything, but I know there will always be things you can't share with me. So all I ask is that you share the pieces you can."

"Fighting helps me burn off steam. I guess you could say it's a way to fight my demons."

She tensed. "But you could get hurt."

"Sometimes I want to hurt. It helps remind me that I'm alive."

"I'm not sure I understand."

"You're not the only one who has spent their life caged, Bambolina. I didn't ask for this life, it was decided for me. And I've made my peace with that, I have. But sometimes... sometimes I need to push back."

"So fighting is your way of retaining some control?"

"I guess you could say that."

"I don't like the idea of you getting hurt." Arianne leaned closer, brushing her nose along mine.

"It comes with the territory."

"What will life be like, for us, I mean?" Her voice wavered. "Will I be expected to stay at home and raise a houseful of babies?"

Laughter bubbled in my chest. "While that image does all kinds of crazy things to me," I grinned, my heart so fucking full I wanted to drag her to the bedroom and make a start, "I will always support your dreams, Arianne."

I wasn't my father. I didn't intend on ruling my household with an iron fist. I wanted Arianne to flourish. I wanted her to be happy.

"I think I want to help people, like at the VCTI."

"You have a big heart."

"But babies," she whispered against the corner of my mouth, "you want that one day?"

"I want everything with you, amore mio. But we're young, we have time."

Arianne was quiet but the contented sigh that spilled from her lips gave me reassurance she wasn't stewing on our conversation.

"I was thinking," she said after a couple of minutes. "Can Alessia come visit?"

"I'm not sure that's a good idea. The fewer people coming to and from the cabin, the better. At least, for now."

"Okay."

"You're not going to fight me on it?"

"I trust you Nicco." She smiled. "I trust you to keep me safe."

"It's all I want," I replied, ghosting my lips over hers.

Until my very last breath.

CHAPTER 22

ARIANNE

"Hmm, morning." I snuggled closer to Nicco. He was still asleep, strands of hair falling over his eyes a little.

I watched him, smiling to myself at how perfect the moment was. Because this time, I wouldn't have to say goodbye.

After Enzo had left us, we'd spent the night curled up on the sectional watching movies. Luis had stayed, but he'd made himself scarce.

I loved it out here, away from everything and everyone, where we could be together without judgment or scrutiny.

I knew it wasn't real. I knew our bubble would soon come to an end. But I intended on savoring every second we had together.

"I can feel you staring," Nicco murmured, his voice thick with sleep.

"That's because I *am* staring." I painted circles on his chest, ghosting my fingers over his scars.

He snagged my wrist, bringing my hand to his lips, sending a shiver up my spine. "Good morning, Bambolina."

"Good morning."

"I could get used to this," he shifted onto his back, fixing his stormy eyes on mine.

"I was thinking the same thing. It's so peaceful out here."

"We'd have to get rid of the bodyguard though." His mouth curved with amusement.

"And change the locks. I wouldn't want Enzo strolling in at any given time." Dipping my head, I brushed my lips over his. "I need a girl's minute and then I'll make some coffee."

"Okay."

I climbed out of bed and pulled on Nicco's oversized MU t-shirt. Enzo had bought us some extra clothes, but I was going to need my own things if we stayed here for any length of time.

It was strange.

I knew I was supposed to be worrying about everything: classes and my volunteer work at the VCTI, but it all seemed so insignificant given the circumstances.

After visiting the bathroom, I quickly brushed my teeth before heading for the kitchenette. Luis was already up and dressed, reading a newspaper.

"Good morning," I said. "Coffee?"

"I wouldn't say no to another." He slid his mug toward me. "Did you sleep okay?"

"I did, thank you. What about you?"

"I got a couple of hours."

"We're safe out here, Luis."

He smiled. "Old habits die hard, I guess. Is Nicco—"

"Right here." He padded into the kitchen, stealing my

breath. He'd pulled on some sweats but left his t-shirt off, the hard lines of his body rippling and flexing.

Nicco's body was a sculpted work of art. Tanned skin pulled taut over cut muscles, broad shoulders and a narrowed waist that was defined by the delicious V disappearing into his sweatpants.

Luis cleared his throat, casting me an amused glance before giving Nicco a nod. "Morning."

"Everything okay?"

"Everything's quiet."

"Good." Nicco advanced on me, curving his hand around my neck and pressing his lips to my head. "I'm going to take a quick shower. You'll be okay?"

It was my turn to nod.

Once he'd disappeared, I joined Luis at the table. "I'm sorry you have to be here."

"I thought we were past all that?" He gave me a pointed look. "I'm here because I want to be here, Ari. You know, you seem different."

"It's him..." My eyes went to the hall where Nicco had gone. "I know you probably think we're too young and foolish..." I stopped myself. Luis didn't want to hear this.

He covered my hand with his. "Quite the contrary. I think what the two of you have found is quite remarkable. That man would die for you."

"I'd rather he didn't." I forced a smile, my stomach clenching at his words. "Can I ask you something?"

"Anything."

"Do you think my father is being blackmailed or threatened by Mike Fascini?"

"I think it's the most likely scenario, yes."

"But before all this happened, when I first started MU, what do you think my father was thinking then?"

"I can't answer that, Arianne. You know as well as I do

your father is a determined and successful man who cares deeply for his family. I think he probably genuinely thought he was doing a good thing. By promising you to Scott, he was securing your future and absolving you of the full burden of one day running Capizola Holdings. I think part of him just wanted to see you cared for and looked after."

"But I'm eighteen. He could have waited."

"I think the likelihood is Mike Fascini has always been pulling the strings and whispering in his ear. Your father is a driven man, Arianne. The opportunity to merge with Fascini and Associates was too good to pass up. But the lines between business and family got blurred along the way."

I scoffed at that, and Luis squeezed my hand. "Hey, I'm not trying to excuse his actions. He has made a lot of mistakes, nothing will change that."

"Do you think he knows who Mike Fascini really is?"

"If he doesn't, he will soon enough."

I pondered on that thought. If my father didn't know, did it change anything?

I didn't have all the answers. Not yet. All I knew, was that in my heart, I felt betrayed. He was supposed to be the man I could trust with anything, the man who would move mountains for me.

He'd let me down too many times to just brush his infractions under the rug.

I finished my coffee before going to the refrigerator. "Are you hungry?"

"I wouldn't turn down the offer of breakfast." Luis gave me a rare smile. "If you're sure you don't mind?"

"I don't see anyone else here to cook, do you? Besides, it'll keep me busy."

And I could really do with that right now.

After breakfast, Enzo returned.

But he wasn't alone.

Nicco's father, his uncles, and Matteo filed into the cabin, filling the room with their somber expressions and larger than life presence.

"Ari," Matteo came over and hugged me, taking me by surprise. "I'm glad you're okay," he whispered.

"Arianne," Antonio said, giving me a nod. He was conflicted, his stormy eyes at war with the faint smile he wore.

"Miss Capizola." One of the other men stepped forward. "I am Michele, Matteo's father. It is nice to finally meet you."

"Hello."

"Vincenzo," Enzo's dad said coolly. He reminded me so much of his son, only scarier. If Enzo was cold, Vincenzo was a glacier. Disapproval radiated from him and I inched closer to Luis' side.

"Niccolò, perhaps Arianne would enjoy a walk. I'm sure Vitelli can—"

"She stays."

"Son, that is not an option."

"It's okay," I stepped forward and laid a hand on Nicco's arm. "I wanted to call Nora and my mom anyway. I'll give you all some space."

He looked at me, his brows drawn tight with uncertainty. "I'll be fine," I urged. "Go talk with your family."

"You stay," he said to Luis who stiffened.

"Are you—"

"You stay."

I went to leave but Nicco snagged my hand, drawing me back to him. "We won't be long." He cupped my face, leaning down to kiss me. My cheeks burned. Everyone was watching. His father, his cousins and uncles, the most important people in his life. Yet he kissed me like I yielded the real power over him.

It was heady.

Overwhelming.

It was everything.

"Go," he murmured quietly against my lips, "before I throw them all out and drag you back to our bed."

I couldn't hide my smile as I left them and went to our bedroom. Closing the door behind me, I grabbed my cell phone off the dresser and flopped onto the bed. I wanted to call Nora, but my mom had been bombarding me with texts since the party, so I decided to deal with her first.

"Mamma?"

"Arianne, thank God. I've been so worried."

"Luis told Father I was safe, no?"

"Yes, but it didn't stop me worrying after what Scott did—"

"I'm okay, Mamma, I'm okay."

"You're safe?"

I smiled dryly. I couldn't help it. She acted like an overly concerned parent, but she had been so willing to force my relationship with Scott before she discovered what a monster he was.

"Where are you?"

"You know I can't tell you that."

"Oh, figlia mia, everything is such a mess."

"Have you spoken to Tristan?"

"I have. He's trying to speak some sense into your father. He's beside himself, sweetheart."

Too little too late.

"You could come home, to the estate. We can keep you safe."

"I can't," I let out a weary sigh. "I won't."

"No." I heard the sadness in her voice. "I don't suppose you will."

"Have you spoken to Suzanna?"

"Not a word since the morning after the party. Once we found out what had happened, your father ushered me back to the estate."

"It isn't safe for you there, Mamma. You could be in danger. Is there somewhere you can go?"

"Whatever are you talking about?"

"Mike. He isn't who he says he is. You can't trust him."

"What do you know that you aren't telling me?"

I hesitated. "Just be careful, okay?"

"I will. Your father has extra security around the house. He's become very paranoid of late."

"You need to try to talk to him, Mamma."

"I'm not sure I can get through to him anymore."

"But maybe if Tristan is there too, maybe the two of you can make him see sense."

"I will try." A beat passed and then she said, "This isn't what I wanted for you, Arianne. I hope you know that."

"I know, Mamma."

But the truth was, I didn't know anything anymore. Not where my family were concerned. There were so many secrets and lies, it was impossible to sort the truth from the falsities.

"I have to go," I rushed out, suddenly overwhelmed.

"What should I tell your father?"

"Tell him, I'm not going back. I won't." Not while Scott was roaming free and Mike Fascini was still pulling the strings.

"Okay. I love you, sweetheart." She let out a small sigh. "Be safe."

"Bye, Mamma."

I hung up, swallowing down the tears burning my throat.

But I didn't dwell on our conversation. Instead, I dialed my best friend's number. She answered on the third ring.

"Hey," Nora said. "How is it being secreted away with your handsome bodyguard and hot mafioso boyfriend?"

"Nor," I let out a strained chuckle.

"Please, you're in hiding with your guy... it sounds like heaven if you ask me."

"Have you forgotten why?"

"No, Ari. God no. But when life hands you lemons and all that."

"You're crazy." A faint smile traced my lips.

"And you love me. So what's up?"

"Antonio and Nicco's uncles just got here," I kept my voice low. I could only make out the rumble of their voices beyond the bedroom. It all sounded very fraught, but I couldn't distinguish words.

It was probably for the best.

"Wait a second, they're having a business meeting, right now?"

"I guess so."

"You have to go listen."

"Nora!"

"You're telling me you're not curious what they're," she lowered her voice, "talking about?"

"It doesn't matter. I would never—"

"They could be making decisions that affect you."

"Nicco will tell me."

"Will he? They live by a code, babe. Secrets. Lies. Cover ups. It's the mafia way." She was so flippant about this stuff.

"You've been watching too much TV."

"You know I'm right."

"Maybe, but I'm not about to go eavesdrop on them. It's... wrong."

"You say that like any of this is right."

What Nicco and I felt for each other was right.

No one would ever persuade me otherwise.

"What do you think they're—"

"Nora, seriously?"

She chuckled. "I should be there. I'd get us some answers."

"How are classes?" I changed the subject.

"Dull. It's not the same without you. The apartment is so empty, and Maurice isn't half as interesting as Luis."

"You could always ask Dan to keep you company."

"I think I have decided Dan and I are more compatible as friends."

"That's a shame."

"Not really. He's busy with the team, and I'm... well, I'm not really feeling it."

"Well as long as you're not throwing away a shot at something good for a certain brooding mafioso?"

"Enzo, really? Please, I have some dignity." The lilt in her voice suggested otherwise, but I didn't argue. We had bigger problems at hand.

A beat passed, and then Nora whispered, "When do you think you might be able to come back?"

"I don't know." My heart ached. We'd never really spent any time apart. Even when we'd lived on my father's estate, she was only ever a stone's throw away in her family's cottage.

"Okay, well, stay safe. That's all that matters right now."

"You be careful too. Scott is still—"

"He wouldn't dare try anything with me," she scoffed. "Besides, Maurice follows me around like my shadow."

I hoped she was right.

"I'll text you later, okay?" she said.

"Okay. Bye."

We hung up just as I heard raised voices coming from the living room. Tiptoeing to the far wall, I pressed my ear against the wood. I didn't want to eavesdrop, I didn't want to be that girl, but Nora had planted a seed. And I couldn't deny part of me wondered what was happening.

"No," I heard Nicco say. "No fucking way."

"Niccolò," Antonio clucked his tongue, "you need to..." His words were swallowed.

"Porca miseria!" I couldn't figure out who that was, possibly Enzo or his father.

"... to our advantage."

"I won't do it." Nicco sounded irritated. Something crashed and then a door slammed, reverberating through the cabin.

I stumbled back, regretting my decision to listen. A couple of seconds later, there was a knock at my door. "Arianne," Luis said.

"Come in."

He slipped inside and closed the door. "How much of that did you hear?"

"Not a lot."

He gave me a pointed look, and I let out a defeated sigh. "I heard the odd word. Is everything okay?"

"Things got a little fraught, but everything will be okay. Antonio and his brothers just left."

"So I can go see Nicco?"

"Umm..." His expression fell.

"Luis?"

"He's..."

I shouldered past him and went into the main room. "Nicco?"

"Hey Ari," Matteo looked sheepish, rubbing a hand through his hair and down his neck.

"Where is he?"

"I... uh... he's..." His eyes went to the door. I took off,

yanking it open, catching Nicco about to take off on his bike.

"Nicco?" I called.

His body slumped back on the bike, his head hung low. I inched closer, sensing his torment. "Nicco, look at me."

"I need a minute." His voice was raw.

"You're leaving?" I rounded the bike.

"No, I would never... I just need..." He inhaled a ragged breath. "I'm sorry."

"I don't want you to be sorry. I want you to talk to me. What happened?"

His eyes shuttered and he exhaled a shaky breath. "Please don't ask me that, anything but that."

The need to know what had happened burned through me but Nicco was hurting and all I wanted to do was make it better.

"Will you come inside with me?"

"I need to ride, Bambolina. I need... space."

"From me?" Pain squeezed my heart.

"Not you, never you. I just... this is how I deal with things."

"So I'll come." I went to climb on the back of his bike, but Nicco hooked me round the waist, pulling me into him. "It's not safe."

"Then it's not safe for you either." I pressed my hand to his cheek, narrowing my eyes as I spoke my next words. "Come inside, Nicco. I won't ask again."

Pulling away, I marched back into the cabin and sat down on the sectional.

"Everything okay?" Matteo asked me.

"We'll see." I rested my chin on my fists, mindlessly counting the seconds.

If Nicco didn't come back, I didn't know what I would do. But if we were going to be together, if we were going to get through this, he had to realize he couldn't just take off every time the going got tough. He might not have been able to tell me everything, but he could *be* with me.

He could turn to me for comfort.

I glanced at the door, waiting for him to walk through it.

"Ari, maybe you should—"

"Don't," I groaned.

"It's not you, you have to know that. This is killing him."

"It's not exactly easy for me either." I met Matteo's sympathetic gaze.

"I know. Trust me, I know. But Nicco is used to being in control. He's used to—"

I didn't need to turn around to see Nicco, I felt him, the tether between us pulling taut.

"I'll give you two a minute." Matteo got up and left the cabin.

The air crackled between us, thick and oppressive. "Do you want to talk about it?" I said, breaking the heavy silence.

"I just want to be with you, Bambolina. Is that okay?"

I nodded, scared that if I spoke, we would lose this moment.

Nicco had relented.

Instead of running away to clear his head, he'd turned to me.

It felt like a turning point.

"I'm here, Nicco. Whatever you need, I'm here."

He finally moved, standing over me. His body vibrated with anger; I could feel it permeate the air. Sliding my hand in his, I stood. "What do you need?"

Nicco's jaw clenched impossibly tight. "Di te, Bambolina, I only need you." He curved his arm around my waist, pulling me close. I slid my palms up his chest, leaning up to kiss him.

"You have me," I breathed, "always."

CHAPTER 23

NICCO

We spent the rest of the day in bed. Matteo and Luis made themselves scarce. There was a fire pit around the back of the cabin. Arianne wanted to check it out, but I'd told her it wasn't safe.

I didn't want to share her, not yet.

Not after earlier.

I hadn't wanted to take off, but after seeing my father and my uncles, I'd needed air. What I'd really needed was to fight, but I couldn't do that, so I'd hopped on my bike with only one thing in mind.

Me and the open road.

Then Arianne had appeared.

I'd seen the disappointment in her eyes; it cut me like tiny daggers. But it was no more than I deserved.

I couldn't tell her the truth, not yet. And the secrets and lies were beginning to feel like a burden too heavy to carry.

When the sun began to sink behind the tree line, Matteo, Enzo, and Luis all returned to the cabin, this time with pizza.

"You seem better," Enzo said as the two of us found some plates and napkins.

"I'm okay." We shared a silent look.

My eyes flicked to Arianne, who immediately averted her gaze. I knew she wanted to know what had happened earlier, but so far she was respecting our privacy.

We joined them, and together we enjoyed an evening eating pizza and drinking beer with her bodyguard and my best friends. Between the food, easy conversation, and laughter it was easy to pretend there wasn't a shitshow happening around us.

"That was so good." She licked the grease off her fingers, and a low growl built in my chest when I noticed Enzo and Matteo watching her. They both chuckled, and I flipped them off.

Luis had been quiet, happy to listen to us regale Arianne with stories of our childhood. But when his cell phone vibrated for the fifth time, Enzo grumbled. "Are you going to get that?"

"It's Roberto." Luis' eyes flashed to me. "He wants Arianne to reply to his messages."

"I have nothing to say to him," she said.

Arianne had left her cell in the bedroom all day.

"If you need to talk—"

"I said I have nothing to say to him." Irritation laced her words.

"It's okay." I squeezed her knee. "Luis will handle it." I shot him a pointed look, and Luis clambered to his feet, disappearing down the hall.

Tristan was buying us time. Mike Fascini knew about Scott's latest attack. He knew Luis had taken Arianne to a safe place. As far as we were aware, Roberto had told him

Arianne needed some space. But he wasn't a fool. Eventually, he would piece together that I was with her, that we were planning to make our move against him.

"Are you two staying?" she asked Matteo and Enzo.

"Yeah, we're going to crash here."

"What about classes?"

"It's all about keeping up pretenses, but maybe after all this, we won't need to—" Matteo elbowed Enzo in the ribs.

"Let me guess, you guys aren't supposed to talk about it." Arianne's expression fell.

"I'm sorry." I brushed my lips over her forehead.

"It's late," she let out a small sigh, "we should probably get some sleep."

"Like you'll be doing any of that," Enzo snorted.

I swiped a bottle cap off the table and threw it at his head. "Watch your mouth."

"I'll clean up first." Arianne got up but I grabbed her hand.

"They can handle it." I glared at my cousins. "We'll see you in the morning."

Guiding Arianne down the hall, we fell into the bedroom in a tangle of kisses and soft moans. "I feel bad," she breathed against my lips.

"What for?"

"Because they're stuck here while we..." Her cheeks flamed.

"They get it."

"Do they?"

"Enzo not so much but Matteo understands."

"What do you—"

"Bambolina?" I advanced on Arianne, not stopping until she was caged between my body and the wall.

"Yes?" She looked at me through her lashes.

"Stop talking."

"Why?" Her lips curved and I lowered my head, capturing them in a bruising kiss.

"Because, amore mio, I'm going to strip the clothes from your body, lay you down, and worship every single inch of you."

"Oh." She blushed.

"Still want to talk?" I cocked a brow.

Arianne shook her head. "I'll be quiet now."

"Good." Kissing the corner of her mouth, I whispered, "The only word I want to hear falling from your lips while we're in this room is my name."

The next morning, I left Arianne sleeping and went to find my cousins. They were already dressed, tucking into a stack of pancakes.

"Smells good," I said to Matteo.

"Hey, what makes you think he cooked them?" Enzo asked, and I frowned at him.

"When was the last time you cooked?"

"I cook."

"Dialing for pizza is not cooking."

He flipped me off. "Where's Arianne?"

"Sleeping."

"Did you wear her out?"

"Watch it." I jabbed my finger at him. "Any news?"

"Nothing to report," Matteo said, passing me a plate.

"Perhaps you need to think about what your old man—"

"Not. Happening," I growled.

"Okay, okay." Enzo's hands shot up. "Forget I said anything."

"We wait and see what Tristan finds out before we make any decisions."

"He needs putting down. He orchestrated the hit on Arianne when she was just a kid, Nicco. And then he let his son—"

"She's not strong enough." Arianne wasn't ready to enter our world, not really. I wanted to shield her from it for as long as possible.

"You're going to have to choose eventually." Enzo let out an exasperated sigh.

"He's right, Cous," Matteo added. "You might have to make the decision for her."

"I need more time. She needs more time."

"I hope you know what you're doing, man." Enzo got up and stalked out of the cabin. It was becoming a regular pattern with us. But at least we weren't solving our problems with fists these days.

"I know you want to do the right thing, but in our life, doing the right thing means something different in their world." Matteo gave me a pointed look.

"Their world?"

"Arianne, Nora, even Roberto. They live by a different moral code to us. I know you know that."

"I won't give her up."

I wouldn't give her up for anything.

"I know. I'm not saying you have to let her go. I'm just saying that you might have to make the hard decisions to keep her conscience clean."

I ran a hand down my face, letting out a strained breath. But Matteo wasn't done.

"If he was here right now, if Fascini walked in here, what would you do?"

My eyes narrowed to slits, anger reverberating through me. "You know."

"So, is Mike really any different? He wants to destroy us,

Nic. He wants to take Capizola Holdings first and then come after us. He is the enemy."

"You think I don't know that?" I seethed, my fist clenched at my side. "It's *all* I think about."

It would be so easy to take them both out. We had several guys on the books who could do it. Hell, I could probably do it.

"We still don't know if he has a backup plan."

"Even if he does, it's nothing we can't find a way around. You're stalling."

He was right, I was stalling.

Because I wanted something better for Arianne. I wanted to be able to give her things, things I might not ever be able to provide.

"This is who you are, Nic. If she's going to be with you, you both have to accept that." Matteo clapped me on the back. "That girl loves you, more than she probably should. You're Niccolò Marchetti, Prince of fucking Hearts. You don't cower and you certainly don't shy away from making the hard decisions."

He left me with my thoughts.

I didn't want to be Arianne's prince. I wanted to be her king. The king of her heart.

The king of her soul.

But I was still holding back. I was trying to divide myself between Niccolò Marchetti, son of the boss, and Nicco Marchetti the guy in love with a girl.

Matteo and Enzo were right.

I couldn't be both.

There was no escaping my fate.

And yet, I still wanted to protect her from the inevitable.

I spent the day agonizing over my father's visit. He wanted to move against Mike sooner rather than later. But he knew what Arianne meant to me. He knew he risked losing me if anything was to happen to her.

But in the end, my torment was all for nothing.

Tristan arrived with news, and it wasn't what we'd hoped to hear.

"Mike has given my father until the weekend to bring Arianne back." He cast his bloodshot eyes to the quiet girl beside me. "I'm so sorry."

"Or what?" Luis barked.

"Or he's going to..." The color drained from Tristan's face. "Kill Uncle Roberto."

"What?" Arianne leaped up, her body trembling. "You're lying... he can't—"

"It's true. Uncle Roberto insisted I didn't tell you. But this isn't a game. Mike Fascini isn't playing around this time."

I grabbed Arianne's hand, gently coaxing her back down onto the couch. "How did he issue the threat?"

"There was a package. A letter and..." He ran a hand through his hair.

"Tristan," I urged.

"A flash drive. It contained live feeds of the entire estate."

"He bugged the house?"

He nodded.

"Fuck." Mike Fascini was more organized than we first thought.

"My uncle's study, the kitchen ... the bedrooms. He has enough to bring down Capizola Holdings at the press of a button."

Arianne clapped a hand over her mouth, smothering a gasp.

"He won't do it. He wants everything Roberto has. He's just trying to show him he holds all the cards."

"Maybe my parents can leave... maybe they can—"

"It won't change anything." I squeezed Arianne's hand in mine. "Mike Fascini has gone too far now. He doesn't care which way it ends, just that he holds all the power."

"I'll go back then. I'll go back and maybe you can—oh God."

"Bambolina, look at me." Cupping Arianne's face, I brushed her cheek. "You can't go back. Not now. It isn't only Mike we have to worry about, it's Scott too. He's unstable." And there wasn't a chance in hell he was getting within two feet of Arianne.

"He's my father, Nicco, I can't just let him..." Arianne let out a garbled cry and I pulled her into my arms, holding the back of her head as she sobbed gently.

"You know what has to be done." Tristan gave me a hard look.

"What?" Arianne eased back, gulping down her tears as she smoothed the hair from her eyes. "What has to be done?" She glanced from me to Tristan and back again.

I inhaled a ragged breath and whispered, "Mike Fascini has to die."

"D- die?" she choked out, edging away from me.

Her reaction stung but I'd expected no less. This was the ugly side of my world. The dark and tainted part I'd hoped never to share with her.

"As in you're going to *kill* him? That's... you can't..."

"If it means keeping you safe, I'll do whatever it takes."

"But killing a man?"

"Bambolina." I gave her a sad smile. "I have done much worse."

"It doesn't have to be you. It can be someone else, anyone else." Her voice rose as tears streamed down her face.

"It doesn't matter if it's me or if it's someone else. This is who I am."

"Okay," Luis said, standing. "Perhaps we should give the two of you some space."

But Arianne didn't look like she wanted space from them, she looked like she wanted space… from me.

"You two stay, I'll go." The words almost choked me. "I could do with some air."

"Nicco," she cried, and I lifted my eyes to hers. But nothing else came out.

She didn't ask me to stay…

She didn't say anything.

"Take your time." I gave him a stiff nod. "I won't go far."

I walked out of the cabin and didn't look back.

Because I knew if I did, I would break.

And a prince with a broken kingdom couldn't protect his queen.

When I finally got back to the cabin, it was dark. I slipped inside with a heavy heart. What would Arianne say? Would she want me to leave and never return?

I braced myself but found only Luis and Tristan in the main room.

"She's sleeping," Luis said. "How are you?"

"It's not me I'm worried about." I sat down and my eyes flicked to the long hall leading to our bedroom.

"It's been a lot for her to process."

"That's what worries me. How much more of this can she take?"

"Don't underestimate her," Luis said.

"What about you, what do you make of all this?" I asked Tristan.

"Honestly, I haven't got a fucking clue what to say. I knew, man. I knew my uncle planned to marry her off to that piece of shit. It cuts me up inside knowing I never saw his true colors until now."

My brow arched. "Arianne spoke like he'd hurt other girls before."

"He's known to be a little forward when he's had a drink, yeah. But he never—fuck, you think there are others?"

"Maybe. But not like Arianne. What he did to her at the hotel..." My spine stiffened.

"How do you do it?"

"Do what?" I asked Tristan.

"I want to kill him with my bare hands for ever hurting her, so I can't imagine how you must be feeling."

I didn't answer. I couldn't verbalize the things I wanted to do to that fucker.

"Do you think she'll come around?"

"Eventually." Tristan's brows pinched. "She hates Roberto right now, but he's her family, her blood. She would never want harm to come to him. That's not who she is."

"So we agree then? This is the only option?" The two of them nodded. "I'll need to call my father and make arrangements."

"You think he'll help?" Tristan asked.

"I know he will. He always knew this was how it would go. You can't negotiate with men like Fascini."

"And after... what happens then?"

I could read between the lines. He wanted to know what happened after Mike was gone.

"I love Arianne and I want a life with her. If she still wants me, I guess we'll be family one day."

He gave me a slight nod. "My uncle will be in the debt of the Marchetti; he won't like that."

"Not my problem."

I was doing this for Arianne.

To protect her.

"I'll talk to him again, try to explain that we have a plan."

I shrugged. "Do whatever you got to do, but just know, I will always put Arianne first. Always."

"Noted." He ran a hand over his jaw. "You know, Marchetti, we might not have always seen eye to eye, but I'm glad she's had you through all of this."

Standing, I narrowed my eyes at him. We were done here. I wasn't looking for his approval or even his gratitude. He hadn't been there when she'd needed him, too busy playing king of the campus at MU.

"Yeah, well she should have had you too." The words spilled out, but I didn't regret them. I couldn't. "Scott was your best friend, your guy. What happened between Arianne and him… some of that's on you."

"Shit, Marchetti, you think I don't know that? You think I don't lie awake at night thinking how different things might have been if I'd have been more clued in?

"Look, I can't change what happened but I'm here and I'm trying to do right by her now. I won't stand in your way. You love her and fuck knows she's made it abundantly clear she loves you."

I smirked.

As if he could actually come between us.

Arianne was a part of me now.

As much as I was a part of her.

CHAPTER 24

ARIANNE

I dreamed of death. Of blood and screams, guns and fists.

I dreamed of Mike Fascini beaten and bloody on the ground, a ruby red halo around him, the life gone from his eyes. And standing above him, like a dark angel, was Nicco.

Startled, I clutched the sheet to my body, willing my heart to slow down.

"What is it?" Nicco asked, pressing his lips to my shoulder.

"Just a nightmare, go back to sleep."

He let out a quiet sigh, but soon slipped back under. But I couldn't sleep, not after the nightmare.

They wanted to kill Mike Fascini.

Perhaps it shouldn't have bothered me. The man was the villain of our story; hellbent on revenge and willing to do whatever it took to see our families fall. But I couldn't help but think there had to be another way. A way that didn't require his life in return for my father's freedom.

For *my* freedom.

Nicco seemed dead set on making me understand that this was his life, that his soul was already tainted.

I didn't doubt it.

But I still wanted to keep it as clean as possible.

Maybe it was a foolish notion, to think it mattered.

It did matter though.

To me, it mattered.

Mike and Scott deserved to pay for their sins, they deserved to feel everything slip through their fingers and fall away.

But death?

My conscience wasn't ready to accept that this was how it had to be.

"Do you wish you had never met me?" Nicco whispered against my skin.

"No. Never." My heart ached at the very idea of it. "But I do wish things could be different. I wish that I was just a girl and you were just a boy."

Nicco looped his arm tighter, tucking me against the hard lines of his body. "I love you with everything that I am. I hope you know that, Bambolina. I hope it's enough."

"I do. It is." I laid my hand over his. "But there must be another way."

"There isn't..."

"It isn't fair."

"Life isn't fair, Arianne. It's cold and cruel and painful. But there are sparks of light in the dark. You are my spark, amore mio. Your brightness outshines the darkness in my soul." He lifted his chin to rest in the curve of where my shoulder met my neck.

"I don't want it to be like this, Nicco."

"Sometimes we must make the hard choices, Bambolina. That's all we are at the end of the day; a chain of decisions, some good, some bad."

I thought back to that night in the alley. If Scott hadn't tried to hurt me, I wouldn't have run. And if I'd never run, I might have never met Nicco.

Scott's bad choice led me here. It was the catalyst of a series of events that had forever changed me. Yet, I still had faith in humanity, in people choosing to do the right thing. The morally just thing.

I closed my eyes and inhaled a shaky breath. There had to be another way.

There had to.

Nicco was gone when I woke up. He'd left a note in his wake. Four little words that eased the knot in my stomach.

I'll see you later.

When I finally dragged myself into the living room, Luis confirmed what I already knew. Nicco had gone to see his father. I felt conflicted. On the one hand, I knew he was trying to protect me from what was to come. But on the other, it seemed cowardly.

"This is the right move, Arianne," Luis said over his coffee.

"Is it?"

"He tried to kill you. That is not a man you want to negotiate with."

"But to murder him?" Bile washed in my stomach.

"I know this is hard for you."

"You don't know anything," I snapped. "I have been lied to and used and... *raped*. Maybe death should befall Mike Fascini. But it feels like the easy way out for him. He deserves to rot in Hell for his crimes."

He'd orchestrated everything.

The failed hit on me when I was younger.

The business merger with my father.

The engagement.

The wedding.

The engagement.

A plan slowly began to take shape in my mind. Mike Fascini had positioned himself as someone of worth to my father. That was something I could exploit.

Something I could use.

"Arianne?" Luis asked as I stared off into the distance.

Blinking, I let my eyes drift to his. "I need you to do something for me."

"Why do I not like the sound of this?"

"I need you to take me to see Antonio."

"Are you out of your mind?" His eyes were the size of saucers.

Quite possibly. But I didn't tell him that.

"I know Nicco has gone there to make arrangements." The word soured on my tongue. "But I need to talk to him."

"I'll call Nicco. We can get Antonio to come here."

"It can't wait." Now that the seed was planted, I knew what I had to do.

"Ari, I'm not sure—"

"I'm going. Whether you help me or not, I'm doing this, Luis. I have sat by letting these... these men trample all over my life, but I won't sit idly by while a man is murdered in cold blood. Mike Fascini deserves to be punished. But this is not the way."

His expression turned grim. "It is their way."

"Will you take me or not?"

"You really want to do this? It isn't safe..."

I glared at him. This was happening. I wouldn't rest until he delivered me to Antonio's house.

"Fine," he grumbled, disapproval etched into his expression. "I'll take you."

"Thank you."

Antonio Marchetti might have been the boss of Dominion, but he was a businessman at heart.

And I had an offer he needed to hear.

We pulled up outside the Marchetti house an hour later. Luis had been quiet the entire ride. He didn't approve of me being here. But it was too late now.

The door flung open and Enzo appeared. "What the fuck?" He marched to the car, yanking open my door. "What the fuck are you thinking?"

"I need to see Antonio."

"You shouldn't be here."

Indignation trickled up my spine. I climbed out and met Enzo's glare with my own. "Well, I'm here now, and I'm not leaving until I speak with Antonio."

"Nicco is going to lose his shit when he realizes you're here. And you." Enzo jabbed his finger at Luis. "You had one fucking job. Keep her at the cabin."

"She was going to find her way here with or without me." His eyes settled on me. "She can be quite stubborn."

"You don't say."

I didn't wait for them to approach the house. Slipping inside, I followed the sound of Antonio and Nicco's voices, finding them in the same room I'd found them in the morning after the gala.

Taking a deep breath, I knocked on the door.

"What?" Antonio barked.

Pushing open the door, I stepped inside.

"Arianne?" Nicco blanched.

"Well, if this isn't a surprise." Antonio glowered at me, sliding his eyes to his son.

"What are you doing here?" Nicco rushed over to my side.

"I need to talk to your father."

"You should have called me."

"So you could talk me out of it?" My lips pursed.

"Niccolò, what is this all about?"

"I'm sorry to just barge in here like this, but Nicco had no idea I planned to come here. I didn't until I woke up," I said, meeting Antonio's cloudy eyes. "But I need to speak to you, Mr. Marchetti. Urgently."

"Please, Arianne, call me Antonio." He relaxed back in his chair. "Well, I am waiting..."

"Actually, I'd like to speak to you... alone."

Nicco let out a low groan. I peeked over at him. He looked confused, betrayal glittering in his eyes.

But I needed to do this.

"Very well. Niccolò, leave us."

"Wait a minute," he shot forward, "maybe I should—"

"Niccolò! Arianne has asked for privacy, and she shall get it. Wait outside."

"Why?" Nicco asked, the hurt in his eyes almost too much to bear.

"I had to."

He stalked out of the room, and guilt snaked through me. But I would worry about Nicco later. Right now, I needed to talk with his father.

"It would seem I underestimated you, Arianne," he said.

"Please, sit."

I took one of the leather chairs. "I am sorry for just turning up like this, but I couldn't just stand by. Mike Fascini and his son deserve to be punished, Mr. Mar—Antonio. But murder?"

"In our line of work, we prefer the term execution." He was so matter of fact it made my chest constrict. "Mike Fascini plotted against my family, Arianne. I'm sure you can understand I can't just let that go unpunished. He has directly threatened you, and now your father." He steepled his fingers. "Can I ask you something?"

I nodded.

"Would you rather sacrifice yourself to save Roberto?"

"No, that's not—"

"Sometimes we must make hard choices."

"That's what Nicco said."

"This life doesn't come easy for Niccolò. I suppose, in part, I am to blame for that. He blames me for his mother leaving. He blames me for a lot of things. And his blame isn't misplaced. I have done things, Arianne. Despicable things. But it is who I am. Just as you sit before me now as who you are."

"Is there another way?"

Antonio's brows morphed into a scowl. "Another way?"

"To deal with the Fascini. You are a well-connected man, you have the evidence of what Scott did to me, surely there is a way to take that to the authorities..."

"There is always another way, Arianne, but it doesn't mean it is the right way."

"I don't want anyone to die."

"Death is inevitable." He stroked his jaw, studying me, as if I was puzzle he was trying to solve.

"I want them to pay, I do. But not like this."

"You know, there are people who might think you should

be sitting here thanking me. I am, after all, offering to save your father. My enemy."

"But you're not doing it for me, are you? You're doing it for you. For the Family. Kill two birds with one stone."

"Explain."

"If you get rid of the Fascini, it leaves my father in your debt. You can use that as leverage to ensure he doesn't come after La Riva. If Fascini is gone, my father's position is weakened. And the Marchetti come out on top."

"Interesting." His eyes twinkled.

"What is?"

"You're more like your father than anyone gives you credit for."

"Whether I like it or not, I am my father's daughter. And I am here to negotiate."

He sat forward; hands folded on the desk. "I'm listening."

"What if you didn't have my family in your debt but as a partner?"

"I'm not sure you are in any position to make that offer, Arianne."

"My father's life hangs in the balance and one day, Capizola Holdings will be mine. I think I'm exactly the person to make such an offer." My brow raised.

"Your terms?"

"Figure out another way to take down the Fascini. You said it's possible. If you can guarantee no one will get hurt, I'll make you a silent partner."

"Your father will never agree to those terms."

"It's not his decision to make." My voice shook. "We both know he's indebted to you either way."

"It's ballsy, I'll give you that. Our families are on opposite sides of morality. Bringing us together—"

"Is righting history."

"This won't change who we are, Arianne. It won't change

who Niccolò is. Do you understand that?"

"I know." My voice was small. "I'm not a fool. I know what you do. I know what your family does. But this is different. This is personal. And I'm not sure I can carry the burden of murder."

"Say I was to consider your offer; I'd need reassurances."

"I give you my word. After the Fascini are dealt with, I'll have my father's legal team draw up all the necessary paperwork." My father would listen, he'd have no choice.

Not after Antonio saved his life.

Besides, he owed me.

My father owed it to me to let me have this.

"I appreciate your tenacity, Arianne. But it is all just words and paper. These things are easily broken."

My stomach sank. This was my Ace card, my final plea. If Antonio didn't take it... I didn't know what would become of me and Nicco.

"I'm sorry," I kept my voice even. "I'm not sure I understand. I can try to have the paperwork drawn up sooner, but we're running out of time. Mike is going to kill my father, Antonio. He's going to—"

He silenced me with his hand. "My son is prepared to kill for you, to *die* for you, Arianne... What are you prepared to do for my son?"

I frowned.

What did he mean?

"I love Nicco, I would do whatever I could to protect him."

"I'm glad to hear that." His lip curved, a dark expression crossing his face. It sent a shiver rippling through me. "The bonds of marriage are sacred in our world. They bind together two people far more than any promise."

Marriage?

"You want me to *marry* Nicco?"

"Mike Fascini might be blinded by his thirst for vengeance, Arianne, but he knew what he was doing convincing Roberto to promise you to his son. One day you will be the Queen of the Capizola empire and your child will be the heir. Fascini knew this. He knew if you gave Scott a child, the Ricci bloodline would supersede the Capizola line."

"I'm not... that doesn't..." It was crazy talk, yet, deep down, I knew he spoke the truth.

"My son loves you, Arianne. He has chosen you as his woman. One day, he will ask for your hand in marriage. It is inevitable. I am not asking anything of you that isn't already written in your destiny."

Antonio's eyes narrowed as he watched my reaction. I realized then, it was a test.

He was testing me.

I didn't belong in their world. I was too pure, too righteous. He wanted to know how far I would go to prove my loyalty to Nicco.

To his family.

Staring him right in the eye, I gave him a small nod. "I'll do it. Do this one thing for me. Save my father, and I'll marry Nicco."

"You will?" Antonio looked oddly relieved.

"Like you said, I love your son, Antonio. I look into the future and see a life with him. So yes, I'll marry him." My body hummed with nervous anticipation, with the idea of binding my life with Nicco's so definitively.

"Do you want to tell him, or should I?"

"Let me talk to him first."

He nodded. "As you wish. But, Arianne, you should know he might not like this. Niccolò has never taken well to following orders, especially my orders."

But this was different.

This was me giving myself to him completely.

Heart.
Body.
Soul.
And in marriage.

∼

"Nicco?" I entered the kitchen and he looked up. His expression was crestfallen, tugging at my heart strings.

"You shouldn't have come here, Arianne."

"Yes, I should." I walked over to him, stopping just out of touching distance. "Can we talk? Somewhere private?"

His eyes swirled with uncertainty. I'd driven a wedge between us by coming here, and I knew he felt betrayed. But there was no going back now, only forward.

"Please," I added.

He pressed his palms against the counter and stood up. "Okay, come on."

It stung when he didn't take my hand, but I took a shuddering breath and followed him out of the back door to the fire pit where we'd once sat with his cousins and Alessia.

That night seemed so long ago, when it was only a couple of weeks. I was different now.

We both were.

But the truth was, I'd never felt stronger.

I no longer had to sit around and let other people determine my fate, I could carve my own path.

I just needed Nicco to see that.

He sat down in one of the lawn chairs and I did the same. The air was cool between us, and not only from the frigid fall temperatures.

"What did you offer him?" Nicco didn't look at me, his eyes staring off into the distance.

"How did you—"

His gaze finally shifted to mine, filled with so much intensity my breath caught. "I know you, Arianne. I think I knew last night that you wouldn't let it rest. So what did you offer him?"

"We negotiated," I said calmly, fighting every instinct to go to him and beg him to understand. "I offered to make him a partner in Capizola Holdings if he'll hand the Fascini to the authorities."

"And he accepted?" His eyes narrowed, dark and menacing. A shiver skated up my spine.

"He has terms of his own."

He scoffed. "Of course he does."

"I love you Nicco, and I want a life with you. I know who you are. I know what it means to be in your world, but I'm not ready to..." I swallowed the words. "I can't just give up my morality. I can't."

"So you decided to make a deal with the Devil?"

"That's not..." I pressed my lips together. Nicco had a point. "I can't really explain it. All I know is in my heart of hearts, I couldn't turn a blind eye to this. Maybe it makes me a fool or naive, maybe it makes me unworthy of your love, but this world has proved itself to me as a dark place. You said I was the light. I'm not ready to give that up."

Taking me by surprise, Nicco stood and came to me, falling to his knees before me. "You are the light, Bambolina, but it doesn't change the fact Fascini needs to pay for his crimes."

"I know." I brushed the hair from his eyes. "But there is always a choice."

"What did he want from you, Arianne?" Defeat washed over him.

"Nothing I wouldn't have one day given anyway." Leaning down, I cupped his face, touching my head to his. "He wants my name, Nicco. He wants us to marry."

CHAPTER 25

NICCO

"No," the word was out of my mouth before I could stop it.

Arianne paled, jerking away from me, leaving me cold and desolate.

"No?" She cried. "But I thought... you don't want me?"

"Not like this." *Never* like this.

I wanted our future to be born out of love, not obligation.

"But it solves everything," she said unable to disguise the pain in her voice. "Your father will help make sure Mike and Scott pay for their crimes, my father's life will be saved, and we'll be together."

"You don't know what you're saying," I ground out.

I wanted a life with Arianne, a future. But she deserved more than... than *this*. She deserved an engagement and a bridal shower. She deserved to enjoy all the planning and lead up to her wedding day.

She deserved so much more than a last-minute wedding arranged as part of a business transaction.

"Your father said you wouldn't be happy." Sadness laced her words. "But I thought... I'm just trying to do the right thing." A soft sigh escaped her lips. "Is the idea of marrying me so unappealing to you?"

"Bambolina, that's not..." I inhaled a sharp breath. "This is not how I want it to be."

I wanted to put this all behind us and enjoy being a couple. I didn't want her to rush headfirst into something she wasn't ready for.

Something *we* weren't ready for.

"I know what I want, Nicco," Arianne's expression fell as if she could hear my thoughts and sense my torment. "Did I imagine I'd be married at eighteen? No, I didn't. But I also didn't imagine that I'd meet someone like you. I didn't imagine that everything I thought I knew would turn out to be a lie."

Frustration laced her words. "Nothing about this is what I'd ever imagined, but here we are. I love you, I love you so much..." Silent tears trickled down her cheeks but I was paralyzed, unable to reach for her.

My father had said all along that Arianne could be the leverage he needed over Roberto, and he had gotten his wish.

It didn't matter if Arianne thought the choice was hers. I knew the truth.

I would always know the truth.

And one day, it would drive a wedge between us.

"Nicco, please, say something."

"I need to talk to my father." I stood, running a hand over my jaw.

"It is already done." Panic overwhelmed her voice. "I made my decision. I don't understand why you're fighting me on this?" Defiance burned in her eyes. "Unless you don't want—"

"Bambolina, stop." I curved my hand around her neck, holding her close to me. "I love you, but I don't want you to do something you'll one day regret." Something she might one day resent me for.

"This will unite our families, Nicco." She eased back to look at me. "It will right things."

The sincerity in her gaze almost killed me. But you couldn't just rewrite a bitter history with a wedding—a wedding born out of business.

"Don't you see," I said, angling her face to mine. "You are just replacing one cage for another."

"No, that's not what this is. I'm choosing this, I'm choosing you. I want this, Nicco. I want you." Her bottom lip quivered. "I thought you felt the same about me. I thought—"

I pressed a hard kiss to her forehead, silencing her. "I need to speak with my father. I'll be back soon." Pulling away, I didn't look at her.

I couldn't.

Because if I did, I was worried I might say something I would regret. Something I couldn't ever take back.

Something that might destroy us both.

"Ahh, Niccolò, did Arianne tell you the happy news?" My father smirked, only provoking the storm inside me to rage harder.

"What the fuck were you thinking?" I seethed.

"Watch your tongue, boy." His eyes narrowed. "Arianne came to me with an offer and I saw an opportunity. You should be thanking me. This will make her your wife. It will bind your life with hers permanently."

"It shouldn't be like this." I shook my head.

"What you would you have me do, Son? Deny your woman and execute Fascini? Make her hate me and resent you? She's not ready to have blood on her hands; you know I speak the truth."

I did.

But it didn't make it any easier to swallow.

"Arianne is strong," he went on. "She has proved that. I have no doubt she will make you a fine wife, Niccolò."

"It wasn't supposed to be like this," I looked at my father, silently pleading for him to fix this. But there was no magical solution.

He was right.

If he took out Fascini, Arianne would never forgive him. Forgive herself.

Maybe even me.

Or if he handed him over to the authorities and became a partner in Capizola Holdings like Arianne wanted, things might be okay for a while. But over time, Roberto would grow bitter and Arianne could end up resenting my family all the same.

And I couldn't let go of the fairytale she deserved.

"You love her, no?" he asked me.

"You know I do. More than I ever thought I could love another."

"Then perhaps it is time you trusted her." My father's expression softened. "Arianne has spent years having her choices removed. Now she is free, and she has chosen. I lost your mother because I couldn't see past my own proclivities, Niccolò. She was a good woman. Strong and loyal and beautiful. God, she was so beautiful." He stared off into the distance, shame washing over him.

It was a strange thing, watching Antonio Marchetti

acknowledge his mistakes, watching him mourn for the woman he'd let slip through his fingers.

"Don't do something you'll regret, Son," my father offered me a sad smile. "That girl is everything I could wish for my son. I see so much of your mother in her, it scares me. But it also gives me hope. Hope that you will get a chance to right my wrongs."

Was he right?

Was I focusing on the wrong thing here?

Arianne seemed so certain, so sure of her love for me. But part of me couldn't accept that. It couldn't fathom that a girl like Arianne Carmen Lina Capizola could love a guy like me.

I kept pondering what Arianne deserved, but maybe the issue wasn't her.

It was me.

What *I* deserved.

What *I* was worthy of.

"Look, I know this isn't how you wanted things to go. But life doesn't always go to plan, Niccolò. Sometimes opportunities arise when you least expect them. If the outcome is the same does it really matter what path you took to get there?" He ran a hand over his jaw. "I cannot give you what you most desire, I cannot free you from this life. But I can give you this."

My body shook with anger, frustration, and uncertainty. I was Niccolò Marchetti. Nothing would ever change that. But a life with Arianne by my side would make it all worth it.

"You know I'm right, Son."

I stared at my father, giving him a sharp nod. I still didn't know what I felt. I was too wired, too volatile.

"Go calm down," he ordered. "And then talk to her. She needs to know you support this, Niccolò. She needs to know you support her."

I didn't go to Arianne.

I sent Alessia instead, asking her to keep my girl company. My father was right, I needed to calm down. Which meant, I needed space and time. But I did text Arianne.

I promise I'm not running. I just need to figure out some things.

Her one word reply had almost gutted me.

Okay.

But when I came back, I wanted to be clearheaded and present. I wanted to be everything she deserved.

A whistle pierced the air, and I saw Enzo waiting over by his car. "So what happened?"

"Not here." I yanked open the door and ducked inside.

Enzo got in and fired up the engine. "Where's Arianne?"

"Inside with Alessia." Leaning back against the headrest, I let out a weary sigh. "I just needed some space."

"That bad, huh?" Enzo backed out of the driveway and pulled onto the street.

"She came here to bargain with him."

"She's got balls, Cous, I'll give her that. Let me guess, she asked Uncle Toni to spare that piece of shit?"

"Yeah, she wants to let the law handle it."

Enzo scoffed. It wasn't how we usually got shit done. We

had our own code, our own justice system. If you betrayed or screwed over the Family, you were dealt with swiftly.

And Mike Fascini had attempted what no other person ever had.

"She's not cut out for this life."

"It's a good thing I'm not asking her to initiate into the family then, isn't it?" Sarcasm dripped from my words.

"Yeah, but you know what I mean. She'll never understand this life, she'll never understand what you do. What we do."

"She's agreed to marry me," I confessed "that's what they negotiated."

"What the fuck?" The car swerved as Enzo's eyes snapped to mine.

"Watch the road," I hissed.

"You can't just drop something like that on me and expect me to keep cool. Marriage... he wants you to *marry* her? Has he lost his fucking mind?"

"Nice, E. Real nice."

"Sorry, I didn't mean... But you're both young. Like really young. Marriage is a huge deal. It's—"

"A life sentence?" I could see that's what he wanted to say. "I love her. I love her so fucking much."

"I sense a 'but' in there..." He cast me a sideways glance.

"It shouldn't be like this. I don't want her to be obligated to marry me to save her father, to save that fucking monster."

My pulse spiked again, but I forced myself to take a breath. I was supposed to be calming down, not getting even more worked up.

"What do you want, Nic?" There was no trace of mocking in his voice, just mild curiosity.

"Her, I just want her."

"So maybe you have your answer. Maybe you just need to accept your fate and go with it."

I glanced out of the window. It was dark, only the headlights of passing cars and streetlamps lighting the way. My mind drifted to Arianne. To how she made me feel every time she touched me, the way my heart galloped in my chest whenever her big brown eyes found mine across a room.

She was my anchor.

My North star in the endless night sky.

And although our time together had been relatively short, I couldn't imagine life without her.

I didn't want to.

"What's going on in that head of yours?" Enzo's voice penetrated my thoughts.

"I know what to do," I rushed out, a sense of peace washing over me.

"So we're not heading to my place?"

"Change of plan. Can we stop by Matteo's?" Officially, he lived with Enzo in their apartment on the edge of Romany Square and University Hill. But more often than not, he stayed with his family at their house in La Riva.

I dug my cell out of my pocket.

"You're calling him?"

"No. Luis."

"Okay..." He frowned. "Going to share your plan with me?"

"I will, once we get to Matteo's."

"What are you up to, Nicco?"

A smile spread over my face. "You'll see."

Almost three hours later, Matteo looked up from his cell phone and said, "They're on their way."

My heart was beating so hard I felt a little lightheaded.

"You okay, Cous?" Enzo clapped me on the back. "You don't look so good."

"I'm fine," I mumbled, taking a long pull on my beer.

We were back at the cabin. I didn't want to do this there. Not with my father, Alessia, and Genevieve hanging around.

Arianne and I needed to talk, and I wanted total privacy when we did.

"You sure you don't want us to stay?" Enzo asked, and I shook my head.

"I've got this."

"Yeah, you do." Matteo grinned. He turned to the overhead cabinets and found three glasses, setting them down in front of us. "Is there any of the good stuff lying around here?" He went over to my father's drinks cabinet. "Bingo." Snatching up a bottle of scotch, he brought it over and poured us each a glass.

"I'm driving," Enzo reminded him.

"One won't hurt. This deserves a toast."

He gave Matteo a sharp nod, accepting a glass. I took mine, swirling the amber liquid around the sides.

Maybe it would settle my nerves.

"To the best cousins, the best friends, a guy could ever have. I love you guys," Matteo said clutching his own glass. "To friendship, family, and the future. Salute."

"Salute." We clinked our glasses with his, downing our drinks in one.

"Shit, that's strong," he spluttered.

"You need to grow some fucking balls." Enzo clapped him on the back.

"Being a cold-hearted bastard does not mean you have big balls." Matteo flipped him off and the two of them started jostling and punching one another.

"Knock it off," I ordered. "You two need to get going."

"We should probably stick around—"

"Now," I said, narrowing my eyes at them.

"Come on, E. Nic's right. We should make tracks."

"Call us after?" Enzo met my stare, concern shining in his icy gaze.

"I'll text."

He rolled his eyes. "Whatever, just let us know, okay?"

"Like he needs to." Matteo smirked.

"Goodbye." I tipped my chin to the door. I appreciated their support, but I wanted a couple of minutes to myself before Arianne got here.

There would be no going back after tonight.

I watched my friends leave. Watched as the headlights of Luis' SUV appeared in the distance. I watched him roll to a stop and climb out, opening Arianne's door.

I watched her climb out, a look of trepidation on her face. "Nicco?" she said, confusion clouding her eyes. "What is it?"

"Will you come inside with me?" I asked, holding out my hand.

Luis caught my eye over her shoulder and gave me a curt nod before climbing back into the SUV. Arianne glanced back. "He's leaving?"

"I wanted to be alone with you." I gently tugged her hand. "Come inside and we can talk."

"Nicco, you're scaring me."

"You have nothing to fear, I promise." I pulled her closer, brushing her cheek. "Do you trust me?"

"You know I do." She gave me a tentative smile.

"Then come inside, Bambolina." I led her to the cabin, my body trembling with anticipation.

"You're shaking," she said, glancing up at me.

"I'll be okay in a second. Go on inside..."

Arianne gingerly made her way up the steps. "Nicco," she gasped when she stepped inside. "What did you do?"

"Every girl deserves their fairytale," I said, wrapping my

hand around her waist and pulling her back against me. Dipping my head, I brushed the shell of her ear and said, "I'm sorry."

But they wouldn't be the most important words I said to her tonight.

Not by a long shot.

CHAPTER 26

ARIANNE

The cabin had been transformed into something out of a fairytale. Twinkle lights hung from the wooden beams, casting a flickering glow around the room. The open fire crackled, filling the room with its smoky scent, and vases of white roses littered the table and breakfast counter. It was so beautiful; I was overwhelmed with emotion.

Nicco walked us forward, keeping his chin tucked into the crook of my neck. "Do you like it?" he whispered.

"I love it. But I don't understand..."

"Sit." Nicco moved around me, guiding me over to one of the armchairs.

My heart was in my mouth as he dropped to one knee in front of me. "Oh my god," I breathed, clapping a hand over my mouth. My body trembled, blood roaring between my ears. "Nicco."

"Just give me a minute." He popped the collar on his dress

shirt. It was then I realized how smart he looked. The black material molded to his shoulders, and he'd rolled up the sleeves to his elbows, revealing his strong forearms.

"You're all dressed up." I smiled.

"Well, yeah, this is a special occasion."

My hands went to his face, as I leaned down.

"God, I love you," he murmured against my lips. But Nicco didn't kiss me. He pulled away gently. "You're distracting me."

"Sorry." My cheeks burned, but he looked so good down on one knee, his eyes burning with nothing but love and adoration. "Okay," I sat up, "go on."

He took a shuddering breath. "If someone had told me four months ago, that I would have been here right now... I would have laughed in their face. I wasn't interested in a relationship. I knew what this life meant for me and, honestly, I wasn't sure I would ever want to drag a girl into that. And then I met you.

"That night I saw you in the alley, my first instinct was to let Bailey deal with you. And then I looked at you, *really* looked at you, and something snapped into place. I wanted to wipe the tears from your face. I wanted to pick you up and keep you safe. That feeling only grew the more time I spent around you."

Nicco took my hand in his, brushing his thumb across my skin. "It was disarming, Bambolina. You disarmed me. But I couldn't get enough of you. You consumed my thoughts and haunted my dreams."

"Nicco..." My breath caught, my heart beating wildly in my chest.

"Your inner strength never ceases to amaze me. Your compassion and big heart. Even when you found out who I really was, you didn't run. You love without limits, Arianne. And I will spend my life trying to be worthy of you." He slipped his hand into his pocket and pulled out a small velvet pouch. "I didn't have much time, so consider this a stand-in until I can get you something new."

The world fell away as Nicco emptied out the simple band into his palm. He discarded the pouch and took my left hand in his. "Arianne Carmen Lina Capizola, you are my heart, my soul, and my future. I don't want to do this thing called life without you." Nicco moved the band to my ring finger. "I want you by my side, always. So will you do me the honor of being my wife?"

"Yes," I cried as he slid the band on. "I love you." Flinging my arms around Nicco's neck, I threw myself at him. He caught me, his laughter and my happy tears filling the space between us.

"Sei la mia anima gemella." He cupped the back of my neck. "The future Mrs. Arianne Marchetti."

"I like the sound of that."

Nicco brushed his lips over mine, sealing the moment with a kiss.

I would be his.

In heart, body, soul, and name.

Nicco pulled me to my feet, peppering my face with kisses. "I'm sorry I acted like an asshole earlier. I was just so shocked that you would do such a thing with no consideration for everything you deserve."

"I only want you."

"I know that now." He took my hand, pressing a kiss to my knuckles, the embedded diamonds of the ring glittering in the light.

"It's beautiful."

"It's a family heirloom of sorts. My Aunt Marcella, Matteo's mom, had it. It was my nonna's. As soon as it's safe I'll take you to pick something—"

"No," I said, already feeling possessive over it. "I love it."

The fact it was a family heirloom only made it all the more special.

"You're sure about this?"

My head almost bobbed off my neck in agreement and I smiled so hard it made my cheeks ache.

"Give me a second." He dropped a kiss to my head and left me standing there while he went over to the kitchen. There was a bottle of champagne on ice, two glasses waiting for us.

"You've thought of everything."

"I had a little help." Nicco uncorked the bottle and poured us each a glass. I went to him, accepting a glass.

"To us."

"To us." I clinked my glass with his. His eyes never left my face as I took a sip of bubbly.

"You are so beautiful, amore mio."

I held out my hand, admiring the ring. It was the last thing I had expected when I'd turned up at Antonio's house.

"What are you thinking?" Nicco asked me.

"I'm so happy... earlier, at the house, I thought that perhaps you were having second thoughts about us."

"It was never about not wanting you, Bambolina. I just didn't want you to make such a big decision out of obligation. Our love isn't a bargaining chip. Our future isn't leverage. You are not some possession to be traded." He spoke with such vehemence it took my breath away.

"What changed your mind?"

"My father, Enzo... *you*." He took the glass from my hand and placed it down on the counter. "You own me, Arianne. I am yours, in this life and the next."

Startling me, Nicco bent down and slid his hand under my legs, picking me up and cradling me against his chest. "What are you doing?" I shrieked, laughter spilling from my lips.

"You'll see."

He carried me into the bedroom, and a sweet aroma flooded my senses. "What is—" I spotted the container on the nightstand.

"Tell me that's not what I think it is." My stomach clenched.

"I called in a favor." Nicco lay me down on the bed. His eyes were dark and hooded as he trailed them over my body. He looked like a man starved, and I knew the tiramisu from the Blackstone Country Club wasn't the only thing on the menu tonight.

I woke to sounds of birds chirping. Nicco's arm was slung possessively over my hip, his body pressed impossibly close to mine. My lips curved at the memories of the night before.

He'd proposed.

Niccolò Marchetti, mafia prince, Prince of Hearts, had gotten down on one knee and promised me forever.

I was floating on clouds so high I didn't ever want to come down.

After carrying me into our bedroom, Nicco had loved me with words and his body. It had been everything, being one with him.

My fiancé.

Uncurling my hands from the sheet, I admired his grandmother's ring. Nicco's fingers ran down my arm, curving around my wrist. "It looks good on you," he murmured, his voice thick with sleep.

"I still can't believe it," I choked out over the lump in my throat. "It's like waking up from the best dream."

"Believe it, Bambolina. Soon enough, I will stand before all our family and friends and declare you mine." Nicco tugged me onto my back and leaned over me. "No regrets?"

"No regrets." Laying my hand against his cheek, I leaned up to kiss him. "I love you, always."

His eyes shuttered, as if my admission was almost too much to bear.

"Nicco, look at me." They opened slowly. "I want this. It's time to rewrite history."

I truly believed I'd met Nicco for a reason. It wasn't coincidence he was there, in the alley, that night.

It was fate.

"I will never let another soul hurt you. You know that, right?"

"I know. What do you think your uncles will say?" I wasn't stupid, I knew Antonio didn't usually solve their problems this way.

"It doesn't matter. My father is the boss. What he says, goes."

"But they won't be happy?" My stomach twisted.

"Uncle Vincenzo is blood thirsty. He'll be disappointed." I winced at Nicco's honest words. "Uncle Michele has a softer approach. He'll be more understanding. But either way, the deal you struck with my father will give the Family a better foothold in Verona County."

"And my father? What will happen to him?"

"I guess that all depends on Roberto."

"He'll come around," I said quietly.

He had no choice.

And if he didn't, well, I was sure Antonio would handle my father.

Nicco lowered his face to mine, kissing me deeply. I could still taste the lingering sweetness of the tiramisu on his tongue. I would never be able to eat that dessert again without thinking about Nicco licking it off the most intimate parts of my body.

"Are you hungry, Love?" he whispered against my mouth.

"I—"

My eyes jerked to the door at the sound of something banging. "What is that?"

"Stay here." Nicco darted off the bed and pulled on his boxers before grabbing his gun from the nightstand. I'd never seen him brandish a weapon before. But this was who he was, who I'd promised myself to.

"Nicco," I whisper-hissed as he crept closer to the door. "Maybe we should—"

"Ssh," he mouthed, reaching for the door handle. I clutched the sheets around my body, fear trickling down my spine.

Quietly, Nicco opened the door and slipped into the cabin. I leaned over, grabbing my cell phone ready to call Luis. But then I heard voices. Laughter. Pushing back the sheets, I climbed out of bed and pulled on some clothes. My heart galloped in my chest as I left the bedroom and moved down the hall toward the main room.

"You have some explaining to do." Nora made a beeline for me. "I knew you were here, I frickin' knew it. But we'll get to that later. Let me see it." She beckoned for my hand, but I was still standing there, gawking at her. "What did you do to my girl, Marchetti? I think you broke her."

"I... what are you doing here?" My brows drew together.

"We thought you might want to celebrate." Enzo gave me a pointed look.

"You did this?"

"And this?" Alessia peeked out from behind Matteo. "Congratulations." She came over to me, and her and Nora swooned over my ring.

"I can't believe you're both here." It was the perfect way to round off a perfect night.

"Group hug," Matteo shouted, bounding over and wrapping his huge arms around the three of us.

"Uh, Matt, you smell of bacon grease."

"Well, yeah, someone had to go and pick up breakfast."

"There's breakfast?" I asked, hopeful. There hadn't been much time to eat last night.

"We got extra." Matteo kept his arm around my shoulder, guiding me over to the breakfast counter.

"Only because you eat like a fucking pig," Enzo grumbled.

"I see you're as delightful than ever," Nora shot back.

"Shut up and eat, Abato."

"Hey, remember that time when she almost ate your—"

"*Matteo!*" Nicco cut him with a harsh look.

"Yeah, yeah, I'll behave. But seriously though, you two, congratulations."

"I can't believe we'll be sisters." Alessia beamed. "Can I be bridesmaid?"

"Me too," Nora added.

"Hmm, we haven't gotten that far." I glanced at Nicco and he smiled.

"Well, for what it's worth, I think you're both fucking crazy," Enzo said as he and Matteo unpacked the breakfast containers. "But if you're happy then I guess that's all that matters."

"Thanks, I think. You didn't invite Luis?" I glanced around, half expecting him to appear at any second.

"He's with Tristan, they're..." Matteo glanced at Nicco and he nodded. "They're with your father."

Silence fell over the six of us. Here we were celebrating, but there was still a difficult uncertain path ahead.

"Nope. Not happening." Nora declared. "This is a celebration breakfast. So less moping and more celebrating."

"Thank you," I mouthed at her and she nodded, pride glittering in her eyes.

"One good thing about weddings... bachelor party." Matteo smirked.

A low grumble spilled from my lips and all heads turned to me.

"Did Ari just growl?" His eyes were the size of saucers.

"I'm just hungry." I averted my eyes, heat burning my cheeks.

"She did, she growled." Amusement laced Enzo's words.

"Yeah, only because she knows what happens at such things," Sia replied. "Remember Uncle Sil? His bachelor party was wild."

"How the hell do you know what happened at Uncle Sil's party?" Nicco arched his brow at his sister.

"I hear things. Aunt Dru made him sleep on the couch for a—"

"Okay, Sia." Nicco clapped his hand over her mouth. "I think we get the picture." He shot me a pleading glance.

"Let the guys have their fun, I say." Nora stabbed her fork into a stack of pancakes. "While the men are away, the girls will play."

"I don't think that's how the saying goes," Matteo said, and she shrugged.

"It is in my world. I'm thinking a stripper, massages, the full works."

Nicco had gone as white as a sheet and I smothered a chuckle.

"Oh, I'm sorry." Nora offered him a saccharine smile. "Did you think we were all going to sit around and braid each other's hair and have pillow fights while you're off getting lap dances and drinking your body weight in liquor?"

"More like sharpen each other's claws," Enzo murmured.

"Careful, E, I bite too." She bared her teeth at him.

"You know you two just need to get it out of your system, right?" Alessia took a bite of bacon.

"Huh?" Nora frowned while Enzo sat deathly still.

"The tension between the two of you." She wagged a finger between my best friend and her cousin.

"Fuck that," Enzo gritted out.

"The feeling is mutual," Nora hissed.

"Okay, why doesn't everyone just take a breath?" I suggested. I was too happy to let their bickering spoil my moment.

"Ari's right," Matteo said. "We're here to celebrate." He grabbed a glass of orange juice and thrust it in the air. To Nicco and his fiancée, Arianne. May your life be filled with happiness, love, and lots and lots of hot newlywed sex."

After breakfast Nicco asked to talk to me.

"What is it?" I said as he led me away from our friends.

"I'm going to go back with the guys to see my father."

"You're leaving?" My heart clenched but I knew it would be like this sometimes. There were still things to take care of.

"Only for a little while. We need to figure out a plan. The sooner it happens," he cupped my face, "the sooner we can get on with our lives."

"Okay." I covered his hand with mine, turning my face slightly to kiss his palm. "Be safe."

"Always. Luis is on his way back. I think Tristan is with him."

"Maybe you should be gone before they get here," I smiled.

"I'm not scared of Tristan, Bambolina."

"I know." We'd moved closer, our lips almost brushing.

"You're mine now," he whispered. "Nothing can ever change that." The sheer possessiveness in his voice made my heart swell.

My hands twisted into his t-shirt. "Don't be too long."

"I promise. I think there's still some tiramisu left in the refrigerator."

My tummy clenched. "Nicco, you can't say things like that to me in public." I breathed, glancing to where our friends sat, as his lips painted a warm trail to the shell of my ear.

"But you taste so damn good."

"Vitelli is here," Enzo called. "We should go."

"I'll be back soon." Nicco pressed a kiss to my head before taking my hand and leading me back to our friends.

"Come on, Sia, let's go." Enzo's cold gaze went to where Nora and Alessia were sitting on the couch.

Nicco's sister pouted. "I could stay."

"Not. Happening. You're lucky we brought you here as it is."

"Fine." She hugged Nora before coming over to me. "I'm so happy for you."

"Thank you." We hugged, Alessia hanging on for dear life. There was something so pure about her easy acceptance. It only reaffirmed the feeling that I'd finally found my place.

Nora laced her arm through mine as we followed them out of the cabin. Nicco lingered at Matteo's truck, locking eyes with mine.

"Damn, Ari. Where can I get me one of those?"

"Hush." I nudged her with my shoulder.

Luis' SUV appeared down the track, rolling to a stop next to the truck. Luis and Tristan climbed out, stopping to talk to Nicco. My breath caught as I watched my cousin extend his hand to him.

"Well, I'll be damned." Nora squealed with delight as Nicco took it.

The two of them glanced over at us before Nicco pulled away and climbed into the truck.

Tristan approached us, a faint smirk tugging at his mouth.

"Sounds like you have some explaining to do..." His eyes went to the band on my finger.

"We should probably talk, yes."

"Fuck, talking." He pulled me into his arms. "You've got balls of steel, Ari."

"I didn't do anything, not really."

"Like hell you didn't. You brokered a deal with Antonio Marchetti and went and got yourself engaged by all accounts."

"I did what I had to."

Tristan eased back to look at me. "But you're happy, right? You want this?"

I nodded, fighting a smile. "I know we're young and I know a lot of people won't understand—"

"Screw what anyone else thinks. All I care is that you're happy and you're safe."

"Have you seen the way he looks at her?" Nora scoffed. "Ari's safety should be the least of your concerns."

Tristan's eyes narrowed, a trace of hurt there. Or maybe it was guilt.

"Yeah," he said, "I'm starting to get that."

CHAPTER 27

NICCO

When we arrived back at my father's house, I half-expected to find my uncles there, ready to toast my news. But the house was quiet when we entered.

"Ah, Nicco." Genevieve rounded the corner. "I hear congratulations are in order."

"You know?" My eyes narrowed.

"Don't sound so surprised, Niccolò," my father moved beside her, squeezing her shoulder, "Genevieve is practically family."

I raised a brow at that.

"Sia, can I borrow you, in the kitchen?" she asked my sister, no doubt sensing the tension rippling in the air.

"Sure thing. I'll see you later." Alessia kissed my cheek before taking off after Genevieve.

"Niccolò, my office." My father turned on his heel and took off down the hall.

"Why do I get the feeling I'm in trouble?"

"Nah," Enzo smirked. "He probably just wants to give you the father/son talk and remind you of the three golden rules."

"Three golden rules?" Matteo frowned.

"Birth control, birth control, birth control."

Shaking my head, I flicked my head in the direction of the kitchen. "Go hang out, I'll be back soon."

Matteo clapped me on the back. "Everything's going to work out," he said.

I wanted to believe him.

Proposing to Arianne, hearing the word *yes* spill from her lips, then sliding my nonna's ring onto her finger, had been one of the most terrifying and best moments of my life.

But our struggle wasn't over yet.

It wouldn't be until Fascini and his piece of shit son were no longer a threat.

"Come in," my father demanded. I slipped inside, closing the door behind me. "How is Arianne?"

"She's fine."

"A toast." He moved to his drinks cabinet and pulled out a bottle of his finest scotch, pouring us both a glass. "Here."

I accepted it.

"I am glad you came to your senses, Niccolò. It is the right move for the Family as well as for your future."

Taking a seat, I glanced up at him, confusion clouding my eyes.

"This job, it can be a lonely life. I look back and realize how much time I wasted. How much I took for granted. Do not repeat my mistakes, Son. When you first brought her here, and I saw the way you looked at her, I was concerned she would be your weakness. But now I see that she can be your strength. Love gives you something to fight for, something to lose. Arianne will anchor you, Son.

"To family." He lifted his glass and I mirrored his action.

"To family. What happens now?" I asked.

"Tommy is waiting for my word to make the tip off to our friend down at the local PD. Michele's guys are handling Fascini's legal team."

One of Uncle Michele's guys, Johnny Morello, was our go-to fixer. With a penchant for extortion and coercion, he rarely failed to secure people's silence or compliance.

"And Uncle Vin?"

"I have ordered him to sit tight. He doesn't like it but the last thing we need is him barreling in all guns blazing."

"He needs to get on board with me and Arianne," I said, pressing my lips together.

"And he will. You're his nephew, my son. One day you'll be the boss. He'll get over it. Besides, once your ring is on her finger, she's family too. She'll be Marchetti."

Fuck.

My heart flipped violently in my chest.

I liked the sound of that.

"Are you sure this is going to work?"

Fascini wasn't stupid. He had to have his bases covered in case his cover was blown—reassurance policies, the best lawyers money could buy, not to mention his squeaky-clean business reputation.

Even if Johnny got to his most trusted inner circle... we couldn't guarantee Fascini wouldn't worm his way out. To the outside eye, Mike Fascini was an upstanding member of society. But everyone had secrets. You just had to know where to look and how to exploit them.

My father regarded me and scoffed, "Niccolò, have some faith. This will work. Mike Fascini and that son of his will pay. No one messes with the Marchetti and gets away with it." His hand tightened around his glass. "No one."

I gave him a small nod.

"I have to ask though, Niccolò. Are you sure you don't want that piece of shit taken care of for what he did to

Arianne? She would never have to know. I can arrange for it to happen discreetly. Make it look like a suicide."

A bolt of anger rippled through me. "He lives. It's what she wants." No matter how much it pained me to say the words.

My father rubbed his jaw. "You are a stronger man than I. Either way, he will never get within a foot of Arianne again."

It was enough.

It had to be.

"It could be a few days before everything is in place. We keep this between us, do you understand?"

"I know the drill."

"There is something else..."

I went rigid.

Of course there was.

"She will need to return to her father's estate until it is done."

"No fucking way." I lunged forward.

"Nicco, hear me out, Son. We can't risk Fascini discovering our plan. There is also the small matter of Roberto sitting tight. She needs to talk to him."

"She can call him—"

"This is how it has to be. She will be safe. The estate is heavily guarded, and Luis will be there with her. Right now, we need to make sure everything falls into place."

"Then I'm going. I won't leave her again. I promised her." I'd promised myself.

My father's hand slammed down on the table. "Niccolò, I am not asking you. I am telling you, this is the way it has to be. The end is in sight, Son. Do not lose your cool now. She'll be safe there."

"If anything... *anything* happens to her, I will hold you personally responsible."

"I would expect no less. But she will be safe. Knowing

she's back at her father's estate will appease Fascini until we make our move."

I didn't like it.

I didn't like it at all.

But what choice did I have?

Arianne had made her deal with the Devil and now we had no choice but to see it through.

My father let out a heavy sigh. "You should go be with her. I'm sure you have much to discuss. She doesn't need to leave immediately. Take the night, she can leave in the morning. And then you stay put at the cabin. Do you understand me?"

The urge to defy him burned inside me. But this wasn't only about me.

It was about Arianne.

"I understand."

"Good." He gave me a swift nod. "It won't be for too long, and then you can look to the future."

"About that... Do you have stipulations for the wedding?"

"Once Fascini has been dealt with, I imagine Roberto will need some time to adjust to our new... arrangement. But I would prefer we handled matters sooner rather than later."

I winced at his crass words. This was my life he was talking about. Mine and Arianne's future.

Our wedding.

But he wasn't my father right now, he was the boss.

"There is much to think about. Where you'll have the ceremony, a honeymoon," his lip curved, "where you'll live, make a home for yourselves."

I sank back in the chair, letting out a heavy sigh.

"It's happening fast." His expression softened. "I understand that."

"Do you?" It came out harsher than I intended.

"You are my son. Arianne is to be my daughter-in-law.

You will want for nothing. Just say the word and you will have everything you want."

"I need to talk to her."

He gave me a sharp nod. "Of course. Go be with her. I can handle things here."

"You'll keep me in the loop?"

I didn't like taking a back seat, not where Scott was concerned, but Arianne needed me. And truth be told, I couldn't trust myself to do the right thing where he was concerned.

"Of course. You can trust me on this, Son, you have my word."

Draining the rest of my drink, I stood up and placed it on my father's desk. He let me get to the door before he stopped me.

"Niccolò," he said. "One day you will understand what it means to sit in this chair. But I have faith in you. And I have faith that Arianne is strong enough to stand at your side. This is your legacy... and now it is hers. And maybe it was always supposed to be this way."

Enzo gave me a ride back to the cabin. Arianne and Tristan were deep in conversation when I walked through the room. Luis caught my attention though, motioning for me to meet him in the kitchen.

"How did it go?" he asked.

"My father will handle it."

"And Roberto?"

"Tomorrow, I need you to take Arianne back to her father's estate and keep her there until this is all over."

"She's not going to like that, but it makes sense. Antonio wants Fascini to believe Roberto is complying."

I nodded, glancing over at her and Tristan. She caught my eye, smiling. God, that smile. "You stay with her at all times. If anything, and I mean *anything* feels off, you get her out of there."

"I will protect her with my life."

"I know you will."

"You know, I never imagined I would grow up to call a Marchetti a friend, but you're a good guy, Nicco, and I am happy for you both. Truly."

"Thanks. Can you take Tristan home and make yourself scarce tonight?"

"Of course. I'll come by first thing for her."

"What's happening?"

I sucked in a harsh breath, turning to find Arianne staring at us. "You're not supposed to be listening, Bambolina."

"Did something happen?"

"My father feels it would be best if you return to your father's estate while he takes care of things."

"When?" She was a picture of composure.

"Tomorrow morning."

"Good."

"Good?" I frowned.

"I should probably speak to my father face to face. It is long overdue."

"Come here." Pulling her into my arms, I held her tight. She'd changed so much in just a few weeks. Arianne was no longer the shy naive girl I'd met in that alley, but a strong woman who refused to bend to the will of the men in her life.

I was so fucking proud of her.

So in awe of who she was... and who she would continue to become.

Arianne commanded the respect of those around her, but

she didn't do it with fear. She did it with humility and compassion.

"Luis will be with you."

"And I'll be around," Tristan said, approaching the three of us. His eyes locked on mine, mutual understanding passing between us.

"It's okay," Arianne said. "I'm okay. This is going to work. It has to. And then," she gazed up at me, "we get to put all this behind us."

"Is your mom okay?" I asked the second Arianne stepped into the room. After Luis and Tristan had left, she'd wanted to call her mother ahead of tomorrow.

"I didn't tell her everything, just that I'd be back tomorrow."

Done adding firewood to the open flames, I stepped back, holding out my hand for her.

"What is all this?" Her eyes went to the pillows on the rug, the strawberries and champagne on the coffee table.

"This is our last night together." My voice cracked.

"It's only for a little while." Arianne pressed her hands to my chest. "And then, when it's over, we have forever."

"Now that," I slid my arm around her back and dipped her, pressing my lips to the hollow of her throat, "I like the sound of."

Her soft laughter rose above the crackle of the fire and the quiet background music playing out through the Bluetooth speaker on the sideboard. "Do you know what kind of wedding you would like?" I pulled her back up to me.

"Honestly, I don't care as long as you're waiting for me at the end of the aisle."

"I thought all girls imagined their wedding day?"

"I'm not all girls, Nicco."

"No, you're not. My father asked us where we'd like to live... have you thought about that?"

Her lips parted on a small gasp, and I knew then, she hadn't.

"It's okay," I said. "We have time to figure it all out."

"It all happened fast, huh?"

"Does that scare you?"

Arianne shook her head. "It should, I know that. But when I think of sharing my life with you... it feels right."

My hand glided up her spine, pressing her closer to me. "Because it is right, Bambolina. I have never been surer about anything than I am about my love for you."

"Maybe somewhere in the middle. University Hill or the city. I'd like to be close to Nora." Her dreamy expression fell. "Oh God, Nora—"

"Will be fine." I kissed her forehead. "She just wants you to be happy."

"I know. I just feel bad. College was supposed to be this big adventure, the start of our freedom..."

"You can still have a life, Bambolina. I will never clip your wings, Arianne." I brushed my lips over hers. "I only want to make you happy."

"You do; so, so much." She deepened the kiss, sweeping her tongue into my mouth and tangling it with mine.

Need pulsed through me, and I picked Arianne up. She wrapped her legs around me as I dropped to my knees gently, before lying her down on the soft rug. "Are you hungry?"

I plucked a strawberry from the container and hovered it over her pink swollen lips. "Open, Bambolina."

Her mouth parted letting me feed the fruit to her. "Hmm," she moaned. "It's good."

I pulled it away and juice spilled over her chin. Dipping my head, I licked the trail of sticky sweet nectar away.

"Nicco." My name was a whispered plea on her lips.

"Tell me what you want, amore mio?"

"You." She twisted her fingers into my sweater, dragging me closer "I want you."

"You have me."

Possession flared in her eyes, making my chest swell. "Then show me," she uttered.

And I did.

All night long.

CHAPTER 28

ARIANNE

"How are you feeling?" Luis asked as we rolled to a stop at the gatehouse. The guard took one look at us and waved us through.

"I'm okay," I said, staring out at my father's estate. The place that had once been my childhood playground no longer felt like home. Instead, it was a lingering memory, faded by time.

"The last time I was here, my father sat me down in front of Mike and Scott and told me I was promised to him. I'll never forgive him for that."

"And I don't blame you."

"But?"

Luis drove up the winding driveway and came to a stop next to my father's town car. "People make mistakes, Arianne, but it doesn't mean their mistakes should define them."

"You're a good man, Luis. But I need time." And even then, it might not be enough to forgive my father.

"I try." He gave me a wistful smile. "Ready?"

I inhaled a deep breath and squared my shoulders. "As I'll ever be."

He climbed out, coming around to open my door.

"Arianne, sweetheart." My mother came running from the house, wrapping me into her slim arms with such force the air *whooshed* from my lungs. "I've been so worried." She held me at arm's length.

"I'm okay."

Her gaze narrowed. "You seem different." She studied me.

"We should probably talk. Where is my father?"

"He's in the sunroom. Since Mike's... warning," the word came out strangled, "he rarely leaves."

"You know about that?" My father had been shutting her out, so I was a little taken aback to find out she knew.

"He finally broke down and told me everything. But don't worry, sweetheart, he's going to fix it."

I grimaced. She was still blinded by my father's empty promises, and it made my heart ache. "We should go inside." I glanced to the security men posted either side of the door.

Luis followed us into the house, moving ahead of me, no doubt as a precaution. Restless energy flowed through me, making my stomach vibrate. Since discovering the camera feeds into the house, my father's men had swept the place and eradicated them all. But I knew Luis and Nicco still had concerns. It was probably why my father was in the sunroom. It was one of the few rooms that hadn't been bugged.

"Father," I said, stepping inside.

The formidable Roberto Capizola was a mess. Dark circles ringed his eyes and his attire was unkempt. He reminded me of some of the clients at the VCTI; people who didn't have the luxury of a hot shower and fresh clothes.

"Arianne, mio tesoro. You are safe."

"No thanks to you." My voice was flat.

My mother inhaled a shaky breath. "Arianne, that isn't—"

"Fair, Mamma? None of this is. But it doesn't matter." I moved to one of the soft leather couches. "Everything will be taken care of soon enough."

"Whatever do you mean?"

"She means... she sold me out." My father's voice held a trace of disappointment.

"I did what is best. You made a deal with the Devil. With the man who tried to kill me and start a war between you and the Marchetti. When that didn't work, he turned to more legitimate options. He wanted to control you, to use you... and you let him." Indignation raced through my veins.

"Roberto?" My mother's mouth hung open as if she couldn't believe it.

"Oh, he didn't tell you?" She'd implied she knew everything, but I should have known he would still keep secrets from her. "It wasn't Antonio Marchetti who tried to kill me, Mamma, it was Mike."

"No," she gasped, "that's not—"

"It is true." He hung his head in shame. "Mike wants to destroy me, to destroy us."

"I did what you could not," I said. "I went to Antonio and asked for his help."

His eyes slid to mine, burning with contempt. "That man is—"

"Willing to save your life."

"At a cost?" he scoffed. "I would rather..." My father swallowed the words.

"Die?" My brow raised. "Nobody is going to die. Antonio

is willing to hand Mike and Scott over to the authorities and in exchange he will become your partner."

"Absolutely not!" He shot up.

"It is done. I am the Capizola heir. I am eighteen now. One day your empire will be mine."

"I won't do it. I won't just hand over the business to that... that criminal."

"That *criminal* took me in after Scott, the man you wanted me to marry, raped me. He promised me protection when my own father wouldn't believe my words. That man is going to one day be my father-in-law. So yes, Father, you will do this. Otherwise, I will be dead to you."

"Arianne!" My mother's face went as white as a sheet, but I kept my attention on my father.

"I am marrying Nicco. You can either get on board with it, or not."

"You cannot trust them..." he murmured, scrubbing a hand over his face.

"Trust is earned, Father. And Nicco and his father have done a damn sight more to earn my trust than you ever have."

Devastation etched into his expression, but he needed to hear this. He needed to understand how deeply his betrayal had hurt me.

My eyes stung with unshed tears, but I would not cry.

Not today.

Not in front of the man who had broken my heart one too many times.

"I may never forgive you, but this is a start to you righting your wrongs."

He slumped down in the chair, a pained whimper leaving his lips. "I guess I don't really have a choice, do I?"

"No, Father." I looked at the man I'd once worshipped. The man I thought could do no wrong.

We were like strangers now.

Two people bound together by nothing more than blood and bad memories.

"You do not."

~

There was a knock at my door. "Come in," I called.

"It's only me." Mom slipped into my room. Although it didn't really feel like my room anymore.

"I just wanted to check and see how you are?"

"I'll be glad when this is all over," I admitted.

"I still can't believe..." She took a shuddering breath, moving to the chair in the corner of the room. "You must hate us."

"I don't..." I let out a weary sigh. "It isn't hatred I feel, Mamma. I just don't understand how we ended up here."

"I find myself asking that same question a lot lately." Her lips quivered as she inhaled a shaky breath. "Your father has always been overprotective, but he had his reasons. And then after the attempt on your life at the school... well, he changed after that. Became obsessed with protecting you. Despite all your father's faults, his actions came from a place of love, Arianne."

"I can't forget... I won't. What Scott did to me... it changed me, Mamma."

"Oh, sweetheart, I know. I know it will take time."

"It will take more than time. They say sons are born in their father's image. Well, I am my father's daughter. If he taught me anything, it's that everything comes at a price. This is mine."

"You're so young though. I knew things between you and Nicco were serious, but marriage, mia cara? That's very... permanent."

"You married Father when you were barely twenty and you were more than willing to give me away to Scott. You weren't worried about my age then, Mamma." Disbelief coated my words.

"Arianne, please…" She inhaled a shaky breath. "You're right, you father and I were young, but we had been together for almost four years by then." She gave me a weak smile and it wasn't lost on me that she'd chosen to ignore my dig about Scott. "This is all so new… and he's—"

"Mafioso?"

She flinched.

"Nicco would give his life for mine. Do you understand that? He would risk everything… for me."

"I know, but—"

"No, Mamma. I am eighteen. I can make my own decisions, and I choose him. I choose Nicco."

Nothing would come between us. Not my father, my mother, or his family.

"You need to talk to him." I lifted my chin in defiance. "You need to make him understand that this is happening. It would make everything a lot smoother if he gets on board."

"Very well." She gave me a small nod and stood. "I will let you get some rest."

I waited until she was almost out of the door. "Mamma?"

"Yes, sweetheart?" Her voice was laced with sadness and regret.

"I would really like it if you were at the wedding. Father should be there too, but I'll understand it if he'd prefer not to come."

"I will speak to him," she said.

They were my parents. To not have them there felt wrong. But they had to decide what they could live with, just as I'd had to decide.

And if they couldn't come to terms with me marrying Nicco, then I wouldn't beg.

~

After spending the rest of the afternoon and evening in the fragile sanctuary of my bedroom, I'd fallen into a restless sleep. I didn't want to be here, but I knew it was the only way, for now.

I showered, taking my time to wash away the lingering pain of yesterday's meeting with my father. When I went back into my room, my cell phone was ringing. My heart swelled at Nicco's name flashing across the screen.

"Bambolina, how are you?" he asked.

"I hate it here," I confessed. "I hate him, Nicco. For everything he's done, for everything he's put me through..." A whimper escaped me, but I steeled myself. We were so close now. So close to putting all this behind us. Antonio and his men would make sure Mike Fascini was no longer a threat, and Nicco and I would be married.

"Amore mio, what is it?"

"I hate him, I do. Yet, I can't help but feel sorry for him."

"He is your father; you can love him and hate him at the same time."

"I guess you're right. Part of me knows that deep down he probably had my interests at heart, but then I think about everything Scott has put me through and I..." My body trembled with pain, with the sting of betrayal.

Nicco hissed under his breath. "I should have killed him."

"No, Nicco," I rushed out. "I don't want you to carry that burden. Not for me." They had the evidence of what he'd done to me. It would be enough to seal his fate. Scott would follow his father to rot inside a prison cell, and I would be safe.

"When are you going to realize, Bambolina? I would do anything for you." The intensity behind Nicco's words made my breath catch. "I love you more than anything. The thought of him hurting you..."

"He can't hurt me anymore. He'll get what's coming to him, Nicco." I had to believe that.

"You are too good for this life, too pure." His torment crackled over the line. "I fear I am a selfish bastard for tethering you to my side."

"It is not your choice to make."

"These violent delights have violent ends..." he whispered the words.

"You're quoting Shakespeare at me?" I chuckled, but it came out strained.

Nicco was quiet, brooding. I knew he didn't agree with the deal I'd made with his father, and part of me wondered if I was foolish to think it could all end peacefully. But I had to believe that after everything we'd been through, we deserved this. We deserved to walk into the future with our hands unbloodied and our consciences clean.

I knew life with Nicco would mean skirting the line between light and dark, good and bad. But this was different. I didn't want this—what Scott had done—to come between us anymore than it already had.

When I didn't reply, Nicco let out a heavy sigh. "I would die for you Arianne." His voice was a low growl, "never forget that."

A shudder worked through me. "Then I would die with you." Because I didn't want to live in a world without him.

"Bambolina..."

"No, Nicco. You don't get to say stuff like that to me without expecting a reply. If something happens to you..." I couldn't say the words.

"Nothing is going to happen to me. You made the deal with my father. He will keep his word."

"I just want to put all this behind us. I wish you were here." With Nicco's arms around me, I felt strong. I felt like we could weather any storm.

"Soon, amore mio. Soon."

CHAPTER 29

NICCO

I snatched up my phone and rushed out, "Yes?"

"Niccolò," my father's gruff voice replied. "Everything is in place. Our friend down at the local PD will hit the Fascini this evening, when they are least expecting it."

A potent mix of relief and anger flooded me.

"Son?"

"I..." I dragged a hand through my hair. "That's good."

"I know it is not what you had hoped for." There was a distinctive lilt in his voice. "But this is a good outcome, for Arianne. For the Family."

"I know, I just..." Fuck, I wanted Scott to pay for his sins. I wanted to watch him bleed, knowing that I would spend my life loving the girl he would never get to hurt again.

"Be strong, figlio mio. Soon this will all be over, and you and Arianne will be able to get on with your lives."

"It doesn't feel right," I murmured. "Arianne is mine to protect, mine to..." The words died on my lips.

"Don't make the same mistakes I did, Niccolò. Don't let your need for vengeance eat away at your soul, not when you have something to live for. Arianne is safe, she is strong, and she will make you a good wife."

His words were like a fist around my heart. I wanted the happy ending, I did. But letting Scott live, it felt like a giant fucking mistake.

"What happened to taking him out and making it look like an accident?" I threw his words back at him, and he chuckled.

"The offer still stands, but I know you won't do it. Because that would be a heavier burden to carry. Arianne wants justice, Niccolò. She wants to believe that the authorities will do the right thing. She is not ready to accept that our world is—"

"Don't, just don't." Pain splintered me in two.

"Let me handle it, Son. Trust me to do this for you. For you both." I gave him a sharp nod even though he couldn't see me. "I know you're probably going out of your mind, so I'm sending you a distraction. Sit tight. It will soon all be over."

Just then, the familiar rumble of Enzo's GTO caught my attention. "They're here?" I asked him.

"You shouldn't be alone, Niccolò. They are your cousins, your brothers, be with them. I'll talk to you when it is done."

We hung up and I went outside.

"We brought supplies," Matteo called, waving two bottles of scotch in his hands.

Enzo tipped his chin at me as he approached carrying a pack of beer. "You good?"

"What do you think?"

He roped his arm around my neck and pulled me back toward the cabin. "I think we need to get lit and fuck some shit up."

Usually, I would have told him to rein it in.

But not today.

Today I needed my friends.

I needed to forget.

"It's the right call," Matteo said later, as we sat around the fire pit, drinking beer and shooting the shit.

"Like fuck it is." Enzo slammed his beer down on the arm of his chair. "That sick fucker deserves to bleed."

"Ari—"

"She doesn't get it, Matt. She doesn't understand this life."

"E," I warned. I had enough anger zipping through me without him making it worse.

"He raped her, Nic. And as if that wasn't enough, he took a gun and pushed it into her mouth and—"

"Don't," it came out a low growl.

I was losing myself, my thin rope of control fraying.

"You should be angry," he went on. "You should be fucking—"

"Enzo," Matteo glanced precariously between us, "this isn't helping."

"No, let him talk," I seethed, my eyes growing thin. "Let him tell us what he really thinks."

"You don't have the balls," he sneered. "You're letting her call all the shots. You're Niccolò fucking Marchetti and you're out here, hiding like a little punk ass—"

I shot up out of the chair, fists clenched at my sides. "Say that again."

Enzo stood up, his cool gaze trained right on me. "You heard me." He stepped up to me, the air crackling with anticipation. "You don't have the ball—"

I wound my arm back and let my fist fly at his face. Enzo jerked back, my knuckles clipping his jaw.

"Come on, guys." Matteo was out of his chair too. "This isn't what Uncle Toni had in mind."

But it was too late.

Enzo had pushed me too far. He'd unleashed my inner beast and there was no going back until it had its pound of flesh.

My cousin rubbed his jaw, smirking at me. "You really want to do this?"

I shrugged. "Scared you can't take me?"

Matteo let out a mumble of disapproval, but Enzo and I only had eyes for each other. He watched me, his jaw set and eyes narrowed, as I shucked out of my jacket and threw it on the chair.

It had been too long since I fought, *really* fought. I'd been too preoccupied with Arianne, and I couldn't deny that she settled me. When we were together, it was easy to get lost in her, to bathe in her light. But sitting here, staring into the flames as they licked the night's sky, I'd succumbed to the darkness again.

And Enzo knew it.

He fucking knew where my head was at and he pushed me anyway.

He came at me like a bull out of the gates, wrapping his bulky arms around me and tackling me to the ground. We landed with a *thud*, the air sucking clean from my lungs. I slammed my shoulder into his, leveraging my weight and we rolled. Enzo glared up at me, and the fucker grinned. He actually grinned.

"Something funny?" My brow raised.

"You need this. I'm happy to oblige. Don't punk out on me now."

"So this is for my benefit?"

He shrugged. "Maybe I have some stuff to work off too."

"You two are fucking crazy," Matteo grumbled from over by the fire.

"I don't—

Enzo thrashed beneath me, bucking me off, and I clambered to my feet, circling him as he stood. Adrenaline raced through my veins as I studied my cousin. Enzo was a decent fighter, quick on his feet and unpredictable, but he'd underestimated one thing.

I was a man walking a razor's edge; fueled by love and tormented by the need for vengeance.

I rushed at him, sending a sharp uppercut to his jaw. His head snapped back, his grunts of pain filling the air. "I'll give you that one." He spat a mouthful of blood at my feet.

Strangled laughter rumbled in my chest. I felt wild, consumed by anger, and shackled by love. I wanted to protect Arianne, to worship and cherish her. But part of me also wanted to deliver Scott's head on a platter, to paint Verona red with his blood.

"Imagine I'm him," Enzo taunted. "Imagine it was me who hurt her. Me who—"

I lunged again, but Enzo anticipated my move, ducking to the left and deflecting my fist with a right hook of his own. Pain exploded in my cheek, but I relished the burn. I soaked it up, letting it feed the fire raging inside me.

"Seriously, guys, maybe we should just—"

We ignored Matteo's pleas. It was on, no holding back. Enzo wanted me to imagine he was Scott? Then he needed to be prepared to be torn limb from limb.

A shiver rolled through me as I cracked my neck. Enzo's eyes grew to thin slits, his lip twisting into a smirk. "There he is, the Prince of fucking Hearts. Time to show me what you got."

I stepped forward; fists ready... I wouldn't just show him.

I'd annihilate him.

~

"Pleased with yourself?" Matteo handed me an ice-cold compress before throwing one at Enzo.

"Watch it, fucker," he grumbled. He was slouched on the couch, his lip swollen and eye split wide open.

I had my fair share of injuries: split knuckles, a bruised rib or two, not to mention the ugly purple bruise around my left eye. But despite the persistent throb of pain radiating through me, I felt better. Lighter somehow.

Enzo had taunted me because he knew I couldn't just sit and do nothing.

And it had worked.

"I don't know about E," I said, glancing over at him. "But I feel great."

He smirked, flipping me off. "You swing like a girl."

"Tell that to the split in your lip."

"It worked though, didn't it?"

"Yeah," my voice grew thick, "it did." I held his glare, silently telling him how much I appreciated it.

"I'll always have your back." He gave me a sharp nod.

"You've lost your fucking mind." Matteo blew out a long breath.

"We can't all be lovers like you, Matt." Enzo nursed his jaw. "Some of us need to fight. We need it to hurt."

"You almost killed each other."

"Nah, I barely scratched the surface," I chuckled.

"Fuck you, Cous." Enzo shoved his arms behind his head, wincing in pain. "I almost had you."

My shoulders relaxed, the tension ebbing away. I hadn't realized how much I'd needed this until Enzo's fist collided with my face.

Fighting had always been my outlet, the way I'd dealt with my demons. But Arianne was changing me, molding me into something new, something more.

"Do you think it's done?" Enzo asked.

"He'll call when it is." It was almost nine, the sun long disappeared behind the tree line.

"Shit, I would have paid to see that fucker dragged away in a cop car. Smug asshole won't know what's hit him."

I grabbed my cell phone and opened my messages. I hadn't replied to Arianne's earlier message, I'd been too busy breaking my cousin's face.

Are you okay?

Her reply came straight through.

I am. Are you? I was getting worried.

Me and Enzo were working through some things...

What things?

I smiled at that. My sweet Bambolina always asking questions.

Just working off some steam.

. . .

You were fighting?

It's not what you think...

So tell me, what is it?

I know this is what you want, Bambolina, but I really wanted to make that piece of shit pay for ever laying a hand on you.

I waited for her reply, my heart crashing against my chest.

I know, and I'm sorry I took that from you, I am. But I couldn't do it, Nicco. I couldn't stand by and watch you lose yourself.

Slipping off the stool, I turned to my cousins and said, "I'll be back."

"Tell Ari we said hey." I heard the amusement in Matteo's voice, and I flipped him off over my shoulder.

I knew they thought I was whipped. That Arianne held my balls—and heart—in the palm of her hand.

But I didn't care.

All I cared about was her.

Doing right by her.

That's why I was sitting here, following orders like the dutiful son—for her. Not for my father or the Family.

Only her.

Inside our bedroom, I closed the door and sat on the edge of the bed before dialing her number.

"Nicco?"

"I needed to hear your voice," I confessed, running a hand over my head.

"Are you hurt?"

"You have such little faith in me, Bambolina?" My lips curved.

"I don't like the idea of you fighting with your cousin." Her voice was small, uncertain, but there was also a trace of disapproval there.

"It's not how you think. He was... helping me."

"Because you need to fight."

"Sometimes, yes."

"Because of me?"

I wanted to tell her no, that my demons were my own. But the truth was, I didn't want to lie.

"Nicco?"

"I want to kill him, Arianne. I want to take my gun and blow his brains out. He deserves no less."

"But don't you see, killing him won't change anything, and if you do it, I might lose you." A beat passed, the blood pounding between my ears. "I can't ever lose you."

"You won't. I'm right here."

"I know you don't understand it, Nicco. But this is just something I needed to do. One day, I hope you'll see that."

"Bambolina..." I breathed through the onslaught of emotion crashing over me. I was a mafia prince, torn between wanting to avenge the girl I loved, and honor her wishes.

The decision had been taken out of my hands, but I knew if I asked my father, he could make it happen. But I also knew that it still wouldn't be good enough. I wanted it to be my hands stealing the air from his lungs as I squeezed his throat. My pistol poised against the small circle of skin between his eyes.

Just then another call came through and I checked the screen.

"Nicco, what is it?"

"My father is calling, I need to go. But I'll call you later, okay?"

"Okay." I heard her sigh deeply and the sound almost splintered me in two.

"It won't be long now, I promise. Hold on for me, okay? I need you to hold on just for a little bit more."

"I love you."

"I love you too." *More then you'll ever know.*

I ended the call and hit answer, striding out of the bedroom toward my cousins. "Is it done?" I asked the second I heard my father's breath.

"It is."

Thank fuck. Relief spread through me. But I quickly realized he didn't sound pleased.

"What happened?"

Enzo and Matteo shot upright, their eyes asking me a hundred questions I didn't yet have the answers too.

"Mike Fascini was taken into police custody. He's down at the local station now."

"And Scott?" My skin vibrated.

"He got away. I don't have all the facts yet, but it looks like he managed to escape."

"You're joking right? That's a joke?"

"I wish it were, Son." Disappointment lingered in his voice.

"You promised me... you fucking promised—"

"I know, I know." He let out a heavy sigh, and I could imagine his dark expression. "I don't know what happened, Niccolò, but I will find out. And I won't rest until we find him. Okay?"

Fuck.

He was still out there.

Scott was out there, and Arianne was—

"I have to go to her."

"I know, Son. Go be with your woman. I'll call you when I have an update."

Enzo and Matteo were both standing now, concern glittering in their eyes.

"We're going to her?" Matteo asked, and I nodded.

"Scott escaped. That fucker managed to get away."

"Fuck," Enzo muttered. "What do you need?"

"We need to go to Arianne, now."

She wasn't safe.

As long as Scott was out there somewhere, she wasn't safe.

Luis met us at the gatehouse. His expression said it all; he was as pissed about Scott evading arrest as the rest of us.

"What the hell happened?" he ground out as I got out of the car to greet him.

"We don't know yet. Have you told Arianne?"

"No, but she knows something is wrong."

"Okay," I let out a small breath.

"Come on, she's inside. Let him through, Harlen." He motioned to the security guard. He glowered at us, but the gates began to recede.

"Don't mind him." Luis gripped my shoulder. "He knows what's at stake. They all do."

"You're a good man, Vitelli."

Luis gave me a firm nod. "I'll meet you back at the house. I want to do a perimeter sweep and talk to all the guards."

"Fucking hell," Enzo said as I climbed back into the car. "This place is like the White House."

He wasn't wrong. The Capizola estate was huge, and right in the center, stood the house with its grand balconies and alabaster pillars flanking the entrance.

"Is that...?" Enzo started to growl.

"Relax." I levelled him with a hard look. "Roberto knows the deal. He might be a piece of shit, but Arianne is still his daughter. He'll want her safe."

He snorted at that, and I knew what he was thinking. Roberto had practically handed Arianne over to Scott and the Fascini, gift-wrapped with a bow.

Anger trickled up my spine, but I shook it off. I wasn't here for Roberto; I was here for his daughter.

The car rolled to a stop, and we all climbed out.

"You," Roberto seethed, his eyes alight with contempt.

"Watch it, old man." Enzo stepped forward, but a voice gave us pause.

"Nicco?" Arianne flew down the steps and didn't stop until she was in my arms, her face buried in my chest.

"Ssh, Bambolina." I held her tight. Roberto caught my eye, a strange expression passing over his face.

"Something's wrong." Arianne eased back, craning her neck to look at me. "What is it? Tell me."

I stared down into honey eyes that had captured my soul and never given it back and whispered the two little words that had the power to push me into the darkness. "Scott escaped."

Her body tensed, her grip on my jacket tightening. "He got away?"

I nodded, watching her expression. But she didn't break. My strong Bambolina steeled herself and inhaled a sharp breath. "It's okay," she said calmly. "You'll find him."

"And if we don't?" someone asked.

"Scott would be a fool to try anything now." Her eyes never left mine, and then she said nine little words that spun my world. "He knows Nicco would kill him if he did."

"I..."

"It's okay." She leaned up, ghosting her fingers across my jaw. Her warmth seeped into me, wrapping around me and taking hold. "Scott is gone, he can't hurt me anymore."

She was too calm.

Too composed.

Enzo glanced at me, arching his brow.

"We need to stay here for now," I said. "Wait for word from my father. He has his men looking for Scott right now. If he's still in Verona, we'll find him."

Arianne took my hand and started moving toward the door. But Roberto stepped forward. "Figlia mia, I'm not sure—"

"Don't," she seethed. "Niccolò is my fiancé, Father. He is here to protect me. To protect us. You are going to make him welcome or you can go retire to your study." Her eyes bore into his until Roberto dipped his head and nodded.

"Please," he almost choked over the word, "join us."

Enzo looked impressed. Matteo grinned. And me? I stared at Arianne with nothing but love and pride for the woman she'd become.

When I'd first met her, she was so unsure and uncertain of her place in the world. But now, standing here, she was strong. And brave. So fucking brave.

She was no longer a pawn in a game she didn't understand.

She was the Queen.

My Queen.

And I was going to spend my life showing her.

CHAPTER 30

ARIANNE

ne month later...

"Holy crap, babe, you look..." Nora fanned her face. "Tears, I have actual tears. Quick someone hand me a paper towel."

Genevieve grabbed a box of tissues and thrust it at Nora. "No crying. We can't have anyone spoiling Ari's make up. Sei bella come il sole." Her expression softened as she took me in.

"My brother is going to freak." Alessia caught my hand in hers.

"Oh, I don't know about that, Sia. The two of you will steal the show."

They looked flawless in their pale lilac dresses. With a halter-style top that scooped low in the front and back, the silk flowed over their hips and skimmed the floor. Their hair had been braided to one side and pulled into an intricate bun, woven with flowers matching the Baby's Breath and Larkspur of my bridal posy.

"Okay," Genevieve held out a tissue for me. "Blot and then I think we're done."

I did as she instructed, leaving a smudge of lipstick behind.

"Ready?" Nora helped me off the stool I'd spent the last hour sitting on while Nora and Genevieve took care of my makeup and hair.

Nicco had wanted to pay someone, but I didn't want any fuss. Besides, there was something special about sharing this moment with my best friend, my soon to be sister-in-law, and Genevieve. I hadn't quite distinguished her place in my life yet, but she had become a fast friend over the last few weeks, the two of us bonding over the Marchetti men in our lives. I wasn't sure if it was official, but I had it on good authority she was Antonio's date for the wedding.

I let her fuss over my dress, smoothing out the lace tail and arranging the long veil over my hair. Finally, they stepped back to look at me.

"Oh my god," Alessia breathed.

Nora had tears collecting in the corners of her eyes as she smiled at me. "You look amazing."

The door creaked behind me, but I didn't move for fear of ruining my hair.

"Sorry I'm late," Mom's voice filtered into our room.

The Blackstone Country Club had gone above and beyond to accommodate us on such short notice, but I wasn't surprised. I was quickly learning that being a Marchetti carried weight. They had transformed the place into something fit for a princess.

"Oh my... Arianne, sweetheart." Tears filled her eyes. "You look…"

"Thank you." My body vibrated with nervous energy.

"That boy has nothing to worry about." I frowned and she chuckled. "Nicco needed some final words of encouragement." A knowing smile played on her lips.

"You spoke to him?" My head whipped up.

"Hair, watch the hair," Nora scolded.

"Oops, sorry." I shot her an apologetic look before turning to my mother once again. "You saw him? Is he—"

"Fine, just some last-minute jitters. Tristan, Matteo, and Enzo are in the bar with him."

"The bar?" I groaned. "I hope someone is supervising them."

I'd witnessed the aftermath of the bachelor party. Nicco had ruined my favorite pair of sneakers after puking all over them before declaring his undying love for me and then passing out on the bathroom floor.

"Don't worry, Enzo is still in the doghouse for letting him get so drunk." Alessia gave me a wink.

"Ready?" Nora had positioned herself in between me and the mirror.

"No," my mom shrieked. "It is bad luck for a bride to see herself before the groom."

I rolled my eyes. After everything we'd been through to get here, I wasn't about to let a little Italian superstition worry me.

Moving over to the full-length ornate mirror in the corner of the room, I inhaled a deep breath.

"Wait," Genevieve said. "At least remove a shoe first."

"A shoe?" Nora balked.

"For luck," my mom added.

"Fine, take it." I lifted my foot and let Alessia slip off my ivory silk heeled pump.

"Ready?" Nora had moved in front of me, blocking my view.

"As I'll ever be." My heart was beating wildly in my chest but the second she stepped out of the way, and I saw myself, it stopped.

"I look—"

"Beautiful, sweetheart." Mom grabbed my hand, coming into the mirror's view.

My skin was glowing, my eyes wide with wonder and anticipation. But it was the dress that took my breath away. Layers of sheer lace gathered at my waist and fell around my body like a delicate waterfall. The batwing sleeves gave the illusion I was wearing a cape, but when I turned around and glanced over my shoulder, I saw the dress cut into a deep V. It ended at the bottom of my spine and flowed into a line of pearl buttons. It was simple yet beautiful, sexy yet demure.

It was perfect.

"I love it." I'd known the second I'd laid eyes on it; it was the one. I hadn't even tried any others. We found each other and it was meant to be.

Just like Nicco and me.

"Okay, now all that's left is your something borrowed and something blue." Nora approached me, a small silver and sapphire hair pin. She leaned over me, sliding it into my hair. Before flinging an ivory and lace garter at me.

"Nora!" My cheeks flushed

"What? It's tradition. Tell her." She looked to my mom and Genevieve who nodded.

"La giarrettiera." Genevieve winked.

"Thank you." I choked out over the lump in my throat.

"And something new." Alessia approached me next, a small jewelry box in her hand. "Nicco wanted me to give this to you." She flipped the lid, revealing a silver bangle. "Can I?"

I nodded, desperately fighting the emotion swelling inside me.

"It's says, 'tu mi completi'."

"You complete me," my mom sighed. "So romantic. My turn." She advanced toward me. "You can't walk down the aisle without your something old. It was my mother's, and hers before that." She lifted the small butterfly brooch and slid it into place on my dress. "Vola in alto, farfalla mia."

Fly free, my butterfly.

"Mom…"

She wiped at her eyes. "I'm sorry, for everything. But today, this is your day, Arianne."

"Damn right," Nora added, cutting the heavy tension. "And Nicco is going to die when he sees you."

"Hopefully he won't," strained laughter spilled from my lips, "I kind of like having him around."

We were currently living in the apartment in my father's building. Nora had officially moved back to the dorms, but unofficially, she still stayed over a lot. I think we both knew once today was over, everything would change, so we were clinging onto each other for as long as possible. Nicco didn't seem to mind. In fact, more often than not, it was his idea to invite her over. Sometimes Matteo came too. Alessia even stopped by on the odd occasion. But never Enzo.

"We have five minutes before Allegra shows up and starts barking orders."

Allegra was the wedding coordinator, but Nora liked to call her Bitchzilla.

"Be nice," I said. "It's her job."

Genevieve ushered the girls over to the door, arming them with their posies. Nora would walk in first with Tristan, and Alessia would follow with Matteo. Then I would enter while Enzo waited upfront with Nicco.

God, I couldn't wait to see him. It felt like it had been days when it had been a little under twenty-four hours.

"Did he come?" I asked my mother, but her grim expression told me all I needed to know.

"He loves you very much, Arianne, but this has been hard on him."

"He made his choice." I stuffed down my feelings toward my father for another time.

Nothing would ruin today.

I'd made my choice just as he had made his.

"You should know he loves you very much, Arianne, we both do. Gosh, sweetheart, this is it. The first day of the rest of your life. Are you absolutely sure this is what you want?"

"I have never been more certain of anything."

She gave me a small nod.

"It is showtime," Allegra's voice rang out down the hall. "Grazie a Dio, you look sensational. Niccolò is going to stop breathing."

"Can we please stop with all the death jokes?" I gave her a tight smile.

"You remember your walk, no?"

I nodded.

"One, two, together. One, two, together... We keep our heads up and our eyes forward."

Nora caught my eye and pulled a face.

I smothered a laugh. "I think we've got it," I said, trying to placate Allegra who took her job very seriously.

"Of course you have got it." She clapped her hands together, sending my heart into a tailspin. "Let's go get your man." Allegra marched out of the room in the same whirlwind she'd arrived in.

"She's really something," Nora chuckled as we met at the door. I inhaled a shaky breath and she frowned. "Nervous?"

"Yes, and excited." There were a hundred butterflies in my stomach. "I just want to get to him."

"I'm so proud of you, Ari." She air-kissed my cheek. "Now let's go get your guy."

~

The Blackstone Suite was filled with one hundred of our closest friends and family. Really, they were mostly Nicco's aunts and uncles, but I'd been shown more love and acceptance from these people in the last month than I had my whole life.

I spotted Michele and his wife, Marcella; Matteo's sister, Arabella, beside them. The Boston family sat behind. Dane must have felt us standing beyond the door because he glanced over his shoulder, offering me a cheeky wink. He was trouble, that much was obvious, and I was relieved not to have to worry about him going after Nora. She might have enjoyed her newfound freedom, but she had boundaries, and Dane was still in high school.

Besides, the second the doors opened, and she took Tristan's arm, she had the attention of almost every guy in the room. Including Enzo.

"Ready?" Luis approached me. He looked mighty fine in his sleek black three-piece.

"I am." He crooked his elbow and I laced my arm through his.

"You look beautiful, Arianne. Every father should see their daughter take their wedding vows... I'm sure he will regret this day for the rest of his life."

"He made his choice."

"Well, his loss is my gain. It is an honor to accompany you down the aisle. Shall we?" We moved into place, waiting for the pianist and cellist to start the entrance music. The soft notes of Christina Perri's *A Thousand Years* filled the room and everyone turned to watch as Luis walked me slowly down the aisle.

I felt their stares, heard their sighs of approval, and whispers of judgment. But they all fell away the second my eyes found Nicco. His gaze grew, shining with pure and unconditional love as he drank me in. I wanted to run to him, to rush into his arms and declare myself his for all eternity. But I knew Allegra was watching, ready to intervene if anything went off script.

With every step closer, my heart beat harder, until I felt sure it would explode in my chest. We finally reached the officiant, and Nicco stepped towards us.

"Bambolina, you look…" the words died on his lips, but I saw the intention in his heated gaze, and color bloomed in my cheeks.

Luis laid my hand in Nicco's before dipping his head to kiss my cheek. "This is your moment, Ari. You deserve it." He backed away and we turned to face the officiant.

"Welcome, family, friends, and loved ones," he began. "We are gathered here today in the presence of God, to unite Arianne and Niccolò in holy matrimony. Marriage is a gift, given to us so that we might experience the joys of unconditional love with a lifelong partner…"

Nicco squeezed my hand, and I peeked over at him. He looked devastatingly handsome. The sharp, black three-piece molded to his broad shoulders and tapered in at his waist. His eyes were dark, swirling with possessiveness. But it was his smile that knocked the air from my lungs. He looked so happy.

He looked… *free*.

The officiant took a deep breath, smiling at the both of us. "Niccolò, do you take Arianne to be your wedded wife, to live together after God's ordinance in the holy estate of matrimony? Do you promise to love her, comfort her, honor and keep her, in sickness and in health, and forsaking all others, remain faithful to her as long as you both shall live?"

"I do."

My heart beat so hard, I inhaled a shaky breath.

"And Arianne, do you take Niccolò to be your wedded husband, to live together after God's ordinance in the holy estate of matrimony? Do you promise to love him, comfort him, honor and keep him, in sickness and in health, and forsaking all others, remain faithful to him as long as you both shall live?"

"I do."

He nodded with approval before looking out to the crowd behind us. "Who gives Arianne to be married to Niccolò?"

"I do," my father's voice rang out clear across the room, and my head whipped around.

He walked toward us, his eyes filled with pride and regret. "Sorry I'm late." He looked at me. "Mio tesoro." It came out choked. "Sei bellissima."

Tears welled in my eyes, but I forced them down. "You're here?"

"I am." My father turned his focus on Nicco. "Take good care of her, Son."

"I will." They shared a lingering look before he took the empty seat next to my mother.

She beamed at me, and a sense of rightness washed over me. I hadn't mourned my father's absence, but him coming here, being here to witness this, gave me hope for the future.

As the officiant continued, I was too lost in my thoughts to hear his words. Lost in a daydream of dark-haired babies with brown eyes, of laughter and happiness, and a home filled with love.

It wasn't until Nicco squeezed my hand again, I realized they were waiting for me.

"Sorry," I whispered.

"It's time for the wedding vows. Niccolò, you're first. Repeat after me...

I Niccolò Luca Marchetti take thee, Arianne Carmen Lina Capizola,

> *to be my wedded wife,*
> *to have and to hold,*
> *from this day forward,*
> *for better, for worse,*
> *for richer, for poorer,*
> *in sickness and in health,*
> *to love and to cherish,*
> *till death do us part.*
> *This is my solemn vow.*

"Now Arianne…"

I, Arianne Carmen Lina Capizola take thee, Niccolò Luca Marchetti,

> *to be my wedded husband,*
> *to have and to hold,*
> *from this day forward,*
> *for better, for worse,*
> *for richer, for poorer,*
> *in sickness and in health,*
> *to love and to cherish,*
> *till death do us part.*
> *This is my solemn vow.*

"And now the exchanging of the rings." The officiant called Enzo forward. "The ring is symbolic, it is without beginning and without end. I believe this exchange of rings not only reminds us of the unending love you have for each other, but also reflects the eternal love God has for each of you. May I have the token of the groom's love for Arianne?" He turned to Enzo who offered up a small velvet pouch.

"Niccolò, repeat after me…"

This ring I give in token and pledge, as a sign of my love and devotion. With this ring, I thee wed.

Nicco slid the band onto my trembling finger, his touch lingering as if he wanted to savor the moment.

"And now may I have the token of the bride's love for Niccolò?" Enzo handed the officiant Nicco's wedding band and he offered it to me.

This ring I give in token and pledge, as a sign of my love and devotion. With this ring, I thee wed.

I pushed the plain gold band onto Nicco's finger. The officiant placed our hands atop of one another's and took them in his. "Niccolò and Arianne, since you have consented together in holy matrimony, and have pledged yourselves to each other by your solemn vows and by the giving of rings, and have declared your commitment of love before God and these witnesses, I now pronounce you husband and wife in the name of the Father and the Son and the Holy Spirit. Those whom God hath joined together, let no man separate." He smiled. "Niccolò you may kiss your bride."

Nicco turned to me and moved in, pressing his palm against my cheek. "Ti amo più oggi di ieri ma meno di domani." His lips brushed mine, but I fisted his jacket, pulling him closer and deepening the kiss.

This man was mine, just as I was his, and I wanted the world to know.

People began to cheer, but it was the officiant who cleared his throat. I buried my face in Nicco's shoulder.

"It's okay, my wife." Nicco coaxed me out. "We have time." His eyes glittered with promise. And I knew he was right.

We did have time.

We had all the time in the world.

"Ladies and gentlemen," the officiant's voice rose over the *thud* of my heart, "it is my privilege to introduce to you for the very first time, Mr. and Mrs. Marchetti."

"You know, Nicco is a good guy, but I think you picked the wrong Marchetti."

"Nice, Dane, real nice." Enzo approached us. "Don't let him hear you say that. He already beat your ass once, but he'll do it again."

"I can take him," Dane scoffed.

"Keep telling yourself that, kid. And lay off the liquor before your old man realizes you're drunk."

"I'm not drunk..." He swayed on his feet. "I'm just happy."

"Yeah, yeah." Enzo clapped him on the back and gave him a gentle shove toward where Arabella and Bailey were sitting. "Go hang out at the kiddie table."

"He's a sweet kid."

"He's trouble." Enzo smirked. "You okay?"

"I'm good." I smiled. "Just resting my feet." I kicked up my dress to reveal my lack of shoes.

"That's just... weird." He jammed his hands in his pockets, his eyes fixated on the dance floor.

"You could go dance with her you know?" I said. I didn't really like the idea of Enzo with my best friend, but the tension between them was undeniable. Only I couldn't decide if they were harboring sheer hatred or burning lust.

"I don't dance."

"Matteo seems to have no problem." He spun Nora around like a rag doll, the two of them laughing and smiling.

"I'm pretty sure the bride isn't supposed to be hiding in the shadows, watching as everyone else enjoys her big day." He cast me a sideways glance.

"I'm not hiding, I'm just... taking a breather."

The Marchetti family was big. Full of loud characters and overbearing women. Nicco had spent the first hour of the evening introducing me to the people I had yet to meet. Everyone was sweet enough, but it was exhausting, and I needed to catch my breath.

"I spent the last five years of my life locked away on my father's estate, this is a lot."

"Welcome to the crazy. And everyone loves Nicco. He really is the Prince of Hearts."

I could see that, watching as he moved from table to table to greet people and check they had all they needed.

"They already look at him like he's..." The words died on my lips.

"The boss?" Enzo's brow went up, and I nodded. "You're not going to break my boy's heart, are you? Because you were just starting to grow on me, Ari. I'd hate to have to—"

"I'm growing on you?"

"Yeah, like a bad rash."

"Hey." I jabbed him in the ribs.

"Seriously, though. You have nothing to worry about. You're his Principessa now. And one day, you'll be Queen.

There is a line of Marchetti men who would take a bullet for you."

There was a time such words would have instilled fear into my heart, but not anymore.

"Including you?"

"Yeah." His expression turned serious. "Maybe even me."

A beat passed and then I asked the question that I'd tried so hard to ignore.

"Do you think Scott will come back?"

"If he knows what's good for him then he'll stay far far away from Verona County. But if he does rear his ugly fucking head again, we'll be ready."

A shudder worked through me. It had been a little over a month since Mike Fascini was arrested and Scott escaped. Antonio's men had searched high and low for him. After a couple of weeks, they decided he had left. Everyone was still on high alert, but life finally felt like it was returning to normal.

Well, as normal as you could get after marrying into one of the biggest crime families in New England.

"Hogging my wife, E?" Nicco found us. He came around to my side and cupped the back of my neck, kissing me deeply.

"I'm standing right here," Enzo grumbled.

"I know." Nicco smirked. "I'm hoping if I make you uncomfortable enough, you'll leave me alone with my wife."

"She has a name, you know?"

"I do. Arianne Carmen Lina Marchetti. Mrs. Marchetti." He kissed the end of my nose. "My wife."

"You're drunk." Curling my hands into his lapels, I leaned in. I could smell the whisky on his breath.

"I had one or two."

"So long as you don't end up like you did at your bachelor party." My eyes shifted to Enzo and he straightened.

"That's my cue to go." He left us alone.

"Will you ever forgive me for that?"

"I loved those sneakers." I pouted.

"And I love you." Nicco fit his body between my legs, careful not to rumple my dress. "I missed you."

"I just needed five minutes."

"You're not having fun?"

"No, I am. Today has been perfect. Your family are just... intense."

His brows pinched. "Has someone said some—"

"Everyone has been very welcoming. I just..."

"It's too much." Dejection washed over him as his eyes dropped to the floor.

"Nicco, look at me." I slid my fingers under his jaw. "It's perfect. I couldn't have asked for anything more. But you have to understand, I'm not from a big family. Sometimes I'm going to need space to catch my breath. That's all it is."

"You're sure?"

I nodded. "I love you, Niccolò Luca Marchetti."

He kissed me, hardly able to contain his grin. "Not as much as I love you, my wife."

CHAPTER 31

NICCO

I watched Arianne as she danced with Nora and my sister. Genevieve and Arabella and some of the aunts had formed a circle around them, cheering and whistling.

"She looks good out there." My father joined me at the bar.

"So does Genevieve." I gave him a pointed look and he let out a hearty laugh.

"She's..."

"More than just the housekeeper?"

"Yeah, Son. I think she is." He dragged a hand over his face. "Do you think it's too soon after—"

"Everyone deserves a shot at happiness. Just promise me things will be different this time. Alessia loves that woman. If you hurt her, I'm not sure she'll ever forgive you."

"Niccolò, I'm not that man anymore."

I gave him an understanding nod.

"It has been a good day, Son. Arianne is glowing." He was about to say something else when a figure stepped up to us.

"May I?" Roberto motioned between us.

"I have to say it, I didn't expect to see you here."

"You're not the only one." Arianne's father was clearly uncomfortable. "But she's my daughter, my blood. And I owe her. I owe more than I fear I will ever be able to repay."

"We all make mistakes, Capizola," my father grunted. "It's what makes us human."

"Thank you." His lips pursed as if the words pained him. And maybe they did. You didn't just bury a century's worth of bad blood.

"You protected my daughter where I couldn't," Roberto went on. "And you saved my life. I will be forever in your debt."

My father regarded him. "That girl is special, and I will treat her as if she is one of my own. But it will never change the fact that she is Capizola." He held out his hand. "I am willing to work for a better future. The future our forefathers wanted us to have."

Roberto stared at my father's hand as if it was contagious. But after a beat, he took it. "To the future." They shared a long look before Arianne's father blinked as if he couldn't believe what had just happened.

"Excuse me, I need to find my wife before she embarrasses herself."

"That was unexpected," I said to my father as Roberto walked away.

"He's finally realized some things are more important than business." He laid a hand on my shoulder and squeezed. "I'm proud of you, Niccolò. Of the boy you were and the man you'll become."

And with that, he walked away.

∼

"So how does it feel then?" Matteo asked me sometime later when the party was in full swing.

I dragged my eyes away from Arianne. "Huh?"

"Being hitched?"

"Fucking amazing," I said around a grin.

"Jesus, you're whipped." Enzo dropped down into a chair with another glass of liquor. As the night went on, his mood had become increasingly dark. I suspected it had something to do with the fact Nora had spent the last hour dancing with Dane.

"She won't go there," I said. "He's still in high school."

"I don't know what the fuck you're talking about," he grumbled.

"No? So you won't care that he's making a mov—"

His head snapped over to the dance floor, murder in his eyes. Matteo bellowed with laughter. "Oh, man. You have it bad."

"Fuck off. I don't even like her. She's... annoying."

"You just need to get her out of your system." Matteo smirked.

But there was something in Enzo's eyes. Something that looked a lot like fear.

"Whatever you do, don't screw her over. She's Arianne's best friend."

"You can rest easy," he grumbled. "I'm not going there."

"Good to know." I fought a knowing smile.

"Are you worried Fascini might show his face again?" He changed the subject.

"I'm not unworried. But our friends down at the local PD have an APB out on him and we've got our guys on it too. He'd be a fool to try anything."

But he was always there, lurking in the back of my

mind. Arianne had taken his disappearance better than I anticipated. But if I wasn't with her, Luis and Jay were. We had eyes on her at all times, and they had eyes on them. That motherfucker wouldn't get within ten feet of her without me knowing.

"Don't let that piece of shit ruin your day. You're married, man." Matteo raised his glass at me. "It's a good day."

He was right. It was a good day.

The best day of my life.

As if she heard my thoughts, Arianne found me across the dance floor and crooked her finger.

"I think your bride wants a dance," Matteo chuckled. "Go get her, tiger."

I undid my cuffs and pushed my sleeves up.

"Oh shit, he means business," Enzo teased and I flipped him off.

The circle of women parted as I made my way towards them. We'd already had our first dance but that was before the drinks had flowed. I wasn't worried about Allegra's steely gaze now, unlike earlier when she'd been dead set on giving us the perfectly timed day. The celebration was well under way and I wanted nothing more than to pull Arianne into my arms and claim her in front of everyone.

Which is exactly what I did.

Our lips met in a passionate kiss as I held her body flush to mine.

"Hi," she breathed, breaking away to look at me.

"Hi yourself." I leaned over her, kissing her again.

"Nicco, everyone is watching."

"Let them watch. You're mine now, Bambolina. Ti amerò per sempre, fino alla morte." She slid her hands up my chest as I twirled us around to the music. "Have you enjoyed your day?"

Arianne's lips curved. "It has been perfect."

"Allegra did us proud." I ran my nose over hers. I couldn't get enough of her.

My attraction to Arianne had always been intense, but when I'd seen her appear down the aisle, it was like seeing her for the first time. Her eyes sparkled with so much love and happiness it made my heart stop. And her dress... It was sheer perfection as if it were made to fit her body. But despite how good it looked, I couldn't wait to peel her out of it later.

The very thought had my blood running hot.

"When do you think we can leave?"

"It's still early, we can't just—"

"I want you, Mrs. Marchetti. I need you more than I need my next breath."

She flushed, staring up at me through hooded eyes. "Soon."

"Room for a little one?" Nora's arms went around us both as she wiggled between us.

"Me too," Alessia called, joining the huddle. Matteo and Dane were next, then Arabella and Bailey. Enzo hovered on the periphery until I beckoned him over and he reluctantly joined the fray.

"Only for you," he mouthed.

"Thank you."

Watching them surround us, witnessing their smiles and laughter, the joy radiating from everyone, it was the best feeling.

I'd spent so long at war with myself, with my destiny. But my father was right.

Love didn't make you weak, it made you strong.

And I had everything I needed right here.

Good friends.

A loving family.

And the other half to my soul.

My wife.

~

Sunlight streamed down on me as I peeked open an eye. Arianne was curled up into my side, snoring gently, the sheet pulled up around her naked body. Hazy memories filled my mind of stripping her out of her dress and making love to her on the bed, and again in the walk-in shower. There wasn't a single inch of her skin I hadn't teased and tasted, branded with my lips.

My dick stirred to life, rubbing against the curve of her ass.

"Hmm," she murmured. "Is that a gun in your pocket or are you just happy to see me?"

Laughter rumbled in my chest as I hooked my arm around her waist and dragged her body closer. "Good morning, Wife." I nipped her shoulder.

"Good morning, Husband." She tilted her head, giving me her mouth. I kissed her, slow lazy licks of my tongue that had me desperate for more.

"How are you feeling?"

We'd barely slept, too lost in one another.

"I feel—"

A loud knock at the door sounded. "If that's Enzo, I will strangle him."

"It could be important. You should go see who it is."

"Okay, but don't move. I'm going to send them on their way and then come back and finish what we started."

"We started something?" Her eyes finally opened, heavy lidded with sleep.

"Don't. Move."

"So bossy." Arianne laughed softly as I climbed out of bed and pulled on my dress slacks.

The bridal suite at the Country Club was secreted away at the back of the property. One entrance in and out, with a balcony overlooking the lake and golf course. A balcony I had hoped to enjoy this morning with Arianne, when they delivered us our champagne breakfast.

"What?" I yanked open the door to be met with Enzo's pale face. "What happened?"

"It's Nora—"

"Nora?" Arianne gasped and I winced.

"I thought I told you to stay put, Bambolina?" I slipped my arm around Arianne's shoulder and drew her into my side.

"Did you hurt her?"

"What? *No!*" Enzo balked. "She's gone."

"Gone? What the fuck do you mean, she's gone?"

"I... we..." He inhaled a ragged breath. "After you called it a night, we stayed up drinking. One thing led to another and I ended up in her room. But when I woke up this morning, she was gone."

"Maybe she didn't want to do the awkward morning after?" Enzo wasn't exactly known for his bedside manner.

"That's what I thought, but all her shit is still in the room." He held out a cell phone.

"That's Nora's," Arianne whispered, taking it from him.

"Is there any sign of forced entry? A fight?"

"Nothing."

"You were there the whole night?" I asked him because nothing about this made sense.

He nodded. "But I think I passed out. Things got pretty wild... Fuck." Enzo dragged a hand through his hair. "I told her security guy to take a hike. I had my gun and knife right there."

"N- no." Arianne dug her fingers into my side. "You think she was... *taken?*"

"It had to be him." Enzo looked murderous. "I'll kill, I'll fucking—"

"Calm down." I levelled him with a hard look. "We don't know what happened yet. There might be a perfectly reasonable explanation." I knew he was most likely right, but I didn't want to worry Arianne unnecessarily.

"Have you raised the alarm with anyone else?" I asked.

"No, I came straight here."

"Call Luis. Go room to room. We search the entire place."

"Got it." He hesitated before settling his stormy gaze on Arianne. "I didn't know... I swear, I didn't think—"

She stepped forward, laying a hand on his arm. "It's not your fault. But please, find her." A shudder ripped through Arianne and I pulled her into my arms.

"Go." I mouthed to Enzo. "And keep me updated."

He gave me a stiff nod and took off down the hall.

"You really think Scott did something?" Arianne stared up at me with glassy eyes.

"It could be something or it could be nothing. For all we know, Nora freaked and is in Alessia's or her parents' room right now sleeping it off."

"Yeah, maybe." She gave me a weak smile.

"Let's get dressed and then we'll go look, okay?"

"Okay."

Anger zipped up my spine, threatening to take hold. This was supposed to be the first day of the rest of our lives and that fucker Scott Fascini had found a way to ruin it.

You don't know it's definitely him yet.

But my gut instinct said it was.

"You think it is him, don't you?" A tear rolled down Arianne's cheek.

"Bambolina," I inhaled a harsh breath, "everything will be fine, I promise."

I regretted the words the second they were out.

Less than one day into married life and I was already making promises I didn't know I could keep.

"Okay, what have we got?" Myself, Enzo, Luis, Maurice, and a couple of our guys were gathered around the club's security camera feeds.

"It's definitely him," Enzo ground out as he glared at a still shot of a guy entering the elevator. "His hair is longer and he's in staff uniform, but I'd know that smirk anywhere."

"He's right." My heart plummeted. "It's Fascini."

"He disappears here." The tech guy pointed to another screen. "It's a blind spot area. But another camera picks him up here and here."

"And then what?" I asked.

"We lose him. It's like he's a ghost."

"Fuck." Enzo slammed his fist into the wall, and I raised a brow.

"Feel better?"

"I'll feel better when that fucker is six-feet in the ground."

The tech guy blanched, but didn't say a word. He knew the score. He knew who we were and what had happened.

"What about the outside cameras?"

"Nothing except this car leaving at," he leaned in, squinting at the screen, "a little after five."

"We have to assume he took her." Luis shot me a concerned look. "Which means he has a five-hour head start."

"Nora is Arianne's best friend," I said. "He knew he wouldn't be able to get to her, so he took the next best thing. He'll use her as leverage to get what he really wants."

"Ari."

I nodded, my stomach twisting violently. "He'll make contact when he's ready."

"So we just wait? That's some bullshit right—"

"Enzo," I warned. "We have to keep our heads. We have no idea where he might be. But it isn't Nora he wants."

It was Arianne.

My Arianne.

"If only I'd have—"

"Don't." I shook my head at Enzo. "You can't blame yourself for this."

"She was right there beside me. I should have felt something. I should have done something. Fuck," he roared.

"We had the place locked down. He was wearing staff uniform and had a keycard to access the elevator," Luis said. "He was prepared."

"Do you need anything else?" the tech guy mumbled, clearly uncomfortable at our presence.

"No, thank you." I flicked my head to the door, and everyone began filing out.

"Anything?" Matteo jogged up to us.

"It's Fascini."

"Fuck."

"Where's Arianne?" I asked.

"She's with her parents and Nora's parents. Mrs. Abato is beside herself."

Enzo kicked the wall before taking off, mumbling something about needing some air.

"Is he okay?"

"He blames himself." I watched him shoulder the door and storm down the hall.

"He was pretty lit when I left them. You know how he can get."

"He says he passed out, but I can't believe he didn't hear anything."

"Maybe Fascini drugged her so she didn't put up a fight. It wouldn't be the first time."

I let out a heavy sigh as I met Matteo's stare. "Did I drop the ball here?"

It had been a month and there had been no sign of Scott.

Not a damn thing.

"We all thought he was gone. You told Enzo not to blame himself, but you can't carry this guilt either, Nic."

"We need to be ready," I said. "When he calls,"—and I knew he would—"we need to be ready."

I was done pussyfooting around where Fascini was concerned.

There was only one way this was going to end.

With a bullet hole through his skull.

CHAPTER 32

ARIANNE

*S*cott had Nora.

It sounded too messed up to possibly be true.

And yet, we'd left the Country Club without her.

She was gone, taken by that psychopath to God only knew where.

Nicco was confident he would call, but it had been almost two hours since we discovered she was gone and still, nothing. Mr. and Mrs. Abato wanted to call the police, but my father and Antonio had talked them down, insisting they would do everything in their power to get Nora back safe and sound.

It had been strange, watching them work together for the common good.

"What's taking so long?" I asked. We were at Antonio's house. Me, Nicco, Matteo, Enzo, and Luis. Maurice was at the apartment with Jay, just in case he showed up, and

Tristan was back at my father's estate with mine and Nora's parents.

We all knew he wouldn't show up anywhere familiar though.

He would want to draw me away from everyone.

"He'll call." Nicco squeezed my knee. The two of us sat on the couch while Matteo sat in the chair. Luis stood over by the door, in his usual bodyguard stance, ready to jump into action at any moment; while Enzo paced back and forth like a caged lion.

He'd been quiet.

Too quiet.

I knew he carried guilt over what had happened, but part of me wondered if it was more than that. If he cared because it was Nora.

God, I hoped she was okay.

I didn't know what I would do if she was hurt... because of me.

Because of Scott's depraved infatuation with me.

My phone sat on the coffee table taunting me. We assumed Scott would contact me, but time was ticking.

"Anything?" Alessia came into the room.

"Not yet," I said.

She sat down beside me. "She'll be okay. Nora is a tough cookie."

Enzo made a strangled sound in his throat.

"Maybe you should get some air?" Nicco suggested.

"No," he said. "I need to be here in case—"

The blare of my cell cut through the air. "It's him." I snatched the phone up in my trembling fingers.

"What does it say?" Everyone moved closer as I unlocked the screen and opened the text.

"It's an address."

"Vitelli," Nicco barked.

"On it." Luis glanced over at the screen and began typing something in his own cell phone. "It looks like it's an abandoned industrial unit right on the edge of Romany Square.

"Motherfucker has a death wish," Enzo growled.

Another message came through.

"Come alone, or she dies," someone read it out.

"Oh God," I cried, and Alessia pulled me into her arms.

"Ssh, it's okay. It'll be okay."

"How are we going to play this?" Matteo said. "We can't just send Ari in alone."

"Yes." I pulled away and wiped my eyes. "You can. You have to. I will not let him hurt Nora."

If he hadn't already.

"You can't ask me to do that, Bambolina." The blood had drained from Nicco's face.

"What other choice do we have? He won't hurt me. Not until he gets what he wants. I can placate him while you make your move."

"No." Nicco looked murderous.

"She has a point," Luis said. "He's obsessed with her. If anyone can distract him, it's Ari."

"I will not risk your life." Nicco shot up. "It is *not* an option."

I stood, taking his face in my hands. "Nora is my best friend. I can't stand by and do nothing."

"It's a trap. If we send you in there alone—"

"I won't be alone. I know you'll keep me safe, Nicco."

"Fuck, Bambolina." His eyes shuttered as he swallowed harshly. "Don't ask me to do this."

"We can send her in with a vest," Luis said. "It's not ideal but it's better than nothing."

"A vest.... fuck." Nicco ran a hand down his face.

"I have to do this," I said with more confidence. "The longer we sat around and decided what to do, the longer

Nora was with him.

"It's our best shot at getting Nora out of there..." Luis swallowed the words.

Words I didn't ever want to hear.

Nora would survive this.

She had to.

We all looked to Nicco, waiting. "Okay," he eventually choked out. "We do it. But you listen to every single word I tell you." I nodded. "I need to speak with my father, and then we head out. Matteo, you stay here with Alessia."

"But, Nic—"

Nicco silenced him with a hard look.

His hands went up. "I'm on babysitting duty, got it."

"Enzo, Luis, you're with us." He moved toward Enzo, lowering his voice so the rest of us couldn't hear.

"Be safe." Alessia pulled my attention from her brother and cousin.

"I will, I promise."

"Arianne," Luis beckoned me over, "we need to get you set up."

I glanced back to Nicco and he gave me a tight smile. "Go. I'll be there soon."

I had no idea where *there* was, but I followed my bodyguard out of the living room and down the hall. He seemed to know his way around the house which surprised me.

"How often have you been here?"

"A few times."

"I see."

He let out a chuckle. "I only ever acted with your safety in mind."

"I know."

I did.

It just seemed weird that a man once so loyal to my father

was now on the other side. Although after the wedding, maybe we were all on the same side now.

Luis kept going until we walked right out of the house to his SUV. He popped the trunk and pulled up the interior flooring revealing a hidden compartment. "One bulletproof vest. Put it on under your hoodie."

My hands trembled as I took it from him. "Is this really necess—

He gave me a pointed look. "Scott is unhinged, Arianne. I know you want to do the right thing, and I agree, I think this is our safest bet at saving Nora, but it doesn't change the fact we could be playing right into his hands."

"I know, I just… okay," I let out a weary sigh. "I'll put it on." Slipping out of my hoodie, I let Luis help secure me into the vest. It felt strange, restrictive, and heavy, like a vice around my chest.

"It's not infallible, but it gives you some protection. Knife." He handed me a blade, the one he'd given me before, the one I'd stabbed Scott with.

"I…"

"Take it." He pushed it toward me. "There is no way I'm letting you walk in there unarmed and you know Nicco will agree with me."

My fingers closed around the handle as I stared down at the blade, remembering how it had felt jamming it into Scott's thigh. A shudder rolled through me.

"Ari, look at me. "Luis' hand landed on my shoulder. "You've got this. We'll be there every step of the way."

I nodded, too choked to reply. Earlier I'd been running on adrenaline, on the sheer desperation of saving Nora. But now I was running on fear.

"Arianne," Antonio's deep voice startled me. "Nicco has filled me in on the plan." He came over to us, and Luis gave the two of us some space.

"I have to do this," I said as if I was talking myself into it.

"I know. She is your friend."

"Nora is family. I couldn't live with myself if I didn't do this and she..."

"She will be fine. It is you Scott wants. Just keep him talking and Niccolò will take care of him, okay?"

"Okay." Tears burned the back of my eyes.

In a rare display of affection, Antonio pulled me into his big arms. "You are a part of this family now. We will not let any harm come to you. Do you understand?"

"I do."

"Good." He eased back. "You and my son have your whole future ahead of you. We shall not let Scott Fascini take that from you, either of you."

"All set?" Nicco stalked over to us. He looked deadly, his eyes dark and stormy. He didn't like this, but I had to do it.

"Call me when it's done," Antonio said.

And I realized then, that this was a suicide mission.

But not for me or Nicco.

For Scott.

The industrial unit was a big place on the edge of Romany Square near the border. We rolled to a stop and Nicco went into full protector mode.

"Luis and E, go scope it out." His eyes were narrowed dangerously as he stared out at the warehouse as if it was the enemy.

Maybe in some ways, it was.

Luis and Enzo left, splitting up and sweeping the area.

"It will be okay," I said, breaking the thick silence.

"Bambolina." He exhaled a heavy sigh, fixing his eyes on me. "Why do I feel like this is a bad idea?"

"It's the only option, Nicco. If you go in there, he could hurt Nora, or worse. I won't take that chance."

"So I'm just supposed to take a chance with your life?"

"Scott is a psychopath. I can appeal to his ego."

"You know how this ends, don't you?"

I nodded, swallowing the lump in my throat. "It's okay. I understand."

Scott couldn't walk away from this. No matter how much I didn't want Nicco to kill him, to carry that burden, I knew they would never let him live after this. And I had to make my peace with that.

"I think I understand now. He threatened Nora and I would do anything to save her." I laid my palm on his cheek. "It's okay. Do what you have to, just make sure you come back to me."

Nicco closed the distance between us, sweeping his tongue into my mouth and kissing me. It was a kiss fueled by anger and frustration, desperation and fear. It was a kiss full of promise and reassurance.

A kiss I never wanted to end.

"They're back." Nicco broke away, touching his head to mine. He inhaled a deep breath before sitting up, his cold mask sliding back into place.

Luis yanked open my door and peered inside. "One way in and out. He's backed himself into a corner."

Nervous energy zipped through me, my body vibrating uncontrollably. I took Luis' hand and let him help me out.

Nicco followed. "Okay. I'll walk Arianne to the door," he said. "Once Nora is clear, you wait for my signal." They both nodded as he took my hand and started guiding me toward the building. Every step was like a gunshot to the heart. Blood pounded between my ears, my pulse so fast I felt a little unsteady.

"Wait," Enzo called, jogging over to us.

"What is it?" My voice trembled.

"Just get her back, okay?"

A faint smile lifted the corner of my mouth. "I will." I laid a hand on his arm. His body seemed to relax at my touch, relief seeping into his expression.

"Come on," Nicco urged. "We should..." He flicked his head to the door. The place was locked down, huge steel chains on the front shutters. But there was a door on the side of the building that was ajar.

When we reached it, Nicco tugged me around to face him. "I'm going to be right behind you, okay? Keep him talking but don't get too close."

"Okay." A tear slipped down my face.

"Ssh, Bambolina. This will all soon be over." He cupped the back of my neck and drew me close, kissing my forehead. "I love you more than life, Arianne."

I hesitated, and then, without looking back, I slipped inside.

It was dark and cold, a cloying smell lingering in the dusty air. My sneakers barely made a sound as I moved down the hall, but I could hear my heartbeat. Feel it as it pounded in my chest. The hall opened out into the main warehouse, floor to ceiling steel shelving creating a network of passageways.

"Hello," I called.

"Ari, don't—" Nora's voice became muffled and I heard Scott grunt and grumble.

Picking up my pace, I weaved in and out of the shelving, until I saw them. Scott had Nora tied to a chair, her hands bound behind her back and ankles bound together. "What are you doing, Scott?" I stepped out into the clearing.

In its day it had probably been a sorting bay of some sort, boxes and crates littered around the place. I stepped over some debris, stopping before them. Nora was gagged, thrashing against her restraints, her eyes pleading with me to run.

"Where is he? Where is that fucker, Marchetti?" His voice rose, echoing around the warehouse, sending a violent shiver down my spine.

"Let Nora go, Scott," I said, keeping to the script Luis and Nicco had gone over with me on the ride here. "She isn't a part of this. You wanted me and I'm here. But you have to let Nora go."

"You think I'm stupid?" He whipped out his gun, waving it around maniacally. I slowly lifted my hands into the air and inched closer. "Scott, look at me."

He was jittery, and part of me wondered if he was on something. "Put the gun down and let Nora go, please."

His gaze darted wildly between me and Nora.

"Let her go," I urged. "If you care about me at all, please, you need to let her go."

He stilled; my words finally reaching something deep inside him. "You'll stay?"

I nodded. He was unhinged, utterly deluded. But it worked. Appealing to the part of Scott that was infatuated with me, made him begin to untie Nora.

The second she was free, I beckoned her toward me.

"Wait." He cocked the gun at her.

"Scott." Fear trickled through me, turning my blood to ice. "Let her go and we can talk. Just you and me."

I silently prayed Nicco was somewhere inside the building. Luis and Enzo too. But I daren't look for fear of distracting him.

"Slowly," he ordered Nora to start walking.

She came toward me and I dropped my hand, brushing her fingers. "Go and don't look back, okay?" I whispered and she nodded, tears streaming down her face. Aside from a split in her lip and some bruising around her cheek, she looked to be okay. But I knew better than most, it wasn't the physical scars that stayed with you.

Nora took off toward the maze of huge steel shelving.

"Thank you." I gave Scott my full attention.

"I had to do something... I couldn't get to you, but I knew you'd come for her. You hurt me, baby. You really fucking hurt me." He advanced toward me and I slowly tracked backwards, trying to keep a safe distance between us. The gun was still in his hand, but he wasn't waving it around now. His eyes were locked on mine. Hatred and lust swirling in their depths. He was at war with himself. Scott wanted me. But part of him wanted to hurt me too.

"You were supposed to be mine," he ground out.

"I'm here now." My conscience screamed in protest at the declaration. I would never be his, but he needed to think I was on his side.

I kept moving, turning us so his back was to the only way in and out. He was fixated on me, exactly as I'd known he would be.

"You betrayed me," he spat the words. "All you had to do was love me. *Me*, Arianne. I would have given you everything. I would have made you my queen. But Marchetti swooped in and ruined everything. I'll kill him. I'll fucking kill him. And then I'll finally take what's mine."

The hand holding the gun grew twitchy again as he waved it in my direction. I was paralyzed, rooted to the spot as pain splintered through me. But I forced down the tears, refusing to show him even an ounce of weakness.

"We can talk about this," I said.

"Maybe I don't want to talk." His eyes were black, soulless, as he prowled toward me. "Maybe I'm done talking. You think I'm stupid? You think I don't know he's out there somewhere, waiting for his moment to strike?

"What are you waiting for, Marchetti?" He yelled. "Come save your woman. Come save her before I—"

"Scott..." I was losing him.

"You. Are. Mine." The venom in his words cut my skin like shards of glass. "If I can't have you." He raised the gun higher. "No one ca—"

Nicco came out of nowhere, grabbing Scott and yanking him backward. "Nicco," I screamed as a gunshot rang out. I was thrown backwards, pain ricocheting through me as I hit the ground hard. Stars exploded in my vision.

"Motherfucker," someone grunted, their voices teetering on the edge of my consciousness.

"I should have done this a long time ago."

Nicco.

That was Nicco.

I blinked, bringing a hand to my head as I tried to sit up. Nicco was on top of Scott, the two of them jostling for control. Nicco rained his fists down on Scott, the sickening crunch of bone on bone filling the cavernous room.

"Nicco," I cried, still disorientated. I patted myself down for any signs of blood but there was nothing. The bulletproof vest had done its job.

"She. Is. Mine," Scott roared. "I had her first. Me. You think you can take her from me?"

Another sickening crunch rang out. "She will never be yours," Nicco ground out, his voice cold and deadly. "I should have done this a long time ago." He pressed the barrel of his gun right to Scott's temple. "You will never touch Arianne again. Never look at her. Never breathe the same air as her."

Time seemed to slow down as I watched Nicco whisper something to him.

But Scott didn't look scared, he looked... pleased, his lip curving into a wicked smirk. I saw his hand move, saw the glint of metal.

"Nicco, he has a—"

My scream filled the warehouse as I watched in horror as the knife in Scott's hand sank into Nicco. His body locked with pain, realization washing over him as Scott shoved him away.

Nicco rolled away, landing with a *thud*, a pool of dark red blood seeping between his fingers as he clutched his chest. "Bambolina..." It was a breathy moan as he reached for me.

"No," I cried. "No." Clambering to my feet, I rushed over to his side. There was too much blood. "You're okay," I said, dropping to my knees. "I'm right here."

"I'm sorry, amore mio, I'm... so fucking sorry." His words were cracked, blood trickling from his mouth.

"Ssh, ssh." I leaned down, kissing his head. "You're going to be okay."

"Ari, I need to look at him." Luis gently eased me away. I hadn't even heard him arrive. Hadn't noticed Enzo apprehend Scott, keeping his pistol trained firmly on his head.

"Talk to me, Vitelli," he called over to us.

"There's too much blood." Luis cast me a grim look and then looked at Enzo. "He needs medical attention, now."

"Nicco." I clutched his hand, blood squelching between our fingers. But I didn't care. As long as he was breathing, as long as I felt his fingers still curled around mine, he was alive. "You have to hold on, okay?" Pain ripped through me. "I need you... I need you."

"He's not looking so good. If I can't have you do you really think I would ever let him have you?" The sick and twisted amusement in Scott's voice flipped something inside me, and without thinking, I pulled away from Nicco and stood up. My hand went to the waistband of my jeans.

"Arianne," Luis yelled, but it was too late. I was consumed with hatred, with the overpowering need to hurt Scott the way he had hurt me so many times.

"Anger looks good on you, Principessa." He grinned as I stalked toward him, as if this was all part of his game.

Well, I was done playing.

"Ari," Enzo warned as I creeped closer.

"Relax," Scott chuckled. "She won't hurt me. She doesn't have it in—"

I barely felt the blade pierce the soft tissue of his neck. Barely registered the blood spraying out of his jugular, coating my hand and clothes like a jet spray of red paint. Barely heard his garbled pleas for help as the blood filled his mouth, trickling down his chin like juice from a ripe strawberry.

"Fuck," Enzo holstered his gun and slowly took the bloodied knife from my hand. "Ari, look at me."

My eyes snapped to his as if waking up from a trance. "He's dead." I glanced down at Scott's lifeless body.

"He is," Enzo said. "He can't hurt you anymore."

But when I glanced back at Nicco, at the pool of blood circling him, his shallow breaths and the pallor to his skin, I knew it was too late.

Scott had taken everything from me.

There was no future without Nicco. No life or happiness. There was only pain and grief and hurt.

Nicco was my heart.

The other half of my soul.

I didn't want to live in a world without him.

As I stared at him, the only man I would ever love, and watched the life drain from his eyes, I wanted that too.

I wanted to die.

CHAPTER 33

ARIANNE

The days were long, and my heart was broken.

It had been two weeks since Nicco died in that building.

Two weeks of unimaginable anguish and pain.

I'd wanted to die that day. To follow him into the afterlife. But Enzo and Luis had grounded me, Nora too. They had stood by my side, watching as the EMTs rushed into the warehouse and began working on Nicco, trying to stem the bleeding and find a pulse.

Tears burned my throat just thinking about it. Within less than twenty-four hours I had gone from a bride so full of love and hope for the future, to a murderer with blood on my hands, mourning a loss so inconceivable I didn't think I would survive it.

But I couldn't regret killing Scott.

I could only regret that I didn't do it the first time around, when I'd had the chance.

Maybe then we wouldn't be here now.

"Arianne." Tristan stood as I entered the room. He came over and pulled me into his arms. "How are you?"

"I feel empty inside." My hand fluttered to my chest.

"You can't think like that. He wouldn't want you to."

"I just don't know how I'm supposed to do this without him, Tristan." Tears poured down my cheeks.

My cousin took my face in his hands. "You have hope. The doctors said he's stable. His body just needs time."

Time.

I'd already survived fourteen days without him, I didn't want to survive another.

"Thank you." I wiped my eyes on my sleeves. "For staying with him." Moving over to the bed, I gently brushed the hair from Nicco's eyes. His skin was sallow, and his eyes were sunken. A tube connected him to the machine breathing for him.

He'd died that day, on the cold floor of the warehouse, but the EMT's had brought him back. Twice, in fact. They'd managed to stop the bleeding and save his punctured lung, but Nicco hadn't woken up. They said his body needed to repair itself.

They said he needed time.

But time didn't feel like our friend, it felt like our enemy, closing in around us.

Sitting down, I took his hand in mine. "It's me," I said. "It's day fifteen without you, and I need you to wake up now. Please, Nicco." I kissed his knuckles. "I need you to wake up."

"I'll give the two of you some space." Tristan's hand rested on my shoulders. I glanced up at him, offering him a weak smile.

"Thank you."

After Nicco was moved out of the ICU into his own room, I'd refused to leave his side. For four nights, I had slept curled up on the couch, before Matteo and Enzo practically dragged me out of there. They made Genevieve and Alessia take me back to the house and make sure I got a shower and ate something other than stale sandwiches from the hospital vending machine.

Now we had a schedule. Someone was always with him so that I could try and look after myself too.

A knock on the door startled me and I glanced back to find Enzo standing there. "I know it's your time with him but I—"

"It's fine, you can come in."

Enzo had taken it the hardest. I knew he blamed himself. It was something we had in common.

"How's Nora?" I asked when he dropped into the chair at the other side of Nicco's bed.

"She's... okay." He frowned.

"It's okay that you're spending time with her, you know?"

"It's not like that." He ran a hand through his hair. "She just helps me—"

My hand shot up. "I don't need to know the details."

That made him smile, but it quickly disappeared when he settled his eyes back on Nicco. "Come on, Cous. We need you to wake up."

"Do you think he can hear us?"

"The doc says talking helps. But I always feel like an idiot, sitting here, talking to myself."

Silence enveloped us. Enzo was still as intimidating as ever, but something had changed between us since that day.

"Killing someone changes you," he'd said to me in the hospital as we waited for news about Nicco.

I felt different but not in the way I'd expected.

I'd been so against Nicco and Antonio dealing with Mike Fascini and his deranged son in their way, I hadn't stopped to consider that maybe we all possessed darkness inside us. It just didn't appear until you were pushed to your limits.

I was hardly surprised my limit was Scott hurting Nicco.

I'd let him hurt me, taunt me, and tease me. I'd let him do despicable things to me. But watching him drive that knife into Nicco had ignited a fire inside me, and in that moment, the darkness had shrouded me.

A shudder rolled through me. We'd been through so much.

Too much.

"You'll learn to live with it," Enzo said, as if he could hear my thoughts.

"There's nothing to live with." I looked him dead in the eye. "I did what I had to, and I'd do it again, a thousand times over."

He dragged his bottom lip between his teeth, studying me. "You know, you're kind of scary right now."

"I'm Capizola *and* Marchetti. You should be scared." My lip curved, and laughter rumbled in his chest.

"He won't like it, you know." His eyes flicked to Nicco.

"It doesn't matter," I replied.

All that mattered was that Nicco came back to me.

Three days later, I'd finally got the call I'd been waiting for.

"He's awake," Alessia had squealed down the line.

I'd abandoned Genevieve in the kitchen and asked Luis to drive me straight to the hospital.

"He's going to be disoriented," Luis said. "The doctors said it could still be a long road to recovery."

"I know." My body hummed with trepidation as we rode the elevator to Nicco's floor. "He's awake, Luis. I didn't think—"

"I know." He took my hand, squeezing it gently. "I know."

The second the doors pinged open, I took off running, skidding to a halt when I spotted him through the blinds. Nicco was sitting up, laughing at something Alessia was telling him. He must have felt me watching because his eyes found me, shining with relief.

I'd been so eager to see him, but now the moment had come I couldn't make my legs work.

"He's all yours." Alessia appeared at the door. "Luis can treat me to ice cream in the cafe." She skipped past me and grabbed his hand, dragging him down the hall.

I entered the room, freezing when our eyes collided again.

"Bambolina." His voice was cracked.

"You're awake," I breathed. "You're really awake." The invisible thread between us snapped taut, pulling me toward him. "How are you feeling?" I reached for Nicco's hand, smothering a whimper when his fingers tightened around mine.

"Ssh, don't cry. Please..."

"I thought I'd lost you." My teary gaze dropped to the bed. "I thought you were—"

"Arianne, look at me." Slowly, I lifted my eyes to his. "It's okay. Everything is going to be okay."

"You died, Nicco. I watched you die." All the pain and heartache of the last couple of weeks hit me like a wrecking ball. Big, fat, ugly tears rolled down my cheeks as I tried to process everything.

"Ssh, amore mio." His thumb brushed my cheeks. "I'm here. I'm right here. He can't hurt us anymore."

I stiffened.

"It's okay. I know what happened. I know what you did, Bambolina. And one day, we will need to talk about it. But not today." He gave me a warm smile. "Right now, I just want to enjoy this moment. I love you, Arianne Carmen Lina Marchetti, and I'll never leave you again."

His words sank into me, flooding me with a sense of peace I hadn't felt since our wedding day.

"I love you too," I whispered, kissing the tips of his fingers.

Nicco always said that he would die for me.

What I hadn't realized then, was I would do the same for him.

Love made us strong.

It gave us something to protect.

Something to fight for.

But, most of all, it gave us something to live for.

EPILOGUE

NICCO

hree weeks later...

"Nicco, put me down," Arianne's shrieks filled the apartment as I carried her over the threshold.

"Welcome home, Wife." I nuzzled her neck. My body ached like a motherfucker, but I wasn't about to tell her that.

Arianne had been watching me like a hawk since I was released from the hospital. It was cute at first, but now it was starting to test my patience. I wanted to touch her. To strip her naked and make love to her. But Arianne took her job as nursemaid very seriously.

"Tonight, we're going to christen our new bedroom, and maybe the kitchen counter, and shower too."

She pressed her hands to my chest. "You're still healing."

"I'm fine." But I wouldn't be fine if she denied me again.

"Nicco..." She pouted.

"I'm fine. See." I twirled us around, wincing in agony as my muscles contracted. "Fuck."

Arianne wriggled out of my arms, sliding to the floor. "I'll call the doctor." She went to move but I snagged her wrist.

"Bambolina, it's just a little pain. The doctor said I need to take it—"

"Aha, I knew it." She glared at me. "Bed rest for you."

"Will you be in the bed with me?" I smirked.

"Nicco... this is serious. You're still healing. You almost—"

I cut her off with my mouth, kissing Arianne with all the frustration and desperation I felt.

"Wow," she breathed. Her cheeks were flushed, her eyes dilated. "He didn't say anything about no kissing, right?" She dived back in, scraping my jaw with her fingers, dragging me closer.

Laughter rumbled between us and I was about to try my luck at taking things to the next level when a voice boomed, "Nice place."

"You have got to be kidding me?" I dropped my head to Arianne's shoulder.

"Nice to see you too, Cous," Enzo grumbled.

"You guys, this place is so freakin' cute." Nora threw her arms around us both, not caring I was sporting a semi and still had my lips attached to Arianne's neck.

"Isn't it?"

I untangled myself from the girls and leaned against the counter. We'd settled on a place in Romany Square, a stone's throw away from the VCTI. Arianne wanted to continue volunteering there and liked the idea of being able to walk. I hadn't broken it to her yet that the only way I would ever let her walk freely around the neighborhood was if she wore a t-shirt with the words 'Niccolò Marchetti's Wife' stamped across the front, or with at least two bodyguards.

Not that Luis ever let her out of his sight.

"How are you holding up?" Enzo glanced down at where I was holding my side.

"If Arianne asks, I'm fine."

"Hurting like a bitch on the inside?" he whispered.

"Something like that."

"I guess you won't be making an appearance at L'Anello's for a while yet then?"

"Never," Arianne called over. "He'll *never* be making an appearance at L'Anello's again."

"Shit, man. Your girl grew balls."

"Like Nora doesn't have yours firmly in the palm of her hand." My brow quirked up.

"It isn't like—"

"That? Yeah, yeah, keep telling yourself that. Before you know it, you'll be planning how to keep her."

He snorted. "I think you own the market share in being pussy whipped. Have you spoken to your old man this week?"

The question caught me off guard. "Not for a couple of days, why?"

"He seems a little preoccupied. I wondered if you knew what was up with him?"

Dread snaked through me, but I pasted on a smile. "Whatever it is, I'm sure it's fine."

"Yeah, you're probably right." He walked over to Nora and roped his arm around her neck. It was a display of total possessiveness if ever I'd seen one.

Arianne threw Nora a questioning look and she shrugged, but I saw the slight flush to her cheeks. Enzo had surprised her.

And she wasn't the only one.

"So, what's the plan?"

"We have a few more boxes to unpack. Matteo is getting

Alessia and Bailey from school and then heading straight here."

"Sounds good. Babe, check the refrigerator and see if Nicco got the beers in." Enzo tapped Nora on the ass before diving over the couch.

"Hmm, what just happened?" She frowned at him and then us.

"I think Enzo grew feelings."

"Heard that," he grumbled.

"Are you two like... *together?*" Arianne whispered. "Because you said it was nothing."

"I thought it was nothing."

"I've known Enzo my entire life," I said. "And that, the way he is with you, isn't nothing. Just be careful, okay?" Enzo was complicated, and the last thing I wanted was for Nora to get hurt. Especially after everything she'd been through.

"Worry less about me and Enzo, and more about when your wife is going to let you get some," she said around a half-smile, moving around us to the refrigerator.

"You told her?" I gawked at Arianne, and guilt filled her expression.

"Well, it's hard not being able to... you know. I had to talk to someone."

"Come here." I snagged her waistband, yanking her closer and dipping my mouth to her ear. "Tonight, when our family and friends leave, I am going to carry you into our bedroom, strip you naked, and spend time reacquainting myself with every single inch of your skin."

Her fingers twisted into my sweater as she suppressed a soft moan. "Any objections?" I asked and she shook her head. "Good, didn't think so."

Arianne turned slightly, brushing my lips with hers. "Until tonight."

"Tonight," I choked out.

Jesus Christ. It was going to be a long fucking day.

∽

The next morning, my father summoned us to the house. We couldn't catch a break. Enzo's words from yesterday lingered in my mind. He was right, something was wrong. I just couldn't put my finger on what.

The arrangement with Roberto was, to my knowledge, going as well as could be expected. Word from our contact down in local PD was that Mike Fascini was looking at serving serious time. Scott was gone, his case open and shut thanks to our friends in the police department. And doctors were confident I would make a full recovery.

"You're nervous," Arianne said as we climbed out of the SUV.

"Thanks." I tipped my chin at Luis. He'd become our personal chauffeur since I was released from hospital. I couldn't ride my bike or drive yet. And Arianne still hadn't gotten her permit. It was on my list of things to do as soon as I was up to it.

"I just don't like surprises."

"I'm sure it's nothing." She leaned into my side.

"Yeah, probably."

We entered the house and headed straight for my father's study. "Niccolò, it's a damn good sight to see you upright, Son."

"Thanks." I accepted his hug but didn't miss the tightness in his expression.

"And Arianne, you look as beautiful as ever."

"Thank you, Antonio. Should I leave the two of you—"

"Actually, this concerns you too. Please, sit."

My senses were working overtime.

"After you and Tommy visited Vermont," my father

leaned forward, steepling his fingers, "Luis Vitelli provided Tommy with some information about the failed attempt on Arianne's life."

"I remember," I said, wondering where he could possibly be going with this.

"Tommy did some more digging..." He inhaled a shaky breath, the blood draining from his face.

"He found something?"

"Nothing. He found nothing."

"But that doesn't make any sense." I frowned. "It had to be Fascini."

"I know, Son. Which is why I sent Tommy to see Mike Fascini."

"What?" Now I was really confused.

"Something about the whole thing had been bothering me. Mike would have needed to pin the hit on us. There would have been a paper trail, something." He scrubbed his jaw. "And then, when Fascini moved the wedding date, I started to wonder, what if Fascini didn't orchestrate the hit, but provided the right person with the right information. But I discounted it because it is not possible."

He was talking in riddles... until everything slammed into me.

"You think we have a traitor in our ranks." It wasn't a question.

I'd wondered myself how Fascini could have found out that we visited Elizabeth Monroe, but I'd assumed he was having us watched.

"I don't think, Son." He expression turned grim. "I know."

"Who is it?" Any traitor to the Family knew what it meant.

They knew it was a death sentence.

"Fuck, I don't know how to say this, Niccolò. It is...Vincenzo."

"Vincenzo?" Arianne's voice was small. "Enzo's dad tried to have me killed?"

"According to Fascini, he made contact with Vincenzo under a guise, drip feeding him the information he needed to organize the hit."

"He wanted war," I said flatly.

It made no sense, and yet, it made perfect sense.

My uncle had always spited my father over his soft approach to handling Roberto Capizola. He preferred to get things done no matter the cost, but my father saw the bigger picture.

"It was Vincenzo who informed Fascini that you and Tommy had been to Vermont, just as it was him who gave them a heads up about the police warrant. But Scott intercepted the call, that's how he managed to evade arrest."

"Figlio di puttana!" My fist clenched. "He betrayed us."

"He did." My father sank back in his chair. "My own brother. I always knew he didn't like the way I ran things, but I never thought..."

"What happens now?" Arianne sounded eerily calm.

"We live by a code, Arianne." My father looked her into the eye, treating her as an equal. Under any other circumstance, it was a moment that would have filled me with pride.

"So he will die for his sins?"

"He will."

She inhaled a shuddering breath. "This will destroy Enzo."

Fuck.

Enzo.

I hadn't even considered my best friend, still trying to wrap my head around the fact my uncle was a traitor.

"Lorenzo is strong. He will survive this."

"When?" I asked through gritted teeth.

"Tonight. It is already set. Me, you, Michele, and Enzo."

"Not Enzo, he doesn't need to witness that."

"You know he must. It is the way things must be done."

I managed a small nod. There would be an interrogation. A chance for Vincenzo to purge his sins and cleanse his soul before death.

"Excuse me." Arianne got up and hurried from the room.

"She needed to know," my father said. "There are some things we cannot protect those we love from."

"I know." Even if my father hadn't asked for her to be here, I would have told her. It just didn't make the reality any easier to process.

"Where?"

"One of the cabins."

I nodded. It wouldn't be the cabin Arianne and I had hidden in, the place I'd proposed. That was sacred now. It would be another one of our places. Somewhere my father had no problem with getting a little dirty.

I stood, desperate to go after Arianne. "What should I tell Enzo?"

"Whatever you need to tell him to get him there."

"You don't have to watch this," I said to my cousin as my father drove his brass knuckles into Vincenzo's face.

"The truth," he roared.

"The truth?" Vincenzo spat, blood oozing from the numerous cuts on his face. "The truth is you don't have what it takes to be the boss..."

Enzo was deathly still beside me, dark energy rolling off him. I didn't want him to be here, to witness this. But my father was right, there was an order to things.

"You know how this ends, Vin," Uncle Michele stepped

forward. "Tell us what we need to know, and all of this can stop." Pain glittered in his eyes. He didn't enjoy this. Few men did. He was offering his brother-in-law an out, but Vincenzo always had been a stubborn fool.

"Vaffanculo!"

The crack of Michele's fist against Vincenzo's cheekbone filled the cabin. His head snapped back, rolling on his shoulders like a rag doll.

"Why?" My father hissed. "Why would you betray us? Your famiglia."

"Because it should have been me. He promised me a spot at the table, you know?" Vincenzo was sneering now, rivulets of blood staining his teeth and chin. "Once the Capizola heir was gone and Roberto came for you, I was going to take the Family into a new future. A strong future. You can't trust them. The Capizola are—"

"That is my wife you're talking about." I yanked out my pistol and stormed toward him, jamming it right against his forehead.

"Niccolò," my father warned. This wasn't over until my father said it was over. But I couldn't just stand here and listen to my own flesh and blood talk about hurting Arianne.

"You don't have the balls, kid," he spat. "That Capizola puttana keeps them in her purse."

I cracked the butt of my pistol across the bridge of his nose, blood splattering everywhere. But he didn't look fazed. Instead, his lip curled into a sneer.

"It was me, you know?" he spat. "I did it. I killed Lucia."

A chill rolled through the air as we all realized what he'd just confessed.

"You lie." My father advanced toward us, dark energy rippling off him. "She left." His voice cracked with pain, matching the vise around my heart.

He'd killed her.

My own uncle had taken my mother's life?

What nightmare was this?

"She didn't leave." Vincenzo didn't show even an ounce of remorse. "She found out what I'd done and threatened to tell you. Always so loyal," he said.

"You're telling me you killed my wife?" My father was shaking, anger radiating from him, making the air around us crackle. "I'll fucking gut you and feed you to the fish." My father went to attack, but a gunshot went off and a hole blew right through Vincenzo's skull.

We all looked at Enzo who stood as still as a statue, not even an ounce of emotion in his eyes as he stared at his father's dead body.

"You good, son?" My father walked over and took the pistol from his hands.

"Better than him." His eyes were black. Soulless.

This was bad. Real fucking bad.

"What do you want us to do with the body?" Michele asked.

"Burn him for all I care." Enzo stalked out of the room.

"Go," my father ordered me. "Make sure he doesn't do anything stupid."

I gave him a tight nod and took off. But when I got outside, Enzo was gone.

And so was his car.

ARIANNE

"Do you think he'll be okay?" I asked Nicco as we cuddled in bed. It was two days after Nicco had returned from the cabin, his face pale and hands trembling, and fallen into my arms.

I hadn't asked what had happened.

I hadn't needed to.

Vincenzo was gone.

Enzo was fatherless.

And everyone in Antonio's most inner circle needed to learn how to adjust to life after Vincenzo's betrayal.

But then Nicco had told me about Vincenzo's final confession. He'd killed Nicco and Alessia's mom when she'd discovered her brother-in-law's betrayal. She wasn't gone. She was dead. Nicco had broken in my arms that night and I'd comforted him the only way I knew how—with my body, heart, and soul.

"He just needs some time," Nicco said. "His dad wasn't exactly a doting father growing up but he was still his dad."

"I can't even imagine how he must be feeling. Nora's going out of her mind with worry. He won't answer any of her calls."

"She should probably back off, give him some space."

"This is Nora we're talking about..." And she didn't know the entire story.

Nicco rolled me onto my side so we were face to face. "They're our friends and I know you're worried, I am too, but what I'd really like right now, is to enjoy waking up in bed with my wife." His hand slipped between us, finding my center.

"Oh, God..." I moaned as he rubbed lazy circles over my clit.

"Does that feel good?"

"Hmm-hm," the words got stuck in my throat as he slowly pushed a finger inside me.

"You were already wet for me, Bambolina." Nicco kissed me, his tongue mirroring the way his fingers glided in and out.

"More," I demanded

"Patience." His laughter tickled my face.

"I need you, Nicco. Please..." I wasn't above begging. Besides, it usually paid off.

Nicco dragged one of my legs over his hip, dropping down the bed slightly to position himself at the perfect angle to rock into me.

"Fuck," he hissed. "You feel incredible." Nicco anchored me to his body, doing all of the work. His mouth was everywhere, on my lips, my neck, latched onto my breast. He was like a man starved, feasting on my skin, savoring every inch.

"Ti amo."

"Always," I said, waves of pleasure rising inside me, threatening to pull me under.

But I wanted to fall.

I wanted to lose myself in him. In the way he loved me so completely.

"Jesus, Bambolina. I don't think I will ever get enough of this." He rocked harder, pushing us both closer to the edge.

I was almost there when my cell phone blared.

"Leave it," he growled, sucking and nipping my collarbone.

"I wasn't going to answer it," I panted, barely able to breathe, too overwhelmed with sensation.

Nicco hooked my leg higher, going deeper. So deep it was like he wanted to consume me. "Let go, amore mio." He whispered against my ear and it was my undoing. I shattered around him, my body trembling with ecstasy.

"God, Arianne." He stilled, clutching my body to him as he slowed his movements, drawing out the moment.

"That was nice." I nudged my nose against his.

"Nice—"

My cell phone began to ring again.

"Don't answer it."

"It could be important," I said, fumbling over my head to try and find it. "It's Nora. Hey..."

Her sobs filled the line. "What is it? What's wrong?"

"He kicked me out."

"What do you mean he—"

"I went over there to see if he was okay and he kicked me out. Said he couldn't deal with me right now..." She hiccupped.

"Nora, he's... it's complicated."

"Secret mafia stuff. Yeah, I know. But he was so... cruel, Ari. You didn't see the way he..." Her voice trailed off.

"Why don't you come over to the apartment and we'll figure things out," I suggested.

"No, I'm okay. You told me not to get involved with him, and I didn't listen. But he was different... he was... Do you think I'm stupid?"

"No, I don't think you're stupid. He was changing." We'd all seen it. Enzo cared about Nora. After the warehouse, it was like a switch had been flipped. But Enzo was in a dark place after finding out the truth about his father.

"I'm going to give him some space but then I'm going back over there."

"I'm not sure that is a good idea, Nor."

"He needs me, Ari. I know he does."

"Just be careful, okay?"

"I'm sorry for disturbing you."

"Don't be silly, you can always call me, always." I hung up and turned to Nicco.

"Let me guess, Enzo broke her heart?"

I pressed my lips together and he sat up. "Shit, Enzo did something? I was only joking." He brushed the hair from my face. "What did she say?"

"She went over to his place to check on him and he kicked her out."

"He's not in a good place right now."

"I know that, and you know that, but she doesn't." And we

couldn't tell her. "I know he's hurting…" I said. It didn't justify Enzo's behavior, but Nora didn't know everything. "Maybe we should have told her the truth."

"It's not our story to tell." Nicco kissed my shoulder.

"I know but I don't like the idea of them both hurting when they were just getting to a good place."

"You can't fix everyone, Bambolina. Sometimes people have to find their own way."

"You're right." I dropped my head to his. "And look at us, we managed to figure it out despite the odds."

"We did." Nicco's lips lingered on mine. "And I'll be forever thankful you stumbled into my life that night."

Our love was fated.

Written in the stars.

A love so powerful and consuming it should have burned us both into nothing but ash. But we'd defied the odds.

We'd survived to tell the tale.

And all that was left now, was to live our happily-ever-after.

NORA

I wanted to heed Ari's words, I did. But I couldn't just sit in the apartment all day, festering on Enzo's cruel words as he'd all but kicked me out of his place.

"You're nothing to me," he'd gritted out when I'd tried to comfort him.

I knew something bad had happened.

I knew it related to Enzo and Dominion. But no one would tell me. Not even Ari.

It stung.

Over the last few weeks, I'd felt like one of them. Part of the inner circle. But when it came down to it, I wasn't.

Enzo had proved that this morning.

Just when he was finally opening up to me.

After the incident with Scott—and I called it an incident because calling it anything else still paralyzed me with fear—Enzo had been different. Maybe even before then.

We'd had such an amazing night together at the wedding, the sex had been rough and dirty, but the way he worshipped me was beyond my wildest dreams. And then he went and ruined everything.

I shook the thoughts from my head. I wouldn't go there. Not now. Not ever. Scott was gone. Arianne had killed him with her own hand.

"Maurice," I yelled. Despite Scott being gone and the threat of retaliation negligible thanks to Mike Fascini being behind bars, Nicco and Ari had insisted my bodyguard stay with me, for now.

"Yes, Miss Abato?" He rushed into the room, scanning for any sign of danger.

"I'm going out."

"Out? But I thought—" He eyed the pile of candy on the kitchen counter. After leaving Enzo's apartment, I may have gone a little overboard and purchased my body weight in sugar.

But screw that. I wasn't going to sit here wallowing.

I was going to fight.

I knew Enzo was hurting. I knew it had something to do with whatever had happened. If only he'd open up and let me in, I could help him.

I wanted to.

"Change of plans," I said, going over to the wall mirror and checking my reflection. "I'm going to need a ride to Enzo's place."

"Are you sure that's—"

I shot him a terse look. "If I want your opinion, I'll ask."

"Very well." He gave me a small nod. "I'll fetch the car."

"You do that. I'll be five minutes." That gave me enough time to add some gloss to my lips and blush to my cheeks. I didn't bother to change out of my skinny jeans and hoodie. I'd never dressed to impress Enzo before, I wasn't about to start now.

But I would make him hear me out.

Because Nora Hildi Abato didn't take no for an answer.

There was something between us. Something undeniable, something I wasn't about to ignore because he decided he couldn't deal with his feelings.

With a new sense of resolve, I grabbed my purse and keys, and headed for Maurice.

Enzo lived in a small apartment building right where the edge of University Hill met Romany Square. I'd been here a few times before. It was a complete man cave, gray walls with dark gray and black accents. The kitchen was all black hi-gloss cabinets and polished chrome handles. It was sleek and edgy and reminded me of the dangerous guy that lived there.

Matteo stayed there too sometimes, but from what I gathered, he often stayed at home with his family. Not Enzo though. He liked his space.

Maurice let the SUV roll to a stop and climbed out, coming around to open my door. I beat him to it though, leaping out. "I'll be okay, you can wait here."

"Miss Ab—"

"Nora. For the love of God, call me Nora," I mumbled.

It had been weeks, but he still insisted on keeping things strictly professional.

"You can see the door from here. I'll be going to Enzo's apartment. He can protect me."

The words did strange things to my stomach, not that I imagined he would be pleased to see me after this morning.

"I'll see you inside."

"Ugh, fine." I took off toward the building, determination steeling my spine. But my plan was quickly thwarted when Enzo didn't answer his buzzer.

Crap.

What the hell was I going to do now?

Then I spotted a guy coming toward the door. He frowned as he exited the building and I grabbed the door, slipping around him to go inside.

Thankfully, he didn't try to stop me, and I climbed the two flights of stairs to Enzo's apartment. Adrenaline coursed through me. I'd lost it. Completely and utterly lost it. Ari had told me to give him space. Hell, even Maurice tried to tell me not to come. But I never was one to listen. Besides, if you wanted something, you had to fight for it.

And I wanted Enzo in all his dark, brooding glory.

Coming to a stop, I lifted my hand to knock when I noticed the door was ajar.

"Miss Abato, maybe I should—" Maurice's concern rolled off my shoulders as I stepped inside, assaulted with the scent of liquor and weed. The place was a mess, littered with empty bottles and glasses.

"Enzo?" I called, dread slithering through me. It had been a few hours since I last saw him, but still, it looked like he'd had a party.

My heart galloped in my chest as I moved deeper into the apartment, down the hall toward his room. I knew I should call someone. Nicco, maybe. But I didn't want to leave without knowing he was okay.

"Enzo?" I called again, checking the bathroom. Then I heard it. A groan coming from his bedroom.

Relief flooded me. He was okay.

Enzo was okay.

Well he obviously wasn't okay given whatever had gone down here in the middle of the day, but he was alive.

I pressed my palm against his bedroom door, taking a deep breath, and pushed it open. "Enzo? It's me—"

The words died on my tongue.

"What the fuck?" He murmured, pushing up, fixing his bloodshot eyes on me. "Nora?" His brows drew together, his icy cold glare pinning me in place.

But I was too fixed on the person beside him.

The naked girl with her hair fanned out around her as she slept peacefully.

Bile clawed up my throat as realization crashed over me. "You bastard." The words tore from my throat in a rush of air.

"Nora?" He rubbed his eyes as if he didn't know if I was real or not.

"And to think I came here to make sure you were okay. Because I care. I fucking care about you..." Pain flooded me. "And this is the thanks I get. I guess they were right." I laughed bitterly, unable to stop comparing myself to the girl at his side.

She was everything I wasn't

Platinum blonde hair down to her tiny waist.

Big boobs.

Tanned skin.

Curves in all the right places.

I had always had a strong sense of self, but in that moment, I felt worthless.

Enzo finally snapped out of his trance, glancing from me to the girl at his side and back to me. "Fuck," he ground out, pushing the covers off his legs. "Nora, I can explain—"

"Save it." My voice cracked as I backed out of the room, crashing into Maurice.

"Miss Abato?" The pity in his eyes made my stomach sink.

"We're leaving, now." I barged past him and all but ran out of there.

I'd come to fight for Enzo, to show him I was there for him, and he'd betrayed me. He'd taken everything that existed between us and cast it aside like it was nothing.

Like *I* was nothing.

And as I fled from his building, tears streaming down my cheeks, I knew Arianne's warnings about Enzo had all been right.

He wasn't a good guy.

Not like Nicco. He was an anomaly. An outlier.

The hero of her unexpected fairytale.

And Enzo Marchetti...

He was the villain.

PLAYLIST

Don't Let Me Down – Connor Maynard
Broken – Isak Danielson
Die for You – The Weeknd
Lovely – Billie Ellish, Khalid
No Time to Die – Billie Ellish
All Goes Wrong – Chase & Status, Tom Grennan
If the World Was Ending – JP Saxe, Julia Michaels
Light Me Up – Ingrid Michaelson
In Case You Don't Live Forever – Ben Platt
No Goodbyes – LEON
Say Something – A Great Big World, Christina Aguilera
Ever – Tiny Deaths
Countdowns – Sleeping At Last
In the Dark – Bring Me The Horizon
Dangerously in Love – Beyoncé
Bad Things – Meiko
Nightcall – London Grammar
Adore You – Miley Cyrus
I Found – Amber Run

PLAYLIST

I Love You – Billie Ellish
Surrender – Natalie Taylor

ACKNOWLEDGMENTS

I can't believe Arianne and Nicco's story is done. Most authors will tell you they love all their books, and it's true. Each book I write is a part of me, the culmination of a lot of hard work and long days at the computer. But there are some stories that are so much more. Stories that become woven into the fabric of your soul.

This is one of mine.

When I had the idea to write a Romeo and Juliet inspired mafia story, I didn't realize how deeply the story would affect me. I know a lot of readers who picked up Prince of Hearts wanted it to be darker. Mafia books hold a certain set of expectations that, it could be argued, I didn't quite hit. But I'm okay with that because this wasn't *my* story—it was Arianne and Nicco's, and I let them tell it as they intended. And I hope you enjoyed their journey as much as I enjoyed writing it!

It goes without saying, there is a long list of people I need to thank for always being in my corner. My alpha reader and friend, Nina. Thank you for always being there! Andrea, for checking those pesky Italian translations (one day, I'll get them right). My translator, Chiara, over at Queen Edizioni, for also helping fix the nuances of the Italian dialogue. Andrea, my editor and friend and all-round legend. Ginelle, my proofreader extraordinaire, thank you for always accommodating my crazy schedule! My awesome promo team who continue to support me and my books. And finally, Give Me Books for handling the promotion side of things. I am grateful to all of you.

And to you: the readers, bloggers, and bookstagrammers. Without you, my books would just be stories lost in an ocean of other stories. Your support and enthusiasm for my characters makes it all worthwhile, and I hope I continue to write the kinds of stories you love…

Until next time,

L A xo

ABOUT THE AUTHOR

Angsty. Edgy. Addictive Romance

Author of mature young adult and new adult novels, L A is happiest writing the kind of books she loves to read: addictive stories full of teenage angst, tension, twists and turns.

Home is a small town in the middle of England where she currently juggles being a full-time writer with being a mother/referee to two little people. In her spare time (and when she's not camped out in front of the laptop) you'll most likely find L A immersed in a book, escaping the chaos that is life.

L A loves connecting with readers.
www.lacotton.com

The best places to find her are

Printed in Great Britain
by Amazon